The Whale H ... g~

Volume 2 - Taranto to Singapore

by David Row

Published by David Row

Copyright 2013 by David Row

This book is a work of fiction. Names, characters, places and incidents either are the product of the author's imagination or are used fictitiously, and any resemblance to actual persons, living or dead, business establishments, events or locales is entirely coincidental

Other titles and further information on David Row's books can be found at

http://astrodragon.co.uk/Books.htm

Table of Contents

Introduction

This is the second book in the 'The Whale Has Wings' series. It carries on directly from the action described at the end of Volume 1 - Rebirth.

While the action described in this book is intended to stand on its own, you may have problems understanding how the Royal Navy (in particular) got here if you haven't read Volume 1. To summarise:

In 1933, the British Royal Navy regained control of its Air Arm (the Fleet Air Arm) from the RAF. This allowed them to build carriers and the aircraft needed for them to their own pre-war plans, rather than be constricted by the limited number and performance of the aircraft grudgingly provided by the RAF. As a consequence, by the time war broke out in 1939, the FAA had better planes, and the building of carriers was a little advanced on our history. In addition, as more planes were available, a class of light carriers was building, and plans had been made for converting merchant ships (in our history, little actual planning for these was done as the RAF would not supply the aircraft required, so priority was very low).

Initially the war doesn't seem to go much differently, until the big raid on the German ships at Wilhelmshaven harbour. Even after this, the diversion isn't yet great, and Norway is still a disaster for the German Navy. However the leverage of the changes in air power are slowly growing. As a result of greater confidence in his carriers, the British are not forced to sink the French ships in Oran, and the attack on the Vichy French at Dakar goes more successfully.

Other changes are less obvious; with more air cover, fewer ships are being lost to aircraft and submarines (as a result, the savings in repair work and new construction more than allows the continuation of the RN carrier building programme). Italy joins the war, and action spreads into the Mediterranean.

This book starts with the British attack on the Italian Fleet at Taranto - this time, the plan is more like the original plans and exercises carried out in preparation for the raid. This books covers the actions through late 1940 and 1941, mainly in the Mediterranean, but also in the Atlantic. As well as the naval actions, details are given of the war on land and air (in particular where this involves British forces), showing how the divergence from our history is slowly increasing.

Chapter 1 - Operation Judgement (21st Oct 1940, Trafalgar day)

The possibility of a carrier strike to immobilize or destroy the Italian fleet had been considered for some years. Indeed, the initial idea preceded that of the Wilhelmshaven raid, and it was only the fact that Italy had not declared war until the summer that led to a raid on Germany being the first such carrier strike.

There were a number of differences with Operation Judgement. First, the location of the Italian fleet had to be known, and ideally this would be Taranto. Taranto was probably Italy's most forward large, well-protected anchorage; as a result it was also the most reachable. After what had happened at Wilhelmshaven, it was considered obvious by the British that Italy would have increased its defensive preparations at all its fleet bases.

The Royal Navy had also learned from their experience in Germany. In general, Taranto was a similar harbour to Wilhelmshaven - it was shallow, so the torpedoes would again need modification. Since the AA defences and the passive protection was considerably heavier, it would be more difficult to hit the capital ships by torpedo - not impossible, but more difficult. So with the exception of the modern capital ships, the attack would be by dive bombers, using 1,000lb bombs and the new 1,600AP bomb - this should penetrate anything but the new battleships decks. The attack would again be at night, and the maximum number of aircraft would be used. The attack would be supported by RAF bombers flying out of Malta, and it was planned that if conditions and Italian actions allowed, a follow-up strike would be made on the following night before the carrier force finally withdrew.

Unlike the North Sea, any attacking force would be in the range of the Regia Aeronautica for some time, especially if the follow-up strike on the second day went ahead. So the strike would go in around 2300 to maximise the effect of the rising moon outlining the targets, to allow the planes to return and land at night. The primary targets would be the Italian capital ships, as many as were in port, followed by the heavy cruisers. These were the two classes of ships most dangerous to the Mediterranean Fleets surface units. Part of the attack would also target the oil tanks, as it was thought that Italy was short on fuel supplies for the fleet, and so destroying the oil stored there would also limit the use of the Italian navy in the period after the raid. After that, targets of opportunity were the destroyers and submarines based there, and the port infrastructure itself. The launch point for the attack was established just west of the Greek island of Cephalonia, about 200 miles southeast of Taranto

In order to do the maximum damage, the Type XIVA torpedo would be used, with the duplex exploder. As it was expected that with all the torpedo protections not many hits would be obtained, it was necessary that the hits be as damaging as possible. It had been hoped to use the new Mk XV, but this had only just finished testing, and production would not be available for a few months. This use of the duplex fuse would prove later to be a very useful decision indeed.

The core of the strike force would be three aircraft carriers, HMS Implacable, HMS Indefatigable, and HMS Courageous. They would be escorted by a force of cruisers and destroyers, and a heavy covering force including the battleships Valiant and Warspite would wait to eastward to join up with them after the raid. While it was hoped that the raid itself would severely damage the Italian fleet, there was always the possibility that some of the modern fast battleships or heavy cruisers would pursue the retiring carrier force, and the capital ships in the covering force were to make sure that they would not be caught. Indeed, Admiral Cunningham was perfectly happy with the idea of Italian heavy ships 'catching' his battleships; he considered it so much easier than having to chase after them.

In order to maximize the strike, a partial deck park would be used on all three carriers; this also would allow additional fighters to be carried, as it was expected that retaliatory strikes would be heavy. While there was always a possibility that the carrier force would escape without interception, after the loss of HMS Venerable off Norway the Royal Navy was going to assume that the Regia Aeronautica would indeed find them and probably manage to make a number of attacks before they got out of range.

HMS Implacable and HMS Indefatigable would carry 30 TBR (strike), 24 Dive-bombers and 30 Fighters.

HMS Courageous would carry 18TBR (A/S,recon), 24 Divebombers and 24 Fighters

This would give the force a total air capability of 60 TBR (for strike use), 18 TBR (A/S, recon), 72 Divebombers and 84 Fighters. In order to fill out this aircraft complement, the reserve units at Alexandria would be stripped of naval aircraft, leaving the forces there in the protection of the RAF for the duration of the raid. It was not possible to launch this number of aircraft as a single strike (the deck space on the fleet carriers limited the number that could be flown off in one strike to about 30 planes), so the strike would go as two groups, first 42 torpedo-armed SeaLance, 36 Cormorant dive bombers and four Cormorants carrying flares and markers. The second wave would be another four flare carrying SeaLance, 12 SeaLance carrying torpedoes, and 30 Cormorants. In addition some of the strike TBR aircraft would carry additional flares.

As Courageous could not launch a fully loaded SeaLance, (her catapult had still not been upgraded, as she had been kept too busy to return to the UK for a planned refit), she would use her Swordfish for A/S and patrol work, allowing the other carriers to provide a heavier strike.

It was hoped to have all the planes landed by 0300, at which point the force would retire to the east to be out of range of the Italian fighters as early as possible. It would also allow them a better chance to evade detection if the direction of their returning planes had been observed. If a second strike was considered unnecessary, then the force would retire on the covering force as soon as the aircraft had been recovered. At dawn they would keep a CAP of 18 Goshawks in the air with another 18 warmed up on deck. It was expected that the air attacks would be heavy.

This force was to be assisted by a strike on Naples by Force H, using the carriers Ark Royal and Victorious, escorted by the battlecruisers Repulse and Renown and an escort of cruisers and destroyers. It had been considered making this force also the cover for a resupply of Malta, but this was discarded as it might have been an attractive enough target for the Italian battleships. For once Cunningham wanted them in port, not at sea. The carriers would launch their attack from southeast of Sicily at long range - approaching 300 miles. This would require the planes to carry a reduced bomb load, but the aim was to distract, not damage, and moving in closer would have led the carriers into the dangerous Sicilian Narrows. The carriers would be taking 30TBR, 18 Divebombers and 27 Fighters each. Their targets would be any destroyers and submarines using the port, and the oil tanks and any other facilities.

The plan was for Force H to strike about an hour before the Taranto attack, to distract the Italians and take their attention away from Taranto. The carrier force would retire on Gibraltar immediately the strike had been recovered; again it was expected that Italian retaliatory air strikes would be soon and heavy. The carriers were also carrying a deck park of fighters (Victorious had carried in extra planes from the UK, and a squadron would be left at Gibraltar as a defence force for the base after the operation was completed. Before the attack Force H would try and imitate a raiding force on the Sicilian airfields (something which had done before).

Finally, a number of submarines had been stationed in the straights of Messina. This was to try and cover possible routes that any damaged ships leaving Taranto would follow. It was expected that due to the rather random nature of an attack, some ships would be damaged rather than sunk. These might try to leave the next day, but in any case it was considered certain they would leave after the second nights attack.

On the 20th, air reconnaissance was carried out from Malta. The island now had six reconnaissance Whirlwinds available, and would conduct missions over Taranto, Naples, and the Sicilian airfields as well as possible targets in close proximity of these in order to try and conceal the actual target. The plane covering Taranto revealed a heavy concentration of ships, including all six of the Italians modern battleships. The photographs were flown out to Cunningham's fleet on a SeaLance which had been sent on to Malta earlier for just this task. As soon as they were looked at, the mission was approved - this was an even better set of targets than had been hoped for.

The photographic analysis showed that Taranto harbour was currently hosting six battleships (the Littorio, Andrea Doria, Vittorio Veneto, Cavour, Duilio and Cesare) and three heavy cruisers in the outer harbour. In addition there were two heavy cruisers, 21 destroyers and 16 submarines and 9 tankers in the inner harbour. There were considerable torpedo net and barrage balloon defences, but the analysis showed that although the coverage of the netting was extensive, it did not completely protect the battleships. It was not in fact realised by the British, but the torpedo netting was in fact far less effective than was thought. Taranto required some 12,800m of netting to properly protect the battleships anchored there, and there was only some 9,000m in place. However the netting was designed to protect against contact fuses - the duplex torpedoes the FAA would launch could slip right under the nets. As a result the torpedo attack would prove to be considerably more effective than anticipated (it should be noted though that not all the torpedoes used the duplex fuse).

Because of concerns that searchlight aimed at the low-flying torpedo planes would dazzle the pilots and cause them problems, the dive bombers would go in at the same time, to confuse and split the numerous searchlight positions defending the port. There was also a supporting attack planned using RAF Wellingtons flying from Malta - the RAF commander there had been busy begging, borrowing and sometimes being suspected of stealing every Wellington he could find in theatre. These planes would not be bombing the ships; they had a different target.

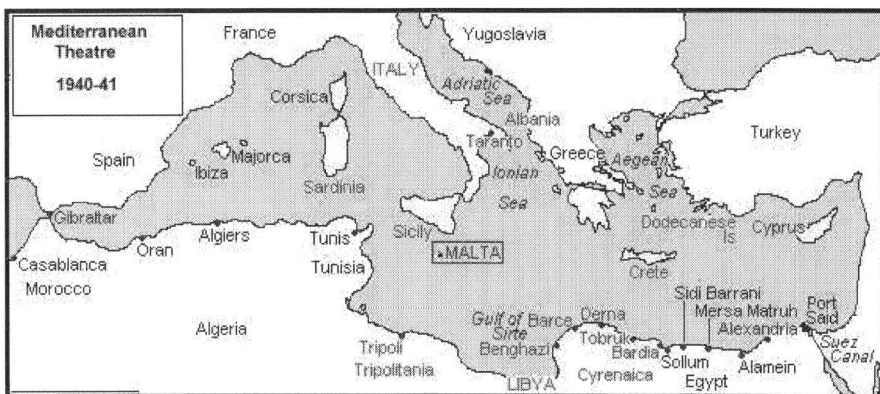

At 1900 the carriers in Force H started to launch their strike. A total of 24 TBR (six of them carrying flares, the rest bombs) and 32 divebombers (carrying 500lb bombs) took off for Naples. A number of planes were non-operational, but there were sufficient spare SeaLance to replace them; all serviceable Cormorants were flown. At the moment, Force H believed themselves not to be under observation; they had been detected the day before by a couple of planes, one of which had been shot down. However for some reason no attack had developed.

At 2230 the main carrier force started to launch. They had also moved into position without detection. Again, a number of planes were unserviceable, but the maximum strike possible was arranged on deck for the first launch - these planes would have the greatest surprise on their side. A total of 42 SeaLance carrying torpedoes, plus 39 Cormorants, six with flares the rest with 1,000lb bombs would soon be heading for Taranto harbour. The carriers had the second wave already armed and fuelled in the hangers ready to be spotted on deck once the first waves had taken off - a dangerous risk, but one which was considered worth taking for a surprise night attack. They would be on their way less than an hour after the first wave and would arrive some 30 minutes after them. This consisted of twelve torpedo armed SeaLance, four Cormorants with flares and another eighteen with 1,000lb bombs. The luxury of an undetected approach to the night attack had allowed a higher than normal number of serviceable aircraft. A number of Cormorants had had to be left behind due to a problem with fuel contamination; although it was possible to fuel on deck using a portable system (this had been instituted after the issue of keeping aircraft ready on deck while attack was imminent was seen to be important), the tight timescale meant four Cormorants had to be left behind.

At about the same time, a force of 16 Wellington bombers lifted off from Malta bound for Taranto. Operation Judgement was on its way.

* * *

The aircraft from Force H neared Naples at about 2200 that night. They only had approximate details of what ships were at Naples (only two destroyers and three submarines, plus some merchant ships), and so the dive bombers had been told to target the oil tanks first, the second group being given the ships in harbour as targets of opportunity. The SeaLance's were tasked with first completing the destruction of the oil tanks, then to bomb as much of the port facilities as they could.

The attack seemed to take Naples by surprise, even though it had been visited by a reconnaissance plane earlier (the RAF had been running reconnaissance flights over various targets for the last week in order to mask the real target areas), and as a result the first half of the dive bombers weren't even fired on before they started they dives onto the oil installations. Even a 500lb bomb starts an impressive fire when it hits an oil tank, and 10 minutes after the start of the attack the oil tanks were burning merrily. The results were so good that the raid commander ordered the bombers to target the ships in the harbour instead of the now-blazing oil installations.

While the first group of dive bombers retired from the oil storage facility, the eighteen bomb-carrying SeaLance engaged the ships in the harbour. By now the defences had been alerted, but seemed rather uncoordinated (the defences had previously only encountered high level raids from the RAF), and only one SeaLance was shot down. In return, two submarines and two merchant ships were left sunk or sinking.

It had only required 20 of the dive bombers to reduce the oil tanks to an inferno, and so the remaining twelve planes were ordered to target the destroyers lying in the harbour. At anchor, a destroyer is a much easier target than when it is manoeuvring at full speed. One destroyer was hit by two 500lb bombs, and was left sinking; a second was hit by one bomb, and although badly damaged was saved by the prompt actions of its crew. One dive bomber was lost in this attack to the destroyers AA fire.

The job finished, the strike headed back to the Force H carriers; as soon as they had been struck below deck, the force turned south to head back to Gibraltar, and readied the fighters on deck ready for the morning. Total losses would be two Cormorants and one SeaLance (which failed to return, probably due to fuel loss), although a further five planes were written off due to combat damage.

Taranto, 2300 (first strike)

Taranto, a major naval base, was rather more awake that Naples. At the first sound of the approaching aircraft, the searchlights lit up, searching the skies for them. It took a while, because they were looking in the wrong place - again, the Italians were expecting a high-altitude bombing attack by RAF planes. This allowed the first waves of attackers to get into position before an alert operator realised what was happening, and the defences started to illuminate the correct areas.

The first planes to attack was a group of twelve dive bombers carrying 1,000 lb bombs - targets the oil storage tanks overlooking the harbour. The tanks were illuminated by one of the flare aircraft, and the bombers turned into their dives as soon as they could see the target. Oil tanks are big, bulky, and don't manoeuvre out of the way of a bomb nearly as well as a ship. One aircraft was hit by AA fire (it ditched in the harbour), but as the other eleven pulled out of their dives the oil storage depot was rapidly becoming a mass of flames.

While the noise of exploding bombs (and a number of exploding oil tanks) was distracting the defenders, a torpedo strike was going in against the battleships. The time of the raid had been carefully planned so the rising moon, as well as the flares, helped to silhouette the targets. The netting surrounding the ships limited the angles of approach of the planes, and once they had been spotted it was clear that the Italian AA guns knew this also. Fortunately for the attackers, the chance of hitting a plane at night was still very low. The first attack by nine SeaLance targeted the modern battleship Littorio. While getting into a good attacking position through the barrage balloons ready to avoid the netting was difficult, the ship itself was a lovely big, stationary target. The torpedo bombers attacked straight into the battleships AA fire, which shot down one of the planes - although it dropped its torpedo when hit, no-one knew where it went. The other eight planes were far more successful - three torpedoes hit the battleship (it was not until much later in the war that the Royal Navy found out for certain that the nets were indeed useless against deep-running torpedoes), tearing large holes in her. The Pugliese Torpedo Defence System was probably the least effective of any in use in WW2, especially against the duplex fuse, and two of the holes were very large for aerial torpedoes.

At the same time, another group of nine planes were aiming their torpedoes at the Vittorio Venetto (the other modern battleship at anchor). Two of the planes were caught in searchlights, and although both escaped without being shot down (although not without damage), this caused them to miss badly with their torpedoes. The other seven planes had more luck. The huge plumes of water showed two torpedo hits, which again caused sizeable holes below the waterline. One plane was shot down by the shore-based AA as it made its escape.

Next to receive the friendly interest of the FAA was the modernised battleship Cavour. In order to work their way around the defences, and also to help reduce the chance of the torpedoes 'bottoming out' the planes were flying as slowly as practical. While the massed AA fire and the searchlights weren't doing a wonderful job of shooting down the attackers, they were causing some confusion and loss of night vision. One of the pilots, somewhat disorientated and concentrating on his target, asked his observer where the balloon barrage he was supposed to be avoiding was. He was told 'we've flown through the bloody thing once, and we're just about to do it again'.

Another strike of nine planes swept in at 50 feet towards the Cavour. The Cavour was an old battleship, which had been completely rebuilt before the war, but she was still small and relatively poorly protected compared to a modern design. Only seven of the planes managed to drop their torpedoes. Two were hit on the way in; one dropped into the harbour, the second managed to get away, damaged, by dropping its torpedo, which went somewhere. Nowhere near the ship, unfortunately. However the remaining planes registered two hits on the old ship. The terrible underwater damage caused to her old hull left her sinking into the mud of the harbour (although this was not immediately realised)

The last of the first four torpedo strikes was aimed at the Cesare, another modernised old ship. Or at least that had been the idea, but the lead crew had got rather confused by all the illumination and pyrotechnics flying about and instead were actually aiming at the Duilio. Again, this old ship had been heavily rebuilt, but was still well below modern standards. By now the defences were beginning to get an idea of what the planes were aiming at, and although the first flight of three planes got their attack off successfully, two of the next flight crashed into the water. The defences also shot down one of the final flight. Despite this, the six surviving planes managed two hits on the ship. Again, the old ship was damaged badly underwater by the hits, although the crew managed to hold the flooding at bay before it got out of control

While the torpedo attacks had been going in at low level, the dive bombers had been circling high above. This had attracted the attention of some of the AA fire, but hitting a small plane at night without radar was proving difficult - so difficult that so far none of them had been hit, and it helped to reduce the fire being aimed at the vulnerable torpedo planes.

The first group of twelve planes dove onto the Andrea Doria. She had been chosen because even though modernised, her deck armour was less than 4" thick. She would be the first ship to be attacked by the new 1,600lb AP bomb, as this should penetrate her deck easily (the newer battleships had much thicker deck armour, and it was not certain if even the AP bombs would penetrate). In fact, even some of the 1,000 bombs would penetrate the poor deck armour of the ship. The first six planes were carrying the AP bombs, and the attack caught the defences by surprise - they were still concentrating on the torpedo planes. As a result the first two flights made a textbook attack on the helpless ship, hitting her with three of their six bombs. One of the AP bombs didn't explode (it was later found it had speared straight through the armoured deck and actually made a hole as it exited the ship!). The other two worked as advertised; although they didn't carry the explosive content of the smaller GP bombs, they sent thick, heavy splinters of their casing in all directions, penetrating bulkheads, and managing to wreck the forward engine rooms. They also caused flooding as the splinters tore their way out through the side of the ship.

While the attack was satisfyingly successful, it did unfortunately alert the defences to what was going on. The next six planes met a hail of AA fire, one of them being hit and diving straight down into the harbour, where its bomb exploded in a huge plume of water. Of the remaining five planes, only one got a hit, the others being somewhat distracted by the AA fire (although two bombs fell close enough to cause underwater damage). The hit, although only by a 1,000lb bomb, actually penetrated the relatively thin armour deck before it exploded, causing severe damage and starting a large fire amidships. The ship was left burning as the planes made their escape at low level.

The final group of nine divebombers were targeting the Duilio. They had seen her hit by at least one torpedo, which was unexpected, but although the ship was listing, she was still above the water. The first flight was again carrying the 1,600AP bomb, and one of these hit - it was this hit that actually doomed the ship. The bomb exploded just as it entered the remaining operational boiler room, where it enthusiastically sprayed every piece of working machinery in range with jagged metal splinters - at which point the working machinery turned into non-working machinery. This caused a total loss of power as the electrical breakers opened automatically, which did nothing to help the crews trying to contain the torpedo damage. The final six planes managed two hits; one plane was lost as it never pulled out of its dive, the others managed two hits on the helpless battleship. One of these exploded above the armour (causing severe damage and fires in the superstructure), the second just under the armour, causing considerable damage, and also ruining the efforts of the crew to handle the increasing flooding. As a result, the list caused by the earlier torpedo damage kept increasing; the crew had no option but to abandon ship before she turned over into the mud of the harbour bottom.

Last to attack were the remaining group of six torpedo bombers. While all the attention was on the battleships, they had been sneaking around to make an attack on the heavy cruiser Fiume in the outer harbour. As the attention was all on the battleships, they managed to start their runs before they were detected. The ships AA was immediately directed against them and one of the planes did not survive to get into range. The other five managed good launches, although one torpedo was dropped poorly and hit the harbour bottom, two of the remaining four hit the ship - one near her B turret, the other near her stern, wrecking both her propeller shafts. The ship immediately started to take on water and list, but at that time was not in immediate danger of sinking.

Taranto, 2400 - second strike

While the first strike had been finishing its efforts in the outer harbour, the group of 16 Wellingtons from Malta had arrived. Finding Taranto had proved easy, the now splendidly-burning oil tanks made it visible from a long way off. As they closed, the sight of all the massed AA fire from the port and from the ships in harbour, as well as the blazing oil tanks, was quite impressive. 'Guy Fawkes night come two weeks early' as one of the crew put it. Their job was not to add to the chaos in the outer harbour. Instead, using the convenience of the searchlight positions to make sure they were on target, they dropped mines around the harbour entrances. Sixteen

Wellingtons carry a considerable quantity of mines, and the task was made easier by them being completely ignored. While it had been realised that there was a small danger of them interfering with the raid aircraft (it would have been embarrassing to lose a carrier plane to having a naval mine dropped on it), the chance was small and it was a perfectly acceptable risk. As it turned out, none of the strike aircraft even noticed they were there. Admiral Cunningham was sure he would have to make a strike on the following night to do the damage he really wanted to do to the Italian fleet. Since it was expected that the Italians might consider this, and get as many ships away as possible during the day, the mines were to dissuade them, hopefully long enough for another strike to do yet more damage. Job done, the Wellingtons headed back to Malta for breakfast. They had more to do tomorrow night as well.

Shortly after the first strike had headed for home (less two planes carrying the raid leaders, who remained to evaluate the damage and suggest targets for the second wave), the rest of the carriers planes arrived. This consisted of twelve torpedo carrying SeaLance, eighteen divebombers and four more divebombers armed with flares. The raid leaders had already decided on their targets.

The first target of the torpedo planes was the Littorio. Already hit badly by three torpedoes, she had just managed to get under way, although it wasn't apparent what a ship obviously damaged was going to do. It fact, the captain had already decided to find a good soft spot to run her ashore so that she was no longer in danger of sinking. Sadly for him he ran out of time. The first attack runs benefitted from surprise; the defences had obviously assumed the attack had finished, and the growl of more aero engines in the night seemed to completely confuse them for a few minutes. Enough time for all twelve planes to make their runs at the slowly-moving ship. Even the ships own AA seemed asleep for the first two flights, and even though they belatedly realised they were under attack, and managed to damage one of the third flight so badly it had to land in the harbour (fortunately the crew escaped), eleven torpedoes were swimming towards the already-damaged battleship. Although she was at least no longer at anchor, she was hardly racing along, and in quick succession three huge plumes of water hung in the night air for a moment. The two hits to the centre of the ship were damaging enough - again, the deep strike with the duplex head doing severe damage, but the final blow was the torpedo that hit her engine room, cutting off the power for some crucial minutes. Having been hit now by a total of six torpedoes, all on the same side, the battleship slowly leant over more and more onto her starboard beam. All the Captain was able to do was to order the crew to abandon ship as the Littorio tried her best to turn turtle. The shallow harbour actually prevented this, but she ended up almost underwater, on her side, and in fact later found to be unrecoverable despite the best efforts of the Italian engineers.

As the torpedo bombers streaked out of the outer harbour at full throttle and zero feet, the first six dive bombers commenced their dives at the Andrea Doria, already on fire from her earlier bomb hits. These planes were all carrying AP bombs. Although the ship was a stationary target, the first flight of three planes all missed. It was the second flight that managed one of the more spectacular hits of the war; two of the bombs hit - it was never certain if one of them exploded or not, as the second sliced easily through the deck armour and buried itself in the forward magazine before doing its patriotic duty. The resulting explosion seemed not only to light up the harbour but also to lift the whole front of the ship. As the aircrew regained their night vision, the ship was seen sinking forward. As one of the pilots later remarked, 'I'd have said she was sinking by the bow, except she didn't have a bow any more'.

The final group of twelve planes were rather put out by this - it hardly seemed fair to hog such a fat juicy target without giving them a crack at it. Instead, they were pointed to the heavy cruiser Gorizia (the Cesare, a higher priority target, had been missed in the natural confusion of the raid - ironically the smoke from one of the burning ships had been effectively concealing her). By now the defences were furious, and they turned into their dive amidst a hail of AA fire - even though it was poorly directed, the sheer volume was dangerous even to dive bombers, and three of the planes crashed into the water, not pulling out of their dives. The remaining nine managed to hit the cruiser with two 1,000lb bombs, which left her listing and on fire (she was to be towed to shallow water to avoid her sinking).

The final act of the raid was for the raid leaders to take photographs for later analysis, as the pilots headed back to the carriers. While the losses during the raid had been heavy, they were less than had been expected. Eight torpedo planes had been shot down during the attack, and three more failed to return (one crash-landed on the Italian coast, the crew being picked up by local fishermen). Only five of the divebombers had been lost during the raid, although four more failed to make it back to the carriers. Total losses were 20 planes out of 115 taking part - the original estimate had suggested up to 50 planes could have been lost.

Chapter 2 - Second Strike

22nd October, Force H

Force H had already started to retire back to Gibraltar; in order to make even a long-range strike on Naples they had had to position themselves between Sardinia and Sicily, uncomfortably close to the airfields on the two islands. They had started to steam Southwest at 0200, and as soon as the returned strike planes had been tucked back into the hangers, the first CAP and A/S patrol aircraft were spotted on deck ready to be launched at first light.

The first of the British fleets to be spotted was Force H. That had been expected; their escape route was far closer to the Italian airfields, and it was far easier to predict where they would be. At 0800 the CAP intercepted a reconnaissance plane out of Cagliari, and although it was shot down there was enough cloud to allow it to dodge the interceptors for long enough to make a sighting report. With the covering heavy ships being two battlecruisers, the force was making 28 knots and it was hoped that they would be out of the range of the Italian planes by the next day.

The first air attack on Force H came from the Italian airfields in Tunisia; this was a mixed force of twelve SM.79 torpedo bombers and fifteen BA.88 level bombers. They were escorted by eight MC.200 fighters. The two carriers carried 54 fighters between them, and had a CAP of twelve Goshawks in the air with another twelve warmed up on deck. The raid was detected on radar at 1200, distance 65 miles, and the ready fighters started to launch. As planned, half the CAP headed for the high level formation (the ready fighters would not have time to get to altitude, but would easily be able to intercept the lower group (the torpedo planes), and half for what where supposed (correctly) to be torpedo planes. The Italian commander had allocated his fighters to guard the torpedo bombers - they were the most dangerous to the ships, and also the most vulnerable to attack.

The first group to be intercepted was the BA.88 formation. With no fighter escort they were terribly vulnerable to the cannon-armed Goshawks, who intercepted them some 25 miles from the fleet, giving them ample time to make multiple attacks on the lumbering bomber formation. After the first two coordinated attacks, 5 of the 15 bombers had been shot down, and two more had been seen to turn away trailing smoke. Still well over 10 miles from the fleet, at this point the bombers all turned and dived for home, although one more was lost to the Goshawks before their controller pulled them back to engage the much more dangerous torpedo planes.

The fighters closing on the torpedo planes had realised that they were escorted when one of their number was shot down by the diving Italian fighters (at this stage in the war, it was often difficult to determine by radar if the planes in the formation were at different altitudes). They turned to engage the fighters, leaving the torpedo planes to be intercepted by the second wave of defenders. As a result of the following dogfight, four Italian fighters were shot down for the loss of two Goshawks (while diving unexpectedly on the Goshawks had been a good start, the poor armament of the Italian planes had only shot down one defender, and the others could easily out-dive and catch the remainder.

Meanwhile the twelve torpedo planes had been boring in towards Force H, diving slowly to reach their delivery height (and also closing faster as a result, leaving the defenders less time to intercept them). The attackers split into two groups of six as they dived, and this split the Goshawks - nine went for one formation while only three headed for the second. The first group, attacked by nine fighters, fared very badly. They were still some ten miles away when first intercepted, and although they continued on to the fleet with great bravery, all six were shot down, the last some two miles from the closest ship.

The second group fared better, as there was insufficient time for the three Goshawks to deal with them. Although two of the torpedo planes were shot down and one was forced to drop its torpedoes early to escape, three managed attacking runs on the fleet, each plane dropping two torpedoes. One pair was aimed at the cruiser HMS Sheffield, but she dodged both of them. The other two planes had aimed for the battlecruiser HMS Renown (the carriers, while the primary target, were hidden behind the protection of their escorting ships). Dodging with a grace that belied her 35,000tons, the old battlecruiser dodged three of the torpedoes, but was hit slightly forward of amidships by the last one. Fortunately the hit was taken on her Torpedo Defence System, and although Renown was forced to slow, the damage was not critical and after 15 minutes she signalled Admiral Somerville that she was still able to make 24 knots.

Despite the damage to Renown, the fleet was still heading for Gibraltar during the afternoon. As a result of the initial attack, it had been decided to keep a heavier CAP on patrol - the carriers had the planes available, and it was thought that the maximum danger was this afternoon - unless they had to slow drastically, they would be out of range of the Italian fighters by tomorrow, and unescorted raids were far less of a threat. As a result a CAP of sixteen planes was kept airborne, and this drove off a series of small raids between 1330 and 1500, which were thought to have come from the airfields in Sicily. In each case, the Italian planes (all small formations), had turned for home as soon as they realised they were being intercepted by fighters. One reconnaissance plane had been shot down, but it was obvious that the Regia Aeronautica still knew where they were.

The largest attack registered on the radar screens at 1600. Obviously someone in the Regia Aeronautica in Tunisia had realised that only large attacks had much hope of causing damage to a fleet operating under heavy air cover. The formation was again in two parts - some 20 high level bombers, escorted by eight fighters, and 18 torpedo planes escorted by ten fighters. This time the CAP was sent straight at the torpedo strike; it was accepted that this meant the high level attack would probably get through the fighters screen, but it was considered far less dangerous. Sixteen fighters were directed at the torpedo planes, while the planes on deck were launched off as fast as possible.

The escorting fighters tried to intercept the Goshawks, but the superior speed of the defenders allowed them to split their attack; eight of them mixed it up with the MC.200's, while the other eight went for the torpedo planes. The dogfight with the fighters moved away from the torpedo planes boring in for the attack, the end result of which was three Goshawks lost for four MC.200's. Meanwhile the 18 torpedo planes had split into three groups of six. Two of these received the loving attention of the eight remaining CAP patrol, as a result of which five of them were shot down, and two more forced to drop their weapons to try and escape. The third flight of six, and the remaining five from the other two groups, were engaged by sixteen more defenders. The third flight never stood a chance; all six planes were shot down, although they did shoot down one defending fighter.

The other five planes had by now scattered all over, and as a result only one fell to a fighter. However this meant that they were attacking individually into the massed AA fire of the fleet. Two of them attacked the carrier Ark Royal, and found out to their cost just how heavy the close in AA defences of a fleet carrier and its escorting destroyer was. Over 40 40mm and a considerable number of 20mm cannon, plus the 4.5" guns of the carrier shot down both planes. Although one of them did launch its torpedo, this came no-where near the carrier.

The remaining two planes came off a little better. One managed an attack on HMS Renown, but even with her reduced speed the old ship proved again how gracefully she could dodge. The final attack hit one of the escorting destroyers - possibly by accident, or possibly because it was the only available target. One of the two torpedoes hit HMS Velox aft. The old destroyer immediately slowed to a halt, her propellers and engine room wrecked. It was obviously impossible to get her under way again, and as soon as the air attack had finished, Admiral Somerville ordered the crew taken off and the ship sunk by torpedo.

Meanwhile the high level bombers had been making an attack undisturbed by anything other than the fleets HA guns (which was, it must be admitted, quite an impressive amount of gunfire). Indeed three of the planes were shot down by the massed guns, while the ships waited and watched for the bombs to start falling before attempting to manoeuvre clear of them. While the attack was pressed home gallantly in the face of heavy AA fire, it was no more successful that high altitude bombing usually was. While bombs falling close added a few white hairs to a number of ships Captains, no hits were obtained, although at one point Victorious almost vanished behind two sticks of bombs that fell to either side of her (leading to an Italian claim to have sunk her).

Fortunately for Force H that was the last attack of the day. By nightfall, they were clear of the Italian fighters, and in fact no further air attacks were made on them before they made it back to Gibraltar. While it had cost a destroyer and damage to the Renown that would take two months to repair, the raid as a whole was considered very successful as part of the whole Judgement operation.

* * *

22nd October, the Mediterranean fleet

After recovering the strike, it was time for the carrier group to count up the cost of the raid and also to withdraw southeast. The intention was to get out of range of the Italian fighters; they were confident they had enough fighters of their own to break up any unescorted raids. Unless these proved unexpectedly successful, they wanted to be in a position to launch a second strike that evening. They began to move Southeast at 0330. Since they had conducted their strike from some 175m from Taranto, it was expected that some three hours steaming at 25kt would put them out of range of the Italian fighters. Once they had done that, they would waste time in order to be able to get back into position for the final strike on the port that evening. It was also hoped that their evasive course would confuse the Italian reconnaissance planes that would undoubtedly be sent after them.

Ironically, after all the excitement of the night strike, and the preparation for heavy air attacks the next day, the fleet wasn't even sighted by the Italians! Granted, there was a lot of broken cloud about, and radar did detect a number of contacts, but nothing came very close, and it was almost with a sense of anticlimax that the fleet reversed course at sunset and headed back to its launch point. They would attack Taranto again at midnight.

While the losses in the first two strikes had been less than anticipated, there were also quite a few aircraft that couldn't be repaired in time to be used again that night (in addition to AA damage a number had been further damaged on landing), although the crews had been busy making sure that the planes that had been unserviceable last night were ready now. The striking force of the fleet was now down to 39 SeaLance and 54 Cormorants. These could be accommodated as a single strike. The final disposition was 39 SeaLance armed with torpedoes, 46 Cormorants with 1,000lb bombs and 8 Cormorants carrying flares.

While a Whirlwind had flown over the port that afternoon, and got some excellent pictures of the devastation, the actual photos were not available to the fleet. Instead, as arranged, a long message giving the details was passed from Malta to the Admiralty, and of course copied by the fleet (who were, deliberately, not classed as a recipient). The final strike plans were made accordingly.

There had in fact been some action already that day at Taranto, although the pilots wouldn't know about it until they returned to Alexandria. At noon, the Italians had decided that in view of the destruction, and the damage to the oil tanks, it would be best to send some of the undamaged ships north. However as the cruiser Trento cleared the harbour, there was a shattering explosion under her bows. One of the mines laid by the RAF Wellingtons had found a customer. The additional confusion this caused didn't help the attempts to handle the situation at Taranto at all. The cruiser returned to the harbour (the damage, while severe, didn't threaten to sink her, especially so close to port), but any further sailings were postponed until the handful of minesweepers available had cleared the channels. This would be done by tomorrow, and the ships were then to sail to a safer location. This was an added bonus for the new attack, although it had been hoped that something like this would happen - the more ships in port, the more targets were available. It was somewhat ironic that it was the Trento that had been the victim - she had only just had the bulk of the damage she had sustained at Calabria repaired, and was in fact due to sail next week to have new turrets fitted (her A and B turrets were inoperable).

The Wellingtons would also visit the port again that night, in fact before the FAA arrived. They had been waiting for the photographs, which showed the damaged oil tanks still burning. The previous attack had damaged or set on fire about half the tanks, and the Italians seemed to be letting them burn out. At 2200, the sirens went off all over Taranto again. This time it was fifteen Wellingtons, and the first thing they went for was the rest of the oil tanks - the already burning ones had proved to be a splendid navigation aid for the RAF pilots. The first ten aircraft scattered 160 250lb bombs over the remaining tanks. By the time they headed for Malta, all that remained of the Taranto oil tanks was twisted metal and burning petroleum. Seeing that the target no longer existed, the other five planes went for their secondary target, the Seaplane base. While the damage done was not tremendous, a couple of planes were destroyed and the facilities damaged. It would also distract the Italians while the real second attack was coming in.

The emergency crews were still trying to deal with the results of the RAF raid when the FAA arrived at 2345. This time the first torpedo strike went in to make sure that the 'lucky' Cesare wasn't so lucky any more. Fifteen torpedo bombers had been assigned to the first attack on the old battleship (they still didn't know that in fact she was damaged and immobile). One of the results of the first raid was that tugs had moved her, which was in fact unfortunate as it meant she was hardly protected by nets - although the ineffectiveness of the nets wasn't known for certain, not having to try and avoid them made the torpedo planes job a lot easier. The other fact noted immediately by the pilots (it was rather important to them!) was the far lower level of AA fire from the previous night. Part of this was because the battleships that had been throwing a lot of it were either sunk or damaged, and partly because the ports guns were now nearly out of ammunition - they had fired off so much they needed resupply, and in all the confusion of the last 24 hours this had not been arranged. As a result the planes executed a textbook attack. Of the fifteen torpedoes dropped, five hit the old battleship. Her earlier damage had not been fixed (her hull had just been temporarily patched, she was waiting her turn in the dry dock for proper repairs), and five torpedoes hitting her on the same side was simply far too much damage for her. In minutes, she was heeling over hard, and ten minutes later was lying on her side on the harbour bottom.

The next target for the torpedo bombers were the cruisers Gorizia and Zara. As the AA fire was proving limited (none of the torpedo planes attacking Cesare had been shot down), the raid leader decided to take the risk of attacking the cruisers one at a time to see how effective each strike would be. Gorizia had in fact been hit by two bombs the previous night, but she was, after all, still above water.

The first attack went in on the Zara - twelve torpedo planes. The heavy cruisers AA did shoot down one plane, but the other eleven launched their torpedoes - three hitting her. Water started to pour into the cruisers port side, although she did not in fact sink. Her captain grounded her in the harbour to prevent this, but she would be out of action for a considerable time. The final group of twelve torpedo bombers went in against the Gorizia. She had in fact had her crew evacuated after the fires from her two bomb hits had been put out, and in any case her only power was from an emergency generator, her main units having been put out of action (although only temporarily) by the bombs. Again, she was a sitting target, and although three of the planes were damaged, all twelve dropped their fish on her. Four hits later, and with no power for her pumps (and only a skeleton crew, unable to control that damage, on board), she was sinking wreck. Sadly one of the damaged planes, unable to properly control its flight, hit a balloon cable and crashed on its way clear of the harbour.

Now it was the turn of the dive bombers. These had split into two groups, nine in the outer harbour, the rest heading for the ships still afloat in the inner harbour. The planes in the outer harbour swooped on the cruiser Fiume, already hit by two torpedoes last night. The ship was a helpless target, and with a surgeons precision the planes hit her with three 1,000lb bombs. These caused terrible damage; worse, they knocked out all her power and one bomb reopened much of the torpedo damage on one side. The ship was left listing and in flames, and she finally sank onto the bottom, her superstructure still above the shallow water. The cost was one of the dive bombers; although no-one saw her hit, she crashed into the water, not pulling out of her dive

The inner harbour was the target of the remaining 37 dive bombers. Eighteen of these were targeting the heavy cruisers Trieste and Pola. This time the AA fire was rather heavier - the ships in the inner harbour had used far less of their AA ammunition last night - and two divebombers were lost to the Trieste. Despite this, she was hit with two 1,000lb bombs. One of these hit her bridge, killing her command crew and also destroying most of her forward superstructure. The second hit her well aft, almost blowing off her stern and wrecking her shafts. Luckily for her an alert officer flooded her after magazines, or it would have been likely that they would have exploded as well. The Pola was less fortunate. For some reason he fire was ineffective - it was thought later than the flares being used to illuminate the ships was confusing and blinding the gunners against the dive bombing attacks - and she was hit by no less than three bombs. Her engine rooms, X turret and much of her superstructure in ruins, and water pouring in, as well as serious fires, she would be later abandoned by her crew - with no power for pumps or firefighting, her fires would burn her to a hulk.

The remaining nineteen planes were attacking the line of destroyers and submarines moored in an appealingly even line across the harbour. No-one was quite sure why the Italian navy had lined them up in such a neat, tidy, and inviting manner, but none of the pilots were complaining. For the loss of one dive bomber, the remainder dropped their explosive presents along the line. A 1,000lb bomb doesn't leave much of a destroyer or a submarine when it hits. As they left, five destroyers and four submarines were sinking rapidly.

* * *

23rd October, the Mediterranean fleet.

The last of the planes from Taranto were struck below at 0400, and the fleet had already turned southwest at 25 knots, heading for a rendezvous with the covering force. CAP fighters had already been spotted on deck - they and the A/S flight would be flown off at first light.

The losses on the second raid had been lighter than anticipated - no-one had considered that the AA fire would be so light this time. The carriers had lost two SeaLance shot down over Taranto, and two more failed to return (one crashed in Italy). Four Cormorants had been shot down, and one more never made it home. Added to the losses from the first night, they had lost 15 SeaLance and 14

Cormorants. Given what they had done to the Italian fleet, it was considered an acceptable loss. In addition some 20 planes were unserviceable; most of these would be written off for parts once they got back to Alexandria.

Morning found the fleet steaming fast on what was looking to be unseasonably good weather (despite the travel brochures, the Mediterranean in October is often quite unpleasant). This was both good and bad news - the good news that it meant interception of Italian planes would be easier, the bad that it would also be easier for the Italians to find them. The first Italian reconnaissance plane was detected on radar at 1000, and although chased off by a pair of Goshawks it was clear from the radio monitoring that the fleet had been detected and reported.

It was not until three hours later that the main attack appeared. The air defence officers had been wondering why it was taking so long for the Italians to respond, and when they saw the size of the blip on their radar sets they realised why. 'It looked like every Italian plane in southern Italy was heading for us' was the comment of the air defence officer on HMS Implacable. The carriers already had 18 fighters on CAP, and as soon as the huge contact was seen they started getting the ready planes airborne. There was then the agonising decision of should they try and get more planes in the air and risk fuelled and armed planes being hit by enemy attack, or hold them back for later use. In the event the Implacable was the only carrier to get another flight of fighters (six planes in this case) airborne; she had been preparing to replace her CAP and the planes were already being prepared. They would not be able to gain any useful height before the attackers arrived. The first of the Goshawks were closing on the raid at about 40 miles from the fleet when they made the first estimate of the size. Judging by the fact it was in two parts, the estimate was 30 torpedo planes and around 60 high level bombers.

The initial CAP of eighteen aircraft was vectored onto the torpedo planes. The Italians had obviously been learning from the previous results of unescorted raids, and they split up into flights of three aircraft, making it much more difficult for the Goshawks to engage them all. As it was, the defending fighters managed to intercept some six of the ten groups before they closed the fleet, and succeeded in shooting down twelve of the torpedo planes. The other four flights were too close in to the ships close range AA defences to engage. The carriers were obviously the priority target, and six planes headed for the Implacable while another six went straight for the Courageous. One fighter was lost during the interceptions, flying into the sea as it tried too radical a manoeuvre to get on the tail of one of the torpedo planes.

The planes attacking the Implacable were met with the same heavy close in AA defence that had deterred the planes attacking the Ark Royal the previous day. Three of them were shot down on their way in, and one more was damaged severely enough that she dropped her torpedo well out of range and limped away. However four torpedoes were dropped at the carrier. Fortunately for her, the attack was not terribly well coordinated, and her Captain threaded through the torpedo tracks expertly.

The Courageous was not so fortunate. While she had a guard destroyer like the other carriers, her own AA defence was far weaker than the modern fleet carriers - the Implacable and her escort could bring 42 40mm guns to bear, she and her escort could only manage 26. The difference was enough to make the incoming planes task much less dangerous. One plane was still shot down, and another was actually on fire when it launched its torpedoes (which as a result went nowhere near anyone). But eight torpedoes were on their way towards the old carrier. Despite the best efforts of her Captain to doge them all, three plumes of water towered over her flight deck , the ship slewing (and nearly running down her escorting destroyer) before slowing to a halt, already listing.

Meanwhile the huge high level attack had been boring in. Twenty Goshawks from the ready flights had been pushing their engines at full power to get up to intercept them, and the six planes launched late from Implacable were also heading for them. Only the ready flights managed to get among the bombers before they reached the fleets HA air defence zone. The bombers showed great discipline, staying close for mutual supporting fire. As a result the fighters only managed to shoot down twelve of them, and the bombers shot down three of the Goshawks in reply (two more were heavily damaged and had to break off attacks). The remaining 48 bombers kept on going, right into the massive black shellbursts of the ships HA fire.

It was obvious that the Italian bombers meant business this time; even though the heavy fire shot down four of them, the rest kept in formation as they swept over the fleet at around 10,000 feet. Even so, it was not easy to get hits at that altitude on radically manoeuvring ships, as the Captains threw cruisers and aircraft carriers around as if they were driving a speedboat, not 10,000 tons or more of warship. The destroyer HMS Jervis was the first to be hit. Two 500lb bombs turned the destroyer into a wreck almost immediately, one blowing off her bows while the other destroyed her engine room. Without power, and already sinking by the bow, her Captain had no alternative other than to order abandon ship.

Next to suffer was the cruiser HMS Liverpool. The first 500lb bomb hit her amidships, destroying her seaplane and hangar, and causing an aviation fuel fire. The second hit her aft, the explosion (and the splinters) knocking out her aft engine room and causing severe flooding. The final bomb to hit her landed on her B turret, destroying it and also knocking out A turret and killing many of the bridge crew. The ship, temporarily out of control, started to slow rapidly.

However the prime target from the bombers was the already-damaged HMS Courageous. Unable to evade, she was hit in rapid succession by four 500lb bombs. While these hits might have been shrugged off (or at least taken with no vital damage) by the fleet carriers, Courageous was a conversion of a WW1 ship, and had little armour protection against bombs. The first bomb hit her aft, directly on the elevator, blowing it right out of its well and onto the deck. The second and third punched through her thin deck; one exploding in the hangar, the second continuing on and exploding in her machinery spaces, the shock taking her generators offline. The final bomb hit on her catapult, wrecking it and sending splinters into the front of the hanger. A heavy plume of smoke rapidly covered the stricken carrier; although the RN was fanatical about fuel safely on the hangar deck, there was still enough combustible material to start quite a serious fire. The problem was that with no power (as well as the main generators being offline, the backup diesel had been wrecked by bomb splinters), it was impossible to deal with the fires and the flooding.

Meanwhile the bombers had been making their escape. The fleet had continued to pound them with AA fire even as the bombs were falling, and another two fell victim. As they headed back to Italy, some of the Goshawks managed a final interception (many of the fighters were out of ammunition after their earlier attacks), shooting down a further seven bombers for the loss of one fighter.

As the last of the bombers fled for safety over the horizon, the Courageous was obviously in a bad way, smoke covering her and her list steadily increasing. It was clear that the ship was finished, and Cunningham immediately ordered her to be abandoned to save as many of her crew as possible. Only 20 minutes after the bombing, the old ship finally turned over and sank. Fortunately the weather was calm, and the escorting destroyers managed to pick up most of the crew, but over 300 men had perished with their ship.

The situation of the Liverpool was more complex; although she had been heavily hit, the modern cruiser was not likely to sink immediately, but neither was she capable of steaming at more than a few knots. The fuel fire had been put out after half an hour, and her flooding at least temporarily brought under control. It was a dilemma for Cunningham; if he left her with an escort, another attack like the one they had just endured would sink her, and quite possibly some of her escort as well; on the other hand he could ill afford to lose a modern cruiser. In the end, it was decided to try to escort her back to Alexandria. Her engineer estimated that with some makeshift repairs, and bearing in mind her damage, she could make 10 knots by the night. The deciding factor was the estimate that in fact it was unlikely that the Italian air force could in fact repeat that intensity of raid immediately. According to their intelligence, that really had been every torpedo plane available, and many of the level bombers. It was also pointed out that she would be in range of escorting fighters until the night, and if things worsened she could be abandoned at daylight.

The fighters were flown onto the two fleet carriers; due to the earlier raid losses there was no problem accommodating Courageous's fighters as well, and the main body of the fleet headed on to the covering force, which it would reach the following morning. As it turned out, the Liverpool did make Alexandria safely - the sky was peacefully clear the following day, and her engineering crew eventually got her up to 13 knots. The main body had arrived back at Alexandria some time previously, whereupon Admiral Cunningham made the rare order to 'splice the mainbrace'.

Chapter 3 - East Africa

21st October (Off the coast of East Africa)

The British Convoy BN7 was attacked by Italian destroyers from Massawa. The escorts, including the New Zealand cruiser HMNZS Leander and the destroyer HMS Kimberley, drive destroyer 'Francesco Nullo' ashore with their gunfire.

Shortly after dawn, the Nullo was overtaken by the Kimberly and two other vessels just outside Massawa. The Nullo and the Kimberly engaged in a one-hour gun battle in which the handicapped Italian destroyer came out much the worse. The Nullo was left dead in the water and sinking, but had meanwhile managed to work its way in under the protection of Harmil Island in the Massawa channel, where the Italians had established a naval 76-mm battery. As the Kimberly closed in to finish off its Italian adversary with a torpedo, the gunners on Harmil Island engaged it, scoring a hit which temporarily stopped the British destroyer (although it had to be towed back to Port Sudan by its companion vessels, the damage to the British ship proved to be minor). While the British departed, the Nullo finally sank .The already-wrecked destroyer was destroyed by RAF Blenheim bombers on the following day.

23rd October (Spain)

At a meeting with General Franco, Hitler fails to persuade him to join the Axis, or to allow him to attack Gibraltar through Spain. Franco's natural caution has been enhanced by the recent destruction of the Italian Navy in the Mediterranean, and he has no desire to see his ports visited by the FAA. Hitler is left un-amused by his 'allies' recaltriance.

24th October (UK)

The first war operation of the Corpo Aereo Italiano (the Italian formation assigned to help the Luftwaffe bomb England) is the bombardment of Harwich by sixteen Br.20s. One of the bombers is lost on take-off and two more were lost upon return, being abandoned by their crews with no more fuel, after a long and unsuccessful night search of their bases. The RAF is underwhelmed by the Italian effort. This will in fact be the only aerial attack by this unit, as it has already been marked for return to Italy in view of the heavy aircraft losses to the FAA. The single operation has been a gesture by Mussolini to show his support.

Britain is still suffering from small daylight raids, but as the losses to the Luftwaffe mount steadily these are being replaced with mixed fighter/fighter-bomber sweeps. While annoying, these do not carry the weight of bombs to do serious damage to the

British infrastructure. Night attacks are still very heavy and the Beaufighter night fighters are still getting to grips with the AI radar.

FAA Swordfish flying from bases in North Africa bomb the Italian-held port of Tobruk and lay mines in the harbour. The aircraft had originally been marked for use as replacements for those damaged in Operation Judgement, but the better than expected success (and the loss of the Courageous) meant they could continue to be used locally.

Mussolini temporarily postpones his planned invasion of Greece by two weeks, in order to allow the Italian navy and air force to recover from the damage and confusion caused by the British raid on Taranto. In particular he is worried that the Royal Navy might pay a visit to some of the Italian Adriatic ports, although there are in fact no plans for this - it would involve any ships used getting far too deep into the range of Italian air cover

The FAA arrange to replace the losses in their squadrons with the pilots rescued from Courageous; the remaining personnel in those squadrons will go back to the UK to act as a core for HMS Bulwark's completion next year. Since only Courageous was still using Swordfish in the eastern Mediterranean, those recovered to the other carriers will be allocated to coastal attacks in support of the Army, working out of North African bases. While no match for a modern fighter, the Swordfish (acting in its bomber role) is still thought to be able to play a useful role in Africa.

26th October (USA)

The North-American NA-73, the prototype P-51(Mustang), makes its maiden flight at Inglewood, California, USA. The Allison V-1710-39 engine had been received in October and after installation, the aircraft began taxi runs on 15 October and two brief flights were made today. It is hoped to have a second prototype flying soon with a UK-sourced Merlin engine; the RAF thinks the plane would make a better fighter/interceptor than close support aircraft (of which they feel they already have adequate designs), and the high altitude performance of the Allison engine is questionable.

A Condor ranging over the Atlantic 150 miles off Ireland damages the 42,348 ton liner 'Empress of Britain' by strafing and dropping two 250kg bombs. The ship was later sunk by a U-boat. This impresses upon the Admiralty that carrier escort of some sort is required further out into the Atlantic, as the large Condors can both sink ships and guide the U-boats onto them. A certain amount of revenge is extracted as the U-32 is in its turn sunk by the destroyers HMS Harvester and HMS Highlander. This will exacerbate the shortage of carriers, as each one will be spending longer with each convoy. This has been anticipated to some extent - the logical result of more successful A/S operations close to the UK was for the U-boats to move west, but that doesn't make it any more pleasant for the Admiralty. The one good effect is that U-boats will have less time on station, able to attack convoys.

27th October (Africa)

Free French forces under General de Larminat occupy Lambarene in Gabon (French Equatorial Africa.) Meanwhile General de Gaulle has arrived in Brazzaville, the capital of French Equatorial Africa, and proclaimed the creation of a Council of Defence of the French Empire. He was welcomed by the governor, Felix Eboue, and huge crowds. Most of French Equatorial Africa, with 12 million inhabitants, rallied to de Gaulle in late July after the arrival of emissaries sent from London led by General Leclerc.

After the capture of Dakar, the Free French have been busy trying to expand their forces. With the men extracted from Norway as their core, a 1st Free French division has been formed, and men to form a second division are undergoing training. Recruitment in the African colonies has been going well, and indeed the French are currently more limited by experienced cadre and equipment than volunteers.

29th October (China)

Japan's strategy for seizing control of southern China suffered a major setback today as its troops were forced to withdraw south into Indochina after losing Nanning, the capital of Kwangsi, China's southern border province. The loss of Nanning, a key city on the Hanoi-Peking line, counterbalances Japan's recent gain in being allowed to station troops in French Indochina. During seven months of bitter fighting for Nanning both sides have suffered heavy losses.

30th October

An Italian attempt to attack British shipping in Gibraltar harbour with "human torpedoes", fails.

In France, Marshal Petain has called upon the French people to collaborate with Germany. This represents a major change from the originally announced purpose of Petain's government, which sought peace with Germany, not alliance, and results from Laval and Petain's meetings with Hitler at Montoire. The appeal does not go down well in the French colonies still obedient to the Vichy regime, and plans are started to recover all the colonial possessions not yet in Free French control over the coming months.

A report by the Royal Navy on the after-effects of Operation Judgement notes that they are in need of replacement aircraft for the Alexandria-based carriers. In addition, the Army is requesting more aid in its operations and defence of North

Africa. While understanding the Army's needs, the Admiralty points out that this is supposed to be the job of the RAF, and that the FAA is not strong enough (particularly in pilots) to carry out this role. It suggests that either the RAF in North Africa is strengthened, or that RAF pilots be assigned to the Navy to form squadrons specifically for this purpose. The Army is quite pleased by this report, the RAF is not.

31st October

A Wellington V high-altitude bomber reaches 30,000 feet for the first time. This aircraft is serving as the high altitude prototype for the RAF's future high altitude bomber program. The first prototype of these, the Supermarine 318, is already flying, but will need changes to reach the altitudes required. As Supermarine are already fully loaded with development work on the Spitfire, the bomber prototype and work have been handed over to Vickers, where a Mr Wallace has been making suggestions for suitable modifications. As soon as the data is in from the Wellington V, a list of changes will be made and a new prototype produced.

As a result of the early wolfpack attacks on convoys, the convoy limits is being extended to 19 degrees west. New escort carriers are expected soon, and the escort building program is delivering a steady stream on new ships, but there is still a drastic shortage of convoy escorts, although the release of the destroyers held against an invasion is helping. There are increasing signs of the Luftwaffe Kondors, and carrier escort is given as a priority to those thought most likely to encounter these aircraft. Two have already been shot down by Goshawks, the FAA being pleased to find that such a large plane seems to be rather fragile when faced with 20mm cannon.

In the Mediterranean, RAF HQ Middle East is looking worriedly at the build-up of Italian troops in Albania. These are seen as a prelude to either pressure or invasion of Greece, and the RAF is worried that if it is required to send squadrons there it has very few planes. Now that an invasion cannot take place until the spring due to winter conditions in the Channel, they want more of the current substantial new production to be sent to the Middle East to provide them with a tactical reserve. This request is heavily endorsed by the Army, but the RAF High Command is reluctant as this means losing planes which could be used to bomb Germany, seen as the main (in some quarters, the only) proper use of the RAF.

Although the night raids on Britain are still very heavy, the RAF removes Air Marshal Dowding from the position of head of fighter command. This raises some eyebrows at the Admiralty, who while finding Dowding an often difficult person to work with, have been impressed by his expertise and technical ability in the job. They have less faith in his replacement, Air Marshal Douglas. However they feel it is not their role to make public comment on the internal allocation of jobs inside the RAF.

1st November

Churchill sends a telegram to Air Marshal Longmore in Cairo, promising additional help will be provided. As well as the request for additional air power, the obvious threat to Greece means that Army reinforcements will need to be speeded up as well. The Navy considers its force in the area adequate (despite the loss of HMS Courageous), as the Italian Navy has for the moment nothing larger than a light cruiser. Many of its ships have been withdrawn so far north for safety from the FAA as to make intervention in the Eastern Mediterranean very difficult. The Navy is currently planning raids on the Italian North African ports and facilities, as well as increased action against their supply convoys, as they see this as currently the best way they can support the Army.

2nd November

In Cairo, Wavell writes to General Maitland Wilson:

"...I have instructed Lieutenant-General O'Connor to prepare an offensive against the Italians to take place as soon as possible.

...in everything but numbers we are superior to the enemy. We are more highly trained and have better equipment. We know the ground and are better accustomed to desert conditions.. Above all we have stouter hearts and greater traditions and are fighting in a worthier cause.

...a striking success will have incalculable effect not only on the Middle East ... but of the future of freedom and civilisation... It is the best way on which we can help our Greek allies."

The operation is given the code name Compass.

In the Atlantic, U-31 earns the distinction of being sunk for the second (and this time, final) time, by the destroyer HMS Antelope with help from Coastal Command aircraft. She was sunk for the first time on March 11th by an RAF Blenheim bomber.

As the output of Spitfires continues to reach the squadrons, the FAA Goshawks have been stood down in the north of England to be replaced by regular RAF formations; in the south the Hurricanes are being withdrawn - it is intended to send these to the RAF in the Middle East. The navy is happy with the new arrangements, as it needs the planes for the new escort carriers arriving during the winter and spring, and the constant operations, while increasing the combat expertise of the more experienced pilots, has left the training of some of the fresh replacements lacking in some of the specialist skills the Navy needs, like navigation.

However on a far more controversial note, the RAF announces (internally), that Court-Martial proceedings will commence against the first two of the pilots who left their desk jobs without permission to fly Goshawks to defend the North. As usual, although supposedly secret, this information spreads rapidly through the RAF.

3rd November

HMS Furious is loaded with Hurricanes for shipment to the Middle East. She will sail with the next Gibraltar convoy and then continue to West Africa. It is intended to make at least two more of these runs to build up fighter strength in the Middle East. Meanwhile Hurricanes are being crated up for the longer voyage around the cape, to go with the next troop and equipment convoy to Egypt.

In addition, Wellington bombers are to be staged through Malta. These planes have been squeezed out of a reluctant Bomber command, who wanted them for bombing raids over Germany. Coastal command is also requesting more Wellingtons to help in convoy protection.

5th November

Franklin D. Roosevelt is re-elected President for a third term, his new vice-president is Henry A Wallace. He wins a resounding victory over Wendell Wilkie, receiving 27,200,000 votes to Wilkie's 22,300,000, gaining a majority in 39 of the 48 states of the Union

In the UK, the decision by the Air Ministry to court-martial two officers is causing massive opposition both inside the RAF and outside it. The squadrons themselves are appalled; as one squadron commander put it, 'punishing an officer who left his desk to defend his country in the air is against all the tradition we have been trying to impart to our pilots'. Most of the comments are less printable. The Navy and Army watch with bemusement. While officially the officers were in the wrong, they cannot understand how anything other than a reprimand is suitable. Unfortunately for the Air Marshals, the news of the action reaches Churchill, not through channels but oddly via Lord Beaverbrook (whose son is a serving pilot in a frontline squadron). Churchill's reaction is reported to be 'volcanic'.

Inside the Air Ministry, an attempt to close ranks comes to grief when Dowding is asked to approve the action. He replies that he is no longer in charge of Fighter Command, personally thinks the action deplorable (pointing out he himself begged for the officers concerned to be allowed to do officially what they did without orders), then calmly announces that as he is no longer in their line of command, he has offered to stand as Prisoners Friend (in civilian terms, the defence council) for the first officer charged. One of the Air Ministry Air Marshalls goes so far as to call this treasonous. Dowding merely regards him calmly, and then suggests that if they wish, he will resign. And stand as Prisoners Friend.

In North Africa, the Free French have been having talks with Wavell. They are aware of his shortage of aircraft, and have offered the use of two Squadrons of US-built Martin Maryland bombers. These were purchased as part of orders made before France fell, and paid for with the French gold recovered in Africa. While there are numbers of French pilots available, they don't have enough to man the planes they have bought. Some of these have been sold on to other countries such as Holland, but these two squadrons, while flying Free French colours, were in any case being piloted by RAF officers. The intention had been to use the planes in support of planned actions against the Italians in Ethiopia, but this will take a while to happen, and in the meantime they will 'lend' them to Wavell.

6th November (East Africa)

The British finally take Fort Gallabat, in East Africa, from the Italians.

There were two frontier stations, Gallabat on the Sudanese (British) side and Metemma on the (Italian) Ethiopian. The two were about a half a mile apart, separated by a wide, dry wadi or stream bed, and connected by a road. The Italians moved across and occupied Gallabat, defended at that time only by a handful of Sudanese troops with British advisers, not long after joining the war in summer 1940. The British attack, by an Indian brigade with attached artillery and tank support under General Slim, commenced on November 6th. The British retook Gallabat rather easily in the first rush, also repelling with heavy losses a prompt and spirited counterattack from Metemma across the wadi.

However, the attempt to move against Metemma failed, as Italian air attacks caused some panic among the British troops, and the combination of rough terrain (very big rocks) and mines put most of the British tanks out of action.

Slim stayed for several weeks, shelling and otherwise harassing the Italians at Metemma, and in the end the Italian losses were probably as great as or greater than the British (on the first day or two the British/Indian forces suffered 167 casualties, including 42 dead, and lost six of their ten available fighter planes, and nine of their twelve tanks (albeit temporarily in the latter case, as most were repairable).

While the Army realises that East Africa is not a big priority for the RAF, they ask if more air support can be sent. Given the relatively old Italian aircraft in the theatre, they propose that once the Hurricanes and Goshawks arrive in Egypt, that the Gloster Gladiators still there can be reassigned. The RAF agrees to consider this.

7th November

(USA) The middle section of the Tacoma Narrows Bridge in Washington State collapses during a windstorm. The film of this will later become famous in science and engineering classes all over the world.

As a result of the court-martial controversy, Churchill calls in the Air Marshalls and lays down the law to them. The officers will not be court martialled, nor will any others of those who joined the Goshawk squadrons. The Air Ministry will put out that this was all a 'mistake'. Since Churchill suspects that the officers will still be penalised if possible, they will be 'lent' on a long-term basis to the Navy, and will form two fighter squadrons in Egypt. The most that will be done is to reprimand the officers. While Churchill's reaction is not surprising to those who know him, it will have a longer term consequence when the anticipated paper on air resources and operations, expected shortly, is released.

The Italian invasion of Greece is postponed for a further 10 days as the air force has still not finished rearranging its plans. In addition the logistics have had to be redone, as with no naval support it is expected that shipping through the Adriatic will prove too dangerous unless heavily escorted by air, and even then will be in danger if the Royal Navy assign a carrier to interdict the shipping. However Mussolini insists that this will be the last postponement - the Italian ultimatum will be presented on the 21st of November.

9th November

Neville Chamberlain died at the age of 71. It is now stated that he was already suffering from cancer of the stomach when he was forced out of the premiership six months ago during the political crisis over how to fight the war.

The 1st Free French division is expected to be operational in the East African theatre within two weeks. The division had been hampered somewhat by its lack of transport - which is in very short supply in Africa at the moment. The RAF has promised that once the division is operation, it will release the Gladiator fighters for additional support (this is a quid pro quo for the French Maryland bombers), as by then it is expected additional fighters will have arrived from England.

The battleship Richelieu arrives at Norfolk Virginia to be completed and repaired. As there are ongoing politics involved with the recognition of the Free French (which ironically haven't stopped the Americans taking payment from them for the purchase orders placed by France before she fell!), the vessel is flying the White Ensign.

The first of the merchant carrier conversions, HMS Athene, has finished her workup - this has been pressed as fast as possible, the increasing U-boat activity has meant the new escort carriers are needed urgently. She will carry twelve Swordfish for A/S duties plus four Goshawks to welcome any inquisitive German patrol aircraft. The second of these ships, HMS Engadine, was commissioned today.

Churchill meets with Dowding to offer him a new job. He realises that Dowding has pretty much burnt his bridges with the current Air Board, but after talking with some of his advisors, he has been given an idea. Dowding will be the head (and Air Force representative) of a small committee looking at the future of the air war - both independently and in conjunction with the Navy and Army. The building plans have returned to normal after the invasion scare, but with a number of new aircraft coming online now or soon, and with a number of existing ones seen as obsolete or downright dangerous, a strategy is needed to use them in the most efficient way to hurt Germany. The committee will report as soon as possible, preferably by the end of the year, so long term building plans can be made.

12th November

Molotov arrives in Berlin, to begin talks with the German Foreign Minister von Ribbentrop, who expounds yet again on the imminent collapse of England. But this collapse may need to be accelerated by invasion.

After lunch Molotov met with Hitler. The Fuhrer said that he had reached several conclusions:

1. Germany was not seeking to obtain military aid from Russia.

2. Because of the tremendous extension of the war, Germany had been forced, in order to oppose England, to penetrate into territories remote from her and in which she was not basically interested politically or economically.

3. There were nevertheless certain requirements, the full importance of which had only become apparent during the war, but which were vital to Germany. Among them were certain sources of raw materials.

Molotov for his part gives a non-committal assent but enquires about the Tripartite Pact. What is the meaning of the New Order in Europe and the Greater East Asian Co-Prosperity Sphere and where does the USSR fit in it? Issues regarding Russia's Balkan and Black Sea interests must be clarified.

Meanwhile Hitler issues his 18th war directive, ordering political measures to bring Spain into the war and death by slow strangulation for Britain. The following day he orders Goering to prepare the Luftwaffe for an invasion of Russia next May.

In Britain the first prototype Mosquito makes its first flight, piloted by Geoffrey DeHaviland.

13th November

Molotov again meets with von Ribbentrop. He presses him on the purpose of the German troops present in Finland. The reply is that the troops are merely in transit to northern Norway and that the whole matter is a "misunderstanding". Hitler also evades the question when he meets with him later, instead launching into a speech on the dissolution of the British Empire and its subsequent carving up between the Axis powers (and the Soviet Union at this point). Molotov also questions Hitler on the recent German-Italian guarantees to Romania which work against Soviet interests, but Hitler evades the question.

That evening Molotov gives a banquet in the Russian Embassy in Unter den Linden and entertains von Ribbentrop. The banquet is interrupted by an air-raid (Churchill states later "We had heard of the conference beforehand, and though not invited to join in the discussion did not wish to be entirely left out of the proceedings."). Carrying on their conversation in an air-raid shelter Ribbentrop talks of the need to divide up the British Empire now that England is so decisively beaten. "If England is so beaten, why are we sitting in this shelter?" asks Molotov.

In the Pacific, The Dutch East Indies agrees to supply Japan with nearly two million tons of oil a year. In Singapore, Air Marshall Brooke-Popham arrives as the new British Commander in Chief.

15th November

The City of Coventry is hit by the heaviest raid so far (proportional to its size), a force of over 400 Luftwaffe bombers attacking the city at night. Serious damage is done to the cities industry and residential accommodation. Sorties are flown by RAF night fighters; AI-equipped Beaufighters as well as Hurricanes and Defiants. Despite the number of bombers, only 15 AI detections were made, and another 11 either unassisted or illuminated in searchlights, and only six enemy bombers were shot down. The day fighters are proving ineffective in night operations, and it is obvious that more proper night fighters are needed. The first of the night-fighter version of the Gloster Reaper is expected in a few weeks; these have been given production priority. A steady improvement is being made in the operation of the AI radar itself, and the number of detections is rising steadily; once there are more night fighters, it is hoped to soon make night operations as painfully expensive for the Luftwaffe as day operations already are.

In Warsaw, the Jewish ghetto, with 400,000 inhabitants, is sealed off from the rest of the city.

At Sidi Barrani Italian troops work to fortify this remote coastal village, the limit of their advance towards the Nile Delta, British troops are meanwhile carrying out clandestine preparations for a major counter-offensive. Moving only by night, and lying low under camouflage netting by day, they are burying large quantities of water and fuel in secret dumps along the 75-mile "no-man's-land" from Mersa Matruh and westward. Marshal Graziani shows no sign of advancing further. An Italian observer reports a "holiday atmosphere" in their ranks as more British tanks arrive in Egypt.

17th November

Air Vice Marshal Park, who commanded 11 Group during the Battle of Britain, has also been relieved of his command and sent off to command No 23 Training Group. This has enraged the pilots under his command (already upset at the fiasco of the court martial episode), and is seen as a direct snub to one of the two men who saved Britain. Air Vice Marshal Leigh-Mallory, who is known to have opposed Dowdings and Parks tactics, gets the job.

Churchill, although not directly involved, is getting reports of this via Beaverbrook. He is fast coming to the conclusion that while there are undoubtedly many good senior RAF officers, there is something rotten at the heart of the Air Board. However he is extremely reluctant to take any direct action (he feels that what he has done already should have made the point), but is becoming receptive to ideas which seem to get around the Air Ministry. He asks the FAA who were involved in the fighter defence of the North to look (informally) into the dispute between Leigh-Mallory and Park over tactics.

Churchill is also concerned at the steady losses of bombers in raids over the continent, which do not seem to be achieving anything, unlike the German raids on England. He sends a telegram to the Chief of the Air Staff "I watch these figures with much concern (aircraft losses). ...we are now not even keeping level, and there is a marked downward turn this week, especially in Bomber Command. Painful as it is not to be able to strike heavy blows after Coventry ... I feel we should nurse Bomber Command."

A delivery of twelve Hurricanes and twelve Goshawks is made to Malta from Ark Royal; one of the hurricanes fails to arrive due to engine failure, but the crew are recovered by a flying boat from Malta.

Off the coast of East Africa, British naval forces bombard Mogadishu. The comment is made that 'it seemed to improve the place...'

19th November

Chancellor Adolf Hitler tells the Spanish Foreign Minister Serano Suner to make good on an agreement for Spain to attack Gibraltar. This would seal off the

Mediterranean and trap British troops in North Africa. But the Spanish dictator, General Francisco Franco, does not want to commit his country to the war, (although he has allowed German submarines to refuel in Spanish ports and German spies to keep tabs on British naval forces in Gibraltar), especially as the situation in the Mediterranean is looking unpleasant for the Axis, and has instructed Suner to stall for time. His intelligence reports that even with specialised German help it is likely to take 4-8 weeks to subdue the fortress, ample time for the Royal Navy's heavy ships and carriers to wreak terrible damage on Spanish coastal cities and ports. There is also the more worrying factor of Britain stopping vital supplies current being let through to Spain. Without these, Spain will starve, and Franco has a lively disbelief in the ability of Germany to replace these items.

In Egypt, four Gladiator Mk. II biplane fighters of the Australian No. 3 Squadron, based at Mersa Matruh, are attacked by eighteen Italian CR-42 Falco biplane fighters. The RAAF pilots claim six Italian aircraft shot down for the loss of one Gladiator and its pilot. The RAAF squadrons have already been promised Hurricane fighters once the next delivery arrives in Egypt; the RAF want to get these operational before the end of November if possible.

20th November

General Wavell sends a message to the CIGS:

"Compass" in active preparation and forward depots already made. Main difficulties transport, spares for artillery and tanks, protection against air attack and secrecy. Can deal with first two locally as far as resources allow but air protection dependent on arrival Hurricanes in time. Am arranging to concentrate all AA artillery I can make available, taking risks elsewhere in Egypt. Shall endeavour to stage operation if air situation makes it at all possible but the less air support the larger the casualties will be and the greater the risk of failure.

The Indian Army arrives at Port Suez in Egypt and at Port Sudan. They bring with them cooks to prepare meals for the separate company messes for British, Hindu, Moslem, Sikh and Untouchable soldiers. . The reinforcements are welcome, as Britain has only 8,000 troops in the Sudan against Italy's 300,000. Further south in East Africa, The RAF bomb military installations at Mai Edaga and Gura in Eritrea.

Japanese warships and transports have arrived off Saigon in French Indo-China, the Japanese having demanded the right to occupy the city.

Chapter 4 - Italy invades Greece

21st November

The Italian invasion of Greece, delayed for some 3 1/2 weeks due to the naval and air chaos after Operation Judgement, starts at last. While his commanders are still pressing for more delays in order for them to reorganise, Mussolini refuses to accept any more delay.

At 0530 Mussolini's army invades Greece. In the firm belief that they would meet little resistance from the Dictator General Metaxas's forces, Italian tanks and infantry crossed from occupied Albania into the mountains of Epirus before dawn. When Hitler was given the news he was furious, but signalled a pledge of military support if Mussolini required it.

In Hitler's opinion Mussolini is making a critical strategic blunder. To Hitler the capture of Gibraltar, with assistance from Franco and Italy's conquest of Egypt, especially the great naval base at Alexandria, would ensure Britain's collapse. Mussolini in turn was convinced that the pro-German Metaxas - who has based his Asfalia secret police on the Gestapo and abolished most democratic institutions in Greece - would succumb quickly offering little resistance. Metaxas, however, rejected the Italian ultimatum half an hour after Italian troops crossed the border.

The first Greek communiqué reads: As of 5:30 am today, the Italian armed forces are attacking our troops protecting the Greek Albanian border. Our forces are defending our native territory.

The first Italian Communiqué reads: "At dawn on the 28th October our forces stationed in Albania crossed over the Greek border and gained entrance at several places. Our advance continues"

General Visconti-Prasca the Commander-in-Chief of the Italian aerial forces has mistakenly not blocked the road to the north, thus allowing three newly-mobilised Greek divisions to move quickly to the front. The Italians are moving slowly, and the Greeks are mobilising quickly.

In Cairo, the British make long-agreed deployments to aid Greece. Air Marshal Sir Arthur Longmore Air Officer C-in-C, Air HQ Middle East (an Australian) orders three squadrons of Blenheims and one of Gladiators to Greece. General Wavell is ordered to send also two AA batteries to Athens and an infantry brigade to Suda Bay, in Crete, to assist in the defence of the Greek islands. It is intended to place Imperial troops on Crete to allow Greece to deploy their troops there on the mainland

23rd November

The Romanian Premier, Ion Antonescu, agrees to join the Tripartite Pact, paving the way for German intervention in Greece, while in Vienna, Romanian officials sign the protocol of adherence to the Axis Tripartite Pact.

In Britain, The first Handley Page Halifax heavy bomber arrives at No. 35 Squadron for familiarisation purposes.

Middle East command receives a telegram from the Chiefs of Staff:

"It has been decided that it is necessary to give Greece the greatest possible material and moral support at the earliest possible moment. Impossible for anything from UK to arrive in time. Consequently only course is to draw upon resources in Egypt and to replace them from UK as soon as possible. Aerodromes must be made ready for three Blenheim and two Gladiator Squadrons with AA protection. One battery HAA guns and one battery LAA guns should be dispatched to supplement Greek AA.

To replace aircraft 34 Hurricanes will be staged through Takoradi, 32 Wellingtons will be staged through Malta. It is intended to increase the weight of attack from Malta by bringing the number of operational Wellingtons to 24. It is appreciated that this will leave Egypt very thin for a period, and we will endeavour to reinforce you from the UK as fast as possible."

In Albania, The Greek counter-attack starts, and reaches the Korce-Peratia road.

24th November

The Governor and C-in-C Malta sends a telegram to the War Office:

"The more I think of it the more troubled I am at the withdrawal of one of our three fighter squadrons from the western desert. This is a very drastic cut and unless we can improve upon present plans, cannot be replaced for some weeks.

AOC-in-C has warned me that we are too weak to give effective support to the army in battle should a major engagement develop. Nor we can we ignore the possibility that an object of Italy's attack on Greece is to induce us to weaken ourselves in the vital theatre of Egypt. In these conditions, it would help us in Egypt if some additional Goshawk fighters could be flown out at once via Malta. Further, while we are glad to have Wellingtons in Egypt, these cannot be used for day bombing and are not the equivalent of Blenheims in value for battle."

It is agreed to send out two squadrons of RAF-crewed Goshawk fighters (these are the ones that were helping defend Northern England and Scotland). The fighters will go by carrier through Gibraltar, the fly on to Malta. They will then use overflow tanks to fly direct to Egypt. The RAF is reluctant to release Blenheims, stating that they are needed for bombing Germany, but it is pointed out that at least two squadrons worth that are no longer considered viable in the fighter role (these were originally intended for use as night fighters, but have been replaced by faster aircraft) can be sent immediately. Churchill orders these two squadrons to be sent at once.

25th November

In Greece, Italian forces reach the river Kalamas, near Epirus. Italian aircraft also bomb Salonika and islands of Corfu and Crete. 300 people are killed in bombing attacks on Piraeus.

The Royal Navy registers its first success at sweeping the new acoustic mine; three are exploded.

In a setback to Hitler, Bulgaria responds to Soviet pressure and refuses to join the Axis pact.

26th November

Churchill telegrams to Wavell:

Re:- Operation Compass... am having a Staff study made of possibilities open to us, if all goes well, for moving troops and also reserve forward by sea in long hops along the coast, and setting up new supply bases to which pursuing armoured vehicles and units might resort.

As a result of this Wavell consults with Cunningham to get his opinion on this (he feels that staff studies in London often deal with the real situation on the ground incorrectly). In fact Cunningham is quite supportive, as he sees any action by the light units of the Italian Navy as an excuse to sink them. However he warns that there will be issues over minefields, and also air cover will be needed.

In Moscow, Stalin informs the German ambassador that Russia is prepared to join the four-power pact provided that:

1. German troops are immediately withdrawn from Finland.

2. That within the next few months the security of the Soviet Union in the Straits is assured by the conclusion of a mutual-assistance pact with Bulgaria, ... and by the establishment of a base for land and naval forces by the Soviet Union within range of the Bosphorus and Dardanelles.

3. That the area south of Batum and Baku in the general direction of the Persian Gulf is recognised as the centre of the aspirations of the Soviet Union.

4. That Japan renounces her rights to concessions for coal and oil in northern Sakhalin.

In Africa, the Belgian Congo declares war on Italy.

In the Western Desert, the British Western Desert Force begins 'Training exercise No 1', which is a dress rehearsal for Operation Compass.

28th November

A small, fast, British convoy which has been escorted through the Mediterranean by Force H splits; two ships enter Malta, the rest of the convoy is escorted by units of the Mediterranean fleet to Alexandria. In addition to supplies, the convoy delivers nearly 1,400 RAF technicians.

Less than two weeks after crossing the Greek border in strength, the Italian army is retreating in total disarray. The Italian commander, General Visconti Prasca, has been sacked and Mussolini's crack 'Julia' alpine division routed with huge losses in men and equipment. The Italians have been taken completely by surprise by the speed and ferocity of the Greeks. Six days after the Italian invasion, Greece's General Papagos ordered the first counter-attack. A small Greek force crossed the Albanian frontier and took Pissoderi, a mountain near the captured town of Koritsa. The main road out of Koritsa was cut by another Greek force. With their superior knowledge of the terrain, the tough and well-trained Greeks have abandoned the valleys and taken to the mountains from whence they can infiltrate enemy positions.

Fighting at an altitude of over 5,000 feet - in the most severe winter for years - Papagos's single division has proved more than a match for the numerically superior Italians whose armour is confined to the lower ground. The Italians have paid the penalty for having allowed the Greeks to hold the mountainous centre of the front. The Julia division found itself trapped. 5,000 men have surrendered, and the Greeks are claiming a further 25,000 dead and seriously wounded. General Soddu will replace General Prasca as the head of the Italian attack on the following day.

In French Indo-China, the Royal Thai Air Force begins aerial bombing after the alleged bombing of Thai positions around Nankorn Panom by French planes. While deploring the action, the Free French commanders feel there is little that can be done to aid the Vichy-controlled colony so far from the centre of the war.

29th November

Romania is in a state of anarchy. There is shooting in the streets as the Iron Guards clash with the army and rival factions of the Guards fight among themselves. The young King Michael is reported to have fled to Yugoslavia. Among the victims of the anarchy are the former premier, Professor Jorga, and Dr Madgearu, a former minister of finance. German involvement is suspected but so far unproven.

30th November

The German merchant raider Pinguin attacks the British ship Port Wellington in the southern Indian Ocean. Unknown to the Pinguin, the Port Wellingtons sighting message has been picked up by HMAS Melbourne, who has been exercising to the north. The raider will encounter one of the light carriers search planes in a few days.

Some 3,000 British military have been ferried from Alexandria to the Piraeus; in addition, forces have been landed on Crete. It is hoped to have RAF units operating in Greece soon to support the Greek army.

3rd December

An RAF reconnaissance aircraft on a standard patrol of the North Sea off the German coast spots a German freighter heading into the North Sea (rather than staying close to the coast which is their normal route). It is marked as a potential blockade runner, and Coastal Command Beaufighters are tasked to intercept it that afternoon. They manage to put two torpedoes into the ship, which is left in a sinking condition. It is later found that the ship is not a blockade runner, but is the armed merchant cruiser Kormoran.

5th December

In the South Atlantic, the German armed merchant cruiser Thor and British armed merchant cruiser HMS Carnarvon Castle exchange 6-inch shells 300 miles south of Rio de Janeiro, Brazil. HMS Carnarvon Castle was hit 27 times (4 killed, 32 wounded) while Thor was able to disengage unharmed. HMS Carnarvon Castle would receive temporary repairs at Montevideo, Uruguay.

The Royal navy does not have any available forces for raider suppression in the area, as the carriers and cruisers are needed for convoy duty and in the Mediterranean. However the battleship Prince of Wales and the light carrier HMS Theseus, with four destroyers, are just finishing their working-up off the West Indies; this group is ordered south to see if it can intercept the raider.

In Berlin, Hitler received the military plans for an invasion of the USSR. He duly approved them all, and proposed a timetable for invasion in May of the following year.

Operation Compass 1940 - 41

Chapter 5 - Operation Compass

6th December

In Egypt, the British 7th Armoured Division, British 16th Infantry Brigade, and Indian 4th Infantry Division began preparing for Operation Compass. To do this the Western Desert Force begins 'Training Exercise 2', which involves a 60m march to their concentration point, 'Piccadilly', 20 miles south of Maktila. The Force will be fully concentrated for 'Compass' by the 8th.

German armed merchant cruisers Komet and Orion stopped freighter Triona with gunfire 200 miles south of Nauru in the Pacific, killing three men in the process. While there is currently no sign of action from the German fleet, the increasing operations of the merchant raiders is causing concern. However the Admiralty is reluctant to release more cruisers to hunting them because of the upcoming Operation Compass.

The Kriegsmarines latest (and currently only operational) battleship, Bismarck, completed her trials in the Baltic Sea and set sail for Hamburg, Germany. She will then join up with the Graf Zeppelin for joint exercises, safely out of range of the Royal Navy.

9th December

In Albania, Mussolini announces the occupation of Erseka by the Greek Army. Erseka is a vitally strategic point as it can cut off all communication and transport and will allow the Greeks a speedy advance into Koritsa.

In Greece, The Italians are driven back behind the River Kalamas. A third RAF fighter squadron arrives in Greece; No.80 Squadrons is the first one equipped with Hurricanes, the initial two being equipped with Gladiators.

The Western Desert Force begins Operation Compass. During the night, forces have moved through the gap between Italian camps Nibeiwa and Sofafi without being detected.

Beginning at 0500 hours, Allied artillery and aircraft bombarded the Italian camp at Nibeiwa, Egypt for two hours. At 0715 hours, ground troops began moving toward the rear of the fort for attack. Troops of the Indian 4th Infantry Division, supported by tanks of the British 7th Royal Tank Regiment, captured the camp at 0830 hours. Italian positions at Tummar West and Tummar East were also captured by dusk. Along the coast, tanks of the British 4th Armoured Brigade cut off the main road to prevent an Italian withdrawal. Meanwhile, the British monitor HMS Terror and gunboats HMS Ladybird and HMS Aphis bombarded Italian positions at Sidi Barrani and Maktila.

In addition to the monitor and gunboats, two forces of the Mediterranean fleet are at sea. The first, and more forward one, is centred around the battleships HMS Warspite and HMS Valiant, the second around the carrier HMS Implacable. The battleships are to give additional fire support to the army in the coastal regions, and to make sure no Italian ships try and interfere. The carrier is covering the battleships and also adding to the RAF reconnaissance fore out of Egypt. In addition Cunningham has lent two squadrons of Goshawks to help make sure the Army has air cover for the start of the operation, until it can capture forward airfields. If necessary he has agreed to move his second carrier forward to help provide this.

In Italy, The newly formed 97 Gruppo of the Regia Aeronautica is deployed with its new aircraft - the Junkers JU87. This Gruppo will operate initially on the Greek-Albanian front, but the Navy is pressing for them to be allocated to anti-shipping strike duties. This time, the Army has won.

10th December

Before dawn, colonial troops of the Libyan 1st Division withdrew from Maktila, Egypt. In the afternoon, the Indian 4th Infantry Division and British 7th Royal Tank Regiment surround Sidi Barrani, pushing the Italian 4th Blackshirt Division and another Libyan colonial division into the desert.

With bands playing and their blue and white flags flying, Greek troops marched through the streets of Koritsa in Albania today as the last Italian invaders fled from Greek soil. Koritsa had been surrounded for several days before the Greeks finally stormed the Italians' shallow trenches with bayonets and trench-knives. The invaders surrendered in their hundreds, with retreat becoming a rout as they abandoned a complete arsenal of heavy guns, anti-tank weapons, food and a huge stock of petrol. The Italian Army retreats to Elbasan as the Greeks advance on the Epirus front.

In Germany, Führer Directive 19 is written. This describes the steps that will be taken if it becomes necessary to occupy the rest of metropolitan France, and to seize those parts of the French fleet still in France. The document concludes 'The Italians will be given no information about our preparations and intentions.'

The carrier HMS Indefatigable with a force of light escorts raids the Italian-held port of Tobruk. The dive bombers sink two merchant ships and the accompanying fighters strafe the harbour and light shipping present before withdrawing. There is no Italian fighter resistance, and only two planes are damages by the AA fire. As a result of the damage and confusion, not to mention the damage to morale, the port will take three days to resume normal operation.

11th December

A report by the Luftwaffe and Kriegsmarine discusses the possibility of conducting a raid on the Royal Navy similar to that conducted by the FAA on Wilhelmshaven and Taranto. While it admits this is possible, there are significant difficulties.

The available torpedo planes and dive bombers are unlikely to get through the RAF daytime defence. This mandates a night attack, for which no units have been trained. Also, the best target, Scapa Flow, is barely in range of the Ju-87R and outside Me109 cover. A raid on Portsmouth or Plymouth would be easier, but the Royal Navy is only using them for light craft now as they consider invasion unlikely until the spring. A raid sinking a few destroyers will not have the propaganda and morale value that one sinking capital ships would. In addition, the dive bombers are currently unable to sink a battleship without a lucky hit due to their thick deck armour.

The report therefore recommends three courses of action.

First, to use the available planes tasked for anti-shipping roles in the Mediterranean (keeping some in Northern Europe to attack British coastal shipping). This would have the advantage of allowing attacks to begin as soon as the force and its logistic train are in place. A second benefit is that ships sunk at sea are not recoverable.

Second, to look into planning a heavy raid on either one of the RN's southern ports, or Scapa Flow (ideally both), which could take place in the late spring if invasion is again planned (or even an invasion scare) which will bring heavy units south into easier range. A raid on Scapa would be easier if one of the Luftwaffe's modern bombers can be adapted to carry torpedoes.

Third, a small unit should investigate the issues involved in a night attack on a port, and suggest training measures (it is pointed out that this may take time). It would also allow the specific aircraft to be allocated. A possible target for a raid would be the autumn (the spring would be too early, while the very short summer nights at the latitude of the UK, and Scapa in particular, make a night raid very difficult).

In North Africa, the British 7th Armoured Brigade attacks Buq Buq, Egypt, forcing Italian 64th Infantry Division to surrender. While this is happening, the Indian 4th Infantry Division and British 7th Royal Tank Regiment force the surrender of Italian 4th Blackshirt Division and two colonial Libyan divisions in the desert.

Off the coast the British battleships HMS Warspite and HMS Valiant heavily bombard Italian positions at Sollum, Egypt. The Allied forces have now captured over 20,000 Italian prisoners of war, 237 guns, and 73 tanks.

The First Free French division commences full operational status in East Africa. This allows Wavell to allocate his 'reserve' formation, the 6th Australian Division, to Operation Compass (it had earlier been considered to be used to replace the 4th Indian Division to allow them to move to the Sudan, but the logistical situation there means they could not have been supported as well as the Free French division. The division is still not fully equipped or ready for action, but it allows his front-line formations to keep more pressure on the Italian Army, which is showing a decided tendency to collapse when sufficient force is applied.

12th December

Hungary and Yugoslavia sign the Treaty of Eternal Friendship. This will be one of the shorter definitions of 'eternal'.

In Greece, the CIC of the Greek Army Papagos meets with General Tsolakogolu, head of the Greek Army III corps which has taken Koritsa. He fears that the troops are tired and need rest. Tsolakogolu insists that the advance continue and recommends that a select group of Greek units be dispatched from those who have taken Koritsa to chase the Italians north

The British 7th Armoured Brigade moves through the desert to outflank Italian forces at Sollum and to cut the road to Bardia in Libya. The port itself was subjected to heavy attack by carrier aircraft attack by HMS Indefatigable, leaving two coastal ships on the bottom of the harbour and the port itself in chaos. Meanwhile, the first groups of Italian prisoners of war began to arrive by truck at the British headquarters at Mersa Matruh, Egypt. Headquarters is surprised by the numbers; even though they had been getting reports from the front-line units, seeing them is a different matter.

13th December

A squadron of Cormorant dive bombers is deployed to Greece. This has been made up from the reserve planes for HMS Courageous and the rescued pilots, and is intended to help interdict Italian shipping supplying the troops in Albania and Greece.

The British 4th Armoured Brigade crossed the desert between Halfaya and Sidi Omar in Egypt in an attempt to cut the road to Tobruk.

The cruiser HMS Coventry is torpedoed by an Italian submarine 40m northeast of Sidi Barrani. The torpedo nearly blows off the cruisers bow, but she manages to make it back to Alexandria under her own power.

The 6th Australian division is not yet considered ready for battle, but O'Connor wants to keep the pressure up on the Italian Army. The biggest issue is their incomplete transport, as this is vital to keep forces moving rapidly in the desert. It is suggested that some of the division could be tasked for an amphibious assault (where lack of trucks would be less of an issue), but at the moment the Army is advancing too fast for one to be easily planned. In the meantime, 16 Brigade is being brought up to full strength at the expense of the other two Brigades. These will be brought up to strength as soon as possible.

15th December

In North Africa, O'Connor presses on with his attacks. Sollum and Halfaya Pass were captured today, followed by the advance to Fort Capuzzo on the Libyan side of the border. All lost Egyptian territory has now been recaptured.

In Greece, elements of the Greek Army's III Corps have been fighting their way North toward Lake Ohrida since the capture of Koritsa on the 22nd. The snow and freezing weather have been affecting the effectiveness of both sides but the Greek advance continues nevertheless.

17th December

The monitor HMS Terror and gunboat HMS Ladybird bombarded Bardia in Libya, sinking Italian ships Galata, Vincenzino, and Giuseppina D. in the harbour. The battleship HMS Warspite and two cruisers bombard Tobruk; as a result the port will be rendered inoperable as the local work force refuse to work. Attempts by the Italian commander to man the port with his men do not work out well.

On the same day, the British announced that they had captured 20,000 Italian prisoners, including three generals, in Egypt (this is in fact an underestimate, the capture figures are mounting so fast they are unable to keep up with them!), and that the 4th Armoured Brigade captured Sidi Omar, Egypt, taking 900 Italian troops prisoner.

The Western Desert force is now getting ready to exploit its victory so far by an assault on Bardia. The 7th Armoured division is concentrating southwest of Bardia while waiting for 4th Indian division to catch up. Meanwhile 6th Australian division is following up (and spending far more time than they wish helping send back prisoners); so far the British have captured 38,000 men, 400 artillery pieces and 50 tanks while losing only 133 killed and 395 wounded and missing.

Bardia, on the Libyan coast, is guarded by about 45,000 Italian and colonial troops (the British are underestimating the defenders, they only estimate some 20,000 men) under the command of Lieutenant General Annibale Bergonzoli, who had orders from Mussolini to fight until the last man. This dismays General Bergonzoli.

18th December

In Berlin, Führer Directive 21 is issued, confirming the plans for Unternehmen Barbarossa. This describes how the intention is to crush the Russian army in a quick campaign, even if war with England (sic) is not completed. Only the navy will continue to prosecute the war against Britain; apart from the need to keep occupied territories under control, all other efforts are to be diverted to attacking Russia.

19th December

Mussolini requests German aid for his troops in Cyrenaica, asking for a Panzer Division, Luftwaffe units, and various logistical support. Given the need to prepare for Barbarossa, this request is not popular, but the German army starts to look at the possibility of supporting Italy. The Luftwaffe is busy getting Fliegerkorps X into operation, and expects to be able to make their first attacks from Sicily by the end of the year. It is pointed out that moving them to North Africa will delay the start of anti-shipping operations, and using them in a ground support role would negate the only specialised Luftwaffe anti-shipping unit. It is suggested that if Luftwaffe units are to be provided, these should be regular ones (rather than the specialised Fliegerkorps X), and that they should ideally provide logistics support so the F.X. planes can be stationed in North Africa quickly if plans change. The Luftwaffe is currently trying to organise training and build-up for Barbarossa, support in the Mediterranean, and a heavy night blitz on Britain, with resources that are becoming stretched.

Bardia is now surrounded by the 4th Indian Division and the 16th Brigade of the 6th Australian division, and being bombarded daily by units of the Mediterranean fleet. The port facilities are now unusable, and the daily attacks, undeterred by the Italian air force (who have so far lost five fighters and seven bombers to FAA Goshawks while trying to attack the British warships) is affecting morale badly

20th December

Aircraft from HMS Victorious attack an Italian convoy off the Kerkennah islands off Tunisia. All three ships in the convoy, as well as an anti-submarine escort, are sunk.

The Western Desert force is reorganised as the British 13th Corps.

23rd December

In Libya, the Commander-in-Chief of Italian North Africa General Rodolfo Graziani replaces General Mario Berti of Italian 10th Army with his Chief of Staff General Giuseppe Tellera after the failures in the initial stages of Operation Compass. Meanwhile the British forces outside Bardia have resupplied and regrouped ready to resume the offensive, but are still short of ammunition. It is hoped to resume the offensive tomorrow, and meanwhile ammunition is being brought forward from the two Australian Brigades in reserve so as not to lose momentum.

24th December

The assault on Bardia begins, started by a heavy bombardment by Royal Navy battleships lying off the coast, and heavy attacks by RAF bombers.

O'Connor's tactical plan for the capture of Bardia, which has a 17 mile of perimeter defended by a continuous anti-tank ditch, wire obstacles and concrete blockhouses, is to send a battalion of infantry in first, establish a bridgehead on the far side of the anti-tank ditch and the wire, then bridge the ditch and clear the wire and minefields for the passage of tanks. The tanks would then be shepherded within the perimeter and fan out in attack, with two more infantry battalions close behind them. The main point of assault was to be the centre of the western face of the perimeter, where O'Connor believed the Italians least expected it.

It was the Australians first major action in World War II. The tank ditch was breached by infantry in less than an hour, crossing places quickly made and nearly a hundred land mines removed. The tanks were into the bridgehead by 7 am. Australian casualties to date are over 100 killed and at least 300 wounded. One Australian battalion suffered heavy casualties when it launched a diversionary attack. After the Australians penetrated the wire, the Italians met one of the companies with machine-guns, rifles and grenades. The troops from 4th Indian Division were equally successful, though the more experienced men suffered fewer casualties. The combined force takes 30,000 prisoners on the first day.

26th December

Bardia is captured by O'Connor after an assault lasting less than four days. The Australian 6th Division and the Indian 4th Division take 45,000 prisoners including four generals, 462 guns, 130 tanks and over 700 trucks; Total casualties of the Imperial forces are 130 KIA and 326 WIA. This is Australia's first major land battle of the war, and O'Connor is impressed with how well the green formation has fought. He urges Wavell to get the other two Brigades fully operational as soon as possible.

Emulating Winston Churchill, British Foreign Secretary Anthony Eden said 'never has so much been surrendered by so many, to so few.' Italian General Bergonzoli and his staff withdraw from Bardia toward Tobruk. Wavell orders British forces to advance into Cyrenaica, to exploit their victory against the Italians. 7th Armoured Division under Major General Michael Creagh detours around Bardia and marches toward Tobruk. Wavell sets out his ultimate objective as Benghazi, to be taken within the next week.

In Albania, Greek troops push Italian troops back 15 miles, capturing Sarandë. To the far south, Italian torpedo bombers attacked the British naval base at Suda Bay, Crete at 1540 hours, damaging British cruiser HMS Glasgow with two torpedoes. This was a surprise to the Royal Navy, whose intelligence had given no sign these bombers were operational in the area. Priority is being given to getting a fighter force operational on Crete, and in the meantime the Navy will limit the ships in the area to lighter craft; the ongoing Operation Compass makes then reluctant to reassign the carriers as the operation is going so well.

In addition to his earlier request for help in North Africa, Mussolini also asks for help against the Greeks in Albania. When this request is passed on to the German planners, they are unhappy at the disruption such help would cause to the ongoing Barbarossa preparations.

27th December

Advance units of Allied force reach the outer defences of Tobruk after taking El Adem airfield eight miles to the south. Patrols to examine the Italian defences begin immediately. The Tobruk garrison is 25,000 men with 220 guns and 70 tanks, commanded by Lieutenant General Enrico Manella.

An amphibious operation is considered to cut off Italian forces as their line of retreat is now mainly along the coastal road. 50 and 52 Commando (a total of some 800 men) is allocated to this, and the Navy agrees to provide support; while shipping is available to carry the men, there is a shortage of the specialised landing draft they need. After the success of improvised operations of this sort at Narvik, it is hoped that the landing craft will not be necessary.

In London, the need for more carriers of some sort leads to the planned modification of some grain carriers and tankers into MAC-ships. These plans, to fit a basic flight deck over the hull, while retaining their cargo capability, were suggested before the war but the carrier build at the time looked adequate. An alternative plan, to catapult surplus carriers off ships, has been rejected - instead the dockyard effort will go to producing a number of MAC ships.

Britain's latest heavy bomber made its first flight at Ringway Airport, Manchester, here today. The Avro Lancaster is a four-engined development of the Avro Manchester, which is just entering RAF service. It has a longer range and heavier bomb-load than any other British bomber. The aircraft that flew today, however, is only a prototype, and it will be some months yet before the Lancaster production lines begin to turn out aircraft. Even so, as the Avro chief test pilot, Bill Thorne, took her into the air, the managing director Sir Roy Dobson turned to the designer Roy Chadwick and said: "Oh boy, oh boy ... what an aeroplane! What a piece of aeroplane!"

28th December

The Greek army capture Premeti, Pogradec and the Albanian port of Sarande.

The AOC-in-C, Middle East, Arthur Longmore, receives a signal from Churchill. "Greatly admire your brilliant support of Army operations. We shall soon be as usual torn between conflicting needs. Probably four or five squadrons will be required for Greece and yet you will have to carry the Army forward in Libya. We will endeavour to send you the maximum number of aircraft we can spare". Having talked with the Dowding committee, Churchill has decided that it will be possible to send additional aircraft, as the number requested to be held at home by the RAF seems to exceed the operational needs over the next few months

29th December

In America, President Roosevelt has drafted a $17 billion budget for the fiscal year 1942, including $10 billion for the armament program. In a "fireside chat" on radio, the President called for the US to become "the arsenal of democracy." The President made "the direct statement to the American people that there is far less chance of the US getting into war if we do all we can now to support the nations defending themselves against attack by the Axis than if we acquiesce in their defeat."

Later polls suggest that Polls suggest that the Presidents "Arsenal of Democracy" speech was the most successful he has ever given. 75% of the population were aware of it and more than 60% agreed with what he said. Henry Stimson urges that US Navy be used to escort convoys to the UK.

In North Africa, the battleship Warspite and three destroyers bombard the port of Tobruk. This bombardment finally saw the end of the Italian heavy cruiser San Giorgio, which has been in the harbor being used as artillery. The ship had established a reputation as lucky, having been missed by earlier bombardments and escaping bombing raids, as well as not being in Taranto harbor during the raid there. Today, however her luck runs out; hit by two 15" shells she is run aground to prevent her sinking.

30th December

The Greeks occupy Santi Quaranta, Albania. Italian Supreme Commander Badoglio resigns 'at his own request', to be replaced by General Cavallero.

The port of Tobruk is now under siege as 13 Corps builds up its supplies ready for an attack. While this necessary pause is underway, the RAF bombs Benghazi harbour, which they have been bombing frequently. Light attacks are made on Tobruk itself to keep the defenders awake and on alert.

The forces for a proposed amphibious attack are allocated, but any attack cannot be made until Tobruk falls. It is then hoped to use the force to trap fleeing Italian forces.

Now that the air usage committee has reported, Churchill has to decide on how to organise Army Cooperation squadrons. The organisational demands of the Army are completely different to those suggested by the Air Ministry. Since things in North Africa seem to be going well, with adequate cooperation between the RAF, Army and Navy, the committee will be flown out to discuss with the field commanders what their thoughts are, then give the War Cabinet its recommendations.

Chapter 6 - 1941

1st January 1941

In Australia, the government approved the construction of tanks in the country in July 1940. They now authorize an armoured division to be part of the Australian Imperial Force (AIF). Australia is also going to be building Beaufighters as a complement to the Sparrowhawks that will be entering service this month. Already producing the Hercules engine, production will be increased to equip both aircraft.

Talks are going on between Australia and Britain over a second light carrier. Britain is prepared to provide one of its existing carriers (which would allow HMS Eagle to come home for a much needed refit, but the present shortage of carriers for convoy escort makes this difficult. The Australian government is considering a suggestion of transferring the ship and crew, but allocating her temporarily to convoy duties until the new escort carriers arrive. This would also allow the crew to gain valuable combat experience.

2nd January

In Britain, the "Twenty Committee", formed to co-ordinate the activities of double agents based in Britain, meets for the first time. Thus the XX or 'double-cross' tactic of using German agents in its service.

Doenitz meets with Jodl in Berlin to ask for better air-submarine co-operation and more air reconnaissance over the North Atlantic. He wants a daily reconnaissance sweep by the twelve Kondors of 40 Group based in Bordeaux. It is pointed out to him that the losses of Condors to the fighters escorting some of the convoys make this impossible (half the Condors assigned to the reconnaissance and attack role have already been destroyed), however the Luftwaffe will see how many planes can be allocated. It is agreed that the production of the aircraft be increased, but this decision will first have to wend its way through the Luftwaffe beaurocracy.

In the USA, President Roosevelt announces the beginning of the Liberty Ship program, 200 merchant ships of a standardized design. Similar ships are already being built by Britain and Canada.

3rd January

A proposed order by the Ministry of Aircraft Production for 250 Warwick bombers is cancelled in favour of additional Wellington construction. It is considered that the Warwick does not offer sufficient improvement over the Wellington to make a new production line viable, instead mass production of the Wellington will be increased and improvements incorporated into the design.

6th January

In London, Churchill promised that Britain would go to the help of Greece in the event of a German advance in the Balkans. In a letter to the Chiefs of Staff Committee the Prime Minister says: "It is quite clear to me that supporting Greece must have priority after the western flank of Egypt has been secured."

He says that more Hurricane squadrons should be sent from the Middle East along with some artillery regiments and "some or all of the tanks of the 2nd Armoured Division, now arrived and working up in leisurely fashion in Egypt."

While the Chiefs of Staff agree in principle that Greece must be supported, they point out that at present that even if all the forces in North Africa were sent they would be well under those needed. The suggest that strength is built up in North Africa, both to drive the Italians as far west as possible before a Greek intervention becomes necessary, and also to have troops prepared in theatre for such an event. It is agreed that now the Hurricane has been replaced by the Spitfire in Fighter Command, as many as practical will be sent to North Africa.

The Excess convoy leaves Gibraltar heading for Malta, covered by Force H. Only the carrier Victorious is available as cover - the Ark Royal is in dock due to a mechanical problem. The carrier is carrying the first of the reorganised fighter squadrons. After reviewing the tactical changes being employed by the RAF after the Battle of Britain, the flights now consist of 4 planes, and the embarked squadron is 20 planes rather than 16. As she will be the only carrier escort, an additional eight planes from the Ark Royal are on board, with 8 SeaLance left behind (as there is currently no risk of Italian heavy ships, there is less need for a full load of torpedo planes).

At the same time the Mediterranean fleet from Alexandria is covering another convoy (MW5.5) to Malta, and will escort an empty convoy leaving. The cruisers Southampton and Gloucester are carrying troop reinforcements to Malta and will then join Force H. Air cover is provided by HMS Implacable as HMS Indefatigable is currently supporting operations in North Africa).

7th January

As a result of the damage done to the Italian Navy and the losses to the anti-shipping wing of the Regia Aeronautica, Italy informs the Kriegsmarine that they will be withdrawing the submarines they have had helping the convoy attacks in the North Atlantic back into the Mediterranean.

In the USA, the results of the trials of the Corsair fighter are mixed. Due to the situation in Europe, and particular the dramatic use of naval air power by the Royal Navy, the acceptance trials for the USA have been accelerated from the original plan. While there are still considerable problems with the aircraft, particularly for carrier use (especially as the USN is still operating with peacetime ideas of risk), a letter of intent is given to Vought. It is hoped to have the production contract by March.

Work on a new version of the Wildcat fighter is continuing. The F4-F3 version has been in operation service since the summer, but after reviewing data from the FAA of its combats, it has been decided to increase the armament to 6x0.5" machine guns, as well as a number of other changes to make the aircraft more survivable. The new model will also have fully folding wings to allow more to be carried. It is hoped to have this model available by the end of 1941.

The speeding up of the naval aircraft has been mainly due to increasing information on the IJN capability. A new fighter, the A6M2, has been deployed in China. While some of the reports on its performance have obviously been exaggerated, (the USN treats reports from the China theatre with deep reservation), it is obviously an improvement over the existing carrier fighter, and the USN feels it needs the Wildcat and the improved Wildcat to keep its advantage in capability. The IJN is also going ahead fast with its carrier construction. The USN has the design for its new Essex class ships ready, and they expect to lay the first ship down in April. Orders for some of the equipment have already been placed, and the ships construction will be a priority.

10th January

Germany and Russia signed a new economic agreement in Moscow today. The agreement is of special value to the Nazi war machine, for the Russians are sending the Germans industrial raw materials, oil products and foodstuffs, particularly grain.

It is believed by the British that among the raw materials are rubber, manganese and chromium. Vital in the production of weapons, these materials are in short supply in Germany because of the British blockade. The Germans will also get petroleum products and trainloads of wheat from the Ukraine. In return the Russians will receive German machine tools to re-equip the Soviet Union's out-of-date factories. According to the official Soviet communiqué: "This new economic agreement marks a great step forward."

On the previous day, Force H had headed back to Gibraltar having handed its merchant ships over to Admiral Renouf's force for escort to Malta. While there had been a number of high-level attacks from Italian bombers, the raids had been broken up by the CAP from Victorious, with the loss of three bombers, and the only result had been the washing of a number of ships under the waterspouts of missing bombs.

At dawn, Admiral Cunningham received a report from the cruiser Bonaventure that she had sighted two enemy destroyers, which had closed the force under cover of darkness. Increasing speed to close the cruiser, he found her and the destroyer HMS Hereward firing into an Italian destroyer which soon blew up. The fleet then turned east to follow the convoy.

Almost immediately the destroyer HMS Gallant had her bows blown off by a mine. It was decided to tow her into Malta (backwards!), and while this was happening two Italian torpedo planes which had slipped in low attacked HMS Valiant, without success. The planes were chased off by the CAP, one of them being shot down. A large formation of enemy planes was then detected to the north by radar, and Implacable turned into to wind to fly off her ready aircraft. As she was the only carrier present, her fighter group had been increased to 24 planes from the normal 24 by using some of the Goshawks normally tasked to defend Alexandria, and her CAP of eight planes would be increased to sixteen once the ready aircraft were in the air.

The new contact was in fact not the Italians, as surmised, but Fliegercorps X. Although the presence of this unit had been detected on Sicily through the use of Ultra and other intelligence, through a mistake the Mediterranean fleet had not been informed. As a result, the defence was working on the assumption that the attack would be by high-level and possibly torpedo planes. This meant they were not in the best formation to defend against dive bombers.

The formation consisted of Ju87 and He111 bombers, escorted by a dozen Me110 fighters. As the defending planes attacked, one of the two groups of eight was drawn off by the fighters. The other group attacked the estimated 45 dive bombers, and succeeded in shooting down 10 of these (the Stuka was an easy target when unescorted), but the remaining 35 attacked, concentrating on the Implacable.

While the carrier had a formidable AA defence, aided by her escorts, this had never been intended to stop an attack by this number of aircraft. Although they managed to shoot down four of the Stukas, and damaged others, this was not enough to stop their attack.

Implacable was hit by a total of five 550kg bombs. One on her forward elevator, which blew the lift itself out of the shaft, one which hit the S2 pompom and exploded against it, two which penetrated the deck and exploded inside the upper hangar, and one which just missed, but exploded very close to her stern, damaging her steering. The ship was left on fire and unable to steer. Although the fighters shot down two more Stukas as they withdrew, they now had no-where to land.

The Navy was paranoid about fuel fires on its carriers, and as a result the shock of bombing did not damage the avgas tanks, and none of the aircraft in the hangers were fuelled. Many were damaged or destroyed, and a number of large (but containable) fires broke out in the upper hangar. Meanwhile the fighters were ordered to head for Malta (fortunately in range) and land there.

It took three hours to get her fires under control and steering with her engines, before she could head for Malta, escorted by the rest of the fleet. As they headed for the island, there were further attacks by Stukas and He111's. Although two He111's and three more Stukas were shot down by the fleet's defences, the Implacable received two more hits from 550kg bombs. One of these hit her port forward 4.5" guns, and although these were destroyed no serious damage was caused to the structure of the ship. The other bomb hit close to the aft lift, putting it out of action and causing damage in the lower hanger.

Despite all these hits from heavy bombs, the ships machinery had not been damaged - the hanger deck armour had successfully protected them as designed, although the upper hanger was effectively destroyed. The ship staggered into Malta harbour, where she would be subject to yet more attacks.

11th January

In Berlin Hitler issues his 22nd war directive, ordering preparations for reinforcements to be sent to aid Italian armies in North Africa (Operation Sunflower) and Albania (Operation Alpine Violets).

"German support for battles in the Mediterranean area. The situation in the Mediterranean area, where England is employing superior forces against our allies, requires that Germany should assist for reasons of strategy, politics, and psychology. Tripolitania must be held and the danger of a collapse on the Albanian front must be eliminated. Furthermore the Cavallero Army Group must be enabled, in co-operation with the later operations of 12th Army, to go over to the offensive from Albania."

The Mediterranean fleet headed back to Alexandria, less the carrier Implacable. In order to provide air cover, the Indefatigable had been ordered to join them (she had been supporting Operation Compass), which she did later that day. Until she arrived, air cover was provided from Malta, but this was not as effective as the fleets own organic air support. Further attacks were made in the morning on the fleet by Stukas, although this time by smaller formations. Most of these were driven off or broken up by the fighters, but the cruiser Southampton was hit by a bomb which caused serious damage, although fortunately it did not explode. The attacks only petered out after the Indefatigable arrived and added to the air cover.

14th January

General Wavell, Commander in Chief Middle East Command, and Air Marshal Longmore are in Athens today and tomorrow for talks with Prime Minister Ioannis

Metaxas and the Greek Commander in Chief, General Aleksandros Papagos. The Greeks ask for nine divisions and a substantial air component to be sent to support their forces. The Greeks have the equivalent of thirteen divisions facing the larger Italian force in Albania and four facing the Bulgarians. At this stage the Germans have twelve divisions in Romania and more in Bulgaria. To meet such a force Wavell is able to offer only a small contribution now, but more later. Since the British have barely enough strength to counter the Italians on the ground, Wavell recommends that the main contribution is by air power and by naval support.

General O'Connor's Imperial force attacks Tobruk at 0830 hours. The attack is strongly assisted by naval and air forces and is led by elements of the Australian 6th Infantry Division. 16th Australian Brigade use "I" tanks to break through the perimeter (these tanks are immune to Italian anti-tank guns) and these are closely followed by the elements of the 4th Indian Division. Free French troops also played an important part in the attack.

The Australians reach their first objectives by midday; but then the Italians brought their coastal and AA guns into action, and there are several hours of fierce fighting around and about the middle of the perimeter. By dusk the Commonwealth forces are ranged along the edge of the escarpment overlooking the town, and the western and south-western portions of the perimeter are safely under control. Meanwhile HMS Gnat, HMS Ladybird and HMS Terror bombard Tobruk.

15th January

Tobruk falls to O'Connor along with 30,000 prisoners.

For the past two days the Italian defenders have had to endure a bombardment of thousands of tons of HE hurled into Tobruk from land, sea and air. The barrage has matched the intensity of that at Ypres in 1917 and stopped only this dawn. Australian sappers went forward to cut the barbed wire on the outer perimeter and clear the way for the infantry who had moved to within 1,000 yards of the Italian trenches during the night. Backed by British armour, the Australians faced stiff resistance at first with many Italians dying at their guns. But eventually the resistance faded and white flags were seen above the defending trenches.

With the outer ring of defences breached, the tanks could attack the defenders from the rear. Of the three forts within the town, the first was taken by the infantry after fierce hand-to-hand fighting, the other two surrendered quickly afterwards. With the forts taken the town surrendered. No Union flag could be found so an Australian "Digger's" hat flies from the flagpole over Tobruk.

HMS Implacable is bombed again in harbour. Although the Maltese-based fighters take a toll of the high level bombers and Stukas, the ship is hit again in the upper hangar. A number of bombs land very close in the water, causing shock damage and leaks. The dockyard is working to get her mobile so she can get to Alexandria, as she is too tempting a target at Malta.

A Greek success has been obtained in Albania by the capture of the Trebeshine massif in early February, having forced the heavily fortified Klisure Pass in late December. However the Greeks did not succeed in breaking through towards Berat, and their offensive towards Vlore failed. In the fight for Vlorë, the Italians suffered serious losses to four divisions, but by the middle of January, due to a combination of Italy finally gaining numerical superiority and their own poor logistical situation, the Greeks' advance was finally stopped.

16th January

An advance guard of the Australian 6th Division, supported by British units, is ordered to advance on Derna located about 100 miles (161 kilometres) by road west-northwest of Tobruk. The Australians, now fully equipped, are leading O'Connors advance, allowing the 4th Indian Division to repair its losses so far in the campaign.

19th January

A chastened Mussolini arrived at Berchtesgaden today to plead with Hitler for military aid. The location is significant - until now, the two dictators have met on "equal terms" on their borders. Count Ciano found the Duce "frowning and nervous" on his special train - clearly worried that Hitler would be insultingly condescending to him after Italy's string of defeats in North Africa, Greece and Albania. Much to his surprise and relief, Mussolini found Hitler cordial and welcoming. The Fuhrer has already agreed to bolster the Italian army in Libya with anti-tank formations and squadrons of the Luftwaffe, and to send an army corps of two and a half divisions to Albania. The price to Mussolini is merely total subordination to Hitler in all military matters.

British forces of the 4th and 5th Indian Divisions in East Africa under Major-General William Platt, acting on information obtained by breaking the Italians' coded messages, invade Italian-occupied Eritrea. British Intelligence had been privy to secret Italian communiqués from Africa for the past five months; every instruction sent from one Italian military unit to another was analyzed by them. The Italian viceroy in Ethiopia was unwittingly receiving and transmitting every Italian military secret and weakness.

A South African Division is to be sent to North Africa; it had already been intended to use this is Ethiopia, but the logistics of the area mean that it would not have been able to support it. The division will serve as a reserve until it is fully operational.

Implacable is again the subject of attacks in Malta harbour; this time a bomb hits her already-ruined forward elevator to cause more damage in the hanger and sending splinters into her forward compartments. This seemed to be the last of the heavy raids (the combination of the initial attacks on the fleet, plus the attacks on the Malta defences have caused heavy losses to the Stukas in particular, and Fliegerkorps X requires time to rebuild to its normal strength.

As a result of the damage to Implacable, the Admiralty reorganises its carrier disposition. Because the Kreigsmarine now has the Scharnhorst, Bismark and Graf Zeppelin operational, it is reluctant to have less than three carriers available to the home fleet in case of a breakout (having to allow for one carrier in dock at any time). Illustrious, Formidable and Colossus will remain at Scapa. The steadily worsening convoy losses mean that the light and escort carriers are needed in the Atlantic. The solution is to send the fleet carrier Victorious around the Cape to join the Mediterranean Fleet. If more than one carrier is needed for a large operation in the Western Med, a carrier can be released temporarily from the Home Fleet. After what happened to Implacable, the Admiralty is reluctant to use the light carriers within range of enemy air bases on a long term basis - they simply are not built to withstand the sort of damage inflicted on Implacable.

21st January

With the Greek refusal to accept British land forces that fall short of the numbers they have asked for, the Defence Committee switch the area of greatest importance back to North Africa. With the impending arrival of German forces in mainland Greece there is a need to capture the islands of the Dodecanese, primarily Rhodes to preserve communications with Greece and Turkey. It is intended to send more landing craft out to be used by the Royal Marine Commandoes training up in theatre.

Meanwhile bad going and poor weather, numerous mechanical breakdowns and a shortage of petrol have brought the advancing troops of O'Connor's force to a short halt, allowing the Italians under General Babini to escape from Mechili.

23rd January

At Derna, for the first time in this desert war, British and Australian troops of the 19th Brigade found themselves facing a major counter-attack as Italian troops covered the evacuation of civilians - most of them Italian settlers - and the bulk of the garrison from this once-thriving seaport town.

Eight days after their successful attack on Tobruk, armour and infantry found the defenders making the best use of the rugged, hilly countryside, their artillery directing heavy and accurate fire with 20mm guns mounted on lorries. The Italian air force, which has not been seen for several days, joined in the attack, dive-bombing and machine-gunning British positions. The Italians have been working as fast as possible to build up their defences, but nearly a hundred tanks are still being worked on in the cities workshops and are unavailable to the defence. The town is taken by the late afternoon, and the Imperial troops regroup ready to follow up the retreating Italians to Benghazi.

It was the intention to place a force of about 1,000 men (mainly Royal Marine Commandoes) in front of the retreating Italians and hold them there while the Australians continued their attack, but the unexpected need to cover the recovery of HMS Implacable to Alexandria has taken the naval forces away. The operation is postponed until the navy can support it.

HMS Implacable sails from Malta to Alexandria. Although still damaged (the numerous misses have caused her underwater damage), the carrier can still make 25 knots, and has an emergency CAP of eight fighters - the dockyard has patched her deck temporarily, and the fighters will be fuelled on deck if necessary (the pilots are worried about landings, as with the damage to the elevators the available deck length has been constrained). Fortunately the ship slips away out of range of the Stukas before this becomes necessary. She is covered by the Malta-based fighters as far as possible, then under air cover from HMS Indefatigable and a task force of AA cruisers and a battleship. When she arrives in Alexandria she will need work to make sure she is capable of making Durban in South Africa, where she will be dry-docked for work on her underwater damage.

It was originally intended to fix her hull damage in Durban, but bring her back to the UK to have her other damage repaired. This was expected to take about four months in total. However the USA has made an offer to fix her free of charge at Newport as soon as her hull is deemed safe to make the trip, and will repair both the underwater and the rest of the damage at once. This is not an entirely charitable offer; the USN is anxious to see how a carrier survived that amount of damage. The RN for its part , and considering the war situation and the growing tension in the Far East, is happy to show them - better US carriers is seen as being helpful to the Empire.

25th January

The keel of the Iowa Class battleship Wisconsin (BB-64) is laid at the Philadelphia Navy Yard. She will be the last battleship commissioned by the U.S. Navy.

26th January

The Australian forces have already advanced well to the west of Derna on the coast and are discovering that the Italians are withdrawing. General Wavel, CinC Middle East Command, agrees with General Richard O'Connor, General Officer Commanding Western Desert Force, that 7th Armoured Division should be sent hurrying across the middle of Cyrenaica in an attempt to cut the Italians off. Supplies are being assembled to support this move but because the Italian retreat is so rapid, the advance will have to start before the preparations are complete.

Wavell also makes arrangements in the rear to prepare 4th Indian to take over as lead division once Benghazi is taken, to allow the Australians to rest and recover. A Free French Brigade is also available, although its transport elements consist of Italian vehicles that have been captured by the Imperial forces during their advance.

27th January

In Tokyo, The Peruvian ambassador to Japan warns his American counterpart, Joseph Grew, that the Japanese plan to destroy the US fleet at the naval base of Pearl Harbor; Grew passes the information on to Washington, where it is promptly filed.

In Eritrea, the British advance from the Sudan has been held up at the mountain fortress of Barentu and the bridge across the river Baraka at Agordat.

The 5th Indian Division, the 1st Free French Division and the Sudan Defence Force began by retaking the border town of Kassala eight days ago. Next day they crossed the frontier.

The 5th Indian Div. found Tessanai deserted, its garrison in retreat, and went onto Barentu. Forty miles north a flying column under Colonel Frank Messervy, "Gazelle Force", penetrated as far as Keru Gorge before being stopped. There the British suffered their only set-back so far. 10th Indian Brigade, trying to outflank the Keru defences, got lost, was strafed by planes, and its commander, Major General Bill Slim, hospitalised with a bullet in his backside. It took two days before Messervy was through the gorge, his artillery fighting off a frontal cavalry charge on open sights, and he is now outside Agordat and the 5th Indian outside Barentu.

Chapter 7 - Cyrenaica Falls

28th January

Led by 4th Armoured Brigade under Brigadier Caunter, 7th Armoured Division strikes out across the Cyrenaica desert to cut the coast road to Benghazi, 150 miles away. British armoured cars occupy Msus, and the forces then move toward Antelat.

Wavell telegrams to CIGS:

'Information indicates that enemy is making hurried withdrawal westwards from Cyrene and possibly south from Benghazi. What remains of 7 Armed Div. is advancing on Msus and may reach there this evening. Tomorrow it will try to cut roads leading south from Benghazi. The RAF is attacking retreating columns.'

29th January

On his way to Great Britain, the Australian Prime Minister Robert Menzies stops at Singapore and is appalled at the neglect of the island's defences, which he considers an easy target for Japan. He sends details of this to Australia, with instructions to investigate what can be done, and will bring it up with the War Cabinet when he arrives in London.

In Berlin, General von Funck reports to Fuhrer headquarters on his fact-finding mission to Libya and on the critical position of the Italian forces in North Africa.

In the Atlantic, the escort carrier HMS Activity is hit by two torpedoes from U-94. The escort carriers are difficult targets, as they are kept in the centre of the convoy at night, protected between the bulk of the merchant ships, but despite the Swordfish covering the convoy by day U-94 has managed to be in a good attacking position. She registers the ship as sunk; a rather overoptimistic assessment, as the buoyancy modifications made to the converted merchantman work well, and although she is slowed and unable to operate aircraft, she is still afloat and moving. She will however require nearly three months in the dockyard to repair due to the damage and stress caused to the hull.

Due to the appalling terrain they are trying to negotiate the tank regiments of 7th Armoured Div. are slowed to the point where they decide to send the faster vehicles and infantry of the Rifle Brigade forward in Bren gun carriers to join the 11th Hussars who by now are now ranging far ahead. This composite forces is under Colonel Combe and hence called "Combeforce". It comprises some 2,000 men of 11

Hussars, a squadron of the Kings Dragoon Guards and the RAF Armoured Car Squadron.

Combeforce reaches Msus, north-east of Beda Fomm late in the morning and hits the coast road near the village of Sidi Saleh about noon. At 1430 the first column of Italian lorries came fleeing down the road from the north to find their way blocked by 'A' company of the Rifle Brigade. As the Italian traffic is brought to a halt and begins to pile up, the Italians fan out west of the road towards the sea and probe south to engage the rest of Combeforce. Fighting continues throughout the day in spite of a growing shortage of ammunition.

Meanwhile the lead elements of 4th Indian have arrived at Derna; the intention was to advance while leaving the tired Australians to hold the town, but instead the Australians, whose advance elements are still in contact with retreating Italians, refuse to be taken out of the line.

30th January

4th Armoured Brigade arrives to strike the blocked Italians in the flank at Beda Fomm further north than Combeforce. The Italians fought hard through the day but by evening their position was critical. 7th Armoured had pinned down a mass of vehicles and men in complete confusion along some 20 miles of the one possible escape road from Solluch to Agedabia. In repeated attempts to break through the Italians lost more than 80 tanks.

O'Connor orders a fast-moving detachment - about a brigade group in strength - along the main road from Barce to Benghazi and on to Ghemines, to complete the encirclement of the Italians. While this is happening, British and Australian troops enter the town of Benghazi.

RAF Middle East signals the Air Ministry to inform them that except for a Hurricane squadron held back to defend the Delta, all aircraft available are being used for support of the Army advance, as well as all spare aircraft available to the navy that the RAF can find pilots for. There is a growing shortage of spares, more are needed urgently.

31st January

After consultations with army and army group staffs the Army High Command has now prepared the first operational plans for the German invasion of the Soviet Union. The deployment plan for the forces is also ready.

Agedaba falls to the British. At 11 am the Italian Chief of Staff surrenders to the HQ of 4th Armoured Brigade. Later General Annibale Bergonzoli surrenders along with the rest of 10th Army. 20,000 men, six generals and a vast horde of weapons, transport and supplies along with a shower caravan and mobile brothel with a dozen women. The cost of the battle to 7th Armoured Division was nine men killed and fifteen wounded. It was a brilliantly orchestrated attack, which took the Italian defenders entirely by surprise when British armour - traversing barren and waterless tracks from Tobruk - suddenly appeared at Beda Fomm cutting any chance of Italian retreat. Australian infantry and tanks then swept in from the north to join the British from the south and west.

With Benghazi taken O'Connor's men continue westwards - advanced units of 4th Indian have arrived at Sirte, with Tripoli itself now under threat. O'Connor intends to use the 4th Indian to keep pressing to Tripoli, his next target. In addition to the Australians, he now has a South African Division assembling, but they are still considered too green to commit. The biggest problem at the moment is the way 13 Corps transport is being ground down by the desert conditions, but O'Connor wants to stop as far west as he can before he is forced to halt and resupply.

While the 7th Armoured has lost few tanks to the enemy, it has lost far more to the terrain and desert conditions. Ideally, the division needs a rest to repair its equipment and supplies, but O'Connor is reluctant to take pressure off the Italians, who show all the signs of collapsing. Given a break, the Italians could reorganise their defences. He suggests to Wavell that a Brigade of the 2nd Armoured is brought forward by sea to Benghazi, allowing part of the 7th to be withdrawn for re-equipping. This will also allow him to strengthen the remaining armoured force.

Wavell is reluctant as he sees a need to withdraw formations in case they have to be sent to Greece, but O'Connor points out that that hasn't been requested yet, and in any case the real problem is supplies and equipment - with Benghazi in his hands, he can get the men easily back to Cairo if needed. Wavell agrees to give him another 10 days to exploit his success; O'Connor hopes that unless Italian defence stiffens he can be at Tripoli by then. If he has to then supply troops to Greece, Tripoli is a much better stopping point as it will compel Italy to bring in fresh troops and supplies further back in Tunisia, and then force them to fight him at the end of a long supply line, while he can reinforce by sea into Tripoli or Benghazi.

Free French troops under General Leclerc besiege the Italian garrison at Koufra.

Air Marshall Dowding and his aides embark for Alexandria on a mission for the War Cabinet, where they will report back to Churchill on the organisation of the Middle East Air Force and how it has been operating to support the Army. Wavell has written to the CIGS expressing his approval of how he has been supported, and Dowding wants to see how this has been done so it can be replicated in other theatres.

1st February

In Ethiopia General Sir William Platt's force captures Agordat, which guards the final approaches to Keren, taking 6,000 prisoners, 80 guns, 50 tanks, 400 trucks and what an official report described as "much material." This is after a three day battle. Italian troops under Lieutenant-General Luigi Frusci, Commander of the Eritrean Army, are falling back to the mountain positions around Keren. To the south Barentu has also been captured by the Indian troops, sealing the approaches to Keren.

2nd February.

On her way to replace the damaged carrier Implacable in the Mediterranean fleet, HMS Victorious attacks the harbour installations at Mogadishu. This causes considerable confusion to the garrison, who have never seen the modern naval aircraft before, and have no idea that the carrier is off the coast.

The British advance reaches El Agheila against scattered and ineffective Italian opposition. Most of the Italian infantry is basically helpless due to loss of transport and any heavy equipment, and the sight of tanks is usually enough to make them surrender immediately. Intelligence indicates there are men making their way west to escape the British, and also some stands by determined troops, but these are not enough to hold back the advance, although a few spots of resistance have been left for the following infantry to clear up.

Due to the loss of armour, a brigade of the 2nd Armoured is being sent to Benghazi by sea, the coastal areas now uncontested by Italy. Indeed, air support from both sides is waning fast, although on the British side it is more to wear and lack of spares and maintenance that is steadily reducing the number or serviceable aircraft. The Italians are suffering if anything more from this, as well as having more aircraft destroyed (along with many non-serviceable planes being overrun and having to be destroyed or captured). O'Connor also wants to bring a brigade of the New Zealanders forward if practical.

Force H with HMS Ark Royal, HMS Renown and HMS Resolution sails into the Gulf of Genoa to allow the battleships to bombard the city of Genoa, firing 300 tons of shells onto dock installations, warehouses and the Ansaldo Electric works, while carrier aircraft bomb Leghorn, a major railway junction at Pisa and other rail connections, and lay mines off Spezia. The incursion is not resisted by the Italian navy, who have nothing available that can damage the British capital ships.

3rd February

In Berlin, The Army General Staff presents detailed plans to Hitler for Operation Barbarossa. Halder estimates that the Russians have about 155 Divisions; German strength is about the same but 'far superior in quality'. Hitler is convinced of the plans and approves them.

•

The British are pushing light motorised units forward to Sirte, but the heavier tanks and infantry are starting to lag behind. Sirte is fortified and the light elements are not enough to take it, although they do keep busy with reconnaissance and rounding up Italians.

4th February

Sirte is now surrounded by the British light forces, who keep it under observation while the lead infantry of the 4th Indian Division arrive, along with a handful of Matilda tanks. Reinforcements arrive at Benghazi by sea today, courtesy of the Royal Navy, and it is hoped to get them moving forward tomorrow. The situation behind the advance is somewhat confused, but is slowly being brought under control. The ships will also take on board some of 7th Armoured most damaged equipment for delivery to the heavy workshops in the Delta. It is becoming obvious even to the rear echelon of the Army that the key to success in the desert is mechanised forces, and the concern now is how long the advance can keep going before the transport arm literally grinds to a halt.

6th February

Hitler offers Rommel command of a new formation to be made up of the 5th Light Division and 15 Panzer Division and intended for operations in North Africa. This force was designated Afrika Korps and equipped with PzKw III and IV tanks. The operation will be codenamed 'Sunflower'. It is hoped to land the initial part of the force at Tripoli in order to block the British advance to the east of the port.

7th February

The British assault the fortified town of Sirte, lead by the tanks of the 2nd Armoured Division. This is the first action they have been involved with, and their lack of experience compared to the 7th Armoured Division shows. Fortunately they are supported by the veteran 4th Indian Division, and the Italians still don't have an anti-tank gun that can stop a Matilda. The 15" shells arriving from the battleships offshore are yet another distraction. By the afternoon the tanks have broken the defensive line, and although some of the defending units fight on bravely, some simply collapse and surrender, leading to the disintegration of the perimeter. Sirte is surrendered by nightfall.

8th February

While the British reorganise after Sirte and wait for supplies, the light units drive on towards Homs, where the Italian army is reported to be digging in to defend Tripoli. Again they are slowed more by the need to accept the surrender of weary footslogging Italian infantry that by any enemy action. However the supply line leading from Egypt is getting more and more frayed, despite the navy running in supplies by coastal convoy. O'Connor is pressing his troops as hard as he can, and the veteran units are responding well, but he will soon be forced to stop.

The first units of the German 5th Light Division leave Naples for North Africa. The convoy also carries Italian reinforcements. Further units will sail tomorrow on a convoy bound for Tripoli. This is at the urging of General Rommel, who has flown in to the airfield at Tripoli, and is convinced of the need to stop the British advance short of the port in order to preserve a forward base of operations. Meanwhile units of the Luftwaffe are preparing to start operations from Tunisia.

In Berlin, the Kriegsmarine sends the first briefing of Operation Rheinübung for discussion with the Luftwaffe; it is hoped to stage the operation by April.

9th February

The 2nd Armoured advance on Homs - while their supply situation is still woeful, they are currently using petrol and food captured in Sirte, which for some unknown reason the Italian commander had not destroyed. They hope to be at Homs by the following day, the lead elements of the 4th Indian following by lorry. There is also a Commando force of some 2,000 men at Benghazi; it is hoped to lane these behind Homs and stop it being reinforced from Tripoli.

While they are doing this, elements of the 7th Armoured are bypassing Homs to get to Tripoli directly, by swinging south through Torhuno. This path seems to have been missed by the Italians, as by the end of the day they find themselves in sight of Tripoli.

10th February

Prime Minister Winston Churchill formally instructs General Sir Archibald Wavell, Commander in Chief Middle East Command, to regard help for Greece as having a higher priority than exploiting the success in North Africa. He mentions the important effect on American opinion of being seen to fulfil promises to smaller nations.

HMS Implacable heads to Durban for a better evaluation of her underwater damage. She is now seaworthy, and after inspection to see that she is ready to cross the

Atlantic, will carry on to Norfolk Virginia for full repairs - the hull damage will be fixed while the hangars and elevators are rebuilt. The repairs are estimated to take three to four months, as some additional refit work will also be done at the same time.

The intention of the Luftwaffe to operate from bases in Tunisia is temporarily stalled due to issues with the French. While the Vichy regime has told the colony to cooperate, there is resistance, both official and unofficial, on the ground. In particular, it is being pointed out that this will lead to Britain legitimately attacking the Luftwaffe bases, and is tantamount to declaring war on Britain. The plan has not gone down well in the other remaining Vichy-controlled colonies, many of whom are facing serious local opposition. Remaining neutral under Vichy is one thing, actively fighting with Germany is something rather different.

Outside Tripoli, the forces observing the city have generated a little excitement of their own. One of the officers in the detachment is a Major Stirling, a British officer who has been championing the idea of fast, light forces able to hit, run and do reconnaissance behind enemy lines where they are not expected. The actions in the desert have given him the opportunity to talk to a number of Australian officers who are quite interested in the idea of being able to hit the enemy when he isn't expecting it. He has pointed out that he has some armed vehicles, and the detachment has armoured cars, and there is this nice airfield close by at Mellaha full of undefended, helpless enemy aircraft.

Later that evening, the air base receives some unwelcome visitors, who proceed to drive around and into it, shooting up anything resembling an aircraft or a fuel dump. The Italians are taken completely by surprise by this, and many of the aircraft present are destroyed or damaged. Indeed they only miss the German General Rommel by hours; he had flown out of the airfield that afternoon to report back on the situation in Tripoli and to expedite the arrival of the lead elements of his division.

The situation in the city itself is almost as confused. Eight weeks ago it was nowhere near the war, only worrying about handling the Italian supply convoys and the troops on leave. Now it is in the forefront of the action, and it is not prepared in any way for this. The RAF are now visiting every night, and although the raids don't do much damage (the RAF is fast running out of serviceable bombers, and in any case the accuracy is poor), the psychological effects are bad. In addition, that morning HMS Terror paid them a visit and landed a number of 15" shells in the port area before withdrawing.

11th February

The news about the problems in Tunisia is given to Hitler, who flies into a rage, condemning the French, the Vichy regime, the Italians, and basically everyone else in Tunisia. The Army, who had also been hoping to send troops via the French North African ports, points out they need to get troops to North Africa if they are to do any good. Hitler instructs that unless the French do as they are told and allow the complete and full use of Tunisia and any other facilities Germany needs in North Africa, they are to prepare for the complete occupation of France.

Wavell replies to Churchill that he understands the need to support Greece, but that the forces currently engaged in North Africa will need considerable refurbishment (in the case of 7th Armoured, basically a complete reconstruction) before they would be ready to send to Greece. He also thinks it's worth allowing O'Connor at least one attempt to take Tripoli, as that would throw the Italians out of North Africa and ease the Malta situation considerably, as well as being a huge propaganda coup. Such a coup could be useful support for Greece in demoralising the Italians. He has reinforcements arriving very shortly, and he suggests that he starts to prepare these for Greece (remembering that Greece hasn't yet actually agreed to British land forces), and planning for their deployment. They would actually be available more quickly, since if they were to replace his existing units it would take a while to prepare their replacements for the desert.

Meanwhile Wavell is meeting with General O'Connor, Admiral Cunningham and Air Marshal Longmore to consider his options. O'Connor, when asked, states that the result of an immediate attack on Tripoli depends a lot on the Italian response. So far, the Italians have tended to collapse when surrounded and attacked, especially later in the campaign where their morale is suffering. However not all Italian units have given in easily, and he considers it likely that the ones who retreated west rather than surrender will be in the Tripoli garrison. If so, the city may hold out from an initial attack, and he does not have the force to take the city against serious opposition until he is resupplied. His idea is to make an attack as soon as possible, in the hope the city will surrender. If it does not, it will be necessary to put it under siege while his units get replenished and rested. To do that effectively will depend on the Navy and the RAF.

Air Marshal Longmore is more than willing to both attack the city and interdict resupply, but he points out his actual serviceable aircraft numbers are very low after the action of recent weeks. He really needs a couple of weeks to repair and service aircraft, give his pilots a rest, and arrange to operate out of airfields nearer the front. So his question is can the Navy give him those two weeks?

Admiral Cunningham's opinion is that, while the navy has also been worked hard recently, that he can stop most resupply reaching Tripoli for that time. He is mainly worried about Italian aircraft and submarines if he uses his heavier forces forward, but is prepared to risk them for the time needed. As long as Malta can also put out a maximum effort during that time, it should be possible to sink a considerable portion of the resupply convoys, and given air cover, those that arrive can be attacked in the port itself. He is also prepared to run coastal convoys as far forward as possible to relieve the supply situation. Fortunately the rapid fall of some of the Italian towns have allowed the Navy to acquire a number of small coastal ships to supplement their existing ships, and the port facilities along the coast are in generally good shape. The Italians often ran out of time to destroy stores and facilities.

Wavell decision is to allow O'Connor one attempt to storm Tripoli, as soon as he is ready, but only if he can be ready inside a week. If that fails, the city will be put under siege and the units will be rested and replenished. Depending what happens in Greece, once this is dealt with an attack can be made to take Tripoli. He also asks Dowding, who is returning to Britain today with his report on air support, to press the CIGS for as many planes as possible to support his operations in North Africa and Greece.

General Ion Antonescu's decision to allow Romania to be used a base for a massive German expeditionary force led today to a diplomatic break with Britain. After a half-hour meeting with Antonescu, later described as "extremely painful", the British envoy, Sir Reginald Hoare, returned to the legation to pack his bags .Most of Germany's oil supplies come from Romania, and German engineers have for some time been running the country's oil wells. When German troops began arriving, Antonescu said that they were to train the Romanian army. The British told him that a full expeditionary force was not needed to train a few Romanians.

12th February

With at least 40 troop trains a day crossing Hungary to Romania, Hitler is building up to a formidable 600,000-strong army on the border with the Ukraine. Much of the equipment carried by the German forces is of French make, having been seized after the French collapse last year. The Germans' next move, now the ice has broken on the Danube, is to float pontoon bridges in the river to enable troops to enter Bulgaria, under a secret agreement reached with the Bulgarian government four days ago. The Germans have promised the Bulgarians a slice of Greek territory to give them access to the Aegean Sea after the war.

The massive German move into the Balkans has set off a wave of speculation that Hitler may be about to go to the rescue of his Italian ally, who has been badly mauled by the Greeks. Some observers, however, believe that this is the advance stage of a plan to invade the Soviet Union.

The Tripoli-bound convoy managed to slip past the RAF in Malta, only to run into first the submarine HMS Upholder, then an airstrike from HMS Victorious. As a result, only three merchant ships survive to retreat to Italy, and a destroyer is also lost. The convoy was ordered to withdraw after Tripoli advised there were RN battleships offshore - in fact there aren't, the 15" shells they assumed were from a battleship were from HMS Terror. Meanwhile Cunningham asks the RAF if they can mine Tripoli harbour whenever possible, as he thinks they may try and run a few fast ships through individually.

The British forces outside Tripoli are being built up as fast as possible. A Brigade from 2nd Armoured is already there, as are advance elements of 4th Indian. The bottleneck is transport, there are broken-down lorries lining the coast road all the way back to Benghazi. The advance is only being kept going by captured Italian vehicles and petrol, but with only one last town to go, the troops morale is high despite their exhaustion. To aid the road traffic, infantry and supplies are being brought forward on coastal shipping, and the Navy expects to be able to land two commando units west of the city tomorrow. As one British officer put it, 'It's all being done on a shoestring. But a very determined shoestring'.

13th February

At Merano, Admirals Arturo Riccardi of Italy and Erich Raeder of Germany meet to discuss naval co-operation. One of the staff officer's present wonders if that means German fishing boats will be sent to support Italian yachts, or vice-versa.

The Royal Navy lands the men of 51 Commando plus supporting forces and their equipment over open beaches west of Tripoli. This completes the surrounding of the city, and O'Connor hopes to be able to attack in two days; he is waiting for the rest of 4th Indian and further ammunition supplies to arrive. That night, the commandos are surprised to intercept a car coming from the direction of Tunisia. It contains a number of men who identify themselves as French officers, and ask to be taken to Cairo to speak to General Wavell. The commandoes are surprised, but after some radio calls it is arranged that they will be taken east where they can be flown to Cairo.

The Vichy government is informed by Germany that they WILL allow their ports and facilities in North Africa to be used by the Germans, or the consequences will be 'severe'. After some hours of agonising, the Vichy regime agrees to obey the instructions and will draw up the necessary orders for the colonial territories. Despite the secrecy surrounding this meeting, a few hours later the news is in London, who rapidly (if secretly) disseminates it.

14th February

The Luftwaffe and the Regia Aeronautica are attacking Malta heavily, in an attempt to close down the ability of the island fortress to interdict the convoys to Tripoli. While they have some success in this, the convoys still have to first evade the Maltese squadrons, then Royal Navy submarines, bombers operating from North

Africa and finally surface forces and carrier strikes. As a result the Italian navy insists they be allowed to send fewer convoys in order to escort them properly, pointing out what has happened to the latest convoy, which was only lightly escorted. Given the Italian navy has no heavy ships, escorts will have to be lighter vessels, but they hope to at least concentrate enough defensive power to fend off anything but the British battleships.

In Italian Somaliland, the Italians are on the retreat. Their latest loss is the port of Kismayu, on the Indian Ocean, which was occupied at 14:00 by West, East and South African troops, under the command of Lt. Gen. Alan Cunningham. The port is the first major prize in what he plans will become a two-pronged drive, up the coast to Mogadishu, the colonial capital, and northwards up the river Juba to Ethiopia. His offensive into Italian territory began in earnest only three days ago, after an eight-week preliminary operation to recapture first parts of Kenya occupied by the Italians and then frontier posts on the Kenya-Somaliland border.

While the supply build-up outside Tripoli is not satisfactory, O'Connor considers it adequate for the one attack he is allowed to make. He has a considerable number of troops available; 4th Indian Division, a brigade of 2nd Armoured, a New Zealand brigade and the commando units and two battalions of the Free French Foreign Legion. His hope is that the Italian defence will crack as it has done in the previous assaults.

Back in England, Dowding has been making his report to the War Cabinet on Air Cooperation between the services. His conclusion is that the success in the desert is the result of close cooperation between the services and a willingness to try and understand the nature of the problems facing each of them. He recommends that each theatre creates a specific team (as the most senior officers have other tasks) to address the problems and solutions for their theatre. They will take as their starting point what has gone on in Africa and develop a doctrine for support operations. He suggests that that any team should include officers experienced in the local problems - he has noted that the requirements of the desert air force is often quite different from those he was familiar with while in charge of Fighter Command in the UK.

In addition, he passes on the requests from Cairo for desperately needed air power. He has spent the previous day checking on the availability of planes in the UK, and points out that there are now ample planes available for defence, and that all available Hurricanes (and Sparrowhawks) would be best used in North Africa and Greece where they can directly engage the enemy. He dismisses the RAF theory of attacking over France with fighter sweeps as inefficient and merely losing more pilots than the Germans. Sending more aircraft to North Africa will help the Army, and if the Germans respond by diverting aircraft from northern Europe that is at least as effective as trying to coax them into fights where they always hold the home advantage.

15th February

The British make their assault on Tripoli, let by 2nd Armoured. The attack is supported by every operational RAF aircraft available; after the attack a few days ago, the Italians evacuated their aircraft from Mellaha, and the only air support now available is bombers from Sicily. The Mediterranean fleet is also out in force, the battleships shelling the city (in particular the port) covered by the carriers. The Italian surface forces are absent, but one Italian submarine is sunk by RN destroyers as it tries to close on the fleet. The dive bombers from the two carriers are also attacking targets of opportunity in the defence perimeter, the idea being to put the maximum pressure on the defenders.

The attackers put pressure on the Italian defensive perimeter as they probe for a weak spot; ironically many of the shells they are using to pound the Italians are Italian in origin - the British have captured more Italian artillery and ammunition than they can use. The assault goes on throughout the day, and by the evening the British have identified a couple of areas they think exploitable. Overnight, air raids and occasional artillery barrages go on, both to wear out the defenders and to make them believe the British have ample ammunition. Meanwhile the troops are briefed on tomorrow's assault, O'Connors final throw of the dice.

Imperial troops capture the port of Kismayu in Italian Somaliland.

Chancellor Adolf Hitler meets the Yugoslav Premier Cvetkovic and his Foreign Minister Cinkar-Markvic at Berchtesgaden to urge them to join the Tripartite Pact. They still refuse to commit their country, in the hope that Hitler will soon be preoccupied with relations with the Soviet Union and that they can get aid from Britain and the USA.

Admiral Stark, Chief of Naval Operations, sends a message to Admiral Kimmel, Commander-in-Chief, Pacific Fleet based in the Territory of Hawaii, regarding anti-torpedo baffles for protection against torpedo plane attacks on Pearl Harbor. The message states "consideration has been given to the installation of anti-torpedo baffles within Pearl Harbor for protection against torpedo plane attacks. It is considered that the relatively shallow depth of water limits the need for anti-torpedo nets in Pearl Harbor. In addition the congestion and the necessity for manoeuvring room limit the practicability of the present type of baffles." The Fleet Air Arm attack on Taranto, a similarly shallow harbour, seems to have been overlooked.

The Vichy government informs the colonies in North Africa of the decision to open its ports and provide support and help for German forces expected soon. The orders do not go down well, even in Algeria, the most pro-Vichy of the colonial areas. It is expected that the first convoys will arrive in about a week, and food fuel and water will need to be provided, as well as turning a number of airbases over to the Luftwaffe. The authorities keep the order secret until they can work out how to present this to their men - more than one governor is worried about actual mutiny once they hear of it.

The officers who presented themselves in Tunisia have reached Cairo, where they speak with General Bethouart, who is currently commanding the Free French forces in Africa, and General Wavell. Following this, Wavell signals to Ethiopia asking how difficult it would be to transfer some or all of the 1st Free French Division to North Africa, and how long it would take.

16th February

The Greek army is again on the offensive, and claim to be pushing the Italians on the Yugoslav-Albania back with large losses in men and equipment. The Italian government denies this.

At first light the British make their final attack on Tripoli. During the night they have positioned troops at two weak spots they have found in the Italian lines. Shortly before the attack, the RAF staged an air raid and the Royal Navy demonstrates their ability to deluge the city with 15" shells from the battleships Warspite and Valiant. Having been practising this sort of fire support for some 200 years, the Royal Navy is by now rather good at it.

Shortly after these attacks begin, the assault begins, led by every available Matilda tank - all 18 of them. The Italians still have nothing that can stop them, and while one of the two assaults gets bogged down by a desperate and fierce Italian defence, the other breaks the perimeter, allowing troops to both attack the rear area and start to roll up the defensive line. For a time it looks like the Italians may throw the attack back - they have, through determined counter-attacks, thrown another one back almost to its starting line - but the second breakthrough is manned by far less aggressive formations. As the breach widens, O'Connor throws in the French troops and his tank reserve. His gamble pays off; under the increased pressure (the Free French troops in particular terrify the Italians), the whole eastern side of the defence collapses in confusion. Shortly after, the Italian commander offers his surrender.

It takes a while to get the ceasefire organised - some of the fascist troops fighting the western attack are reluctant to surrender - but by evening Tripoli is in the hands of the British. Wavell is able to signal Churchill that night that 'all of Italian North Africa is now under our control'. Not technically correct, there are units and some small towns holding out, but essentially correct.

Chapter 8 - Greek Adventures

17th February

The heavy emphasis on mutual goodwill and friendly relations in the treaty signed in Ankara today shows the deep mistrust Turkey and Bulgaria have long felt for each other. Bulgaria has never ceased to fear that one day Turkey will seek to regain the territory lost after the Great War and in the Balkan Wars before it, while the build-up of German troops in Bulgaria in recent weeks has alarmed the Turks, who are worried that the Germans' next blow will be delivered in the Balkans and threaten Turkey.

In Japan Foreign Minister Matsuoka Yosuke states that the white race must cede Oceania to the Asiatics. "This region has sufficient natural resources to support from 600 million to 800 million people. I believe we have a natural right to migrate there" says Matsuoka. This speech is not well received in US government circles or in Britain. The Chinese government has serious doubts that 'we' means anyone other than the Japanese.

The British 6th Infantry Division is reconstituted in Egypt. It is intended to use this force in Palestine, allowing the Australian division there to be allocated to the proposed Greek campaign. Another Australian division, the 7th, is due to arrive in a few weeks.

18th February

General Thomas Blamey, General Officer Commanding I Australian Corps, meets with General Archibald Wavell, Commander in Chief, Middle East Command. Wavell explains the composition of a force designated "Lustreforce" intended for operations in Greece. The force is to consist of the New Zealand Division, the Australian 7th and 9th Divisions, the HQ of the I Australian Corps, the 1st Armoured Brigade and an Independent Polish Brigade Group.

Australian troops, 12,000 strong, arrived in Singapore today to reinforce the British garrison. Already the 11th Indian Division has arrived in the theatre, and the III Indian Corps headquarters under Lieutenant-General Sir Lewis Heath is due to be set up in May. The build-up of British strength is in response to the growing menace of Japanese military expansion to the south. Nazi Germany has been urging the Japanese to attack Singapore at once, but the Japanese have their own timescale for offensive operations in the area.

The southward advance of Japan continues to cause anxiety in Australia at a time when the greater part of the Australian forces is engaged in the Middle East. The Singapore base is regarded by Australians as the keystone of defence against Japan, and Britain has assured Australia that if a Japanese attack appeared imminent, a British battlefleet would be sent at once to Singapore. However, there is obviously a need for an army and air force strong enough to hold out in Singapore and Malaya until the fleet arrived. Australia has therefore contributed a brigade of infantry to the garrison.

The Australians are worried about the report they have received from their Prime Minister regarding the poor quality of the troops and defences in the area. As the price for reinforcing, they have asked for a review by a senior officer with operational experience, suggesting that as 6th Australian is currently being refitted in North Africa a suitable officer can be spared to report. The CIGS is rather unwilling to meet this requirement, but the Australians have made it clear that in view of the troops they are providing they consider it only reasonable, and after some controversy in London the idea is approved.

News reaches the British that the Greek Prime Minister, Ioannis Metaxas, has died in Athens. The planners in London prepare to ask again if the Greek government wants British Army units to help - this has been resisted by Metaxus, who was only prepared to accept RAF help.

In Britain, the light carriers HMS Ocean (recalled from convoy duty) and HMS Colossus are preparing to transport as many Hurricane fighters as they can carry to Malta. From there the planes will be flown to the newly-acquired airstrips in Libya.

Admiral Darlan flies to Algeria to 'look into the situation and encourage the acceptance of the new orders regarding cooperation with Germany'. The visit is the Admirals idea, and he has merely informed the government as he is about to leave for Africa.

19th February

The British Secretary of State Anthony Eden and Field Marshall Sir John Dill (Chief of the Imperial General Staff) have arrived in Cairo to discuss with the local commanders, General Archibald Wavell (Commander in Chief Middle East Command), and General Alan Cunningham (Commander in Chief East Africa Command), whether they can send help to Greece and if so how much. The British political leaders are strongly in favour of sending all that can be spared and Wavell, the military commander who is responsible, believes that this can be done effectively and is, therefore, prepared to recommend it.

Now that Tripoli has been taken, he hopes to be able to rest and reconstitute the formations which have been attacking for the last couple of months. He has been promised more convoys both to replenish their stocks and to build up a force for Greece, once the Greek government actually agrees to one. The visit is useful as it also allows Wavell to discuss some possibilities in French-held North Africa that he has recently been appraised of. One of the results of the discussions is that General Leclerc is summoned to Cairo.

As the troops used will be mainly inexperienced, Wavell brings in General Blamey and General O'Connor (who is taking an ordered two week rest after exhausting himself during Operation Compass) to ask about the state of 6th Australian Division, which he is considering using in place of one of the fresh Australian divisions. During the course of their discussions, Blamey asks, as the force will basically be a Australian/New Zealand operation, if it has been agreed with the Australian Prime Minister who is currently in London. Wavell assures him he is sure that it has, but will verify that for him. O'Connor is reluctant to recommend the use of 6th Australian, as he feels they desperately need a rest, and taking them out of North Africa for Greece will make it look like they are being used too heavily.

In Ethiopia, Free French troops capture Jumbo after heavy fighting with Italian forces. In three hours the Italian Artillery fires over 3,000 rounds.

Emperor HaileSelassie, who was brought back to Abyssinia in January to help organize resistance to the Italians, arrives at Dangilla along with Brigadier Orde Wingate's Gideon Force. During the next two weeks, they harass the Italian troops around Bahrdar Giorgis and Burye with considerable success, despite the fact that the Italians have four brigades in the area and the Gideon Force is only 1700 strong. Meanwhile in Italian Somaliland Cunningham's troops cross the river Juba and head towards Mogadishu

One of the Brigades of the 1st South African Division is prepared to move south to replace a brigade of the 1st Free French Army, which is being brought north. While swapping the two divisions has been considered, the transport infrastructure is poor, and would involve considerable disruption of a currently successful campaign. Once one Brigade has been replaced, command will look into replacing a second. In the meantime, the Free French Brigade that has been fighting in North Africa is consolidating near Tripoli, and is being given priority for replacement supplies. There have been political issues involved with the use of South African divisions - initially they were only to be used in the southern part of the continent, but agreement has been reached that they can now be deployed 'in Africa'. The arguments in favour of wider use have been influenced by the success of the Australian and New Zealand troops in defeating the Italians - after all, if they can come all this way to defeat the enemy troops on the African continent, surely so can

South African troops. This has not stopped some political parties in South Africa complaining, but they have at present lost the argument.

21st February.

An Italian convoy is assembling in Naples, loaded with men of the Arête division and the German 5th light division. Its destination is Tunis.

Eden, still in diplomatic discussions in Cairo, receives a telegram from Churchill with the advice, "Do not consider yourselves obligated to a Greek enterprise if in your hearts you feel it will only be another Norwegian fiasco."

In a second telegram, O'Connor is promoted to Lieutenant-General and made a Knight Commander of the Order of the Bath. He will take over the command of the Imperial troops in North Africa, which are expected to be expanded soon both with new units and once Somaliland and Ethiopia have fallen. The victorious British forces are currently recovering from nearly two months of campaigning, except for the engineering and maintenance men who are busy repairing as much as possible of the armour and transport that has been savaged by the desert conditions. Having possession of all the battlefields, and the well-equipped Italian maintenance facilities, more than expected can be repaired or cannibalised, but it will take time. Since the 7th Armoured is in by far the worst shape, it is being pulled back to Egypt for a full reconstruction while its working equipment is used to strengthen the 2nd Armoured.

The Royal Navy has also pulled its heavy units back; they too need maintenance work done on them, and the carriers airgroups are in poor shape. For the next few weeks the waters off Libya will be covered by the light cruisers and destroyers, unless it is necessary to intercept a convoy. The RAF is also busy in its workshops; it has a huge number of unserviceable aircraft that need maintenance and repair.

22nd February

German military staff arrives in Sofia, Bulgaria as 17 divisions, eight of which are heading for Greece, cross the border in a gesture of fascist good-neighbourliness.

Heavy night raids by the Luftwaffe are still causing serious damage in Britain. However the new night fighters, aided by steadily improving AI radar and training are taking a steadily increasing toll of the Luftwaffe bombers; nearly 60 were shot down in January (as well as the losses to the AA defences), and the success rate is increasing steadily. Fortunately night bombing isn't accurate enough to target precise targets, although the damage and deaths caused by the area bombing is unpleasant, it is not doing serious damage to the British war industry.

The Reaper night fighter is now being produced in sufficient numbers to allow the Beaufighter production to be reassigned to its original role (the limits on the night fighters are currently radar sets rather than fighters). It is hoped to have the first Beaufighter squadron operational in their new role in about three months.

A new order is placed for more light bombers from the USA, partly for the RAF partly for the French Air Force (although again most of these will be 'lent' to the RAF)

23rd February

The British Foreign Secretary, Anthony Eden, arrived in Athens today with a senior military mission including Sir John Dill, CIGS, General Wavell, Admiral Cunningham and Air-Marshall Longmore. The main item for discussion with King George and his government is the question of British military aid to Greece. There is some reluctance on the part of the Greeks to accept the help offered by Eden, on the grounds that insufficient British help might serve only to precipitate an attack by the Germans.

Eden's task is to reassure the Greeks that, although the forces being offered, which would have to be withdrawn from the army in North Africa, are all that Britain can spare at the moment, they are well-equipped and trained and will acquit themselves well. Talks are well under way this evening and look like lasting well into the night, with the Greeks insisting that they will fight with or without British help.

Representatives of the French Colonial governments of Syria and Lebanon are received, very quietly and unofficially, in Cairo where they have requested to talk with General Wavell and the Free French leaders.

In Italian Somaliland the main Italian forces defending the line of the Juba River have been defeated. The troops of General Alan Cunningham are now advancing very rapidly toward Mogadishu.

The first Corvette built in the USA as their part of the 'Ships for Bases' deal starts sea trials. Due to the still-delicate nature of the US state of neutrality, the British crew are dressed as civilians. Once the ship has passed trials, she will sail to Britain for Asdic to be fitted, and then work up. It is hoped to have the rest of the Corvette order completed during the next four months.

25th February

In Cairo Wavell decides against the projected bombing of the Ploesti oilfields. First it would necessitate violating Turkish airspace, and secondly it might attract the attention of the Germans to a British presence in Greece. The RAF is in any case against it for at least a month due to the need to rest the aircrew and repair the aircraft after the all-out effort to support O'Connor.

British Nigerian troops of the 11th African Division have begun to occupy Mogadishu after a day's lightning advance up the coast from Brava, 120 miles away. Meanwhile, the 12th African Division pushes up the river Juba towards the Abyssinian border town of Dolo.

A meeting is held in Washington D.C., concerning defences in Hawaii. The minutes state that "in view of the Japanese situation the Navy is concerned with the security of the fleet in Hawaii, and apparently the new commander of the fleet there has made a check and reported it to Washington and the Secretary of the Navy has outlined the situation to the Secretary of War. Their particular point is the type of air force in Hawaii, particularly Pursuit (fighters). They are in the situation where they must guard against a surprise or trick attack. It is necessary for the fleet to be in anchorage part of the time and they are particularly vulnerable at that time. I do not feel that it is a possibility or even a probability, but they must guard against everything. We also have information regarding the possible use of torpedo planes."

The Italian convoy which has been assembling in Naples is ready to sail, but the Italian Navy refuse to let it proceed until they have mustered a stronger escort. In particular, they intend to wait a few more days to allow a number of submarines to get into position against possible Royal Navy attacks.

The results of the trials of the new Mosquito aircraft are encouraging enough for the Ministry of Aircraft Production to place a production order before the trials are complete. The plane has the advantage of not needing much in the way of some limited resources, like aluminium, but will require a unique method of construction to be planned and implemented. DeHavilland promise that despite this they can get at least 60 produced by the end of the year.

26th February

After talks in Athens lasting all night and much of the day, the Greek Premier Alexander Korizis, agrees in principle to Eden's proposal for British aid.

The Greek government agrees to accept a British force which at this stage is intended to be 100,000 men with suitable artillery and tank support. The Greeks are very reluctant to accept anything less since it would not be enough to fight the Germans off and would only encourage them to attack. The disposition of the British and Greek forces is also discussed. The British prefer a position along the line of the Aliakmon River but the Greeks are unwilling to give up the territory which this line does not cover. A final decision is postponed until it can be discussed with General Blamey, the proposed Army commander.

A Free French Brigade is now outside Tripoli, having been resupplied. Tripoli itself is supplying part of 6th Australian Division. The Australians are happy to be in Tripoli and its entertainment; the authorities in Tripoli are rather less enthused.

As well as the 2nd Free French division which has been forming (the first Brigade of which is at Tripoli), the French have also been forming an Armoured Brigade. Unfortunately no tanks will be available for it for some months (the first tanks ordered from the USA by France are not expected until June). However there are considerable numbers of captured Italian tanks, including nearly a 100 Italian M13 tanks (not dissimilar to the US tanks on order), over 80 having been captured in the Benghazi maintenance depot. There are also a considerable number of lighter Italian tanks, considered useful for training, as well as spares and support equipment. These are offered to the French until the US tanks arrive, which will enable the Brigade to be operational in a few weeks.

27th February

At a meeting of the British War Cabinet to discuss the situation in the Middle East, Australian Prime Minister Robert Menzies agrees to send Australian troops to Greece. He has been informed by telegram by General Blamey that the task is far more uncertain that some of the proponents of the plan have been making out, and he sets the condition that an Australian be put in command (as it is basically an Australian and New Zealand force), and that he is responsible, in case a German invasion forces a withdrawal, for deciding when and where this will happen. Churchill is unhappy about this, but as the only alternative is to give Libya back to Italy by withdrawing the troops there (who in any case will not be ready to fight for some weeks), he agrees.

28th February

France capitulates to Japan's ultimatum to accept its proposals for settlement of the border dispute between its colony in Indochina and Thailand.

The Vichy cabinet's decision in the early hours of the morning came only hours after the Japanese ultimatum expired. Throughout yesterday Japan made it clear that it was ready to implement its proposals by force if necessary. When the agreement is signed Indochina will cede to Thailand all of Laos west of the Mekong and an important part of north-western Cambodia. Japan wants military bases in southern Indochina and Thailand, and expects to capitalise on its intervention by making a military pact with Thailand.

1st March

The 11th African Division begins a lighting pursuit of the retreating Italian forces in Somaliland north from Mogadishu towards the Ogaden Plateau.

General Cunningham reports on the East African front to Wavell:

"Enemy evacuating whole of Italian Somaliland. Force at Ischia Baidoa apparently withdrew via Neghelli. Free French Div. was unable to cut it off through lack of petrol. Light forces are moving to occupy Lugh Ferrandi and Dolo. Bardera has been occupied.

...Force at Mogadishu has outrun supplies. Harbour cannot be entered for some days pending sweeping operations. Movement of motor transport by ship to Mogadishu not possible, and the rains beginning to render road from Kenya precarious."

An Italian convoy finally sails for North Africa; it carries the advance units of the German 5th Light Division and the Italian Ariete Division. The convoy's first task is to avoid the aircraft from Malta searching for it; accordingly for the last three days Malta has been heavily bombed by the Luftwaffe and Italian Air Force, which has caused considerable damage as well as reducing the number of aircraft operational on the island. It has also reduced the number of Axis aircraft available, if needed, to support operations in North Africa. The convoy also carries Luftwaffe personnel to allow a fast preparation for an airbase; in particular, Rommel wants Me109 fighters to secure his air cover as soon as possible.

2nd March

Eden finds out from General Heywood that the Greek government had failed to carry out the agreement reached at Tatoi and that no order for the withdrawal of troops from Macedonia and Thrace had been given.

Mussolini flies in to Albania, hoping his presence will raise the morale of his troops. It doesn't.

Germany officially admits that its troops (of the XII Army) had entered Bulgaria. According to a High Command communiqué: "The German army, in agreement with the Royal Bulgarian government, has been marching into Bulgaria since Saturday." In the Bulgarian parliament the Prime Minister, Professor Filov, said that Germany had asked permission to send in the troops on a temporary basis in order to "safeguard peace in the Balkans".

All day today the Germans have been pouring into Bulgaria by way of pontoon bridges across the Danube. Meanwhile there are reports that the vanguard of the

German forces is already approaching the Greek frontier at four points. With the Luftwaffe present in strength, the German attack on Greece seems imminent.

In London, the Chiefs of Staff estimate that one German armoured division and three motorised divisions could reach the Bulgarian-Greek border by March 6, with an infantry division arriving by March 11. This is thought to be the maximum strength that the Germans could field until April 15.

General Wavell is asked how soon his troops will be ready. He replies that the New Zealand Division can sail as soon as transport is arranged, but that it would be unwise to send this formation on its own. He suggests they are immediately sent to Crete, which he needs to hold in any case. Meanwhile General Cunningham has light forces on to Ferfer (about 200 miles north of Mogadishu and Dolo) which will complete the occupation of Italian Somaliland.

Chapter 9 - Tunisia

3rd March

During the early morning there are no less than four meetings between the Greek and British military staffs in Athens, trying to agree on a defensive strategy. In the event of an attack on Macedonia the British urge a quick pull back to the Aliakhmon line whereas Papagos clings to the more advanced Nestos line, "If the Yugoslavs should fight, that is where we Greeks should stand", declared Papagos. Dill snapped, "General, you will have to fight that battle."

General Wavell arrives later in the morning in Athens, and some time later General Blamey, the commander-designate of the British forces in Greece, arrived at Tatoi airfield.

In Tunisia, the preparations of the Vichy government for the arrival of the convoy, and the obvious intent of the Italians and the Germans to base themselves in Tunisia to attack the British, has led to considerable civil unrest, and more than a few riots. The local population is quite unwilling to see their country turned into a battleground for the benefit of Italy. Fighting for themselves is one thing, becoming a German-Italian battlefield is something quite different.

At 3am, a military force led by de Tassigny occupies key positions in Tunis, in particular the harbour. The force meets little opposition; in fact many of the men supposedly guarding the installations offer to help. Meanwhile there is confused fighting on the streets of the capital as forces and police loyal to Vichy contest the city with the rebel forces.

The Italian consulate immediately informs Rome of what is happening; it is obvious that unless the city and harbour area can be secured quickly, there will be nowhere for the convoy to dock. Having the convoy stand off until the situation is resolved is considered unacceptable, as this will just tempt the Royal Navy into sinking it.

At the Tunisian border, Free French troops are put on immediate alert as soon as the news from Tripoli is received. They will move out once it is daylight, having been preparing for a situation like this for some days. With Wavell in Greece, the orders have been issued by O'Connor (who is still the commander of the units), with agreement from the Free French in Cairo.

The RN delivers some 80 Hurricane fighters to Malta. The planes have been flown of the carriers to the west of the island; half of the planes will remain at the island (where the available fighters have been reduced due to the high level of enemy raids), the other 40 will fly in stages to Egypt.

4th March

Free French motorised forces and a number of British tanks (flying the tricolour with the crews trying, rather unsuccessfully, to look French) enter Tunisia from the forward base at Tripoli. The formation is led by the Foreign Legion (it is hoped that the Legionnaires reputation will help ease the way of the column), who find that there is little opposition. They are held up a number of times by local forces, but in only one case does this lead to any fighting, when a group of pro-Vichy police attempt to ambush the column. Indeed, they have to actively stop some of the forces they meet joining them. By the afternoon, the column is most of the way to Tunis, and the rest of the Brigade is preparing to follow them. The RAF has put aircraft on alert to aid them if necessary, but it is hoped that the use of French troops will be enough to persuade the locals that this is not a British invasion. Leaving their rear unguarded is a risk, but the forces in Tunisia aren't huge and the rest of the Brigade is following them.

In the city itself, the situation is somewhat of a stand-off. De Tassigny has control of the harbour and its defences, as well as being the official commander of the men under his command. However the Vichy governor has had the bulk of the men he considers particularly loyal to Vichy in the city (recent events have made many of the Vichy authorities thoroughly paranoid, and they have been trying to organise men loyal to them), and as a result there are small to medium sized bodies of troops and armed police in various parts of the city. The situation is tense, and firing has broken out on a number of occasions, but neither side want to start a war inside the city if it can be avoided. De Tassigny has a trump he has yet to play, thanks to some officers he sent to Tripoli recently, and is prepared to wait till it comes into play.

Meanwhile, the orders given to the convoy are confused. The Italian navy wants it to return to Naples immediately. The Germans insist it should land. The Italian commanders, who have a better idea than the Germans of the defences of Tunis (which are still under the control of de Tassigny), don't care as long as they don't go anywhere near Tunis.

The issues are resolved on the convoy itself, where General Rommel has been reading the various conflicting despatched. He instructs that the convoy should head to the port of Bone in Vichy-held Algeria. When the convoy commodore objects, he is persuaded by the pistol of one of Rommel's aides.

The draft operation orders for Operation Rheinübung are agreed in Berlin. In order to complete preparations, the Bismark, Scharnhorst, Prinz Eugen and the carrier Graf

Zeppelin will commence final training in the Baltic. The operation is scheduled for the new moon period around the 25th of April.

Britain's new raiding force, the Commandos, have destroyed 18 factories producing fish oil - a commodity which is made into glycerine, a basic ingredient of high explosive - on the Norwegian Lofoten Islands in Operation Claymore.

"Herring oil factories and trawlers at Svolvær, Henningsvær, Stamsund and Brettesnes were destroyed". About 800,000 gallons of oil and petrol were burnt, 11 ships totalling 19,000 tons are sunk and 215 Germans and 12 Norwegian collaborators (dubbed "Quislings" after Norway's Nazi puppet leader) taken prisoner. 314 volunteers also left with the commandos. Led by Brigadier Charles Haydon of the Irish Guards, 500 commandos with 100 other specialists went in escorted by five destroyers and a submarine.

This is the first major raid to be undertaken, and is far more organised than recent small actions. It has become obvious that the pre-war operational requirements (which for some reason were discarded once war broke out) for amphibious assaults are highly relevant to a successful action, and as resources permit the forces are being built up using these as guidelines.

More important that the actual raid damage is the action of the destroyer HMS Somali. While leading the commandoes, she happened upon a German patrol boat, which was foolish enough to open fire. Fire was returned, and the crew abandoned the patrol craft as it was beached on an islet. The British boarding party recovered papers which included the daily Enigma settings for February.

Prince Paul, the regent of Yugoslavia, was summoned to the Berghof, the Fuhrer's mountain retreat, and given the usual treatment accorded to small powers. After listening to Hitler's threats and ranting into the early hours, Prince Paul buckled and agreed to follow Romania and Bulgaria into the German camp and sign the Axis Pact. Hitler did offer the prince the Greek port of Salonika, which would give Yugoslavia access to the Aegean. Paul, aware that joining the Axis will be unpopular at home, has arranged for the signing of the treaty to take place in great secrecy in ten days time.

General Blamey, the commander of the the Imperial expeditionary forces being prepared for Greece, arrives in Athens to arrange the final details with the Greek general staff. A major convoy is about to leave Alexandria in Egypt, with the first large contingent headed for Crete, and other forces are ready to follow. The British have only just discovered that the Greek forces in Macedonia have not retired to the Aliakmon Line and will not be able to persuade them to do so because of the damage to morale that would result if territory is obviously given up without a fight after the German move into Bulgaria.

Blamey is not happy about the situation (something he puts forward in typically Australian blunt detail). While he realises and accepts the use of his troops in Greece is political, he is not prepared to sacrifice them 'on behalf of the bloody Greeks who don't even keep to their bloody agreements with us'. The staff are kept busy working out how the Allied troops can be deployed in Greece with some hope of a secure line of retreat, given the Greek obstinacy.

The Turkish government turns down Hitler's personal plea to join the Axis powers. The Turkish President replies that he is grateful for the assurance that German troops would be kept a safe distance from the Turkish border, and tells the German ambassador that Turkey will do everything in her power to avoid war with Germany. He points out his concerns about Bulgaria's mobilisation, which he feels can only be directed against Turkey. The German ambassador, Von Papen, assures him that this is not the case. Fortunately for Von Papen the President does not press him on exactly who it is aimed at if not at them.

5th March

Free French motorised units reach the outskirts of Tunis, to the general appreciation of the populace They are greeted by units of de Tassigny's men, but do not enter the city immediately, though they do put out a screen to the west of the city as a precaution. The town is still in turmoil, as the initial fights between de Tassigny's forces and the Vichy supporters have turned into a tense armed standoff; neither party really wishes to turn Tunis into a battlefield. The arrival of the column of French troops outside the town finally forces a resolution of the situation. The French commander enters the city under a flag of truce, to talk to the Vichy authorities, and later to de Tassigny, in the hope of avoiding a full-blown attack on the city. While this are happening, the rest of the Brigade (less some troops detached on the way to secure the route, and a number of tanks, are arriving and assembling outside the city. No attempt is made to conceal this. Officially of course the authorities are only talking to the French commander.

Britain has broken off diplomatic relations with Bulgaria. George Rendel, the British minister, handed the Bulgarian government a strongly-worded note protesting against Bulgaria's active co-operation with Germany which, it declared, constituted a grave threat to Britain's ally, Greece, and was "incompatible with the maintenance of British diplomatic representation in Bulgaria.

In Greece, Eden reports that the Greeks are reluctant to evacuate their forces from Albania if Yugoslavia does not attack from the north, and who are only offering the British 23 battalions of troops to delay any German advance into Salonika until British reinforcements arrive.

General Blamey is increasingly unhappy about the position he seems to be expected to put his troops in, and the constant refusal of the Greeks, as he sees it, to follow the military logic of their situation. In order to play for time, he suggests to Eden that, until the exact deployment can be arranged, his troops concentrate as an operational reserve, while the New Zealand Division holds Crete as a base for the RAF if German attacks force them to withdraw. Blamey's position is strengthened by a telegram from Menzies who basically gives him carte blanch to dispose his men as he sees best.

Meanwhile Operation Lustre officially begins as troopships head out of Alexandria for Crete; the cruisers Gloucester, Bonaventure and York are carrying the advance elements of I Australia Corps directly to Greece.

On patrol off the east coast of Tunisia, the submarine HMS Upright torpedoes and sinks an Italian cruiser as she covers the Italian convoy heading for Bone. This change of direction has in fact caught the Royal Navy unprepared, they were expecting to attack the convoy as either it entered Tunis, or as it retreated back to Naples, and Cunningham's ships are not disposed to intercept it.

6th March

Churchill issues his Battle of the Atlantic directive. Merchantmen modified with a deck to carry 4-6 Swordfish are to be fitted out as a priority, merchant ships to be given AA weapons as a first priority (in particular any ships to be used on the Gibraltar and Coastal convoys), and more Coastal Command squadrons formed and fitted with radar. Port and dockyard congestion is to be dealt with and the defence of ports greatly improved. These and numerous other matters are to be dealt with as a matter of the very highest priority. The survival of Britain depends on them. Overall direction is to be exercised by a Battle of the Atlantic Committee chaired by the Prime Minister himself.

The picture is not entirely black; the presence of Goshawks on many of the southern routes have turned the Luftwaffe Kondors into an endangered species; they are now only to be seen doing long range reconnaissance where they think they won't encounter a carrier. This has reduced the early losses due to them bombing ships, and made the U-boats task of finding a convoy much more difficult. However the Coastal and Gibraltar convoys are still suffering air attack as the intercepting of the Ju88's and He111's used is more difficult, and often a fast attack is made before the fighters can intercept.

The first of the US-built escorts will arrive soon, and Canadian-built corvettes are now starting to arrive (although they need additional work on arrival as Canada cannot produce all the equipment they need). The British corvette program is now delivering significant numbers of ships, and the new twin-screw Corvettes are on the slips. The Free French have also contributed six destroyers to form an escort group.

However despite better air cover, the U-boats Wolfpack tactic has not been defeated, just made more difficult. While they only manage an occasional concentration, the boats are still taking a heavy toll of any straggler, and U-boat sinkings are not affecting their numbers thanks to the construction programme.

In Tunis, an arrangement has been made between the Vichy governors and the Free French forces (for reasons of face, de Tassigny isn't mentioned even though he has been involved in the negotiations). The governor realises his position is completely untenable (outside the city where the bulk of the forces loyal to Vichy had been stationed, the situation is far worse for the regime, and with the harbour out of their control, there is no hope of reinforcement), and the result is a resignation of certain people in the government structure. By agreement, there are no individual reprisals and later a number of people and their families will be repatriated to metropolitan France.

The first aims of the new regime are twofold. To restore stability in Tunisia (while the government in Tunis has made agreements, there are some units in the country who are still loyal to Vichy, and it would be preferable to disarm them peacefully), without too much of a blood-bath, and to find what has happened to the Axis convoy that was heading for them. The position of the convoy is cleared up later that evening when they hear first of the actions of HMS Upright, and then from Bone that the convoy has docked there.

Fortunately Bone is not a major port, and while Rommel is keen to get his reconnaissance elements ashore and headed for Tunis as fast as possible, practicalities mean this will take a few days. It is agree in Tunis that the Free French troops will dig in to the west to impede any invasion, and the local forces are being mobilised in support. There is considerable French military equipment in the country, and while not up to modern standards will be very useful in a defensive position, but it will take a few days to get a suitable force together and then get it into place. The local forces are not strong, but they know the country well and will be attached to the Free French forces in the west of Tunisia. Another brigade of Free French forces is expected in Egypt in a few days, and this will follow immediately to Tunisia. There are also allied formations in Libya who can be used if needed, although many of these are still short of transport and supplies. However it is not thought that the Vichy forces in Algeria will attack themselves (one of the reasons for the generous terms to the governor is to stop Vichy using the excuse of civil war to intervene). As part of the hurried defence activity, an airfield is being prepared to handle some of the RAF Hurricanes supporting 13 Corps.

Churchill telegrams to Eden agreeing that the situation in Greece had worsened - so much so that he War Cabinet found it difficult to believe that Greece could be saved unless Turkey or Yugoslavia came in on the allied side, which now seemed most unlikely. Another telegram confirming this opinion is sent to General Blamey, with the (top secret) instructions that, while a commitment of some sort in Greece is necessary for political reasons, things should be arranged so as to risk as little as necessary to meet our commitments.

8th March

Wavell receives a signal from the British Military Mission in Athens. "General Papagos yesterday gave an impression of greater optimism. He states indications led him to hope Yugoslavia might yet fight. He therefore reverted to question of holding Nestos position if Yugoslav collaboration at last moment made this possible. From the point of view of morale he emphasised fact that troops in Eastern Macedonia were recruited locally, and that, if fighting in forward positions would be defending their own homes. He remains anxious about lorry situation in view new supply difficulty, and urges that every available lorry be sent as early as possible."

Wavell views this with some misgivings; he is fast losing belief in the ability of the Greek government to come to what he feels are the hard but necessary military decisions, but feels that he has to work with them as much and as long as possible.

Meanwhile in order to try and reduce any interference from Malta, Axis aircraft drop 76 tons of bombs on this 122 square mile island. While not good for Malta, no-one seems to have pointed out that bases on Crete and the Royal Navy's carriers are probably far more of a problem should they intervene.

In the United States, the carrier USS Ticonderoga is launched. The last of the Yorktown class carriers, she has been built as fast as possible, considering the steadily worsening situation in Europe and the Far East, and the role aircraft carriers seem now to be playing. It is hoped to have her commissioned by next March. The first of the follow-on class of carriers, the USS Essex, is expected to be laid down next month.

The 1st Free French Armoured Brigade is formally declared operational at Benghazi. This is a trifle optimistic, as while they are now equipped with ex-Italian tanks, they are as yet not properly trained up with them. The unit will now conduct training exercises aimed at allowing them to move to Tunisia as soon as possible. Until they are ready, a brigade of the 2nd Armoured will move into Tunisia in case the force under Rommel attempts to attack into the country.

The first prototype of the Canadian-designed Ram tank is completed. This tank is based on the US M3 chassis, with a new turret designed large enough to take the new

British 6-pdr AT gun (although the prototype only mounts the 2-pdr). The development has been funded jointly by Canada and France, who want the tank for the armoured divisions they are currently training. Building the tank in Canada will allow easy access to the US components for the tank, and production is expected for August. The first batch will mount the 2-pdr if the 6-pdr is not available in sufficient quantities. The tank also interests the British army, who have supplied guns for a second 6-pdr prototype. General O'Connor has stressed the need for a new tank to include a bigger gun (to allow HE fire), and also that it must be reliable - his experience in the desert has shown that tanks that break down too frequently are of little use. The British want to compare the tank with the Valentine; the new turret for the Valentine has space for three crew, but is too small to accept the 6-pdr gun. One possibility would be to use the Ram turret on a new version of the Valentine chassis (allowing complete construction of the tank in Britain).

9th March

The Italian spring offensive in Albania begins, around Bubesh on the Albanian front, between the Devoli and Vijose rivers, and led by Mussolini himself. The goal is to gain a victory against the Greeks before the Germans intervene, and Mussolini has come to Albania to watch.

The Italians will employ nine divisions (including one armoured and two alpini), plus many smaller units of up to regimental size, against about 20 miles of front straddling the Vojussa river. The Greeks defend with the 1st and 15th Divisions in the line, and the 6th Div and half the 17th Div in reserve. The Italian preparations have long been detected, and the Greeks are established in well-hidden hilltop positions with interlocking fields of fire for their machineguns, mortars, and highly effective mountain artillery. The Italian attack is preceded by a two-hour barrage in which 300 guns fire off 100,000 shells, but these are mostly light field pieces (100mm or smaller) and their effect on the deeply dug-in Greeks is minimal. There are also air attacks by Italian Stukas. The main push will be north of the Vojussa in the 6.5-mile sector of Gastone Gambarra's 8th Corps.

In Bone in Algeria, General Rommel, commanding the Afrika Korps, sends a message to the German High Command suggesting that it might be possible to go on the offensive before the hot weather begins. He suggests four objectives, (1) The occupation of Tunisia, (2) the re-occupation of Cyrenaica, (3) the occupation of northern Egypt, and (4) the capture of the Suez Canal. He proposes 8 May to begin the campaign, but points out he will need the rest of his division plus at least two good Italian divisions under his command. The report is greeted in Berlin with a certain amount of scepticism.

He now has a small force unloaded and ready (the local dockworkers not having proven terribly keen or efficient at unloading his ships), consisting of the 3rd Reconnaissance Battalion, elements of the 39th anti-tank battalion and infantry from the Italian Ariete Division. Despite his bold assumptions about taking Suez, Rommel's force is short of tanks (the bulk of 5th Light Division is sitting outside Naples, and the Ariete division lost most of its heavy tanks when they were sent on ahead to Benghazi (ironically they will soon face them again in the hands of the French). Rommel is also very short of petrol, although he has asked for supplies to be sent from Algiers. The result is that his advance only moves close to the Algerian-Tunisia border where it forms a covering force. At the moment the Axis have little concrete information as to what exactly is happening in Tunis, and how strong the allied force there is. Rommel has suggested an immediate attack, but he has been ordered to wait. The German High Command has rather more pessimistic reports of Allied forces in Tunisia.

The Italian navy estimate it will take about a month to get the rest of the 5th Light and Ariete divisions to North Africa, assuming that they will land at Algiers (they consider Bone both too small and ill-equipped, and altogether too close to the RAF). The biggest problem is that the convoys have to travel considerably further to Algiers than they would have had to reach Tripoli, and they are allowing for losses to the Royal Navy. They point out that they can only continue the convoys if they can get control of the air in their vicinity, otherwise there is nothing to stop Royal Navy heavy units from destroying them. Assuming losses to the Royal Navy and RAF are not too severe, they believe they can meet Rommel's requirement for a fully supplied three-division force by the beginning of May. Rommel considers this 'unacceptably long', and is pressing the German High Command to 'push the Italians as hard as possible'.

10th March

In what will prove to be the only success of the entire Italian offensive, the alpini of the Pusteria Division capture the fortified peak of Mali Spadarit, on the extreme left wing. However, this leaves them far in advance of any friendly troops, and heavy fire from adjacent Greek positions on their flanks and rear forces them to withdraw somewhat back down the slope. In Gambarra's sector, attempts to manoeuvre against Monastery Hill get nowhere, and Gambarra already has to bring up troops from his reserve Bari Division to reinforce the Puglie and Cagliari.

The French battleship Richelieu arrives at Gibraltar with an escort of three French destroyers, having finished her repairs in the USA. In addition to repairing the damage she suffered during the invasion of Dakar, she has also been refitted with modern AA guns and had equipment modified to allow her to work more easily with the RN. She will be attached to Force H, whose current role is to harass and strike

Italian shipping in the Mediterranean and conduct strikes on shore targets. Her arrival allows the Admiralty to send HMS Renown back to the UK for a refit, and to free up four destroyers for much-needed convoy escorts.

11th March

President Roosevelt this afternoon signs into law the Lend-Lease Bill, Public Law 11, 77th Congress. The bill passed both the House of Representatives and the Senate with large majorities. It seeks, as its congressional sponsors put it, to give "legislative form to the policy of making this country an Arsenal for the Democracies and seeks to carry out President Roosevelt's pledge to send these countries in ever-increasing numbers, ships, aeroplanes, tanks and guns." The bill empowers the President to lease to Britain munitions owned and paid for by the US government.

Debate on the bill was fierce, and its isolationist opponents in the Senate filibustered against it. On 6 March, however, Senator Walter George, the influential chairman of the Senate foreign relations committee, made a powerful speech in favour of its passage, arguing "the collapse of the British Empire would mean chaos in this world." Two days later the bill was finally passed by the Senate - by 60 votes to 31.

Immediately after the bill was signed the US Army and Navy approved the export of the first material to be released under the terms of the act. Though what is involved is being kept secret for military reasons, it is believed that the first shipments will include 24 motor torpedo boats already ordered to British design which have been held up by the US attorney-general and will help to defend Britain against invasion.

Most of the material released today will go to Britain. Some will go to the Free French forces, Greece, and some to China. The president's assistant, Laughlin Currie, has been sent to determine what the Chinese need. A few hours after the vote the president sent Congress a request for $7,000 million for munitions. The New York Times predicted that if American convoys are needed to deliver the products from the arsenal to the democracies, they will be sent.

There has been much discussion between the USA and Britain over the way the act will work, particularly with regard to items that Britain and the Free French can still pay for, and the British in particular are unhappy about some of what they see as severely restrictive trade clauses. In the end a compromise is reached; since it is in practice impossible to distinguish the end use of war consumables such as ammunition and fuel, these items will be supplied to Britain with the agreement she will distribute these to the various allied forces in exile as well as use them herself in support of them. For capital items, Britain (and also the Free French) will continue to pay for items they wish, and can use these however they wish (the French, in view of the German occupation of their country, are rather less concerned about trade clauses). In practice, it is known to the US government that many items such as tanks and planes 'given' to the French and others will end up used by British forces, but the facade helps the bill gets passed. The US government is taking the practical approach that it is better to have Germany defeated than worry too much about trade clauses (and in fact is assuming that the British will have to sign them anyway in about a year when they estimate their money will run out)

12th March

In Hawaii, the Commander-in-Chief, U. S. Pacific Fleet, Admiral Kimmel, sends the following message to the Chief of Naval Operations, Admiral Stark: "In view of (your letter of 15 February), the Commander-in-Chief, U. S. Pacific Fleet, recommends that until a light efficient net, that can be laid temporarily and quickly is developed, no anti-torpedo nets (for protection against torpedo plane attacks) be supplied this area."

The Australian government informs London that it expects the first production Beaufighters made in the country to become operational in October. Since the night fighter situation is easing in the UK, they ask for one, preferably two squadrons as soon as possible for pilot training and to develop tactics with the planes. The RAF was in fact hoping to use the first of its operational squadrons in the North Sea (against light German coastal shipping), and in the Mediterranean against light shipping. They suggest as a compromise that at least one squadron to be formed in the Mediterranean be from the RAAF, to give the necessary training and useful operational experience in the over-water role.

The development of a Torpex (an improved high explosive) warhead for the Navy's torpedoes is basically complete, and the first production units will be tested in May. They will be used on the new Mix torpedo, initially on Beaufighters and Wellingtons, and on the Fairy Spearfish when it enters service later in the year. The torpedo can be fitted with attachments that allow it to be dropped at up to 225knots, and it hoped to develop these further to allow a drop at 300knots, to take advantage of the performance of the new planes. It has already been seen how vulnerable torpedo planes are against any sort of fighter defence, and the new torpedo will, it is hoped, make the attacks more survivable. The new heavier torpedo will, with the more effective explosive, be nearly as destructive as a pre-war 21" submarine launched torpedo.

Two further Audacious class carriers are laid down, intended to be in service in 1944. The navy is currently examining the capability of the Audacious class against the expected further development of naval aircraft with a view to designing a new, larger ship to follow on from the Audacious. There has been opposition to so much of the navy's limited warship building going on the carriers rather than other heavy ships, but the FAA point out that apart from the fleet carriers, the other ships are intended for convoy duties, to work with the huge escort building program. In any case, shortages of armour, fire-control equipment and heavy guns mean they simply cannot build any more cruisers or battleships at the present, so fleet carriers are the obvious alternative. By early 1942 they expect to have some 19 battleships and battlecruisers in service and with the lack of capital ship opposition in home waters and the Mediterranean the need for additional battleships is reduced - indeed the Navy is looking at the possibility of putting the old R-class battleships into reserve to free up trained manpower for the carriers.

The US Navy announces that as a result of its increased production rate (instituted last year) the Grumman 4F Wildcat fighter will have replaced all the older Brewster Buffalo fighters in navy and marine service by June of this year. A number of the 'Martlet' version of the fighter are being used by the Free French in the Mediterranean and Africa (a version of this was offered to the RN but they decided it was inferior to the later models of the Goshawk fighter). The US will expedite orders of the Buffalo to the exiled Dutch government (who want them for the Dutch East Indies). The rest of the planes will be used for training or put into war reserve.

Chapter 10 - Afrika Korps

16th March

Two He111's of the German 10th Air Corps went on an armed reconnaissance mission during which they attacked units of the British Mediterranean Fleet west of Crete. Upon returning to base, the crews report torpedo hits on two heavy naval vessels which they describe as battleships. This supposed success meant a substantial reduction in the Royal Navy's strength in the Mediterranean. German leaders urge the Italian navy to get involved and to co-operate with the German attack on Greece that is planned for April 6, by sending their vessels forward into the eastern Mediterranean north and south of Crete. The Italians point out that the ships they are most worried about are the carriers and the Luftwaffe seems to have missed these, but they will do what they can with the light forces available to them.

British convoys are still bringing units of the army into Greece and Crete. Priority has been given to take the New Zealand Division to Crete (as it is considered vital to protecting a line of retreat if needed), but the Australian formations are steadily growing in Greece itself. The defence infrastructure of Crete itself is considered inadequate, and the New Zealanders are being used in an improvement program; this will take some time, especially as vital equipment such as AA guns is not available in the needed quantities.

The supply situation is made worse in Egypt due to mining raids on the Suez Canal by German aircraft. As a result badly-needed supplies are unable to get ashore. The British solution is, almost bizarrely, to hang nets over the canal so they can at least see where the mines land and deal with them.

20th March

In Hawaii Admiral Bloch states in a letter that the depth of water at Pearl Harbor is 45 feet, and for that and other reasons, he does not recommend anti-torpedo baffles. CINCPAC agrees, until such time as a light efficient net is developed. No-one seems to have pointed out to the Admiral how shallow Taranto harbour is (some 40 feet).

It has taken Rommel much longer than he anticipated to get all his force unloaded and ready for operations. Losing two of the supply ships to air attack didn't help (although at least one of the two ships was already unloaded). In fact is has taken so long that the following convoy is already on its way to Algiers with the next part of his force. Fortunately for the Italian navy, the Mediterranean fleet is preoccupied with the operations planned in the Eastern Mediterranean in support of Greece, and so far the convoy has only been harassed by aircraft from Malta, sinking one transport ship.

The Vichy government is doing everything it can short of declaring war on Britain to show it is cooperating with Germany, whose veiled threats about what will happen if they DON'T co-operate are becoming increasingly blunt. Fortunately for them, Hitler is preoccupied with the preparations for Barbarossa at the moment. Their current position is to offer the Axis all help possible in Algeria, including port facilities, fuel, and food supplies. There is growing opposition and resentment to this, which is being suppressed by the regime with an increasingly heavy hand.

In Egypt, General O'Connor is looking at how best to allocate his troops to deal with what he expects to be an attack on Tunisia once Rommel's force is established in Algeria. His main problem is that no sooner do more forces arrive, they are tasked to something else, and as a result he has had little in the way of substantial reinforcements. Currently XIII Corps consists of three divisions, 2nd Armoured, 6th Australian and 4th Indian. He has 7th Armoured refitting in the delta and a South African Brigade as his reserves. The Free French expect to have about a division in Tunisia once they have finished relocating from Ethiopia, plus what will effectively be a somewhat under-armed armoured brigade.

His main problem is equipment. While considerable supplies have been arriving, much of this has gone to Greece and Crete with the ANZAC forces. While the base workshops have repaired what was repairable after the campaign across the desert, much of the transport simply had to be written off for spares. Fortunately a considerable amount of Italian equipment is available; indeed the Free French are outfitted with Italian trucks and support vehicles. Because of the transport shortage and the poor infrastructure in Libya, he intends to position his forces in a number of locations where, as far as possible, they can be supplied at sea until he can build up enough strength to foray into Algeria (assuming, of course, that the politicians will let him). One brigade of 2nd Armoured will be forward in Tunisia in support of the Free French forces until their Armoured Brigade is ready to deploy. The 4th Indian Division will be at Tripoli. The 6th Australian Division plus a brigade of 7th Armoured will be at El Agheila and Benghazi. He is still not happy with the state of training of 2nd Armoured, who he feels are insufficiently prepared compared to 7th Armoured, so the remaining two brigades will be held around Tobruk where they will keep training (the advanced Brigade is the one which saw combat in the Cyrenaica campaign).

He would prefer to have his forces further forward ready to intervene faster in Tunisia when it proves necessary, but at the moment his logistics simply don't allow it. He takes comfort in the fact that Rommel has equally troublesome logistics problems to solve, and at least his transports aren't being sunk out from under him by the Royal Navy and RAF. The Free French are occupying forward positions on the Tunisia-Algeria border, and if attacked will fight a delaying action until he can reinforce them.

22nd March

The Italian convoy to Algiers, which had managed to avoid interception by the Royal Navy so far, runs into a force of cruisers and destroyers from Force H. The forces fleet carrier is unfortunately in dock, so instead a surface force of cruisers and destroyers has been sent. Air cover for the convoy is limited; there is now a Luftwaffe airfield operating near Algiers, but this so far only consists of a squadron of fighters and one of Stukas. The Royal Navy attacked the convoy just after dawn, and sank four merchant ships and three escorting destroyers for the loss of one destroyer and damage to two cruisers. The Luftwaffe dive bombers attacked as the force was retreating west, but only managed to land one hit on HMS Southampton. Fortunately the Stukas are not from Fliegerkorps X, and are more used to dealing with army support than with ships

23rd March

Luftwaffe Stuka dive-bombers, with a fighter escort, conduct a raid on Malta. A total of thirteen German planes are shot down while the British lose two fighters. British authorities decide to withdraw all bombers and flying boats from Malta as a result of the raid. As air bases are now available in Tunisia, there is less need to have the longer-ranged aircraft so vulnerable to enemy attack, and it seems likely they will next be needed to intervene in Tunisia or Greece in any case.

The Vichy regimes in Syria and Lebanon, which have been in secret discussions in Cairo with the Free French and the British, come to an agreement. In a similar manner to Tunisia, a considerable number of people will resign; those who wish will be transported to France, or to a neutral or allied country of their choice. In return, the two countries will declare for the Free French. The decision has been helped along by subtle hints pointing out that the forces in the desert have little to do at the moment, and Syria and the Lebanon are really quite close. The British are keeping quiet about the fact that they are still short of equipment and transport, while the presence of the veteran 7th Armoured Division is being mentioned. However the agreement will not be made public for some days. The more cynical among the allies reckon this is to allow certain parties to get away with ill-gotten gains; they are quite correct in this assumption.

This will leave Vichy as only controlling French Morocco, Algeria and (oddly) Madagascar out of its former colonies, a serious political blow to them when it becomes public.

The Italian convoy that had scattered when intercepted by the Royal Navy straggles into Algiers. The Vichy regime, desperate to show its compliance with German 'requests', starts unloading operations immediately. This is just as well, as that night the RAF pays a visit in the form of a bombing raid by Wellingtons, which sinks one of the ships in the harbour and sets another on fire. With the convoy losses at sea, and now this, the supply convoy has lost over half the equipment sent.

25th March

In Vienna's ornate Belvedere Palace today, the Yugoslav premier, Dragisa Cvetkovich, put his signature to the pact which binds his country to Germany and the Axis. He had left behind in Belgrade a government and country deeply divided, with the Serbs passionately pro-British and the Croats equally pro-German.

After the signing, the premier said that his chief aim was peace and security for the Yugoslav people. Von Ribbentrop welcomed Yugoslavia as a "new partner", and promised that Germany would respect the country's territorial integrity and not make military demands. Nobody believes him, least of all the Yugoslav premier, and there are disturbances in Belgrade when it becomes known that Yugoslavia has signed the Tripartite Pact with Germany.

Increasing Axis activity in the form of air reconnaissance has been observed south and west of Greece and Crete and there are daily attempts to observe the harbour at Alexandria. It is suspected from this additional interest in the activities and whereabouts of the Royal Navy's Mediterranean Fleet that the enemy was planning some form of surface action. Secret intelligence intercepts confirmed that there would be attacks on British convoys but in planning the response it was most important to ensure that the Italians did not get any idea that this was known or suspected. While a number of the infiltrating reconnaissance planes have been shot down, they are starting to come over at high altitude, and this is making it very difficult for the Goshawks to intercept them (like most carrier planes, they are optimised for performance below 20,000 feet). A request is made to London for a squadron of Spitfires to make interception more likely.

Despite the damage done to the previous convoy, another one is ready to leave Naples. Rommel is pressing hard for more men and equipment, as he wants to attack Tunisia before the allies can rebuild their strength. Intelligence reports show that Imperial troops are arriving in Greece in numbers, and if they are in Greece they obviously can't be in North Africa. Indeed, Rommel wants the men and equipment brought forward as soon as they land, which raises the problem that the mechanised equipment requires desertification - modifying the equipment on arrival had been normal practice when the Italian workshops in Cyrenaica had been available, but apparently no-one in the supply services seemed to have realised these were now were now being used by the Allies. Rommel sends off a blistering telegram to Berlin, as a result of which the equipment will be modified in Naples so as to be ready to operate as soon as it lands.

At the moment, the contact between the Afrika Korps and the Allies is in a series of small units dug in around the western border of Tunisia. It is the aggressive patrolling of the German units that makes Rommel eager to attack immediately, as he sees the Free French as the weak link in the Allied forces.

26th March

The heavy cruiser HMS York was hit by Italian explosive motor boats launched from the destroyers Crispi and Sella while she was lying in Suda Bay, Crete. Badly damaged, the ship was beached in shallow water, with both boiler rooms and an engine room out of action.

Although the shipment of Hurricanes via Malta has helped, the RAF in the Eastern Mediterranean is still short of planes, and more are requested from Britain. There is currently a good supply of fighters available in the UK, as only limited operations are being undertaken against France, and it is hoped another delivery run can be made as soon as the carriers are ready again. This delivery run will become a steady process; a carrier loaded with aircraft will escort a Gibraltar convoy, then the fighters will be delivered to Malta where some will remain and others will fly on to North Africa. Priority will be given to planes other than the Hurricane, which is still being delivered via the cross-Africa route.

Given the build-up of Rommel's forces in Algeria, plans are being made for a fast convoy to be escorted through the Mediterranean direct to Alexandria carrying equipment and tanks. The base workshops have repaired most of the vehicles that were repairable, but shortages in certain classes remain.

27th March

At 2.30 this morning in Belgrade the Yugoslav regency council, headed by Prince Paul resigned; his nephew, King Peter, who is 17, took over and appointed as his Prime Minister General Dusan Simovich, the chief of the air staff. Simovich had organized the coup after two days of anti-Nazi demonstrations. Soon after a radio announcement of the successful coup, King Peter was cheered as he drove through Belgrade. Hitler does not take the news well.

In Washington, the secret Anglo-US staff talks (ABC1) which began in January ended today with broad agreement on plans for strategic co-operation in the event of US entry into the war against Germany or Japan or both.

In fourteen meetings since 29 January the two sides have discussed the American plan, put forward by Captain Turner of the US Navy and Colonel McNarney of the US Army. The result is plan ABC1. Its main argument is that Germany must be defeated first. The US would therefore give strategic priority to the Atlantic and to Europe, although the US navy would be used offensively in the Pacific as British staff officers have drawn attention to the vulnerability of Singapore.

Britain leases defence bases in Trinidad in the West Indies to the U.S. for 99-years, in exchange for another 30 Frigates to be built in the USA.

In a US research laboratory, a team of physicists reports the discovery of a new isotope of uranium which it calls plutonium-239.

30th March

In Belgrade the new Foreign Minister makes efforts to remain on good terms with Germany. He assures the German Minister that they would respect international treaties concluded by their predecessors, including accession to the Tripartite Pact. However the Yugoslav Army takes up positions on the frontier anticipating a German invasion. Meanwhile Hitler has approved the plan to invade Yugoslavia on the 6th April.

HMS Implacable arrives in the United Stated for her full repair work. She will also get a refit and some new equipment, and is expected to be operation again in July. The USN personnel and naval designers who board her to start arranging the work are amazed at how well the ships structure has stood up to so much damage; indeed, the hangar deck armour had not been seriously penetrated. Although the damage above this was severe, it was mainly to the easily-repaired hangars, and the report sent to the USN points out that similar damage would have sent any US carrier to the bottom. Although the Essex class carriers are too far along to redesign, consideration is given to modifying the follow on class according to the lessons of the Implacable's survival.

The Richelieu makes her first raid on Algiers; accompanied by destroyers, a night bombardment of the port area causes considerable damage and disruption. Unfortunately it doesn't catch any ships in port, but the damage done to the facilities will slow loading and unloading of the next convoy. The battleship retired west after the bombardment, covered by FAA fighters. The mission itself is pushed by the Allied propaganda machine as a sign of how the Free French are still in the fight against Germany (with the obvious comparison that the Vichy regime is not).

31st March

The new night fighters and the first of the centimetric AI radar sets are taking an increasing toll of Luftwaffe bombers. Night fighters and AA guns destroyed over 70 planes this month, and more are damaged. The losses are starting to be a problem for the Luftwaffe, who in addition to mounting heavy raids on England are committing increasing number of planes to the Mediterranean and are trying to prepare for Barbarossa. It is suggested that the raids on England are paused now summer is approaching to allow the planes and men to be rested and made ready for deployment in the east.

The cruiser HMS Bonaventure with a Mediterranean Fleet cruiser force is escorting a convoy from Greece to Egypt when she is torpedoed and sunk by the Italian submarine Ambra some 90 miles south of Crete. The need to protect the troop convoys to Crete is occupying Cunningham's fleet, and only occasional forays can be made against the convoys from Italy to Algeria, which are being left to Force H and the strike force at Malta.

The Vichy governments in Syria and the Lebanon publicly declare for Free France. To those familiar with the region, there is an interesting lack of the politicians who used to be in charge in the current regimes. The British 6th Infantry Division will move into the area (one Brigade to the Lebanon, two to Syria) until Free French forces can take over. In the meantime the Free French will take over the running of the two colonies. While the declaration is as recently agreed, Middle East command is worried that the deteriorating situation in Greece might make some of the Vichy representatives reconsider, and they want to make sure they have forces on the ground in case.

The acquisition of Syria is particularly important to the Free French, as there are some 35,000 troops in the country which are now under their command. This will allow them to form a full Corps within the next few months. Heavy equipment will still be a problem, but it is hoped that orders from the USA will fill much of this shortage. They hope to move a Brigade to Tunisia to strengthen its defences once transport and support is available - this will give them a full division and an armoured brigade in the colony, backed up by British forces in Tripoli, which it is hoped will be sufficient to deter a German attack at least in the near term.

2nd April.

The New Zealand division under Major-General Sir Bernard Freyberg finish their concentration on Crete. It had been intended to then transport them onto Greece to join the force there, but the Australians in Greece have still not taken up the originally agreed positions, and so they are to wait on Crete until the situation is clear. In the meantime, they are busy improving the defences and facilities of Crete, which are in poor condition, and making an airbase ready for staging Sparrowhawk fighters to help guard the convoys between Greece and Alexandria

The Italian navy extends the time it expects to take to fully build up the German 5th light and Italian Ariete divisions in Algeria to the end of the month. The convoys have been taking significant losses from the British; air strikes from Malta and Tripoli, attacks at sea by destroyers and cruisers, carrier strikes from Force H, submarine attacks and mines in the harbour at Algiers have sunk over 40% of the ships sent. In addition to having to make these losses good, the amount of material needed was underestimated. Unlike the earlier convoys to Tripoli, there are no Italian stockpiles in Algeria, so as well as the German equipment all the Italian supplies need to be built up as well. The Vichy government in Algeria is supplying water and food, but they have no petrol spare for the Afrika Korps to use. This is all having to be brought from Italy, and the Royal Navy is singling out tankers for specific attention.

3rd April

A coup d'état in Iraq is led by the nationalist politician General Rashid Ali el Gailani and a group of officers calling themselves the "Golden Square". The group is opposed to the British presence in the country. The Regent Emir Abdul Illah escapes to Transjordan and by 3 April, a new government has been installed. The Soviet Union recognises the new government at once. It was the first to do so, and the Luftwaffe makes plans to set up an airlift to Iraq, although at the moment the distance to Iraq means that any substantial airlift will be impossible. A 1930 agreement between Iraq and Britain had granted the British two bases there: Shuaiba, south of Basra, and Habbaniya, an important RAF base and training camp in the Euphrates Valley about 48 miles west of Baghdad. As a result of the coup, the British send troops from India and the Middle East to ensure access to the vital oil supplies.

In the Red Sea the eight Italian destroyers and torpedoes boats remaining at Massawa, Eritrea, sortie from the port. The destroyers are sighted north of Massawa and are attacked by SeaLance aircraft of No 813 and Swordfish of No 824 Squadron assigned to the aircraft carrier HMS Victorious but operating from Port Sudan to cover local troop activities. The destroyers Daniel Manin and Nazario Sauro and the MAS-213 are sunk and the destroyers Pantera, Tigre and Cesare Battisti are scuttled near Massawa.

4th April

In Berlin Hitler meets the Japanese Foreign Minister Matsuoka Yosuke again, and promises to join Japan in fighting the USA if it should declare war. The Foreign Minister has been on an official visit to Rome and Berlin.

The first two squadrons of Beaufighters arrive in the Mediterranean theatre. The original intention had been to base one at Malta and the other in Cyrenaica, but in view of the current heavy air attacks on Malta both squadrons are sent to North Africa. One squadron is the first RAAF unit to be involved in the Mediterranean; it will be used to give the Australians familiarity with the plane in preparation for their own version currently in production. The Beaufighters will initially be used as long range fighters and torpedo planes to attack the Italian convoys to Algeria and force them further west (and into easier range of Force H).

6th April

German, Italian and Hungarian forces move on Yugoslavia and Greece, supported by a heavy concentration of Luftwaffe aircraft. Although the Allied expeditionary force is not complete (it consists of the 9th Australian Division, the 7th Australian division and the 1st Armoured Brigade), units have moved forward to man the Aliakmon Line along with three Greek divisions. The Imperial and Greek forces are supported by seven RAF squadrons.

8th April

In Eritrea, the Italians in the seaport of Massawa, the main Italian naval base in East Africa, surrender to British and Free French troops. Of the 13,000 men defending the town, 3,000 have been killed and 5,000 wounded. The Allies capture 17 large Axis merchant ships in the port along with many smaller military and civilian vessels. The 5th Indian Division, which has played a large part in the Allied campaign in Eritrea, starts to prepare to be shipped to Egypt to form the basis of a new Army Corps. The priority in the East African campaign is now to clear the road between Asmara and Addis Ababa and troops are being sent to this task from both ends of the road.

In Greece the German armour is pushing the Greeks back through the Dorian Gap, and the British 1st Armoured Brigade is moved forward to help. Meanwhile the infantry formations make ready to defend the Aliakmon line.

9th April.

The Metaxas Line in Greece collapses. Within three days of crossing into Greece from Bulgaria, German forces have captured the key port of Salonika, and forced the surrender of the whole eastern wing of the Greek army between Salonika and the Turkish border. This brings them close to the defence line manned by British and Australian troops.

The danger to the Olympus-Aliakmon line is also an outflanking move from Yugoslavia through the Monastir Gap. The 1st Armoured Brigade and the 19th

Australian Brigade are detached from the 1st Australian Corps and placed under command of General Mackay, to form a blocking force in the Florina valley.

An additional four destroyers led by HMS Jervis are detached to Malta to help interdict Rommel's supply convoys. While Admiral Cunningham is short of destroyers, Middle East command needs to slow the build-up in Algeria while the situation in Greece is deteriorating so quickly.

11th April

With the destruction of all Italian war vessels in the Red Sea announced by the British, President Roosevelt declares the Red Sea and Gulf of Aden are no longer "combat zones" and therefore open to American shipping. The President also cables Churchill to tell him that he proposes to extend the US Security Zone to 26 degrees west. He asks for details of British convoys to be relayed to the US Navy so that patrol units may meet them. In return the Americans will pass on intelligence of U-boats operating within the Security Zone.

12th April

The Imperial forces deployed along the rugged terrain from the Gulf of Salonika to Edhessa in the Vermion Mountains, have been pulled back to Mount Olympus, the next defensible line some hundred kilometres to the south. The Germans were pouring into Greece through the Monastir Gap, and with the Yugoslav resistance crumbling, General Blamey was left with no choice.

The 45,000 strong Imperial forces have had little or no time to prepare their defences, and their strength is insufficient to organize a defence in depth. If the Germans are not stopped at Monastir they will soon be turning the British left flank, at which point the Corps will have no choice but to withdraw.

Admiral Cunningham has put the Mediterranean fleet at notice to sail, and supplies which were due to have been delivered to Greece have instead been diverted for the time being to Crete. The situation in Greece is deteriorating much faster than anticipated. In a private meeting with Wavell, Cunningham assures him there are sufficient ships to evacuate the expeditionary force, and probably a considerable number of the Greek army as well, but enemy air power will cause him losses, which he is prepared to accept. There is a limit to how long the carriers can give air support, but he feels this will suffice for the main evacuation effort.

13th April

In a treaty designed to safeguard both parties' borders, the Soviet Union and Japan today signed a neutrality pact for the next five years. The pact acknowledges existing borders, giving Russian recognition to Japanese Manchuria (now known as Manchukuo) for the first time. Under the pact, should either the Soviet Union or Japan become the object of military action, then the other party will observe neutrality.

In Greece the Imperial forces retreat to the Thermopylae line. This is only 50 miles long, and should be much easier to hold that the Olympus-Vermion line. However Blamey warns Middle East command that if the Greek army continues to give way, he will soon either be forced into an untenable defensive position or withdraw from Greece. Meanwhile the Luftwaffe continues its heavy bombing of Malta in an attempt to reduce the interference with the Algerian-bound convoys.

In London, the Australian Prime Minister Menzies criticises the way he sees Australian troops carrying an unfairly heavy part of the fighting in the Middle East. It is agreed that General Blamey will be given authority to withdraw from Greece if he thinks it necessary to preserve his force. To placate Menzies, it is promised that more British troops will be sent out to the Middle East as soon as possible, and commitments made for further support of Australian concerns in the Far East.

In secret talks between Iceland and the US government, Iceland agrees not to resist US forces replacing the British forces on Iceland.

15th April

Wavell and other senior British Middle East commanders meet and decide that the evacuation of all forces from the Greek mainland is unavoidable. General Blamey is informed of their decision, and the RN and RAF units in Alexandria and Crete put on alert. The New Zealand division on Crete is told to speed up preparations to defend the island from possible attack.

The first of a new class of convoy escorts, HMS Exe, is launched. A large building program of this class the twin-screw corvette (later to be called the frigate) has been started, and more of this type are being built in the USA as part of the bases deal. It is hoped to have her in commission by January 1942. Due to the severe convoy losses, the escort program is currently the highest priority naval building program, but due to the larger size and more complex nature of the ship, they will take 12-15 months to build rather than the 6-9 for the current, simpler corvettes.

There has been much discussion as to the ships armament; in the end two versions are under construction. The first, intended as a specialised A/S ship for the North Atlantic, carries a single 4" gun plus up to eight 20mm cannon. The second class, intended for use where there is a larger air threat, carries four 40mm cannon as well as twelve 20mm. Both types will carry a large number of depth charges and the new hedgehog AS spigot mortar. Faster than the single-screw corvettes, and with a longer range (allowing them to cross the Atlantic without refuelling), as well as modern refinements in sonar and radar, it is hoped that once they arrive they, and the new escort carriers which will then be available in numbers, will reduce the current merchant ship losses to U-boats.

16th April

Off Algeria, Capt P. J. Mack with destroyers HMS Janus, HMS Jervis, HMS Mohawk and HMS Nubian operation out of Malta intercept a German Afrika Korps convoy of five transports escorted by three Italian destroyers. All Axis ships are sunk including the destroyers Baleno (foundered next day), Lampo (later salvaged) and Tarigo. In the fighting HMS Mohawk is torpedoed twice by Tarigo and capsizes. She is eventually sunk by gunfire from HMS Janus.

The race to build up forces and supplies in North Africa by both sides continues, although as one British General pointed out, it was not so much a horse race as two tortoises straining to get ahead of each other in search of a particularly tasty lettuce leaf. While the Axis had ample forces available to ship to the theatre, they were severely limited by shipping (not helped by the fact the British were sending up to 40% of the equipment to the bottom of the Mediterranean Sea), poor port facilities and the need to build up all the supplies they would need almost from scratch. On the British side, the supplies had to come the best part of 12,000 miles, and each time a convoy arrived much of its contents seemed to get diverted to other demands such as Greece.

Wavell orders that no more troops are to sail to Greece (the Polish Brigade was about to leave, but instead will be held in reserve in Egypt), ships with unloaded cargo should return with it immediately and ships loading in Egypt will stop loading and unload. While the airfields are not yet in a satisfactory state, fighters are dispatched to Crete in order to help cover an evacuation from Greece.

In Tokyo, an Associated Press dispatch quotes Ko Ishii (the spokesman for the cabinet board of information) as denying absolutely that "Japan intended to send an army or navy force against Singapore." He added that Premier Prince Konoye already stated that "Japan's southward intentions are clearly and entirely peaceful and economic. This report (about Singapore) is entirely groundless and the propaganda of war mongers"

17th April

Churchill agrees to a secret appeal from General Papagos, the Greek C-in-C for British and Empire forces to evacuate mainland Greece in order to save it from further destruction, but insists that Crete must be held with force. He also offers to evacuate as many Greek troops as possible to Crete in order to allow it to continue as a centre of Greek resistance. In Athens the British staff begin detailed plans to evacuate the Imperial troops to Crete and Egypt.

Although recent night attacks have caused considerable damage over Britain, in view of the need for additional aircraft in the Mediterranean and to prepare for Barbarossa (and also due to the steadily increasing toll the British night fighters are taking), the Luftwaffe suspends major operations over Britain. The Luftwaffe bomber force is in need of the temporary rest; it is actually weaker now in planes (and even weaker in experienced pilots) than it was before the start of the French campaign last year, while the RAF and Allied forces are considerably stronger.

19th April

The Yugoslavs surrender after twelve days fighting. Many troops will stay in the hills after the surrender, continuing the struggle as partisans.

The first Imperial troops arrive in Iraq when the British 20th Indian Brigade lands at Basra. Although Rashid Ali's new government objects, these movements are covered by a 1930 treaty and with no German support available, the objections are ignored by the British.

General Student, leader of the new XI. Fliegerkorps which now controls all air transport units, suggests to Goering that an attempt be made to invade Crete from the air once Greece is taken. The idea catches Goering's interest, and he agrees to put it before Hitler.

21st April

Evacuation starts of Imperial troops and equipment in Greece. The troops will be evacuated to Egypt (or to Crete if sailing on local vessels). At the same time it is suggested that the Greek army starts to use small craft and fishing vessels to evacuate trapped troops to Crete. The British have a fair number of landing craft available to them as well as the usual shipping, and it is hoped to recover at least a part of the expeditionary forces equipment to Crete using these.

In Australia, there are political moves against Menzies, blaming him for high Australian casualties in Greece. The movement is opposed by those pointing out that the forces there are under Australian command, and the additional commitments Britain has made to Australian concerns about Japan. The arguments will go on for some time

22nd April

British tank regiments are to be re-organized as more effective fighting units. In future they will have their own support arms in the front-line, including motorised infantry, combat engineers, artillery, anti-aircraft and anti-tank units. This change has been worked on for some time, after the reports of the success of such a mix in the desert, and reports of the effectiveness of it when used by the German Panzer units. The regiments in North Africa are already following this pattern where equipment allows, and it will be replicated with the forces held at home.

The formal evacuation of Greece begins; The Royal Navy will cover convoys to bring out the troops, as much equipment as feasible and also Greek troops (who will be landed in Crete). Air cover will be from the Navy's carriers and from fighters based on Crete. The situation in the Eastern Mediterranean means little can be done for the time against Rommel's supply convoys; Force H will undertake further operations against them and the ships in Algiers. The Greek King and his government will be evacuated to Crete tomorrow - it is hoped Crete will serve as a part of Greece not under occupation and allow the Greek government to continue to play a part in the war against Germany

25th April

Hitler issues Directive No. 28 - Operation Mercury, the invasion of Crete. Planning will begin immediately so the operation can be launched after Greece falls.

Germany and Italy undertake to give financial and military aid to Rashid Ali's government in Baghdad. However the Basra: Reuters News Agency reports that "strong British and Imperial troops have arrived in the area of the Mosul airfields and, with the consent of Iraqi military authorities, have occupied positions of strategic importance". British troop movements are still continuing.

At 2100 on the 25th April, the rattle of heavy anchor chains echoed around the peace of Bergen fjord. Operation Rheinübung was finally starting.

Chapter 11 - Operation Rheinübung

Post-war opinion is divided on this operation. Some see it as the best attempt of the outnumbered German Navy to inflict considerable damage on the Royal Navy and the British convoy system; others consider it a 'Death-Ride' in keeping with the Nazi mentality.

The basics of the operation itself were simple. The Kriegsmarine had four heavy surface units available; the battleships Bismarck and Scharnhorst, the heavy cruiser Prinz Eugen and the carrier Graf Zeppelin. There were a number of destroyers that would accompany the heavy ships for the first part of the operation, but these short ranged craft would then return to Norway. The preparations for the operation itself had been carried out in great secrecy; the heavy units had slipped out of port and up the coast of Norway as far as Bergen under cover of cloud and poor weather, and had in fact managed to concentrate in the fjord without having been spotted by the RAF.

Sadly, all that careful forethought was wasted. The code-breakers at Bletchly Park had given the Admiralty news that German heavy ships were heading up the Norwegian coast, and confirmation that the Bismarck and Prinz Eugen at least were involved was confirmed by a member of the Norwegian resistance. As a result, although they didn't all go to sea, the units of the Home Fleet were put at four hours readiness for steam. The Prince of Wales was hurried out of her hull cleaning in dry dock, and all boiler cleaning cancelled. The old battleships Barham and Ramilles were ordered to join two of the most valuable northern convoys; their slow speed made them unlikely to be useful in a chase, while putting them in front of a potential breakout meant they might be able to intercept.

The main force of the Home Fleet was the fleet carriers Illustrious and Formidable, the light carrier Colossus, the battleships KGV, Prince of Wales, Nelson and Rodney, and the battlecruiser Hood. A number of cruisers were also available. Coastal command was also put on alert, both to try and keep the German ships under surveillance in Norway, and then to hopefully track and attack them if they ventured out. In addition, two other carriers were put on readiness to join the Home Fleet; the light carrier HMS Ocean, currently at Liverpool having just escorted in a convoy, and HMS Glorious, just finishing working up after a recent refit.

The aim of the operation was to cause as much damage and disruption to the British convoys as possible, then slip back home. The fleet would then be a constant threat to a repeat foray, and would require the Royal Navy to keep heavy units tied up in Scapa Flow as a response. This would then make them vulnerable to a heavy air raid on the base itself (provisionally planned for the autumn). The start of the operation would be the breakout from Norway. The ships would be covered for the first part of their trip by land-based Luftwaffe fighters, allowing them to proceed without having to worry about the Graf Zeppelin flying off aircraft. As this was going on, high level Luftwaffe reconnaissance planes would check Scapa Flow. If the British Home Fleet was still an anchor, then the Graf Zeppelin would conduct an air strike on the base (aided by Norwegian based bombers) as a distraction, and would then retreat to Norway, allowing the surface units to slip past to the north before the British discovered them. If the Home Fleet heavy units were at sea (especially the carriers), then the Graf Zeppelin would accompany the surface force to provide air cover and a strike capability against the Royal Navy. While the carrier could only launch a small strike, it was thought this would be adequate against the biggest threat to the breakout, patrolling Royal Navy cruisers.

While the Luftwaffe kept up a constant air patrol over the fjord to discourage the RAF, a reconnaissance Whirlwind managed to get over the ships and get a set of photographs. The results concerned the Royal Navy; they had assumed this was one or two of the German heavy ships aiming to slip out to raid, not all four. The disposition of the Home Fleet was therefore split into four parts.

First, the carrier Glorious and the cruisers Norfolk and Suffolk, along with a number of destroyers, would cover the Denmark straight between Iceland and the Greenland ice barrier. The cruisers would be deployed to the east of the carrier in order to protect her if they ran into the German ships without warning. Second, the light carrier Colossus and her escorts would cover a light cruiser force consisting of Galatea, Aurora, Kenya and Neptune between Scotland and the Faroes. The most likely route between the Orkneys and Iceland would be covered by the fleet carriers Illustrious and Formidable with the battleships Prince of Wales and KGV, and the battlecruiser Hood. This force could also reinforce either the northern or the southern force if the Germans used one of those routes. Finally the battleships Nelson and Rodney would remain at Scapa to block the escape route. They would be joined by the light carrier Ocean as soon as she arrived (she was currently escorting a convoy). The biggest worry was the weather. Poor weather, not uncommon at this time of year, could allow the German force to slip past, or catch one of the light carriers by surprise. The risk was, it was felt, worth taking, as such a powerful force could not be allowed to break free into the Atlantic convoy lanes.

In addition to the naval forces, Coastal Command was also put on alert and asked to add its reconnaissance planes to the search north of Scotland, In particular the A/S-radar equipped Stirlings. There were only a small number of these available, and so far they had been kept busy on the convoy routes looking for and keeping down submarines. It was hoped their range and radar would allow them to spot the raiding force even in bad weather. For the next few days the convoys would have to take the risk of less air cover. While the chances of them being intercepted by the German carrier was of course a risk (the RN knew, from its own experience of intercepting Kondors, how vulnerable a large plane could be to fighters), the hope was that the radar would allow discovery at sufficient range to keep safely back and in range of cloud cover. Finally a squadron of SeaLance torpedo planes, normally based in East Anglia in case of an attempted invasion, were put on alert to move to Scotland at short notice to provide a strike capability off Scotland in case the German fleet attempted to slip by closer to land.

At 2100 on the 25th April, Operation Rheinübung began.

Admiral Lutjens's fleet had first headed north towards Trondheim. Reports from the Luftwaffe had indicated that the Home Fleet seemed to not be in Scapa, so he intended to keep his carrier with him. Shortly before dawn the destroyers accompanying the force were detached to Trondheim, having insufficient range to accompany the heavy ships. He intended to take the ships out through the Denmark Straight, rather than through the Iceland/Faeroes gap, as he felt this would be too heavily patrolled by British aircraft. By midnight on the 26th the ships had turned west to head directly for the Straight.

Meanwhile the British had confirmation that the force had sailed; reconnaissance over the fjord had shown the absence of the heavy ships, and it was assumed that a breakout into the convoy lanes was intended. However until more was known about what route the German fleet would take, Admiral Tovey decided there was no reason to change the disposition of his ships. The ships had left the fjord before a strike on them could be arranged; the weather in Norway had delayed the possibility until it was too late. He had therefore moved his fleet carriers to cover the capital ships, and be ready to move north or south if the German fleet didn't take the central passage into the Atlantic. In case the Germans slipped past them in bad weather, Force H was ordered to leave Gibraltar and sail north to take up a blocking position.

The weather on the 27th was poor, and as the British ships took up station only the ASV-equipped planes were of any use, and searches from the fleet carriers and Coastal Command found nothing. The situation was of course the same for the Germans; with no ASV equipped planes, they were operating without any aerial reconnaissance at all. The German ships were not in fact spotted until late in the evening, and not by an aircraft but by the radar of HMS Suffolk, on patrol in the Denmark straight. The large echoes on the radar set could hardly be anything other than the German force that was expected, and the cruiser radioed a sighting report even as she retired westward, keeping the enemy under contact by radar.

The cruiser had also been spotted by the German radar, and although the one, smaller echo could have been anything, the fact that it was retreating at 27 knots to keep the distance between them indicated a warship of some sort. Meanwhile Coastal Command on Iceland was asked to send out a radar-equipped Stirling to confirm the sighting; this was done at 0100, and an hour later a confirmation was received. Four large echoes (assumed to be capital ships) heading west out of the Denmark Straight.

While a night strike from the nearest carrier, HMS Glorious, was a possibility, the poor weather made the attempt difficult. With the enemy now under observation, Tovey decided to have the carrier retire west to keep the range open (she was around 120 miles from the German fleet), in preparation for a dawn strike, when the weather might not be better but at least they would have daylight.

Lutjens had no night strike capability at all (the planes carried by the Graf Zeppelin were modified Me109 fighters and Ju87 dive bombers), so the only option seemed to be to cripple or sink the cruiser tracking them at first light, and then search for any other ships in front of him. If the cruiser was alone, he still felt he had a good chance of breaking out before other ships could intercept his force.

The strike from HMS Glorious was spotted on deck well before dawn on the 28th. The Admiralty was still uncertain as to the number of planes that the German carrier could handle. Intelligence had given the ship's displacement at around 25,000 tons, about the same as a British fleet carrier. They estimated she could be carrying up to 60 - 80 planes, probably split evenly between dive bombers and fighters (no sign had ever been found of a carrier-operable torpedo plane). Glorious was carrying 18 TBD, 18 DB and 20 fighters. The fleet carriers and the battleships had altered course to the north during the night, but they would not be in a position to send off a strike until the afternoon. The decision was made to have Glorious attack the carrier, as without air support it would be relatively easy to hunt down the rest of the German force. With luck, Glorious would hit the carrier before she got her own strike off.

At 0430 the Glorious started to fly off her planes. Given the unknown quantity of aircraft on the German carrier, it was a maximum strength strike in two waves. First eighteen SeaLance armed with torpedoes, escorted by six Goshawks, then a second strike of eighteen Cormorants with another six Goshawks. The remaining eight Goshawks would be retained for defence.

Meanwhile Lutjens was still only aware of the cruiser loitering at the edge of his radar range. During the night, it had been decided to send out an air search at first light, to sweep in front of the ships. While the weather was still poor, he needed to know if there were any British ships apart from the cruiser close to him. The Graf Zeppelin was carrying 20 Me109's and 24 Ju87. The Ju87 had a secondary function as a search plane, and twelve would be flown off to start the search as soon as it was light. The other twelve would attack and sink the cruiser, who's shadowing was beginning to annoy the German Admiral. As a result the German planes would have cleared their carrier by the time the FAA strike arrived.

The first ship to be subject to air attack that morning was the cruiser HMS Suffolk. The weather was clearer today, although the German ships were not quite visible over the horizon, and the ship was at action stations at dawn. Radar emissions from the German ships made it possible they had been spotted, and the intelligence reports indicated that there may be a carrier with the group. If so, it was going to get interesting when the sun rose.

At 0600 the cruiser saw the black dots of a flight of Stukas heading for them. The ship worked up to full speed and puffs of AA fire started to pockmark the sky around the dive bombers as they moved into their attack formation. As soon as the planes turned over into their dives, the close range AA joined in as well. Despite the lack of fighter cover, the Stukas did not escape without loss; two of them were shot down by the cruiser. This did not stop them getting three hits on the ship with 500kg bombs. The first hit just aft of the bridge, splinters killing and wounding many of the men on the bridge, and penetrating deeper to put the forward boiler room out of action. The second hit further aft, destroying the aircraft hangar and killing many of the crews serving the AA weapons, although fortunately none of the splinters from the bomb caused serious damage to the machinery space below. The third struck her on X turret, destroying the turret and causing additional damage to the engine room forward of the turret. Prompt action to flood the aft magazine prevented an explosion, but the ship was on fire and temporarily out of control and not under power.

While the attack on the Suffolk was taking place, the German ships radar reported the echo of the first strike from Glorious, her torpedo planes. These were escorted by six fighters, who moved to intercept the four Me109's that were the German CAP. As the fighters wove into a dogfight, the torpedo planes moved into attack formation. It was only when they dropped their torpedoes that things went badly wrong. In order to achieve the maximum damage, the torpedoes were using the magnetic duplex fuse. When the torpedoes hit the rough water of the Denmark Strait, instead of heading for the carrier they exploded on contact with the water. Only two torpedoes launched successfully, and the carrier managed to avoid both of them. The shooting down of two Me109's and damaging one more for the loss of one Goshawk hardly compensated for this, especially as two of the torpedo planes were lost to AA fire.

By now, it was obvious to Lutjens that a British carrier was in the area. Since his force was now located, the direction the British planes had come from was passed to his scouting force. It did not take long for one of the Ju87's to spot the Glorious and her two escorting destroyers. While that plane dodged in and out of clouds to avoid the attention of defending fighters, and a second plane was sent to join her as a backup, the remaining scout planes were recalled. They would hopefully be recovered after the second British strike, already visible on the radar screens, had been fought off.

All the available fighters had been launched, seventeen Me109's. Facing them were the 18 dive bombers and their escort of six Goshawks. While the Goshawks did their best to keep the fighters off the dive bombers, it was almost impossible, and as a result the attack was severely disrupted, five of the Cormorants and four of the Goshawks being shot down for the loss of two Me109's. Only eight planes managed to attack the carrier, and the need to keep dodging the fighters and the AA fire from all four of the German heavy ships meant that only one hit was achieved on the Graf Zeppelin. The 1,000lb bomb penetrated her flight deck well forward, wrecking her forward elevator and causing serious damage to the forward part of the hanger. Luckily for the ship, all her planes were in the air, and as a result there were no large amounts of inflammable material or fuel to spread the blaze. However the thick plume of smoke towering in the sky over the ship did little to reassure the worried pilots, who were wondering if they would have anywhere to land shortly. Even as the last of the British aircraft headed back to their carrier, the damage-control parties were racing to bring the fire under control.

It seemed that the Graf Zeppelin was a lucky ship. While it took some time to get the (thankfully minor) fire under control, the position of the hole in the deck was far enough forward that planes could still land, although moving them around to allow more to land on was a complex undertaking, especially as it was necessary to strike the dive bombers below to rearm them - a strike on the now-located British carrier was urgently needed, and being pushed by the Admiral.

While this was happening, Lutjens was deciding on the course of action for his force. He obviously needed to sink, or at least incapacitate, whatever carrier was out there, or his heavy ships would be attacked before they could break clear into the Atlantic. The question was, should he scatter the ships now, and leave the carrier on her own, or should they remain together until the carrier was dispatched. In the end he decided to remain together for the time being. As it turned out, a mistake. His decision was, however, fortunate for the Suffolk. Taking advantage of the delay and confusion in the German force, she had cross-connected her remaining boiler and engine rooms and was limping Northwest at her best speed, hoping to close the icepack where she was likely to find fog to hide in. If the German ships had split up at that point, it is likely one of them would have been close enough to finish her off, however as a result of the flying operations the force was in fact heading south.

On Glorious, there was consternation as to the problems with the torpedoes, and the resulting survival of the German carrier. While a bomb hit had been reported, it was not clear if this would be enough to cripple her or even stop her making an attack on them. So while she recovered her planes, the carrier and her escorts turned south to close on the approaching fleet carriers and battleships, hoping to draw the German fleet after them.

It was still only 0900, and even though the British force was indeed drawing the Germans towards the heavy Home Fleet units, it would be a few hours before the fleet carriers could launch. The information as to the torpedo problems had already been passed on, and preparations were underway on Glorious for a second strike, using the contact fuse on the torpedoes. The Germans were still being tailed by a radar-equipped Stirling out of Iceland, and the carrier air commander was sure he could get off a strike before the German carrier, even if the damage done wasn't enough to stop her flying off aircraft.

This estimate was in fact quite accurate; it had taken the Graf Zeppelin well over an hour to get the fire under control and land her planes, and by the time the fire was out two hours had passed. Under normal circumstances this would have given the Glorious ample time to rearm, refuel, and get a second strike on the way before the German carrier could respond. However something was to happen which made this impossible.

At 0955, a lookout on the Glorious yelled a warning as he saw three torpedo tracks heading for the port side of the carrier.

Almost immediately the carrier swung hard to port to try and comb the tracks, an emergency action which was hardly appreciated by the crews trying to attach torpedoes onto planes. The carrier nearly managed to evade; two of the torpedoes missed by a matter of feet, watched by the men on the AA guns with a sort of horrified fascination as the white wake passed close down the port side, but the third hit the old carrier about 1/3 of the way down her hull. The shock caused chaos in the hangar, a number of crewmen being injured as they and the equipment were thrown around - the attack had been so unexpected there hadn't been time for any of them to prepare for the impact. The carrier slowed drastically to prevent more damage due to the flow of water into the gaping hole, rapidly taking on a list which increased to 15 degrees.

Meanwhile the carrier's two escort destroyers were attacking the underwater contact which they hoped was the submarine, who had given herself away by the torpedo attack. No-one was sure how a U-boat had slipped in so close with the carrier moving at speed, but it was later assumed this was some expert German planning to aid the breakout (in fact, as came out after the war, it was pure chance - the U-boat was on anti-convoy work, and had stumbled upon the carrier and found itself in a position to attack - just good luck, at least from the German point of view). While the

119

damage control parties on the carrier worked to shore up bulkheads and bring the flooding under control, the ocean heaved in white columns as the two destroyers enthusiastically depth-charged their contact. Some 30 minutes later, they were rewarded by a thick film of oil on the water, and debris floating on the surface

After an hour, the Glorious was able to resume her now-limping course south at some twelve knots. Despite the best efforts of her engineers, the carrier still had a list of some six degrees, which was going to make flying off of aircraft 'rather tricky' (in the words of her deck officer). The carriers air staff were hopeful that the damage to the Graf Zeppelin had been enough to put her out of action (although the thick cloud cover had allowed the shadowing planes to stay safe, the carriers radar made it clear that they were under observation). As soon as the submarine attack on the Glorious had been reported, and it was realised she might be unable to send up aircraft, the British force altered course slightly to intercept her and allow the carrier to be brought under the fleet carriers CAP.

The fleet carriers were making their own preparations for a strike. Unless there was a drastic change in course by the enemy, they expected to launch around 1200 and hit the Germans about an hour later. Indeed, such a change, and a dispersal of the German fleet into individual raiding units was being suggested and discussed on the Bismark at that very moment. However Lutjens had decided he wanted the British carrier sunk or put out of action before he did so. At 1130 the Glorious spotted a large radar return closing from the North. It looked like whatever damage had been done to the Graf Zeppelin, it had not been enough to prevent her launching an air strike. It had made taking off difficult; the shortening of the take-off area meant that the Ju87's were only carrying 250kg bombs, but this was considered adequate to sink or cripple a carrier. The take off had been difficult - two Ju87's and an Me109 had floundered on takeoff, but the rest of the carrier planes were heading for the Glorious, the Graf Zeppelin's captain having decided to use all his available planes on the strike. Twenty Ju87's and fourteen Me109's were closing the British force.

The Glorious currently had twelve Goshawks available (three planes had been damaged by the shock of the torpedo hit), and no-one had ever taken off from a carrier with a six degree list. Nevertheless, the pilots were prepared to take the chance. In what was to become one of the legendary feats of launching, the deck officer timed the movement of the carrier perfectly. All twelve of the fighters got off into the air (although with more than one takeoff that came close to disaster). While this was happening, a flight of eight more Goshawks was on its way from the fleet carriers, who had vectored in their CAP. However they wouldn't arrive until the strike had reached the Glorious.

Her fighters in the air, the carrier and her escorts prepared for the attack; the two escort destroyers to either side of her, and the cruiser Norfolk (who had closed the carrier during the morning once the torpedo attack had been reported) astern of her. With the torpedo damage having opened her hull the carrier could do little to evade the dive bombers once they were into their attack runs.

First contact was made between the two groups of fighters. The British had split into two groups, one of eight which went for the escorting Me109's, the other four heading for the dive bombers. The German pilots were expert, but as often happened the lure of a dogfight meant that all fourteen attacked the Goshawks. The resulting fight lasted until the divebombers had closed and attacked the carrier, six of the Goshawks being shot down for the loss of two Me109's. However this had allowed four fighters to intercept the dive bombers, and five of the Ju87's were despatched before they could fall into their dive.

The fifteen Ju87's left had been somewhat disrupted by the fighter attacks, but nevertheless turned and fell into the attack in groups of three, into a ferocious AA barrage from the British ships. A barrage heavy enough to shoot down two of them, and damage another so badly it had no hope of attacking. The dive bombers were following their orders, which were to sink the carrier and ignore any other ships until this was done. This they did with commendable dedication and accuracy.

Four of the twelve bombs hit the old carrier. One of them did not explode due to a faulty fuse, but the other three did her serious damage. Two exploded in her hangar, destroying many of the aircraft there and starting a number of fires (although the RN doctrine of not having fuel or explosives in the hangar limited the intensity). The third went through the flight and hangar decks, exploding in her machinery spaces, and causing damage to the temporary work holding back the water from the torpedo damage. As a result, water started to flood into the carrier, causing her list to increase again. Despite all this, the ship was still under control; her aft machinery was still in operation, but the necessity of reducing the pressure of the water into the torpedo hole meant she had to slow to five knots, barely under way. It was fortunate that the damage to the German carrier had forced the Ju87's to reduce their bomb load to 250kg, as if they had been using heavier bombs it was likely the damage would have sunk the old carrier. As it was, she was almost stationary and on fire, but not yet in any danger of sinking.

Meanwhile, and sadly just too late to stop the attack, the CAP from the fleet carrier had arrived. This was obviously completely unexpected by the Germans, and as a result they shot down four Me109's and three Ju87's before the German planes could disengage to the north. They stayed circling the burning carrier in case another attack emerged; the British overestimate of the planes on the Graf Zeppelin made them think she would have enough planes available for a second strike.

The manoeuvres of the two forces during the morning - the German fleet heading south, the British force heading north - had now brought them only 120 miles apart, and while the dive bombers had been closing on the Glorious, the Illustrious and Formidable had been launching their first strike and spotting the second ready to launch. Even before the last of the Ju87's was retiring from the attack, 21 TBR, 18DB and 12 fighters were getting into formation and heading north, a second equally powerful strike warming up on the carrier decks.

To the north, Lutjens was happy about the results of the strike. With the British carrier out of action and almost certainly sinking, his ships could break out into the convoy lanes. It was a shame that the Graf Zeppelins airgroup had been ruined by the effort, but that was why she was there, and now his powerful battleships could do what they had been designed for. Once the carrier had recovered her planes, he would split his force, leaving the Prinz Eugen to protect the carrier while the Bismark and Scharnhorst went on to sink record numbers of British merchantmen.

Unfortunately this plan came apart even as the Graf Zeppelin was landing on her planes. A large echo was picked up from the south - obviously another British strike. The damage to her flight deck made the landing-on a slow process, and the fighters were ordered to intercept the inbound strike rather than try to land. This was a tactic of desperation; many of the planes were low on ammunition after their previous combat and intercepting and engaging the new attackers would likely mean they had to ditch due to lack of fuel. Nevertheless, all eight fighters turned south as ordered.

The inbound attack was intercepted some 10 miles from the German ships (while the Graf Zeppelin had radar, the Germans had not developed anything like the FAA's techniques of combat management, and the fighters were simply sent in the direction of the strike). The SeaLance were already losing altitude for their torpedo attacks. However the fighters sent with them outnumbered the defenders, and as the Me109's started an attack on the torpedo planes they were intercepted and kept away from the attack planes by a dozen Goshawks.

The first planes to attack the carrier were the Cormorants. The Graf Zeppelin was in the middle of the heavy ships, who were adding their firepower to hers, but the AA, while heavy, was not of the intensity that an RN force was used to putting up. All eighteen of the planes were tasked to attack the carrier, to put her out of commission and ideally sunk before the second strike arrived, and only one of the planes was shot down by the defences. As the planes levelled off into their escape, the carrier was reeling from four 1,000lb bomb hits.

Unlike the RN and the USN, the German navy had not really appreciated what a fire hazard a carrier was. The precautions and protection against avgas fires was thus less. In addition, she had managed to strike all nine of her returning dive bombers below. As the attack had been at a fairly short range, this meant she had nine partly-fuelled potential bombs in her hangar. All four of the bombs had penetrated her flight deck easily. Two had exploded in the hangar itself, causing major fires; the other two had sliced through the hangar floor and exploded lower in the ship. Shock damage cut power in the vessel, that and serious machinery damage due to the bomb hits caused the ship to slew to a halt.

Smoke was already billowing from the ship as the divebombers made their escape, and it was only minutes after before a number of secondary explosions shook her as partly-fuelled planes in her hangar exploded like small bombs, causing additional fires and decimating the damage control parties trying to bring the original ones under control. As they watched pieces of the flight deck hurled into the air, the torpedo planes were certain that this carrier at least wouldn't be launching any more strikes today.

While the orders to the first strike were to make certain of the carrier, they did have a problem, in that the carrier was surrounded by three rather large pieces of moving steel, making her quite a difficult target for a torpedo run. In view of the damage already done, the raid leader decided to expend some of his torpedoes on the Scharnhorst, in order to make a clear path to the carrier. Twelve of the SeaLance curved into an attack run on the battlecruiser, while the remaining nine started an attack run behind them aimed at the carrier itself.

As expected, the captain of the battlecruiser really had no choice but to take violent evasive action against the torpedo tracks heading for his ship. Indeed, the Scharnhorst managed to evade ten of the twelve torpedoes, but in doing so the carrier was left completely uncovered against the remaining torpedo planes. The two torpedoes that hit the battlecruiser caused only moderate damage against her heavy Torpedo Defence System, but even so a considerable amount of water entered the ship through the damaged parts of her hull, and her speed was reduced to 24 knots.

The Graf Zeppelin, almost stopped now, could do little to evade the attack. It was a textbook example of how to torpedo a ship - four of the nine torpedoes hit the helpless carrier on the same side. While the attack was somewhat mitigated by her TDS, the damage caused let so much water in that in minutes the ship had developed a list of over 15 degrees, and made it impossible to restore power. As a result, the fires and petrol burning in the hangar (and already starting to leak down deeper into the ship) were obviously uncontrollable, and as yet more explosions rocked the ship the captain had no choice but to give the order to abandon.

The whole attack had barely taken 15 minutes, and as the aircraft headed south, the German force was left trying to recover from the loss of its carrier and the damage to the battlecruiser. Without any destroyers present, the Prinz Eugen came close enough to launch her boats to try and pick up survivors, but the heat from the burning carrier made it difficult to get close enough for effective rescue work. Meanwhile the Scharnhorst was starting to make temporary repairs to the torpedo damage.

Less than half an hour after the attack, with the Graf Zeppelin capsizing into the North Atlantic amid clouds of black smoke and steam, the Bismarck's radar picked up another large echo of aircraft heading towards them from the south.

The second wave of aircraft had no difficulty in finding the German force - the pillar of smoke sent up by the Graf Zeppelin could be seen 50 miles away. It was just as well they had the help, the weather was steadily worsening, the tops of the waves beneath being blown into spray. With no enemy fighters to worry about (the three Me109's who had survived combat with the Goshawks had been forced to ditch as they ran out of fuel), they could take their time to make a deliberate attack. With the carrier gone, their orders were to damage and slow the two capital ships so they would not to be able to evade the British force. The first strike was a combined one on the Scharnhorst; a hammer and anvil attack by twelve torpedo planes while ten Cormorants dive bombed her. While the battlecruiser was slowed by the earlier torpedo hits, she was still fully under control and attempted to avoid the torpedoes. However with a dozen torpedoes cutting in from two directions, it was simply impossible to comb all the tracks. Two more of the aerial missiles struck her on the port side, and she was forced to slow to reduce the new inflow of water.

While she was manoeuvring to try and evade the torpedoes, the dive bombers were making their near-vertical attacks. Armed with 1,600lb AP bombs, they were quite confident of penetrating the ships armoured deck. Faced with the almost impossible task of combing two groups of torpedoes and a simultaneous dive bombing, the battlecruiser was hit three times. One of the bombs failed to explode (although even so nearly a ton of armour-piercing steel did considerable damage to one of the ships engine rooms). Of the two that exploded, one hit her amidships close to the port side, slicing through the deck and exploding in one of the secondary magazines. Not designed to withstand a direct hit of that size, the magazine itself detonated, blowing a large hole in the side and deck of the ship. The final bomb did by far the most serious damage, even though it almost missed. The armour piercing missile cut through the stern of the ship, its fuse detonating it just after it hit the water close to the ships propellers

The Scharnhorst was unusual among capital ships as having three propeller shafts. While a ship with four shafts might have survived being incapacitated by the bomb, the explosion wrecked the starboard and centre shafts. It also severely damaged and jammed the rudder, leaving the huge ship unable to steer, and in fact do anything than curve around in a huge circle.

The other eight dive bombers made for the Bismark. Her AA defence was heavier than that of the Scharnhorst, and this time the dive bombing was not well coordinated with the attack by the torpedo planes. Despite this, they managed one hit and one near miss. The miss did some damage to the ship's hull, but nothing serious. The other bomb was more successful, hitting directly on top of B turret. The bomb didn't penetrate - Bismarck's main turrets had almost 8" of armour protection - but it did disable the turret. The explosion also sent heavy splinters from the bomb across the upper deck, causing the bridge crew to duck reflexively, but more importantly sending a jagged shard of steel straight through the battleships main fire control radar.

The men on the bridge were getting back to their feet when a lookout saw the torpedo planes approaching. Nine planes were left, and they were attacking in two groups to make Bismark spread her defensive fire and to make it hard for her to evade both launches. The rough sea was already causing a problem as the torpedoes dropped. Two of them broached and failed in the rough water and of the remaining seven only one hit the huge battleship. Bismark had a very deep TDS, and while she was slowed slightly by the underwater damage, and started to lose fuel oil from a ruptured tank, no major damage was done.

The planes turned to fly back to the carriers, now some 90 miles to the south, disappointed that they hadn't done more damage to the Bismark. At least the Scharnhorst had been rendered incapable of action, and they looked forward to coming back and doing the same to the Bismark.

On the Bismark, Lutjens was reviewing his options. Scharnhorst was not going to be under control any time soon; either a propeller shaft had to be got back into action so she could steer on engines, or her rudder had to be repaired enough to be useful. Doing either in the worsening seas seemed unlikely. That left him with two heavy ships, the Bismark and the Prinz Eugen. While the battleships radar was, temporarily at least, out of action, the heavy cruiser reported that the raid had also left a couple of watchers. So even if he abandoned the Scharnhorst, it was unlikely he would get away, though there was always the possibility that the cruiser might break free into the convoy lanes. However a cruiser alone was not enough to seriously inconvenience the Royal Navy; most of the important convoys were now escorted by a light carrier or a heavy cruiser or battleship. While the Bismark could handle these, the cruiser could not. He needed some way of dealing with what was obviously a second carrier to his south. His own planes had already sunk one (judging from their reports). If he could sink the second, he had a chance. Especially if the weather kept on worsening, it was possible he could catch her with her planes on board. The weather had deteriorated since the captain of the Graf Zeppelin had been worried about getting his planes off and back again in, and the same would surely apply to the British carrier.

In the end, it was perhaps the thought of at least getting revenge on the British carriers which had done so much damage to the Kriegsmarine over the past year that made him take the decision he did. Leaving Scharnhorst to her best efforts at damage control, the remaining two ships turned south and brought their speed up to 27 knots. It was 1445 on the 28th March, a day that would be remembered in the German Navy.

Back at the British force, the two carriers were still landing their planes (a process slowed by the now quite rough seas) when the aircraft shadowing the Bismark reported two heavy ships heading south in the direction of the carrier force. This posed Admiral Holland a problem. He would have all the planes down in another half hour, in plenty of time to manoeuvre his force to stay away from the German ships and arrange another strike that day. However Glorious was still in poor shape. While all her fires had now been put out, the old ship still had serious damage from the torpedo hit, and in the current weather conditions couldn't do much more than 6-7 knots - preferably in an easterly direction in order to reduce the pressure on the damaged area.

He therefore decided to split his force into three parts. The Glorious, escorted by the cruiser Edinburgh and three destroyers, would make for Iceland in a course intended to keep her clear of the German ships. The Illustrious and Formidable, with their escorting destroyers, would drop back to keep about 80 miles from the Bismark, while readying a full strike. The third part of his force, the KGV, Prince of Wales, Hood and the heavy cruiser Norfolk would intercept the Germans. The carrier's would intervene when they were ready, although in view of his superiority he felt that unless the Germans changed course again his capital ships could finish the job by themselves. He wasn't too concerned about the weather unless it worsened into a full storm; while the carrier evolutions were slowed, they signalled that they saw no problem in getting another strike off in daylight.

The three capital ships and the cruiser turned north, battle ensigns snapping in the growing westerly wind. They were guided by the plane still shadowing the Bismark, the closing speed of the two forces some 50 knots. At just before 1600 a lookout in the crows nest of the Hood confirmed the sighting. Smoke on the horizon to the north. All the ships involved were already prepared and at action stations, the only thing remaining was to see what the surface action would bring. Holland had been informed that the Formidable would be ready to launch in about half an hour; the two carriers were ordered to launch their first strike, but to wait for the target. Depending on how the surface action worked out, he was considering using the strike to finish off the Scharnhorst.

The German ships were in line ahead, the Prinz Eugen leading the Bismark. The British ships had broken into two groups; the KGV and Prince of Wales in one, the Hood and the Norfolk in the second. Holland's tactics were for his two heavily armoured ships to attack the Bismark at odds, while the cruiser and Hood worked around, keeping the German cruiser occupied and allowing the Hood to close the range to avoid an engagement where her thin deck protection would make her vulnerable. Once all three heavy ships were in range, they would concentrate on the Bismark. The seas were coming in from the west, making things a little difficult for the men manning the optical rangefinders, but the radar sets on the two ships were giving him accurate ranges. His sighting report had already gone off, and with the enemy in sight there was no longer any need to not use his radar. The Hood, with her older systems, was having a bit more of a problem, but if things went according to plan his two newer ships would be keeping the Bismarck's attention.

The first shots were fired by the Bismark at a range of 22,000 yards. Unknown to Holland, her main fire control radar was still out of action, but in any case the British preference was to close to decisive range if the enemy allowed. The first shells from the Bismark were accurate for bearing, but with only optical rangefinding the range was not terribly accurate. Thirty seconds later, the six forward guns of the KGV replied, followed a few seconds later by those of the Prince of Wales. Meanwhile the Hood and Norfolk were curving around to take the German force from the side.

The first hit was obtained by the Bismark; despite her lack of radar, her gunnery department was still superb, and on her fifth salvo registered a hit on the KGV. The heavy armour of the battleship took the 15" shell without allowing serious damage; despite her size and reputation, the British battleships were more heavily and better protected than the Bismark. The Prinz Eugen was also firing by this point, but as yet hadn't hit either of the British battleships.

It only took one more ranging salvo before the British started scoring their own hits, three hits from the sixth salvoes of the two battleships hitting the Bismark hard. Meanwhile the Hood had finally closed to under 20,000 yards, and turned to expose her after arc, allowing her to fire all 8 of her guns at the Bismark. With three capital ships targeting the Bismark, the Norfolk started to aim her 8" shells at the Prinz Eugen.

As soon as they saw the hits, Holland ordered his ships to turn and expose their after turret as well; the range was now down to 18,000 yards, as Bismark also turned. The battle became a pounding match, one in which the British ships outgunned the

Bismark by 26 heavy guns to 8 and the result was never in doubt. While the Bismark showed the usual ability of a German heavy ship to absorb damage, the heavy 15" shells did her terrible damage, soon leaving her superstructure riddled and all but her Y turret out of action. Indeed, by this time Lutjens was already dead, the bridge having taken a direct hit from one of the Hoods main guns.

Despite her damage, the Bismark continued to fight, and Holland's force continued to pound her until all her main guns were silenced. The ship was now a blazing wreck, the heavy smoke now being the biggest deterrent to accurate British gunfire. The Prinz Eugen had not escaped either; hit by a number of 8" shells herself, as soon as the battleships realised the Bismark was finished, she had been the recipient of a number of 15" salvoes which had left her blazing and sinking.

The British ships had not escaped unharmed. The KGV had taken seven hits from the Bismarck's main guns, and her A turret was out of action as well as having serious, but not fortunately crippling, damage to her superstructure, especially as three of the shells had not exploded. The PoW had been hit four times, and twice by 8" shells from the cruiser; her most serious damage had been a hit close to the bridge which had killed most of the people on the bridge, but despite this her fire had never slackened. The Hood had closed to 17,000 yards to fight, and while having been hit a number of times, had taken the hits on her heavy main belt. She had a number of fires, and the belt had been penetrated twice, causing damage to her machinery spaces, but by that time the German ships were already clearly finished.

Despite all the damage she had suffered, the Bismark had still not struck, and so Holland ordered Norfolk, who had managed to avoid being hit by more than a couple of 6" shells from the Bismarck's secondary armament, to close and sink her with torpedoes. The cruiser made two runs, each time firing four 21" torpedoes, three of which hit. A short while later, the Bismark was seen to be listing and settling, men jumping over the side as they abandoned ship.

While the battleships had been completing the destruction of the Bismark and Prinz Eugen, the carriers had got their first strike spotted and flown off, a rather tricky operation in the current weather, but one they were used to. 28 torpedo planes and 26 dive bombers were heading north (with no enemy aircraft carrier above water, the strike was unescorted). Since Holland's battleships had nearly finished the German fleet by now, he ordered them to head back to the Scharnhorst and finish her off. This time there was no problem in dealing with the damaged, and still circling, battlecruiser. The dive bombers were carrying 1,000lb bombs (more effective against the battlecruisers relatively thin deck armour), and seven hits left her ablaze and helpless. It hardly needed the following five torpedo hits on the helpless vessel to send her sinking beneath the icy waters of the North Atlantic. As the last of the planes turned for home, they could already see her capsizing behind them, ensign still flying, the first battleship to be sunk at sea by enemy aircraft alone.

Sadly, although Holland did order a destroyer to close the Scharnhorst and pick up survivors, only 90 men had survived the sinking and the icy waters. Over 300 were picked up from the Bismark and Prinz Eugen before the British ships turned to rejoin the carriers and head for home. The last heavy ships of the German Navy were no longer a threat to the convoys keeping Britain alive.

Chapter 12 - Retreat from Greece

26th April

Imperial and Greek troops retire over the Corinth canal. A German airborne force attempted to capture the bridge to prevent this, but the bridge was already rigged for demolition and is brought down before they can capture it. British troops from the armoured brigade (and some of their tanks) are evacuated from the beaches around Athens, and Australian troops are already being evacuated.

27th April

The part of Force H not returning from its abortive run into the Atlantic makes a sweep in the western Mediterranean in the hope of finding Italian merchant ships, but these are at the moment prudently in port. Somerville has suggested shelling and bombing Algiers to make it unusable as a port, but this is currently not permitted for political reasons. Perhaps ironically it is the British Foreign Office who is most concerned; the Free French show a somewhat more bloodthirsty attitude towards Vichy-owned territory.

Off Greece, German air power is attacking the evacuation force and the RN ships covering it. They are only moderately successful as some cover is being provided by Goshawks flying from the airfields in Crete. However a number of ships have been attacked by Stukas, who succeed in sinking the destroyer HMS Wryneck off Cape Malea

28th April

Reinforcements of Malaya and Singapore are temporarily suspended due to the situation in the Middle East. This is not popular with the Australians, who point out that they are providing most of the manpower in the Middle East. It is agreed that the situation will be reviewed in a month, once the situation in and around Greece has stabilised.

A troop convoy arrives at Alexandria with 50th British Division. This will allow the establishment of the new XXX Corps to allow the British to take the offensive in North Africa once the men are acclimatised. The situation in Greece means that using the division will have to wait until the Greek situation is resolved. There has been some concern in Britain about sending out more troops in view of the fact that the weather in the Channel would allow the Germans to invade if they wished, but the Navy and RAF have pointed out that there are no signs of this, and in any case the German situation is far worse than the previous year - they are still limited by sealift capability, while the Army is hugely stronger than a year ago. The German Navy in particular is extremely weak, having nothing larger than a destroyer to support any invasion attempt.

Also arriving in Malta is Air Marshal Keith Park, who has been brought out to advise on how to improve the fighter control and radar setup on Malta. Once he has reported on the situation on Malta, he will review the situation in Egypt as well. While the defences have taken a toll on the Italian and German planes, it has been noted that everything is rather improvised rather than planned, and as air activity increases it is causing problems.

29th April

Hitler is told of the result of Operation Rheinübung, and flies into one of his increasingly common rages. As a result, Raeder hands in his resignation and goes off to tend his garden - the naval war from now on will be conducted by the U-boats. Hitler orders them to be given priority in construction (a rather redundant command, as this is already happening in the shipyards); the light destroyers and escorts will stay operational to protect the coastal convoys. Goering manages to gloss over the poor performance of the German aircraft by pointing out that it's now obvious planes are far superior to ships, and if the Kriegsmarine had only built up a proper naval air arm before the war....

Hitler does get some better news later that day. Greece falls, with the loss of most of the Greek army. The Imperial forces have lost some 5,000 men and considerable equipment. However the rest of the force has been evacuated safely, and considerable number of Greek troops have made it to Crete, some on British shipping but many on Greek small ships and craft, although with no equipment. A number of ships have been sunk, including one of the destroyers taking men off, and a number damaged - the RN has two cruisers out of action until they can be repaired, and HMS Malaya's X turret is non-operational after a bomb hit. The carrier fighter squadrons have been providing cover where possible, but losses and the heavy pace of the action are exhausting them.

The Luftwaffe continues its heavy bombing raids on Valetta harbour in Malta, hitting a light cruiser and a destroyer. However the steady stream of reinforcements is allowing the RAF to take a steady toll of the bombers. It is decided to bring the cruisers back to North Africa, leaving only the less-vulnerable destroyers at Valetta.

General Paulus arrives in Algiers to check on the situation himself. He is unhappy about the supply situation, although Rommel assures him it is adequate and expects to be able to attack very soon with two divisions. He explains that once Tunis and Tripoli have been recaptured the supply situation will ease, as the RAF will be forced much further back. Paulus remains unconvinced.

30th April

The new pro-German Iraqi government orders approximately 9,000 troops to march on the RAF station at Habbaniya, a few miles northwest of Baghdad, and to set up their artillery on the surrounding plateau. There are 2,000 British troops and 9,000 civilians sheltering at the airbase. The Iraqi's have been heartened by the fall of Greece, although the takeover of Syria by Allied forces is worrying to them.

2nd May

In the USA, a joint Army-Navy Board completes the Rainbow-5 War Plan calling for abandonment of the Philippines upon the outbreak of war and the sacrifice of the garrison. Admiral Hart is advised by Navy Department that he would be given at least four days' notice prior to the start of hostilities. Hart instructs his staff to base all plans on a two days' warning. In view of the plan effectively abandoning the Philippines, it is kept a close secret.

The Iraqi Army has concentrated a force of more than a division overlooking Habbaniya. The British Flying School Squadron in Habbaniya armed with Gladiator fighters and supported by Wellingtons from the RAF base at Shuaiba bombs the Iraqi troops in their positions only a mile away from the airbase. The Iraqis responded to the raid with an artillery barrage, supported by bombs and machine gun fire from their own aircraft. The British are aided by five companies of Kurds. Rashid el Gailani asks Hitler for military assistance, and is assured that his request will be given 'immediate attention'. However with the nearest German forces in Greece, and the former Vichy colonies of Lebanon and Syria now under Allied control, there is little Germany can do except conduct long-range bombing raids.

Allied troops occupy Basra and the oil installations, and start to evacuate women and children from the Habbaniya air base. There is local unrest and opposition to the landings.

The first complete RAAF squadron arrives in Egypt, flying Sparrowhawks. This is to give them operational experience to take back to Malaya, where they have been for the last few months.

In Algeria, the Africa Korps is being assembled ready for their first operation. Thanks to the poor security at the American Embassy in Cairo, Rommel has a good idea as to the disposition of the Imperial forces. Unfortunately he has far less detail on his immediate opposition, the Free French, as their relations with the Americans are rather less cordial. He feels that they are the weakest of his opposition, and plans to drive through them to attack Tripoli before having to consolidate.

3rd May

British troops attack on Iraqi positions around the Habbaniyah Airfield, and air attacks are mounted against the Rashid airfield.

The American United Press News Agency reported:

"A reliable source confirmed tonight in London that Rashid Ali al Gailani has asked Hitler for help against the British troops in Iraq, but he is believed to have initiated hostilities prematurely so that he is unlikely to play a role in future German war plans. The special military significance of Iraq lies in its oil, which supplies the British Mediterranean fleet and the Mediterranean based units of the Royal Air Force with a large part of their fuel."

In Britain, the Westland jet development aircraft makes its first flight, powered by two 860-lb thrust Whittle jet engines. The initial 17-minute flight is said to be 'most promising'

The 5th Indian Division is established in Egypt, and starts training with units of 7th Armoured. The Division is experienced, having finished campaigning in Ethiopia, but has limited experience with coordinating with tanks. They will be joined by 50th British Division once the men are acclimatised, and will form the new XXX Corps. Once this is operational, it is intended to combine it with XIII Corps to form the new 8th Army under General O'Connor.

Meanwhile the Australian 7th and 9th Divisions are put into reserve while the equipment losses in Greece are made good. 1st Armoured Brigade has lost most of its tanks, but it is considered necessary to deploy some tanks at least to Crete to support the New Zealand division, despite the attack on Tunisia. After necessary repairs are done, the Brigade will deploy to Crete with about 60 tanks. Once tank supplies allow a second armoured brigade will be added to I Australian Corps. The Corps commander, General Blamey, is made 2nd IC in the Middle East. While there has been some criticism of the Greece action, it is generally felt (and also by Wavell) that he did as good a job as possible in what was always a situation that would end in failure once Germany invaded. While it would be preferred to keep 1st Armoured as a reserve in Egypt, intelligence reports are indicating that at attack on Crete will be made soon.

Chapter 13 - Rommel Advances

"I never realised the Pyramids were so large" - comment by General Erwin Rommel, 1941.

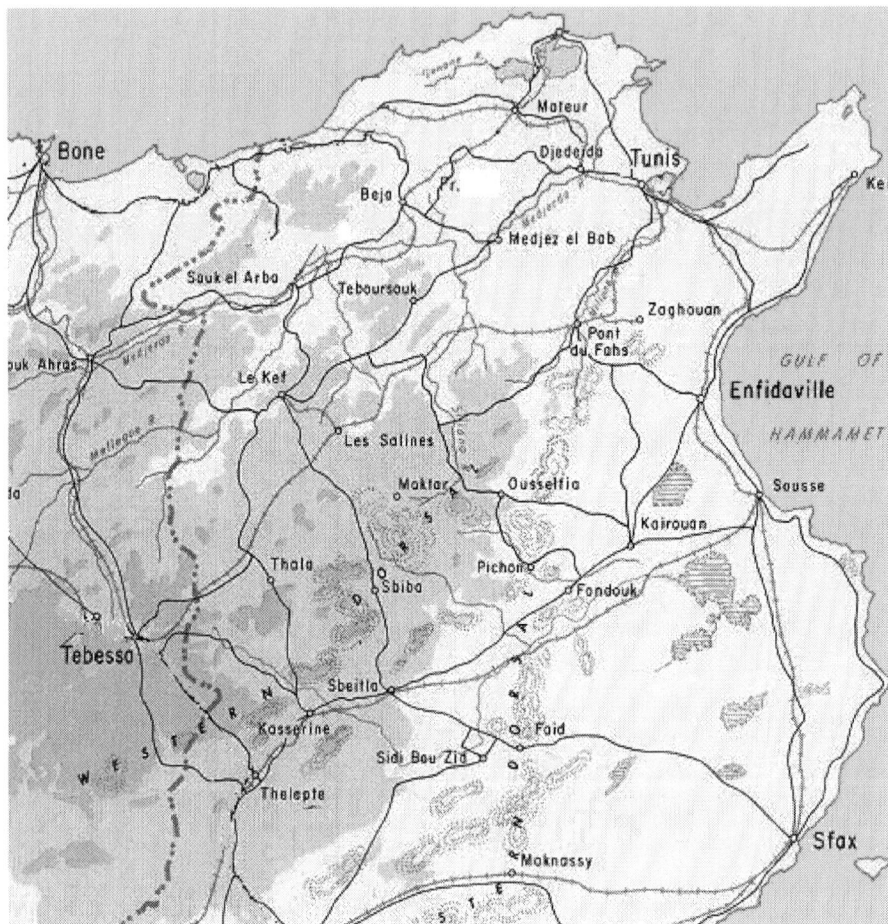

On the night of the 4th May, the rumbling of tanks on the move heralded the first elements of the Africa Korps moving out from their forward positions near Bone. Although under strength thanks to the depredations of the Royal Navy and RAF, Rommel considered it to his advantage to use the confusion in the British command caused by the recent Greek debacle. He hoped that this would have affected the troops morale and allow him to cut through the defenders to his main objective, Tripoli.

His main units were the German 21st Panzer Division and the Italian Ariete Armoured Division. Both were under strength in tanks and heavy equipment, although it had been possible to bring them up to full troop strength. Between them they had some 260 tanks, plus some light tanks really only useful for reconnaissance. He also had two infantry regiments of the German 90th light division. While his tank force was substantial by the standards of North Africa in 1941, he was short of infantry. However Rommel believed that O'Connor's earlier campaign had shown that it was mobile armoured formations that were important in the desert rather than sheer masses of infantry.

Up until now, the Algerian/Tunisian border had been fairly quiet. Both sides had been content to keep their activity down to observing, patrolling and occasional night raids to capture a patrol for questioning. This had suited the French, who were steadily training and increasing their forces. They also had a good idea of what forces Rommel had available, thanks to copious reports from sympathetic officers and officials in Algiers and Algeria - shortage of their own men had forced the Germans to use Algerians in the ports and railways, plus of course the normal problem of soldiers talking. Their basic plan was simple; fall back slowly while inflicting damage on Rommel, and identify his main axis of advance while waiting for XIII Corps to arrive. Rommel had managed to keep exactly how and where he was going to attack secret - indeed, he intended to reinforce whichever attacks was most successful, rather than keep to a predetermined line of attack.

Given the geography of Tunisia, the only good place to attack was in the north. The only good attack route into the south was protected by the Mareth line, a pre-war defensive line built by the French and now reoccupied. Between this and the north the only entry was a few easily-defended mountain passes. Rommel had considered a feint to Tunis, followed by an airborne drop to allow him to rush one of these passes and take the defenders by surprise, but he was informed that no airborne units or transports would be available for some time. He therefore intended to use his armour superiority to break through in the north, and then use the superior mobility of his armoured formations to roll up the French southwards down the coast. While he knew that the French had some ex-Italian armour, he dismissed this in view of the terrible performance of the Italian tanks in the Cyrenaica campaign. Apparently German intelligence did not realise that the tanks the French armoured brigade under LeClerc were using were the modified ex-Ariete tanks, considerably better than most of the early Italian armour.

While Rommel expected to be able to manoeuvre on a tactical level, the terrain meant that the initial assault would be quite straightforward. The German armour would push forward, and when the French responded they would either simply brush the ex-Italian tanks out of the way or, if resistance was stronger, draw them back onto his anti-tank guns. Once the French armour was out of the way, his armour would punch through the French lines and make for Tunis, leaving the motorised troops to mop up. He was sure that the French would collapse once they realised his armour was behind them and heading for Tunis.

5th May

Haile Selassie, the Emperor of Ethiopia, has returned to his capital of Addis Ababa in triumph. The streets of the city were lined with black and white African troops. After being welcomed with a 21-gun salute, he spoke of his gratitude "to Almighty God that I stand in my palace from which the Fascist forces have fled."

In Washington DC the White House announced: "We can offer no official confirmation that 26 American merchant ships loaded with tanks, anti-aircraft guns, and other war material arrived at the Suez Canal. We can only say that we do not rule out the possibility."

The carrier HMS Illustrious arrives at Gibraltar carrying an airgroup heavy in fighters (she has left her TBR strike squadron behind). She will join the Tiger convoy and carry on to Alexandria to provide some relief to the exhausted FAA fighter squadrons (the operational fighter strength of the two carriers in Cunningham's force is down to 16 planes, even after scouring Egypt for all available replacements)

The Afrika Korps attacks Tunisia at dawn, artillery laying down a barrage on the light forces observing the frontier. The tanks warm up, ready to head for Tabarka as soon as the divisional artillery has suppressed the defenders. The attack was led by the 21st Panzer Division, as Rommel thought the heavier and better-protected German tanks would have a better chance of overrunning the defenders and causing them to panic. While there was indeed a certain amount of this among the Tunisian units, the 1st Free French Brigade was an experienced formation, and was the main unit blocking the rote to Tunis (it had small units of the Tunisian army attached to exploit their local knowledge, but the bulk of the acquired Tunisian force was undergoing training). It slowly pulled back in front of the barrage, and when the first tanks appeared out of the dust they ran into the Brigades anti-tank guns. These were well-positioned and immediately took a toll of the advancing Germans, knocking out six Mk III Panzers before the Germans pulled back. However Rommel had assumed that, at the frontier at least, there would be anti-tank defences, and half an hour later the French were the recipient of an attack by twelve Stukas, which caused serious casualties and broke up the defence line.

The setback, while unwelcome, did not cause the experienced troops to panic. They knew that their mission was to delay rather than stop a heavy attacks, and slowly pulled back, hoping to lure the Germans onto their guns again. In the meantime, the commander of the 1st Free French Division, General de Bethouart had put the rest of his force on alert as well as informing the British that the expected invasion of Tunisia had started. The 4th Indian Division and a brigade of the 2nd armoured were ordered to proceed from Tripoli into Tunisia and aid the Free French (leaving one brigade behind to guard Tripoli). Further back towards Egypt, the 6th Australian Division was also put on alert. General O'Connor would go by air to Tripoli later that day, where he intended to set up his command post. His initial intention was to concentrate the bulk of his armour here ready to move on the Axis forces as soon as they had put themselves in a vulnerable position.

While the fighting in Greece had reduced the number of planes available to the RAF in the desert, they were still able to respond to the request for air support from the French. While no dive bombers were available, the tail of the German formation was a tempting target and a raid at noon from fourteen Wellingtons escorted by Hurricanes caused the loss of a number of the divisions support vehicles as well as causing considerable disruption.

Despite the defenders efforts, the panzers advanced steadily towards the first target, the town of Tabarka. Once the heavier German tanks had cleared the initial border defences, the Ariete division moved forward to widen the breach as they advanced in parallel to the south of 21st Panzer, heading for Djebel Ariod. He intended to be in control of and past Tabarka by sunset, and the slow but steady withdrawal of the French allowed him to do this, at the cost of a steady trickle of losses from his lead units. It was clear to Rommel that now the frontier had been breached the French had little immediately behind it.

The Italian advance to Djebel Ariod was not quite so easy. It seemed that the bulk of the French border force and its artillery had retreated in this direction, and as a result they had to stop and clear numerous small blocks to their advance. Nevertheless by nightfall they were well on the way to their target.

General de Bethouart was not displeased by how the battle had gone so far. The Germans had got further faster than he had anticipated, and the quality of their tanks was allowing them to smash through defences that would have held up an Italian formation, but his reserves were getting into position and 4th Indian and 2nd Armoured were motoring up the coast ready to support him. While the Luftwaffe was indeed a nuisance, the Allied air force was able to stop them dominating the skies, although overall the Luftwaffe held the balance of power. His control of the interior lines of communication in Tunisia was helping, the relatively good rail and road links allowing him to move his reserves ready to block the German advance. Although at the moment he was happy to allow the German tanks to keep moving deeper into Tunisia

The build-up of the French force was hardly unexpected to Rommel, indeed his plan required them to concentrate so he could flank and destroy them, leaving the way to Tunis open. The Luftwaffe and his radio interception service was giving him a reasonable idea of what was happening, and so far his only worry was that the French armour would not allow him to pocket and destroy it.

6th May

An urgent supply convoy sails from Gibraltar, escorted by Force H and also the carrier Illustrious, which will continue on with the merchant ships to Alexandria. This convoy will be run straight through the Mediterranean despite the misgivings of the Chiefs of Staffs. The situation has improved since the last time a fast convoy was run through, and the armaments and especially the tanks are needed urgently, even more so now Rommel's long-awaited offensive has started. With three fleet carriers and 80 fighters to protect the convoy, it is hoped that this will succeed. The major opposition is thought to be air and possibly E-boat attacks when they are close to Sicily. The dangerous Sicilian narrows are now easier to negotiate due to the Allies holding Tunisia; one of the main problems, the minefields which made negotiating the narrows so dangerous, are now cleared close to the Tunisian coast, and it is far more dangerous for the Italians to try and renew them. A section of minesweepers have been based in Tunis to keep the convoy route clear.

After four days of non-stop British air raids, the Iraqi troops are forced to leave the high ground around Habbaniya and retreat to Baghdad on the night of Tuesday 6 May. Meanwhile the British 21st Indian Brigade arrives at Basrah.

In Tunisia the Afrika Korps continues to advance towards Tunis. The French forces have been slowly falling back according to the pre-arranged delaying plan while XIII Corps moves in from Cyrenaica.

The 21st Panzer has taken Tabana, which was not heavily defended, and units of the 21st and the Ariete Division are close to Djebel Abiod. Rommel had hoped that the French might have been induced to stand closer to the border and allow him to destroy more of their force, but the French are using the limiting geography of the area to slowly fall back along the constricting road system. By the late afternoon his armoured formations are close to Djebel Aboud, and taking fire from French artillery and anti-tank elements around the town. So far Rommel's losses in armour have been light; some 15 medium tanks to anti-tank fire and irrecoverable breakdowns, while Ariete have lost about 20 - mainly to mechanical issues, as they do not have the frontline workshop support the Panzer division enjoys.

The French armoured brigade is concentrating West of Tunis; assuming he takes Djebel Aboud, there are a number of routes Rommel's armour could take to get to Tunis, and LeClerc wants more information before he commits his force. The first elements of the 4th Indian Division and the 2nd Armoured are expected to reach Tunis by nightfall. Meanwhile O'Connor has started the 7th Armoured Division moving forward to Tripoli before their forward move into Tunisia. A Brigade of the 6th Australian Division will move after them once they have cleared the roads.

In the sky above Tunisia the RAF and the Luftwaffe continue to contend for air superiority. The Luftwaffe has superior numbers (the RAF is still depleted after Greece), but is insufficient to stop the RAF mounting reconnaissance missions and intervening on the battlefield. While the air attacks are causing a problem for the French Tunisian forces, the veteran 1st Free French Division is treating them as an annoyance at the moment.

7th May

The town of Djebel Aboud falls to Rommel in the morning as the French defence crumbles under the assault of the tanks of 21st Panzer - the French have only small numbers of anti-tank guns capable of stopping the newer tanks at other than close range. Rommel then sends two forces forward. Units of 21st Panzer move east along the road to Djefna, while the Ariete follows the southerly route that eventually leads to Medjez el Bab and Tebourba. The 4th Indian is concentrating its first Brigade at Chouigur, just in front of Tebourba, and its second will follow the road down to Medjez el Bab, which they expect to reach before the Ariete division. A brigade of the 2nd Armoured is now at Djedeida. With the arrival of the British forces, the French Brigade has moved forward to Djefna where it is digging in. Their armoured brigade is now at Mateur, ready to move once the main axis of Rommel's advance has been identified. The French have been ordered to delay the advance for as long as possible to allow the new reinforcements to dig in and prepare defences.

8th May

Rommel is still pressing his forces forward as fast as possible. He wants to engage the French at odds before the British can arrive in serious numbers to help them. The British are doing exactly that, the premade plans and the good (by North African standards) road and rail net in Tunisia is allowing them to advance rapidly from their forward bases - O'Connor has already made it clear what will happen to any commander who is tardy about getting into position in Tunisia.

Rommel's advance force has run into the French Brigade now protecting Djefna, and after losing a number of tanks to the well dug in French, has halted until more armour and the supporting artillery can arrive. The French use the time to continue to dig in in front of the town. The Ariete are on their way to Medjez al Bab, which they hope to reach tomorrow. They have also put out a covering force along the Chouigui road. Rommel is not happy with their speed of advance, which he considers too cautious and may allow the British to reinforce; in fact the first units of 4th Indian are already at the town and busily imitating moles while awaiting the rest of the brigade. They also have 30 tanks of the 2nd Armoured to help them when the Italian armour arrives

9th May

The Polish Brigade sails on a coastal convoy for Tunis. The brigade had originally been reserved in case it was needed in Crete, but Wavell and O'Connor consider Rommel's attack the more urgent problem. In any case, the biggest problem facing Crete is supplies and some types of weapons rather than more men.

In Tunisia, Rommel's forces continue to advance, but more slowly. Having failed to panic the defenders in their initial assault, Rommel needs to bring up more of his force in order to make his first major attack. He expects this to be at Djefna; he wants 21st Panzer to push the French defenders back to at least the town of Mateur, which will give him the option of taking (or at least threatening to take) the port of Bizerte.

The lead elements of the Ariete division have still not reached Medez el Bab, suffering from frequent French ambushes - not terribly costly, but each one costs them time. The occasional interference from the RAF is also unwelcome.

By now, a brigade of the 4th Indian is in place in the town and busy on defensive works. While Luftwaffe reconnaissance has informed Rommel of this (it was, after all, hardly unexpected that the town would be defended), he is unaware that it is now held by experienced troops with a limited armoured capability.

General de Bethouart considers the force defending Djefna to be a delaying option, and expects to fight the main battle in front of Mateur, where the bulk of his forces are preparing, backed up by the French armoured brigade. The British 2nd Armoured is now at Tebourba in brigade strength, and a light force supported by infantry has been sent along the road past Chouigui to warn them if the Italians decide to push along this route.

Part of the 6th Australian Division has moved forward to Tripoli, but is being held there until O'Connor can see where best to use them. Elements of 7th Armoured are still moving into Tunisia, but slowly, moving mainly at night. They will start to concentrate on the eastern side of the Kasserine pass tonight, but he expects it to take a few more days for an adequate force to be assembled there.

South of Iceland U-110(Captained by Lt-Cdr Lemp of the 'Athenia' sinking) attacked Liverpool outbound convoy OB318 protected by ships of Capt A. J. Baker-Crewsswell's escort group. Blown to the surface by depth charges from corvette HMS Aubretia, the crew abandoned ship, but the submarine failed to sink. A boarding party from the destroyer HMS Bulldog manages to get aboard, and in a matter of hours they transfer to safety the submarine's entire Enigma package - coding machine, code books, rotor settings and charts. It will prove to be a major breakthrough in the breaking of the Naval Enigma. Although the U-boat is taken under tow, it will later sink on the way back to Iceland.

Admiral Cunningham is concerned about the losses his fighter pilots have taken recently in supporting the Army. The carrier air groups were never intended for this sort of heavy commitment, and replacements are urgently needed both to fill up his squadrons and if possible to allow the pilots a rest. This is looking increasingly difficult as it looks like yet another naval effort will have to be made very soon off Crete. He hopes to get some relief when HMS Illustrious arrives with the Tiger convoy; given the current operations in the Med, her air group currently consists of 12 TBR, 18DB and 40F (although some planes are having to be carried on deck). While the various options are being debated with his staff, an interesting suggestion is made by his Air advisor. He has been chatting with some of the recently arrived RAAF pilots and found out that, in order to help move aircraft around in the Far East, the Australian Sparrowhawks had retained their arrestor hooks, and the RAAF pilots given basic training in landing and flying off a carrier. He wonders if this squadron could be used to supplement the FAA pilots, and indeed if one of the RAF squadrons could do the same? As a de-navalised plane, the addition of a hook to RAF Sparrowhawks would be a straightforward job for the base workshops at Alexandria.

The Tiger convoy has passed the most dangerous part of its route, the Sicilian narrows. It has been helped by bad weather throughout its route - the heavy CAP's from the carriers have not been needed as the weather prevented the convoy being found by the Italian Air Force. The convoy is now in swept waters and heading for Alexandria, along with the Illustrious. Force H also bombards Bone before retiring to Gibraltar, which does nothing to help Rommel's logistics or advance into Tunisia.

10th May

21st Panzer assault the French defences in front of Djefna. While the French hold firm for some hours, the pressure of the German panzers forces them back into the town. That afternoon, a heavy air raid is made on the town, causing much civilian damage and lighter damage to the French force, which retires in some confusion down the road to Mateur. The 21st pushes on through the town but then pauses overnight to reorganise; they have lost eight tanks in taking the town, and Rommel is starting to become more confident as to the inability of the French to stop him before Tunis.

The Ariete division lead units finally arrive at road junction north of Medez el Beb - or they would have, except they discover that 4th Indian is dug in blocking the way. The British artillery and AT guns are an unwelcome surprise for the Italians, who lose six tanks and a number of vehicles in the initial ambush. The division is also the recipient of the first attacks by RAAF Beaufighters. Carrying 4x250lb bombs, as well as 4x20mm cannon and 4x0.5" guns, the heavy fighter causes chaos and considerable damage to the support elements on the road between Djebel Abiod and the front.

Stung by a heavy retaliatory raid by some hundreds of RAF bombers against Hamburg which has caused a considerable amount of damage to the city and the shipyards, the Luftwaffe makes a final large night raid against London using over 500 bombers. The raid causes huge damage, killing or injuring over 3,000 people, mainly due to the large number of incendiaries used. The defences and the night fighters shoot down over 40 aircraft, and with those lost and written off due to damage, the loss rate is some 15%, unsustainable by the Luftwaffe. From now on raids will be by small forces of bombers.

11th May

On the night of the 10th/11th May, a raiding force of light armoured cars and lorries led by a Captain Stirling moves through the desert from one of the small passes in the mountains in central Tunisia, heading for the Luftwaffe airfield south of Bone. The men cause considerable damage as the blow up everything they can lay their hands on and machine gun everything else with great enthusiasm. The Luftwaffe loses a total of 23 Me109's and Ju87's, which have been supporting Rommel.

The Polish Brigade disembarks at Tunis; their job will be to defend the city in case the Afrika Korps break through the French defensive line. Not all the convoy that left Alexandria has ended up at Tunis. Part of it was detached and entered Tripoli at night, where some of the craft it comprised were hidden and camouflaged.

The Ariete division tries a frontal assault on the defence works north of Medjez el Beb, hoping they are as fragile as they look hurriedly constructed. While they are indeed recent, the 4th Indian is a very experienced division, and the works are supported by anti-tank guns and the Brigade artillery. The Ariete's tanks are halted on the defence line, then the British counterattack led by a detachment of Matilda tanks. While the British are impressed with the bravery and resolve which with the Italians fight, they are driven back from the British defences with the loss of 17 tanks.

The 21st Panzer consolidates east of Djefna, building up for an assault on what they see as the main French defensive position in front of Mateur. Rommel's intent is to press the defences, then hook an armoured force around to take the defenders in the rear. The Luftwaffe has reported Italian tanks in the area, obviously ones now under French command, but Rommel is confident that if they venture forward they will simply allow him to destroy them as well.

12th May

The Ariete division make another attempt to penetrate the 4th Indians defences, this time with an infantry attack. Against the well-prepared Indians it makes a few small penetrations before being driven back. The 4th Indian has lost about 400 men to the attack, the Ariete considerably more, without gaining any useful ground. The British have lost six of their Matildas to breakdowns - the tank is not the most reliable in North Africa

The 21st Panzer starts its attack against the French defences. These go slowly (as the intent is not specifically to penetrate them unless an unexpected opportunity presents itself), but once the defenders are occupied a significant part of Rommel's armour sets out to the southeast to get behind the defensive works. This has been anticipated by LeClerc, and the French armoured brigade at Mateur moves out to force an engagement.

The ex-Italian tanks do better than anyone had anticipated, causing considerable losses to Rommel's mobile force, but while the tank-tank combat is somewhat in favour of the Germans, they manage to draw the advance elements of the Armoured Brigade onto their 88mm guns, destroying eleven tanks in 15 minutes. The French then pull back, and the German armour also stops and pulls back a little in order to consolidate and recover damaged tanks.

The French have lost more than the Germans; 50 of their 80 tanks have either been destroyed, damaged or have broken down and cannot be recovered. The Germans have lost only 25 (although some ten more will not be operational again for 1-2 days)

After the destruction caused by the British night raid on the airfield, the Luftwaffe commander in the area rounds up 200 locals (including French), and accuses them of spying and aiding the British. To show what will happen to any further treachery (as he puts it), all 200 hostages are shot. Once this becomes know, the political effects will be serious.

The much anticipated Tiger convoy arrives unscathed, bearing a considerable quantity of weapons - 295 tanks and 40 Sparrowhawks for the Allied desert army. The tanks include 135 Matildas, 139 of the new 2-pdr-gunned Valentine tanks and 21 light tanks, as well as the first 24 6-pdr AT tanks to reach the Middle East. It also brings badly needed drop tanks for the RAF fighters, which will allow them to cover Crete from North Africa if needed. This is more than enough to re-equip a complete armoured division.

As a sign of defiance against the latest Luftwaffe raid, a march past goes through central London of representatives of the crews of the ships engaged in the recent Atlantic operation which finally destroyed the German fleet.

That night, a force of tanks, armoured cars and support vehicles moves out through the Kasserine pass, first into Algeria at Tebessa, the heading north. A light force of Tunisian French had infiltrated and attacked the small force left to cover the pass into Tunisia, completely surprising them, and the armoured column met little resistance.

That afternoon a convoy, heavily escorted by the Royal Navy, left Tripoli headed north towards Tunis. Cunningham has two fleet carriers and two battleships in support, hoping that the carrier planes and the RAF will prevent observation of the transports and landing craft by the Luftwaffe

13th May

Both sides in Tunisia take the opportunity to reorganise. The big decision is whether to pull back from Djefna and pull Rommel even further forward. There are two arguments against this; first that 7th Armoured thrust north may not succeed, and second that a withdrawal under fire is going to cause the French losses, particularly in material. In the end it is decided that Rommel is far enough forward anyway, and that engaging him and occupying his attention at Djefna will do what is required. Since the Polish Brigade is now in Tunis, the French can reinforce at Djefna with the men they were holding back in front of Tunis. However they cannot replace the tanks they lost, so part of the 2nd Armoured force at Tebourba is brought north (some 60 tanks) to reinforce the French armour. Since Ariete don't look like breaking through at Medjez el Beb in the next day or so, it is considered a low-risk option.

With the departure of 7th Armoured, a brigade of the 6th Australian Division is moved further north into Tunisia close to the town of Sfax. This will allow it to be used either as a reserve in case anything goes wrong in the north, or to exploit the 7th Armoured advance.

The 21st Panzer continue to press their attack at dawn, and by now they have pushed the French back into Djefna itself. Losses are about even on both sides; the French don't have tanks, but they are well supported by artillery which is slowing the German infantry. Even so, there are some worrying moments when the German armour almost breaks the defensive line, and the brigade reports that unless the situation changes they will have to withdraw during the night.

As the situation at Djefna is looking good (from a German perspective), the 21st again sends its armour around to flank the defences - this time they are only using the Mk III Panzer as the 75mm-armed Mk IV's are needed to support the infantry attack. After what they see as the destruction of the French armour on the previous day, they anticipate an easier time of it. Unfortunately they run straight into the lead elements of 2nd Armoured, who were (perhaps optimistically) thinking along the same flanking lines as themselves. The result is a confused tank battle, with the British cruiser tanks showing they are not a match for the panzers. Although they had been warned about the German tactic of drawing the armour onto their AT guns, the 2nd still gets caught in a similar trap.

The net result is another stand-off as both sides withdraw to refuel and reorganise. The British have lost some 40 of their 60 tanks (mainly to the German 88mm and to breakdowns), while the 21st has only lost eighteen tanks (although another eight will need to be fixed, they have been successfully recovered by the German forward maintenance units)

Having not got very far with an attack into Medjez el Beb from the north, the Ariete has been probing further south, and today tries another attack, this time along the road leading in from the southwest. This is not as heavily defended, but even so the presence of the heavily-armoured Matildas stops them from getting to the town. The defenders lose another ten Matilda tanks while the Ariete lose eighteen of their M13/60 tanks. The British brigade is now having problems holding the advance, and asks that reinforcements from the brigade held in reserve be sent forward that night - they are worried about the southern road into the town as well, which again is only lightly held.

Later in the day, Rommel receives reports of some sort of force moving north along the Algerian border. At first he discounts this, assuming it is another of the light raiding forces like the one that hit Bone airfield recently, but a later Luftwaffe report indicates a large force which includes tanks. This, if true, is far more worrying. Rommel only has a very small reserve in Bone, and he begins to wonder if it can hold whatever this attack is. The Luftwaffe is ordered to attack it and slow it down, and to get more information as to the nature of the attack. Reluctant to consider a retreat at this point, he considers the option of a final strong attack to break through the French lines. If he can take Tunis, he can get his supply sent there rather that to Algeria. He also orders the Ariete to make a decisive attack tomorrow to break through onto the Tebourba road.

The 7th Armoured are happily motoring north during the day, led by some Tunisian French officers familiar with the territory, as well as a number of Algerian French who were 'captured' having 'accidentally' strayed into Tunisia. They expect to be in sight of Bone at nightfall. Meanwhile the convoy heading north along the Tunisian coast is closing on Tunis; heavily escorted, and with constant fighter cover, it has yet to be spotted by the Luftwaffe (who are currently occupied with trying to observe and attack the force in Algeria and in assisting Rommel). The RAF is successfully stopping them achieving air superiority in Tunisia itself.

The news of the massacre of hostages at the airfield near Bone reaches the French in Algeria. The reaction is, to put it mildly, angry. The Germans have insisted that the Algerian authorities supply troops to protect their bases against more 'terrorist attacks' as they put it. The Vichy governor finds that the first two units told to prepare to move to Bone and do so are in open mutiny and refusing to move. The feelings in much of the rest of the army in Algeria are similar, if perhaps not quite so militant as yet

Chapter 14 - Counterstrike

"Rommel has stuck his neck out, now's the time to wring it for him." Conversation between General O'Connor and General de Bethouart in Tunisia, 1941

14th May

On the previous evening Rommel had finally received a detailed report of what was happening south of Bone. This was obviously not a mere raid; it was far too strong, and already dangerously close to cutting him off from his supplies. After the battles of the previous day, it looked unlikely that the defences would collapse and let him into Tunis before he was attacked from the rear; the only option was to turn back and retreat to Bone, fighting his way in if necessary.

The 21st Panzer was very well trained, and despite the difficulty of reversing themselves while still maintaining contact with the enemy and stopping him from interfering, was on the march west by the afternoon. The Ariete division had also been informed of the situation and had already started retreating towards Djebel Aboud; their situation was easier as the defenders they faced had only a few tanks. They were however subject to RAF raids, which while causing little damage slowed them considerably. The destruction on the Bone airfield had noticeably reduced the Luftwaffe's strength, and as soon as it had been realised how strong the force heading up from the south was, the remaining planes had moved back to Algiers. The Ariete, and in particular their soft-skinned vehicles, were subject to bombing from RAF Wellingtons and the attentions of the new Beaufighters, none of which helped their speed of retreat.

The 7th Armoured had actually stopped short of Bone during the night; they did not want to get caught up in attacking a large town (they were a mainly armoured and mobile force). Instead they moved east of the town during the morning, setting up a blocking position between Rommel and the town. Their lack of infantry did not last long. The convoy from Tripoli had finally made its way around the Tunisian coast, where it stopped and unloaded some 1600 Commandoes from landing craft onto the beaches covered by 7th Armoured. Due to the need to break through the French lines, all the Africa Korps armour was at the eastern edge of their advance. While the mobile force was somewhat light on tanks (a number of which were spread out behind them along their route), they easily stopped a move against them by Rommel's rearguard, who on realising the strength of the force stopped to wait for their own spearhead to return.

Once the commandoes had been unloaded, the convoy and its escorting RN ships heads east to meet up with the fleet carriers still at sea off Tunis.

The British and French forces took a while to realise that the enemy was actually retreating; both the Africa Korps formations were highly trained and managed to look as if they were still advancing until the retreat was well under way. Once this was realised they started to follow up the retreat, where possible putting the closest elements under fire. The situation was especially dispiriting for the Ariete, who were starting to find it all too familiar. Meanwhile O'Connor released the 2nd Armoured reserve to join up with the 4th Indian and chase the Ariete; he wants to make them keep heading west rather than north.

That night, the 21st Panzer start to move back through Djebel Aboid, heading for Bone. Rommel is close to the new front of the division; he wants to see what in fact is between him and Bone, hoping to break through to the port where he can set up a defence and wait for reinforcements. The situation is confused, resulting in him losing contact with the armoured car that was supposed to be escorting him, and at 0215 he finds his car bouncing along what passes for a road in those parts when he sees two lorries running parallel. Both of which seem to be heavily armed and full of rather aggressive British and Australian troops. Rommel's luck has finally run out in the shape of one of Captain Stirling's patrols

15th May

Most of 21st Panzer had made it back through Djebel Abiod by dawn. This was just as well, as shortly after dawn the town, and the German troops pouring through it, received a visit from the FAA. The carriers that had earlier covered the amphibious landing had a final part to play, as 72 TBR (acting in their bombing role) and dive bombers plastered the road junction and any vehicle that looked like it might belong to the Afrika Korps. While this wasn't one of the main roles the FAA was trained for, the attack was a surprise and the train of vehicles moving westward quite an easy target. While only three tanks were destroyed, a good third of the divisions transport and soft-skinned vehicles were destroyed, trapped, or damaged - with the French now pushing up behind them, anything damaged simply had to be abandoned. This job done, the carriers headed back to Alexandria, where they would be needed shortly.

The Ariete division had meanwhile decided that it was on its own, and instead of trying to move west then north towards Bone (with the likely chance of being attacked from the rear by more British forces moving out of the south of Tunisia), had headed back down the road to Constantine (on the way to Algiers). This allowed them to break clear of the pursuit, who had made the initial mistake of assuming that they would head north to join up with the 21st Panzer. While the retreat was reasonably straightforward, the division did lose some 20 of its tanks to breakdowns - as with the 21st, any vehicle which broke down had to be left. Tanks which suffered this fate stayed to delay any pursuit, allowing the rest of the division to reach Algiers safely.

The Axis forces in Bone itself were hardly capable of attacking the British forces to the east of the town, being basically support troops. However the British force did come under increasing pressure from the retreating 21st Panzer, and in fact was slowly being forced back by the desperate attempts to break free of the trap, taking a steady toll of the enemy as they did so. The news of Rommel's capture wasn't made known until the afternoon, and in fact did not seem to make much difference to the attempts of the division to break west. The presence of the Luftwaffe was by now mainly that of bombers flying from bases in Sicily, the relatively small force in Algeria either having been worn down to very few operational planes. The RAF was also suffering from a lack of available aircraft, attacks mainly being made to reduce the impact of the German bombing.

At Vichy, Marshal Petain announces the replacement of the Franco-German armistice agreement by a new collaboration scheme. Concerning the meeting between Admiral Darlan and the Führer, Marshal Petain declares his complete approval. No-one has bothered to ask the French forces in Algeria what they think of the new scheme.

A private message was sent to the Vichy government, insisting that the Vichy forces in Algeria assist the Afrika Korps by directly attacking the advancing British and French. This led to a meeting of the government in Vichy that was 'contentious' in the words of the official report. Despite internal opposition, that evening they ordered the French troops in Algeria 'to resist the invasion by the English (sic) and the rebel French elements by whatever force was necessary'. This was greeted with despondency by the commanders in Algeria, who were not at all sure they could get their troops to obey. Indeed, at that point, while only a handful of units were in open revolt (mainly due to the Bone massacre), many others were simply not acknowledging orders, and sitting tight (an army unit sent to arrest the units in revolt had, for some mysterious reason, not seemed to have received its instructions).

Aircraft of the Fleet Air Arm attack the Al Amarah military barracks in Iraq, 48 miles from the Persian Gulf.

Relations between Vichy France and the United States degenerated sharply as the Senate passed a bill empowering the government to seize foreign shipping in US harbours. Under the Ship Seizure Bill the US can take over vessels "by purchase, charter, requisition" or may take them "into protective custody." Although not specifically aimed at Vichy, the measure is a clear response to Petain's decision to collaborate more closely with Germany. Armed guards have already been placed on board all French ships in US ports, including the liner Normandie. Other French merchant ships will be put in "protective custody" as they arrive.

16th May

At dawn, the men of the 7th Armoured blocking the way to Bone saw a group of German officers approaching under a white flag. Trapped between them and the French and British armour pressing forward from the east, and fast running out of fuel and ammunition (the remaining tanks of the division were by now virtually immobile), and having lost their commander, the divisional commander felt he had no choice but to surrender for the sake of his men. The surrender was quickly accepted, and messages sent to the pursuing troops to inform them. The 21st Panzer thus achieved the distinction of being the first German division to surrender to the Allies in WW2.

The Ariete division arrives in Algiers. The mood in the city is poor; indeed the troops are the subject of jeering crowds as they make their way into the city. The local French police don't seem very interested in doing anything to disperse the crowds, the reason for which becomes obvious once the division commander meets with the local commander - Algeria is now in all but open revolt. The orders to attack French troops entering the country have apparently been too much for anyone but the most dedicated Vichy supporters. The only place still under control is Algiers, due to the support troops stationed there, and in fact they are most relieved to see the arrival of the Ariete division. Their leaders are less relieved when they find out about the losses the division has taken - their commander informs them bluntly that if the Allies make a determined attack he cannot stop them.

17th May.

The carriers arrive back at Alexandria, and are hurriedly refuelled; intelligence is indicating they will be needed very soon. They also fly off some of their TBR aircraft in exchange for more fighters. To supplement the naval Goshawks, a squadron of Sparrowhawks have been refitted with arrestor hooks at the base workshops, and volunteer RAF pilots given a crash course on basic carrier landing and takeoff. Since the expectation is of an airborne invasion of Crete, it is hoped that they won't have to worry about bad weather (for which they are certainly not trained up for), as the Luftwaffe will not be trying to land troops in bad weather. There is also an additional RAAF squadron available who have already had similar training, and these two squadrons allow Cunningham to have some 100 fighters available to him. The rest of the Mediterranean fleet is on alert, and a cruiser/destroyer force is already at sea between Egypt and Crete.

Due to increasing Luftwaffe bombing on the island, General Freiburg has asked that the last of the RAF aircraft be withdrawn to Egypt; the air attacks are simply too heavy to allow them to remain. It is hoped that the carriers, operating south of the island, can supply him with the necessary air defence, although Cunningham has warned that their endurance may be limited.

Hitler hears about the surrender of the 21st Panzer and flies into a rage. When he calms down, he asks if implementing Operation Anton immediately will affect Barbarossa. He is told that it will not; the invasion of Russia is ready, and just waiting for the roads to dry out. He orders it to be implemented as soon as possible - the loss of the 21st Panzer would never have happened if it wasn't for the French stabbing them in the back. (Hitler's view of the situation is, it must be said, somewhat biased).

In Algeria, the British have stopped their advance on the border (apart from the force already near Bone), allowing the French to move forward to take the city. Given the surrender of the 21st and the overwhelming allied force heading west, the supply and maintenance troops in the city have surrendered without a fight. The French column has halted outside the city, where its leaders are having (highly unofficial) talks with a number of local French military commanders who have arrived quietly.

18th May

While O'Connor and the French have been holding and defeating the incursion into Tunisia, preparations have been going on at a furious rate for the defence of Crete. In fact, this was actually the higher priority in the mind of Wavell at the moment, as it wasn't considered likely that, no matter how well they did, the Afrika Korps could get further than Tripoli before Crete was all over.

Crete was defended mainly by the 1st New Zealand division. Having been diverted there instead of Greece when it became obvious to General Blamey that Greece was going to fall, the division is fully equipped. This is helpful as the road and communications network on Crete was very poor, and moving troops around without transport was going to be time-consuming, The division had spent its time on Crete preparing defensive works; little had been done during the time Greece was at war with Italy. The invasion was expected to be in two parts; an airborne attack, followed by a seaborne landing. The Allies had considerable information as to the nature of the invasion from their Ultra intercepts, but to preserve the security of these the New Zealanders had only been given partial information. Also a number of additional units had been sent to bolster the division. AA units from the newly-arrived 50th British division were shipped to increased the defences (it was considered likely that the Luftwaffe would be able to make the airfields untenable for defending fighters before the invasion, as was in fact the case), along with one infantry brigade, and a dozen infantry tanks sent to make life difficult for any airborne troops

There were also a substantial number of Greek troops on the island, making up about a brigade of armed and ready troops. There were also some 35,000 men evacuated from Greece, some with the British but mainly on small craft and fishing vessels. As a result they had very little equipment. Initially it had been hoped to equip at least some of the Greek troops with British weapons - they were experienced, and once recovered from their evacuation ordeal, would help to defend the island. The British had their own shortages, and did not have sufficient weapons to outfit any large number of men. While the discussions over this had been going on, one nameless staff officer had pointed out that they had warehouses "stuffed to the rafters with captured Italian weapons and ammunition", and while Italian equipment wasn't the best, it was a lot better than nothing. Accordingly enough small arms and a few other weapons such a mortars, plus ammunition, had been shipped on to the island. As it was simply impossible to provide transport, light weapons only were sent, as the men would have to fight and move on foot. Three brigades were formed using this equipment, and another two from the existing defenders.

The Royal Navy had promised that they would prevent any seaborne invasion, and as far as possible interfere with any transport planes used, but pointed out that the carriers simply couldn't be risked north of the island, and so they could not provide a constant air presence. Light forces of cruisers and destroyers would be covered by the FAA in order to sink any ships trying to get to Crete from the north.

19th May

The largest Italian army still fighting in Ethiopia formally surrendered today. 18,000 Italian and colonial troops have marched out and into prison camps. Few Italian troops now remain to be dealt with in Ethiopia. The Duke of Aosta also surrenders with 7,000 more Italian troops. Of the 230,000 Italians that started this campaign in East Africa only 80,000 remain.

By the morning of the 19th, Axis forces had completed their preparations for Anton, the complete occupation of France, which had been anticipated for some time. The German First Army advanced from the Atlantic coast, parallel to the Spanish border, while the German Seventh Army advanced from central France towards Vichy and Toulon. The Italian 4th Army occupied the French Riviera and an Italian division landed on Corsica to capture the island. By the evening of the 20th, German tanks had reached the Mediterranean coast.

Vichy France limited its active resistance to radio broadcasts objecting to the violation of the armistice. The 50,000-strong Vichy French Army initially took defensive positions around Toulon, but when confronted by German demands to disband, they lacked the military capability to resist the Axis forces.

The Germans had formulated Operation Lila with the aim of capturing intact the demobilised French fleet at Toulon. French naval commanders managed to delay the Germans by negotiation and subterfuge long enough to scuttle their ships, before the Germans could seize them, preventing the fleet from falling into the hands of the Axis. This was just as well, as the RN had plans ready to attack and sink the ships with a carrier strike if the Germans had gained control of them.

Chapter 15 - Crete

20th May

During the previous evening and night, the demolition of the airfield runways had gone ahead as planned by General Freyberg. This proved to be none too soon, as at 0800 the first German paratroops were dropping on the airfield around Maleme airfield and the town of Chania. The drop, while nominally successful, suffered terribly at the hands of the Greek and New Zealand defenders, who did especial damage to the gliders that landed with the paratroops - almost all of them were wiped out by mortar fire on landing, and the rifles of the defenders. Indeed the only surviving units were those who had landed off course, and while some of these managed to prepare temporary positions, others were engaged by the Greek infantry. The more mobile New Zealanders were busy engaging and trying to contain the force that had landed at the airfield.

Although the carriers south of the island were trying to mount a CAP over the airfields, the distance meant they could only manage intermittent cover, and sadly were not present when the first wave of the German attack began. They had more luck that afternoon, when a second wave of paratroops and gliders attacked Rethimnon and Heraklion. Twelve Goshawks intercepted the drop at Heraklion, and slaughtered the vulnerable transport aircraft. They destroyed at least 20 planes, and it is estimated that half of the attacking force never made it to the ground. Heraklion was defended by a British and a Greek brigade, and with the losses and disruption of the fighter interception the German force had no choice but to form a defensive perimeter and try and hold until reinforcements arrived.

The most progress made by the attackers was at Maleme, where they gradually extended their perimeter, although not without heavy losses at the hands of the defenders. It was decided that the main reinforcement would go into Maleme tomorrow, as that assault seemed to have made the best progress. So far the Luftwaffe has lost some 40 Ju52 aircraft, more than expected, and mainly due to the unexpected interception by the FAA. The Luftwaffe started the operation with some 450 transport planes, so the losses, while annoying, are not considered a problem - yet.

21st May

The Royal Navy decides to try a different tactic to keep air cover going over the island. They lost five planes yesterday to Me109's flying from Greece, so realise that there is no point in patrolling in small numbers. So instead they mount a covering force of sixteen fighters. Since this means they won't have much available to defend themselves in case of attack, the air defence for the carriers themselves is taken over by Sparrowhawks, flying out of Egypt with auxiliary fuel tanks. This is a risky tactic, as the RAF planes are not used to defending the carriers, but it is felt that unless a heavy raid is mounted on them it will prove sufficient. In addition, the two squadrons of Beaufighters that had later been amusing the Afrika Korps have moved back east, and will be mounting patrols over the island from dawn - they have the range to do this from their bases in Egypt, although there is some worry about their chances against Me109's.

The cruiser minelayer HMS Abdiel lays mines off the west coast of Greece, which sink an Italian destroyer and two transports. However the destroyer Juno is sunk and the cruiser Ajax damaged as they withdraw southwest of Crete.

Given the poor results yesterday, Student decides to concentrate today's landings on the Maleme area. This decision was helped by the fact that overnight the paratroops had pushed the New Zealand forces back from Hill 107, which dominated the airfield. With this in their hands they expected fewer problems in landing reinforcements.

During the morning, more transports and gliders land troops at Maleme. However the New Zealanders AA defences are still unsuppressed, and a number of fighter sweeps by the FAA and the RAF catch the transports and the gliders, leading to heavy casualties among them. The paratroops are forced to enter combat almost as soon as they have left their aircraft, suffering more casualties to rifle and machine gun fire. By the evening, they had managed to control the airfield sufficiently to allow Ju52's to start flying in the 5th Mountain Division. While delivering a considerable number of troops, losses to the planes were heavy. The runways had been damaged two days ago by the defenders, and as a result planes were lost as they crashed on landing, often killing their occupants. The Allies artillery still dominated the airfield, and the last wave of transports were unfortunate enough to land as the Beaufighter sweep was about to head for home. The fighters expended their ammunition on the helpless transports, destroying 16 on the ground.

The actions at the other two airfields were not going well for the Germans. Using the tactics of holding the paratroops with the Greek units while the more mobile Allied force made attacks was whittling down the German numbers steadily, and their position was not helped by the two dive bombing raids in support that the fleet carriers launched. While the navy pilots were not really trained to attack ground targets, they did considerable damage and disruption to the paratroops. By night, it was looking like both these bridgeheads would be eliminated by morning.

At sea, the Germans attempted to land the first of their invasion convoys. The result was a disaster. Force D, consisting of three light cruisers and four destroyers intercepted the caiques and their single escort at midnight, and despite aggressive action by the Italian ship overwhelmed it and sank most of the transport craft before withdrawing. It is estimated that some 1200 German soldiers and Italian sailors were killed, for the loss of two British seamen. Force D then retired under the carriers' protection by daybreak.

In Algeria, the 'secret' talks between the Free French and the local commanders have borne fruit, aided by the full invasion of France by the Germans. Leaving the British to guard their backs, a strong Free French force heads slowly east to Algiers, joined by a number of the local French units in passing. By nightfall, it halts outside the city, and an officer is sent in under a flag of truce to talk to the Vichy commander there. While this has been going on, the situation in the rest of the country is tense; many of the local forces have put some of their more Vichy-friendly commanders under arrest (usually peacefully, but a number of people have been killed during these operations). It is now an open secret that, no matter how denied by Vichy, Algeria will very soon be a part of the growing Free French forces.

22nd May

Freyberg realises that Hill 107 is the key to using his artillery to suppress the airfield, and orders at attack soon after dawn to recover it. This is supported by all 40 of the carriers available divebombers and a full squadron of Beaufighters. They are escorted by the FAA Goshawks, and as a result are uninterrupted in the loving attention they give the hill. As the dust and smoke slowly clears, the ground attack come in, the men advancing with fixed bayonets. In fact, they are hardly needed, the ferocity of the air attack has stunned the defenders, and inside 30 minutes the hill is back under allied control, and artillery fire is again making the German position uncomfortable. The allies had destroyed some 70 aircraft the previous day, 50 of them Ju52 transports, and although the Luftwaffe continues to fly in planes and gliders through the day, another 45 are lost, often to ground fire after they are unable to take off immediately from the damaged runway. The Luftwaffe has now lost well over a hundred of them, as well as Ju87's which have been the preferred target of the British fighters - indeed, Squadron Leader Pattle claimed his 50th German plane during the day as he led his squadron of Sparrowhawks off HMS Illustrious. The Beaufighters are proving to be a dangerous ground attack aircraft; although not really a match for the Me109, it can hold its own or better against any of the other Axis aircraft.

A force of cruisers and destroyers are spotted north of the island by the Luftwaffe as they move south to get under their air cover. Caught before this is possible (due to the fighters supporting the attack on Hill 107), the cruisers HMS Naiad and HMS Carlisle are damaged before the FAA fighters arrive. The Luftwaffe is still conducting sweeps around the island, and later that day HMS Warspite is hit by a bomb, without serious damage. HMS Gloucester and HMS Greyhound are attacked, but this time the Goshawks shoot down three Ju87's and drive the rest off. HMS Fiji is not so lucky, struck that afternoon a number of times and left powerless. Fortunately she is south of Crete and an escort of RAF fighters keeps her company until she can be towed slowly back to Alexandria.

General Freyberg signals to Admiral Cunningham that he thinks his men can defeat the airborne troops as long as they do not get any substantial support from seaborne landings. Cunningham replies that as long any of his ships remain afloat the Germans will not get through by sea. A second attempt to land troops is made that day; a number of the caiques were sunk by gunfire, although the lack of sufficient air cover north of the island had led to losses for the Royal Navy. However the ships had forced the German force to retreat.

As predicted, the lack of reinforcements and constant attacks, especially by the Greek troops, has finally reduced the landings at Rethimnon and Heraklion. The only remaining German bridgehead is at Maleme airfield, and despite the men being flown in, is not making any progress. The commander begs for support, particularly heavy weapons and, if possible, tanks - the few British tanks, invulnerable to the paratroops light weapons, and being used as mobile machine gun posts and causing considerable losses. He is informed that a new landing attempt will be made tomorrow.

In Algiers, talks between the Free French and the Vichy commanders have reached a deal, not dissimilar to that obtained in Syria. The Vichy commanders will surrender the country, and they, their families, and any other Vichy supporters who wish to will be granted safe passage back to France or a neutral country. The decision will be announced the following day.

23rd May

With only one landing left to worry about, Gen Freyberg releases his reserves to bolster his attack. The Germans continue to try and drop paratroops - the defenders are noticing that they seem to have run out of gliders, and that today few transport planes try to land. The reason for that may be the wrecked Ju52's covering a considerable part of the airfield and surrounding countryside. Despite their situation, the German paratroops hold on, fighting fiercely as their perimeter is slowly reduced. The Allied force still has to contend with attack from the air, but this is lighter than on previous days and they are getting used to it (even if it is just as much of a nuisance as before).

Late that afternoon, a convoy of small craft and lighters is spotted by a RAF patrol plane heading to Crete. Despite the daytime and the reduced availability of fighter cover, Cunningham orders his ships to sink or stop it - preferably both. He is asked by a worried Army command if he can spare the ships for such a risky operation. His reply is "It takes three years to build a ship, it takes 300 to build a tradition". The Navy will make sure the Army is supported".

The ships are in fact an Italian force from Rhodes, with some 3,000 men of the 9th division. They are first visited by the Cormorants from Illustrious, who sink two steamships and three tankers. Then, under fighter cover, the convoy sees five British destroyers. Despite ordering the ships to scatter, two reefer ships and a number of the small craft are sent to the bottom. The destroyers are attacked by dive bombers during part of the action, but their manoeuvrability allows them to survive until four British fighters arrive to chase them off.

The final attempt to reinforce by sea takes place that night, when a German convoy attempts the run to the island. They are intercepted close to dawn by the same group of destroyers, who again break up and sink many of the caiques, sending another 1,800 Mountain troops to the bottom. However staying to turn back the convoy has left the ships exposed. While they get fighter cover for an hour, the pressure and losses on the British fighters has been growing and they have to leave the destroyers to fend for themselves. As a result they only have their speed and AA guns to protect them when attacked by 24 Stukas, who managed to sink HMS Kashmir and HMS Kelly.

That evening the announcement that Algeria is now behind the Free French cause is broadcast. Gen De Gaulle states "thanks to the brave men of our army, and with the help of the British Empire, the first part of metropolitan France is recovered from the grip of Nazi tyranny". The only part of Africa now not in Free French hands is French Morocco.

24th May

While tired, the defenders on Crete continue to press the paratroops, aided by their artillery and the fact that the Greek troops are determined to drive them off the island come what may. The fighting does not seem so determined today, and in fact the paratroops were running very short of ammunition - the losses of the transport planes, and the turning back of more due to reports and interceptions by British fighters, had not allowed them to be resupplied. Additionally, as their bridgehead shrunk, more and more of the supply drops that they did get were falling outside the area and were lost to them. Although they fought on till in some cases they were completely out of ammunition, they finally surrendered at 1800 that evening.

Despite this, the defenders are still the subject of attacks from the air, but without troops on the ground the affect is fairly limited. Like the British, the Luftwaffe formations are also exhausted after five days of continuous fighting. They do take a final revenge on the Royal Navy, who have perhaps moved rather too far north in order to better support the Army and the ships making anti-convoy sweeps. A force of 20 Ju87's finds HMS Illustrious southwest of Crete, and despite her CAP, (only six planes due to the use of most of her fighters over Crete) manages to hit her twice. Fortunately for the carrier these are only 250kg bombs due to the range the divebombers have to attack from, but she takes damage to her deck, central elevator and rear hangar. While a dozen planes are destroyed in the hanger, and it takes four hours to bring the fire under control, the damage is not serious, nothing having penetrated the ships hangar deck armour, and she is escorted back to Alexandria, where her repairs will take a month.

27th May

As it is now obvious that the Germans have stopped trying to invade Crete, at least for the time being, the British start to reorganise and rebuild their forces in North Africa, in particular the air force, which has suffered heavy losses over the last few weeks (although inflicting heavy losses on the Luftwaffe as well). With the welcoming of Algeria into the Allied camp, Churchill immediately wants to know when convoys can be pushed though the Mediterranean again. The Admiralty points out that while this is indeed very desirable (the route is only some 40% of the distance around the cape, and basically halves the shipping needs), the Tiger convoy was lucky with the weather. They need time to repair the ships damaged in the previous operations, establish air bases and air cover, and reorganise. In any case, as they point out, the convoys already in operation can't just be turned off, and the recommend the possibility be reviewed in 4-6 weeks with the resumption about a month after if things are going smoothly. It is also pointed out that the FAA in the Med has been very heavily worked - indeed overworked - recently due to operational needs, and they need a short period to incorporate new pilots and give them a rest.

The losses in transport planes for the Luftwaffe in Operation Mercury have been very heavy. The gliders were expendable, but the best part of 200 Ju52's lost or seriously damaged are not. The losses to the fighters and bombers were also high, and with Barbarossa about to start, it will be difficult for the Luftwaffe to rebuild its strength quickly. The situation is not so bad for the Italians, but they are looking at defending the Dodecanese before attempting any more attacks on Allied territory. Accordingly it is decided that for the next few months the theatre will be in a defensive posture.

The British, who don't realise yet that the Axis is not going to be renewing the attack soon, is looking at building up the defences on Crete before taking any offensive actions. The Greek force there needs to be properly equipped and more defensive and infrastructure work done as a matter of urgency; the airfields will be out of action for at least a week, more due to broken German aircraft littering them that the deliberate destruction done by the defenders. Luckily they will have time to do this

In Washington today President Roosevelt today warned America of Nazi designs on the Americas. He promised to extend US patrols in the Atlantic to protect the sea-lanes to Britain, and announced that he had proclaimed an "unlimited national emergency." requiring that its military, naval, air and civilian defences be put on the basis of readiness to repel any and all acts or threats of aggression directed toward any part of the Western Hemisphere. The US was rearming "only for self-defence", he said.

Meanwhile in Germany 100 troop trains a day are heading east.

Representatives from French Morocco arrive in Algiers to conduct secret talks with the Free French. Given that the position of Morocco is untenable in the face of any allied attack now, it is expected that a similar deal will be struck to those in Tunisia and Algeria. That evening, the Vichy governor of Madagascar restates his dedication to the Vichy cause. It is thought that the governor considers himself too far away from anyone for it to matter.

30th May

British troops of the 4th Cavalry Brigade of 1st British Cavalry Division arrive outside Baghdad after travelling 500 miles across the desert from Palestine. Rashid Ali, the German and Italian diplomats in Iraq and the Grand Mufti of Jerusalem have all bravely fled to Persia. A cease-fire agreement has been signed by the remaining government with the British, whose main force is at Ur, and the Regent has been restored.

The British anti-tank gunners, disappointed that the Afrika Korps had fled before they had a chance to try out their shiny new 6-pdrs on them, has been testing them against the copious supply of dead Axis tanks, the results of which leave them quite enthusiastic. Permission is given for a couple of guns to go to Tunis and be tried out on the German tanks left there.

O'Connor has noticed that there were problems with the British tanks employed in the latest operations, in particular their tendency to break down and the lack of a decent HE round. While these points have been made already in the Cyrenaica campaign, the latest action has reinforced the point that these problems have not been fixed. According he selects a group of experienced officers to evaluate the performance of both the British and German tanks, with a view to putting out a formal request for a new (or at least modified) tank to fix these problems. As it looks unlikely they will have to conduct major armoured operations in the near future, he thinks this is a good time to review the current tank designs and policies.

2nd June

The USS Long Island, Aircraft Escort Vessel Number 1 (AVG-1), the first USN escort aircraft carrier, is commissioned at Newport News, Virginia. The Long Island was a flush-deck escort aircraft carrier converted from the cargo ship SS Mormacmail in 67 working days. She will be used to give the USN experience of operating this type of ship, which the RN have been using successfully in the Atlantic.

After examination of the damage she sustained in the German breakout, it is decided not to put Glorious through a full repair and refit. Dockyard space is full, and she is already old. Instead she will be repaired sufficiently to be able to act as a training carrier - the increasing numbers of aircrew needed mean that the Furious needs help, and the light carriers which were originally intended for training are proving more useful as convoy escorts.

It had originally been intended to build a second light carrier for Australia to supplement HMAS Melbourne, however at the moment the building slips are full of new construction and repairs. It is agreed that the Australians will take over HMS Theseus, allowing HMS Eagle to be brought back for a badly needed refit. The RN currently has adequate heavy ships; when the new carrier goes out to the Far East, HMS Renown will accompany her to bolster the strength in the area and allow the carriers to exercise and work with a capital ship.

The prototype of the Canadian Ram tank finishes testing, with a generally satisfactory result. The tank has been ordered off the drawing board; while modifications are desired after the completion of the testing, these will be brought in after the initial batch. The tank will be named the Grizzly as it comes into service with the British Army and the Free French, and will mount the new 6pdr gun. It is expected to have the first models available by the end of August. The prototype is now to be sent to Britain for study and evaluation against the latest model Valentine; it is hoped that the turret can be fitted in place of the 2pdr currently on the Valentine. If this proves successful, a new version of the Valentine will be produced with this turret.

Meanwhile the USA expects to be delivering the first of the French order for the M3 tank (with 2pdr gun) in June. They will also be supplying parts for the Canadian tanks until Canada is in a position to produce them locally.

3rd June

From today until the 6th of June the Finnish and German military leadership will be negotiating at Helsinki on co-operation in event of a Russo-German war. An agreement regarding the Finnish Army and Air Force is reached. Although formally the idea of a Russo-German war is hypothetical, the Finns have already worked out that the Germans are in all probability about to invade the USSR.

In the Atlantic Ocean, the Royal Navy has now sunk four of the support and replenishment ships prepositioned for the abortive breakout by the German heavy ships.

4th June

Air Marshal Park arrives in Egypt after his review of the Maltese air defence system. He has left recommendations there for implementation, and is expecting to be asked to do the same thing for Crete. Instead he finds himself in conversation with General Blamey.Blamey has been concerned for some time with the state of the defences in Malaysia and SE Asia in general, as these have long been seen as the outer defence line for Australia. He has also been asked by Menzies to find out what the current state is, and advise if the British preparations are all they could be. Having met some of the RAAF men moved to the Middle East, he is becoming more and more concerned as to the condition of the admittedly insufficient forces there. He has also been introduced to a British army officer currently recovering from a somewhat embarrassing wound in Cairo. He wants the two of them to fly out and give the defences in Malaya and Burma an unprejudiced look, and report back to him and to General Wavell. His also points out that with the recovery of North Africa some limitations that have been assumed in the past might not apply any more. The two of them are to be back with their recommendations in no more than six weeks.

7th June

French Morocco formally declares for the Free French. As with the earlier declarations, those senior officials and their families, plus others who want to leave, are given transportation to France. The French are currently arguing about what to call themselves. Since Algeria is technically a part of France, not a colony, should they still call themselves the Free French or just the French Army?

It has been agreed that once the army has listed the military resources available in its new acquisitions, a new plan will be drawn up for a new Army, although it isn't expected that this will be fully formed until next year, mainly due to supply constraints. The current expectation is that they will be able to field some eight divisions, two of them armoured, provided that the equipment can be supplied.

11th June

At a Liaison conference between army and navy, the Naval Chief of Staff Nagano Osami astounded his colleagues when he vehemently calls for the Southward Advance. He and the navy's powerful "First Committee" were anxious to move before the American navy's huge "two-ocean" building programme was completed, although the preparations for the planned attacks will take some 6 months to complete.

The USA agrees to garrison Iceland in place of the British force. This will free up a division for use elsewhere.

130 Army divisions are reported to be massed on the border facing Russia. The official news agency TASS says "rumours of a German intention to attack the USSR are without foundation."

14th June

Discussions are taking place with the French in Cairo about the most efficient way to start to run convoys through the Mediterranean again. The obvious way is to run the convoys through by sea, but this will involve having to escort and probably fight them through the Sicilian narrows. The final decision is to run all normal (i.e. bulk) shipping through in convoy, however high value cargoes, such as military equipment, will be landed at Oran to go on by rail (or in the case of aircraft unpacked and flown on where necessary. In order to ease supply in Egypt, XIII Corps will relocate to Tunisia/West Cyrenaica, where they can be supported via the rail link. The committee is also investigating the resumption of exports from North Africa to Britain, in particular some items such as iron ore which are badly needed by the British steel industry. These exports will reduce the load on shipping across the North Atlantic, and will be more efficient as the ships will be loaded in both directions (many ships on the North Atlantic route travel west in ballast). Having most shipping use the Mediterranean rather than the Cape route will also amount to saving over a million tons of shipping. It is expected these changes will start to take place in about a month, allowing for the placements and loading of shipping to be prepared in advance. There is also the suggestion of joining the rail line in Tunisia as far as Egypt, but this will take a considerable time, and require items such as rails to come from the USA. It is being looked at as a long term action.

18th June

The first of a series of bombing raids on German ports starts with a heavy raid on Hamburg. The RAF has been carrying out limited attacks over the last four months, mainly in order to keep the Germans devoting effort to air defence. The bulk of their effort has been in gardening (which has caused considerable loss and disruption to coastal shipping in particular), and in heavily escorted daytime raids against limited targets in the Low Countries and France. These daytime raids have suffered casualties, heavy in some cases, but have also been shooting down a considerable number of German fighters. Although the loss ratio favours the Germans, it is not by much (although the Germans do save more pilots). There have also been a number of experimental raids on inland waterways by bombing and mining.

The main direction has been to allow Bomber Command to build up its strength in heavy and medium bombers, and to improve the accuracy of its bombing. The new pathfinders have steadily been gaining experience, although their methods are by no means perfected, and the new raids are intended to see how well the new system works with heavy raids. In order to simplify the navigation problems, coastal or near-coastal cities such as Hamburg have been selected.

The US government formally adds Greece to the countries which will be supplied with lend-lease. It has been agreed that for practical reasons they will use British equipment and ammunition where possible, and as the supply situation eases in the Middle East it is intended to make the Greek troops on Crete into two divisions plus some auxiliary units. The local population fought fiercely in defence of their island, and surplus Italian equipment will be used to equip the local equivalent of the Home Guard

21st June

In response to a failed attack on the US battleship Texas Doenitz instructs his U-boats thus: "Fuhrer orders avoidance any incident with USA during next few weeks. Orders will be rigidly obeyed in all circumstances. In addition attacks until further orders will be restricted to cruisers, battleships and aircraft carriers and then only when identified beyond doubt as hostile. Fact that warship is sailing without lights will not be regarded as proof of enemy identity."

Soviet fighter pilots are ordered not to fire on a German plane which flies over Soviet airspace. The border guard is put on alert, but forbidden to take any "provocative" action.

In Ethiopia the Italian garrison at Jimma surrenders to Ethiopian troops under British command.

The U.S. State Department informs the Italian Ambassador that all Italian consulates in U.S. territory are to be closed by 15 July 1941 at which point all Italian diplomats will have to leave. The German consulates have already been closed

Chapter 16 - Barbarossa

22nd June

The German attack on the Soviet Union, Operation Barbarossa, begins, taking the Soviets (or at least their leadership) almost completely by surprise. The Germans have 140 of their own divisions, including 17 Panzer and 13 motorized divisions.

There are also 14 Rumanian, two Hungarian, and 21 Finnish divisions. Facing them are the 230 division of the Soviet Army. 170 divisions are in the western part of the Soviet Union and 134 are directly opposing the Germans. The attacks began at 0300 hours with ground and air attacks. Most German operations are going according to plan.

24th June

A new version of the Supermarine 318 high altitude bomber enters testing. This has now incorporated the lessons learnt from the High Altitude Wellington program. Due to Supermarine now being fully occupied with the Spitfire, the program is now being run directly by Vickers. Preliminary arrangements have been made for production, as it is being seen as an integral part of the future bombing campaign against Germany.

In Berlin the German News Bureau announced: "An attempt by the Soviet air force on Tuesday morning to fly weak forces into East Prussia has been frustrated by the German air defence. The enemy aircraft encountered such accurate flak fire that they were forced to turn around at once and to jettison their bombs over open country. Since early Monday morning the Luftwaffe has continued its successful attacks on Soviet military airfields. Large numbers of Russian aircraft were destroyed on the first day of battle, and we can now report that a great many more aircraft have been shot down on the same day."

Vilna and Kaunas fall to the Germans on the Eastern Front while another assault is begun on the citadel of Brest Litovsk.

The USA starts delivery of Brewster Buffalo fighters to the Dutch East Indies. These fighters are no longer considered a first-rank fighter by the USA, and have now been completely replaced in the USN by the more powerful Wildcat. A modified version of the Corsair is undergoing trials; reports of the combat in Europe have speeded up the need for a high performance fighter, and work has been speeded up on fixing some of the problems with the aircraft.

27th June

Stalin accepts Churchill's offer of an alliance to fight Hitler. It has been agreed that military collaboration between the two nations will be on a "mutual and reciprocal basis." Military and economic missions are to be sent to Moscow to coordinate the joint war effort.

In his broadcast last Sunday after receiving the news of the German invasion, Churchill, who has been outspoken in his opinions of the USSR, said that no-one had been a more consistent opponent of communism than he. "I will unsay not a word that I have spoken about it," he said, "But all this fades away before the spectacle which is now unfolding. Any man or state who fights against Nazidom will have our aid. Any man or state who marches with Hitler is our foe... We have but one aim and one irrevocable purpose. We are resolved to destroy Hitler and every vestige of the Nazi regime."

He forecast an even greater alliance: "The Russian danger is therefore our danger and the danger of the United States, just as the cause of any Russian fighting for his hearth and home is the cause of free men and free peoples in every quarter of the globe."

The Soviet Information Bureau announced: "Our troops are fighting fiercely against large Fascist armoured units in the Minsk area. The battle is still going on. Violent armoured conflicts have been waged all day near Lutsk. Our operations have proceeded favourably."

29th June

Finnish troops push towards Murmansk. A joint Finish-German attack starts on 29 June at 3 am. The attackers are German 2nd and 3rd Mountain Divisions and Finnish Detachment Petsamo which protects the attack's right flank. Soviet resistance is initially quite light and the Finns' and 2nd Divisions advance is rapid.

The fortress of Brest-Litovsk finally falls after a siege lasting a week when it is bombed by squadrons of Ju88's. Guderian's Panzer Group links up near Minsk with the Panzers of General Hermann Hoth, creating a huge Soviet pocket.

British forces in the Middle East are reorganised.

A new army will be formed, 8th Army. It will initially consist of XIII Corps and XXX Corps, with a further Corps to be added later.

XIII Corps consists of 2nd Armoured, 4th Indian and 6th Australian divisions.

XXX Corps consists of 7th Armoured, 50th British and 5th Indian divisions.

I Australian Corp currently has 7th Australian Division, 9th Australian Division and a British armoured brigade; the armoured brigade will be expanded to a division as in the other Corps.

The New Zealand division will remain on Crete for the time being; after the Greek divisions are properly equipped and ready, a decision will be made to redeploy them

There is also the 1st South African Division, a Polish Brigade and some Commando units in reserve, and a number of Indian divisions occupying Iraq and other strategic points.

It is intended to expand the commando forces, and additional landing ships and craft are to be expected from Britain. The next task seen for Middle East command is to look at reducing and occupying the Dodecanese islands to help secure Crete and the western Adriatic.

General O'Connor will be in charge of 8th Army. His Corps commanders are Gott (XIII Corps), and Montgomery, sent out from England to command XXX Corps. Wavell remembers him from amphibious exercises in the area before the war, and the amphibious operations being considered will need well-trained troops and good planning, both areas in which Montgomery is considered to excel. General Blamey will remain in command of I Aus Corps.

30th June

The Maud Committee, set up last year to study the feasibility of producing a bomb based on nuclear fission, has presented its findings to the government. It concludes that such a bomb containing 25 pounds of active material would produce an effect equivalent to 1,800 tons of TNT, as well as large quantities of radioactive substances, and the material for the first bomb could be ready by 1944.

The German Second Panzer Group captures Bobryusk, Russia. Army Group South captures Luvov. In the north the Germans advance toward Kiev. The western front commander, General Dmitri Pavlov, and his leading officers are executed for incompetence on Stalin's orders.

The French islands in the West Indies declare for Free France, after a rather extended period of secret negotiations. This will also allow the ships exiled there after Mers-el-Kebir to be refitted in US yards and brought back into service, a useful addition to the Allied navies.

2nd July

Marshal Semyon Konstantinovich Timoshenko is appointed western front commander.

Heavy rains have affected the roads being used by the German advance. The armoured reconnaissance detachment of the German 7th Panzer Division under General Baron von Funck reported that it had been forced to halt its drive "because the prescribed roads have been reduced by heavy rainfall to an untrafficable swamp."

Hoeppners Fourth Panzer Group attacks toward Ostrov. The Romanian Third and Fourth Armies and the German Eleventh Army begin full scale attacks in the South.

At Debra Tabor in Ethiopia a force of 4,500 Italians and levies besieged by Ethiopian patriots surrender to a British force of one squadron and one company.

Japan is preparing for war against Britain and the US over Indochina by conscripting one million men and recalling all its merchant ships from the Atlantic. While 400,000 conscripts will reinforce the Kwantung army in China, the rest will be committed to south-east Asia. The decision to open up the southern front - to be known as the Greater East Asia Co-Prosperity Sphere - has been spurred by the speed of the German successes in Europe. Ironically the British success in North Africa has been used to point out the effectiveness of fast action of an army supported by naval and air units, which the Japanese intend to deploy in the new theatre.

At an Imperial Conference at which the emperor made a rare appearance, the war minister, Hideki Tojo, urged the cabinet that now is the time to secure a greater empire or risk missing the opportunity. These are repeats of Liaison Conferences which are held between military and political leaders. Imperial Conferences repeat the information for the Emperor and obtain his approval. This Conference ratifies the decision to attempt to take bases in French Indochina, even at the risk of war.

3rd July

After heavy fighting against Soviet tanks, General Nehring's 18th Panzer Division reported the existence if a new kind of Soviet tank, quite different in appearance from the all the known types, which seemed "very advanced and was indestructible by German antitank guns".

Panzergruppe 2's 3rd Panzer Division (General Model) reaches the Dnepr River when it captures Rogachev, south-east of Minsk.

Stalin broke his silence today and, calling his people "brothers" and "sisters" rather than "comrades", called on them to fight a total war against the invading Germans not only in the modern sense but also in the grim "old Russian" way. In a speech broadcast throughout the Soviet Union, he called on the people to lay the land waste before the invader. Everything possible must be removed, he said, and that which cannot by moved must be destroyed.

The mopping up of the Italian forces in East Africa continues as the Italian garrison at Debra Tabor surrenders to the British, and General Gazzera's 7,000 strong army in the south surrenders to a Belgian force.

With the Italian surrender at Amba Alagi, all that remains for the Allies in East Africa is clearing up. A few Italian divisions remain around Gondar in the north-west, and in the far west, and the rains - which make all roads impassable - will give them a few months life, but they present no strategic threat to anyone. This allows the allies to start considering the redeployment of some of the troops in the area; while some will need to remain in the country, the other units will be withdrawn for use elsewhere.

The USS Hornet enters commission. The newest of the USN's fleet carriers, she has been brought forward in completion date due to the increasing tension between the USA and Japan and the increasing importance carriers are playing at sea. The last of the Yorktown class carriers, Ticonderoga, is expected to be ready in 8-9 months.

5th July

A 49-year-old Communist who organized groups of his fellow Yugoslav's to fight Franco in the Spanish Civil War today issued a call to his country "to rise like one man in this battle against the invaders and hirelings." Josip Broz, alias "Tito", has recruited many partisans from the Yugoslavs who have fled to the mountains to escape forced labour under the Germans.

The German Sixth Army breaks through the Stalin line near Lwow. The Soviet defence line west of Zhitomir is also breached by the German Sixth Army. To the north, east of Minsk, the German advance reaches the Dnepr River.

7th July

The United States takes over the protection of Iceland from Britain and lands troops to start building naval and air bases. The American security zone is also extended eastwards to longitude 22 W, to embrace Iceland. The US assumes the responsibility for the direct protection of all convoys of American ships bound for Iceland and of any such ships of other nationalities as wished to attach themselves to such convoys.

The Admiralty report on the possible composition of a fleet for the Far East in case of a Japanese attack is sent to the War cabinet. It stated than in a few months seven fleet carriers will be available (after HMS Bulwark commissions in September). Three should be left in the Mediterranean, two at Alexandria and one at Oran. One would be held at home, but that would usually be in refit/modernisation. A light carrier would be retained at Scapa in case one was needed urgently, but carriers could be quickly released from Atlantic convoys if need be. Three fleet carriers would be available. Later this year the RAN will have two light carriers in operation. It recommends at least one and preferably two more be sent. With no German surface unit heavier than a destroyer still afloat, the retention of heavy ships in Home Waters can be kept to a minimum, and the invasion of Russia means no attempt an invasion will be possible this year.

Now that there are virtually no enemy heavy or capital ships left in home waters and the Mediterranean, the navy can actually spare battleships more easily than carriers. They recommend the Warspite and Queen Elizabeth (both of which have been modernised) are sent to work with the light carriers (as the light carriers are slower than the fleet carriers, the older battleships speed is a better match). HMS Duke of York will commission in September, and has had the additional work done requested some time ago to make her more suitable for operation in the tropics. HMS KGV and HMS Prince of Wales are having similar modifications and modernisations done while the damage caused by the Bismark is being repaired. They suggest either Repulse or Renown is given a short refit and modernisation. This will give a squadron of one battlecruiser and three fast battleships to work with the carriers.

They point out that even this powerful force will be inadequate if attacked by the whole Japanese fleet, but even in the worst case (the USA remaining neutral), they feel that with the support of land-based planes it will be adequate, as the Japanese would have to retain ships to cover themselves in case of American intervention.

In addition to the usual support of cruisers and destroyers, two submarine squadrons should also be sent (as per the pre-war plans); eight T-class and eight U-class. These are less needed in the Mediterranean now as the only targets tend to be small and close to land; given the number of minefields the Italians have laid, better and cheaper results will be obtained by torpedo-armed Beaufighters and naval planes.

Given that the Mediterranean is now relatively quiet, they suggest Admiral Somerville as commander, in view of his experience with air and fleet operations.

9th July

Vitebsk and Pskov fall to the Germans; 300,000 Soviet prisoners have now been taken and 40 Divisions eliminated. The 2nd and 3rd Panzer Groups have encircled them at Vitebsk and Pskov forming the 4th Panzer Army. It has now crossed the Dnieper and Dvina Rivers and is advancing to encircle Smolensk.

Lieutenant Brabner, just back from Crete, spoke in the House of Commons: "In Greece, Crete, and Libya there has been an almost chronic lack of the most important war materials. It sounds incredible, but when we were at Malemi (the aerodrome at Canea, capital of Crete) we rarely were in a position to put more than two aircraft into the air for a continuous patrol during daylight hours."

He then told the House that "70% to 80% of our tanks broke down before they saw the enemy."

These statements will have an impact on the disposition of British resources and the development of new tanks. In fact his assertions are somewhat exaggerated, and considerable efforts have been made to improve the situation, but much more remains to be done. Fortunately the lull in action in the Mediterranean theatre allows the issue of tank performance and reliability to be addressed more easily.

10th July

Units of the Soviet 5th Army counterattack SW of Korosten, but are held by Kleist's Panzer Group. Four Italian divisions leave Italy bound for the Eastern Front - this causes controversy in Italian military circles, where many feel Italian troops are needed in the Mediterranean, but this commitment is in exchange for the earlier German commitment to the short-lived Afrika Korps.

General Guderians forces have crossed the Beresina and are preparing to cross the Dnieper in sight of Smolensk, the gateway to Moscow. Meanwhile the 3rd Panzer Division under Model makes an assault crossing of the Dnepr at Starye Bykhov, about 110 miles downriver from Smolensk. General Hoth is sweeping north to by-pass Smolensk and cut the road to Moscow.

On Stalin's orders Pavlov, the failed commander of the Bialystock sector, has been shot, and a new line of defence has been established under the command of the defence minister, Marshal Timoshenko.

The progress of the American defence program is announced to the Congress. Only $3.6 billion out of $20 billion voted was actually spent on the army. During June 1,476 aircraft were produced out of a planned 3,000 a month. Last August the army has 300 modern combat planes, today it has 250. There are also fewer anti-tank guns than there were a year ago, but the number of rifles has increased by 200,000 and the number of motor vehicles rose from 745 to 125,000. Many members of Congress are unimpressed.

15th July

Britain and the USSR have signed a mutual defence pact. Importantly, the treaty includes clauses that neither party will conduct separate peace negotiations. It also allows Britain to consider the Russian requests for material aid.

Brigadier Slim arrives back in Cairo with a report on the state of the defences in the Far East. It includes reports on the air situation from Air Marshal Park, who has remained behind to prepare a situation report on the air defence of Ceylon for Admiral Cunningham.

Slim, Blamey and Wavell discuss the report, which is scathing in many areas of what has been going on. Blamey in particular is shocked, the situation, though obviously not perfect, had been reported as being far better than seems to be the case. The current plans assume a pre-war invasion of Thailand, which all three men consider to be politically impossible, and there are insufficient men, poorly trained, and no tanks. The air situation is nearly as bad; following the Dowding report of last year, a number of modern squadrons of fighters have been deployed by the RAAF. However there are few modern planes apart from these, and a shortage of all other types, as well as AA guns.

Wavell and Blamey will shortly go to London to discuss further operations in the Middle East, and Blamey intends to show the report to Menzies. The report does point out that the situation is not irretrievable, but that prompt action needs to be taken in a number of areas. As the Middle East is looking far more stable, they see no reason why the resources cannot be made available; if the Japanese scare comes to nothing, the force can quickly be brought back into the Mediterranean theatre. Indeed it would be in some respects easier to pull trained men from Southeast Asia to North Africa, especially if (as may be the case if such a need came to pass) the Mediterranean became too dangerous for direct convoys.

16th July

A production line for the new Mosquito light bomber is being set up in Canada, although the first production versions are still be waited on in Britain. The trials of the prototype have proved very impressive, and in view of the different techniques required to manufacture the bomber, the Ministry of Aircraft Production feels that an early start will be beneficial.

The bombing campaign against the U-boat pens being built in Germany and France is intensified. The targets are easy to find, helping the still-poor RAF navigation, and it is hoped to do as much damage to any U-boats present and to the pens before they are completed. Intelligence has shown that once the pens are complete they will be immune to all current or planned RAF bombs, and investigation is started on if it will be possible to destroy them; since it is obvious any bomb will have to be heavy and ideally dropped from altitude to aid the penetration, the new high altitude bomber is the suggested delivery system.

In the Führer's headquarters, the German leaders plan how Soviet territory is to be divided after the final victory. All the resources are to go to Germany. The Ukraine and Crimean peninsula is to be German. Finland can have East Karelia, but the Kola Peninsula is for Germany. Hitler also orders that the preparations for the annexation of Finland into Greater Germany should be started in utmost secrecy. Alfred Rosenberg is appointed to the post of Reich minister of the occupied territories following a conference at Angersburg; he will be responsible for the exploitation of subject Soviet peoples and the elimination of Jews and Communists.

Prince Konoye resigns as Japanese Prime Minister. The Foreign Minister, Matsuoka, has been advocating joining Germany in the attack against the USSR; he will not be in the cabinet when it is reformed on the 18th, being replaced by Vice Admiral Chyoda Teifiro.

19th July

Churchill has decided to send the Russians high-level secret intelligence based on Enigma decoding. The Russians will not, however, be told that Britain has cracked the Enigma secret, for the Soviet Union's own codes are being read by the Germans. Instead, the "sanitized" messages are being disguised under the cover of "a well-placed source in Berlin" and passed on through the military mission in Moscow.

In the Mediterranean, General Montgomery is preparing for the first of a series of amphibious landings in the Dodecanese islands. At the moment there are shortages of landing craft and aircraft, and he considers the training of the bulk of his troops quite inadequate for the task. The first landings will be based around the Commando units, already better trained for such work, on small targets, while an intensive training program continues. As more landing craft become available, tougher islands will be targeted. He has also asked Cunningham for a skilled naval assistant (as while the current targets are small, it is obvious that at some point a large and far more complex landing will be needed), and Cunningham has suggested Admiral Ramsey, who planned Dynamo and is now at Dover, which is steadily becoming a less important command.

The Germans are continuing their thrust towards Leningrad in the face of increasing Russian resistance. There was heavy fighting yesterday near Lake Peipus where the German infantry has still not been able to break through in support of its advance tank units. Leningrad is now under attack from three directions: the Finns are approaching from the north and north-east, on both sides of Lake Ladoga, while the Germans are attacking through Estonia and the Luftwaffe are mounting heavy raids on the city and on the rail link with Moscow.

Guderian is ordered to move south and join the Kiev battle after the action at Smolensk is complete. He objects strongly that he should continue towards Moscow, but is overruled by Hitler.

Chapter 17 - Preparation in the East

20th July

Generals Wavell, Blamey and O'Connor arrive in London for discussions on the future of operations in the Mediterranean and the Far East. While the plans for operations in the Mediterranean are not contentious, and the situation for the next six months seen as readily achievable, there is far more concern about the Far East.

Blamey has discussed the Slim-Park report with Menzies, who is seriously upset. It seems like little that was planned had been done, and there are many issues to be addressed. Blamey agrees, but points out that Wavell feels that the situation is by no means irremediable, and that the recent successes in the Mediterranean theatre will allow much to be done. The discussions go on for some days. Churchill is reluctant to send too much East, however it is pointed out that after all, he's happy to send equipment to Russia, who was an enemy up until a few weeks ago. Menzies also points out that early and substantial forces being sent east, with more to follow, would be very beneficial to the Australian political issues and encourage Australia to do more to help the war effort.

The argument is decided by the views of the Chiefs of Staff, who surprisingly are in favour, particularly the RN and Army. Their arguments are as follows.

The actions possible in the Mediterranean by the Army are currently limited by the availability of landing craft and associated ships. A large scale operation is impossible before next spring due to the available numbers. So the troops can only be used in small numbers. Eighth Army is more than large enough at the present to cover contingencies, as anything more than a raid on North Africa is well beyond the Axis at present. While the situation in Russia may change and allow Germany to bring more pressure on the Middle East, this isn't going to happen suddenly, and with the action in Ethiopia basically over they have troops there available to be redeployed. The Army therefore suggests that I Australia Corps be sent to Malaya, and the armoured brigade enlarged to a full division (as already planned). There are already two divisions in Malaya, although they both require considerable training. An additional British division would be useful, and politically important to show Britain was defending with its own men, not just Imperial troops.

In Burma, at least one and preferably two more divisions are needed, as well as more armour. They suggest a good Indian division and one of the two African divisions soon to be available in East Africa. Again, the existing troops are in need of training, and sending experienced formations allows them to be given the intensive training they require.

The Navy is actually all in favour of sending carriers at least to the Far East. This is partly due to their current shortage of pilots, which they expect to weaken their air groups for some 4-6 months, due to the intensive effort they have put into Mediterranean operations. Deploying 2-3 carriers to Ceylon will allow them to use them to train up new air groups to full efficiency in a relatively safe area. The remaining four fleet carriers will allow one to be in refit, one in the Western Med, able to cover the Atlantic at short notice if required, and two in the Mediterranean fleet for operations against Italy and in support of the Dodecanese operations. It would be easy to move one of these east if necessary. As to battleships, they have no need of more in the Med, and moving 3-4 east again allows them to be worked up in quiet. They point out that if anything happens it is easy for them to pull these ships back into the Med, and indeed the same applies to the Army divisions.

The RAF is more reluctant to send too much east, as it is still foreseeing a heavy commitment in the North Sea and the Mediterranean, as well as increasing raids over Germany. The Australian production will not really start to feed in until the end of the year. The Dowding report did recommend a higher commitment, and so do the defence plan for the area. They agree they can spare some squadrons of Sparrowhawks and Beaufighters until the Australian production line comes on stream, but they dig in their heels over Wellingtons. The Navy wants more air assets for use at sea, given the strength of Japanese air power; they offer to supply three squadrons of Cormorants and three of SeaLance (including some radar planes), although they will need to borrow RAF pilots. They suggest more Hudsons can be acquired from the USA, and a reconnaissance squadron would be most useful in the area. Again, these squadrons can be relocated to the Middle East in case of emergency,

The final needs are for improvements in support. Air Marshal Park has already pointed out that the radar and air defence organisation in both Malaya and Burma are quite inadequate and will lead to misuse and inefficiency. There are also Naval issues, as now the Japanese are much closer to Singapore they wish to use it only as a forward base, making Ceylon their main centre of operations. They would also like at least one northern Australian port improved as a base for submarine operations.

Menzies is delighted with the suggestions, and points out that this will allow him to go home and point out the success of his working with Britain - he is sure he will be able to use this to get Australia to also increase her forces available to defend the area.

It is agreed that the Chiefs of Staffs recommendations be accepted (subject to material limitations), and arrangements will be made to move I Australian Corps east as soon as shipping is available. The Navy will look at deploying the battleships and carriers as soon as they can get them ready (they wish to do a minor refit on some of the ships before they leave), but submit that the first heavy ships will be on their way before the end of August.

RAF squadrons can be deployed all the way by air now that North Africa is cleared (although fighters may still need to be shipped as far as Gibraltar). One of the points Parks made was inadequate support and maintenance for the RAF and as a start a base in eastern India will be prepared to be the end point of the air route, before the planes are deployed to active squadrons. The RAAF Beaufighter squadron in the Med will be sent out as soon as a replacement squadron can be supplied from Britain, and the new Mediterranean convoy route will make the supply of stores and equipment far easier.

In reality it will take longer than estimated to get the formations and their support in place, but it is seen as important to have the process underway; Menzies because of the political bonus it will give him, the British because they are hoping that the scale of the force will make the Japanese think twice about any offensive action. Unfortunately they do not realise that due to the oil and resource squeeze forced on Japan by the USA, the Japanese decisions have already been made, and it is too late for British action to change them.

24th July

The Japanese government presented an ultimatum (decided in the Japanese Imperial Conference on July 2) to the Vichy government of French Indo-China on the 19th, demanding bases in southern Indochina. They conceded today, and the Japanese will begin to occupy these bases on the 28th. This is viewed with great concern in Britain and Australia, as this will move Japanese aircraft into much closer range of Malaya and Borneo. The action is also denounced by the American government. It does however remove much of the remaining opposition to deploying more forces to the Far East.

25th July

In response to the Japanese takeover of French Indo-China, the British government announces that 'considerable' Imperial forces will be sent to SE Asia over the next months.

With the Grand Harbour at Malta unusually full with merchant ships from a newly-arrived convoy, high-speed Italian motor boats, their bow packed with high explosive, made a reckless attack at night. Fifteen Italians died when their MTL's came under fire from harbour defences manned by the Royal Malta Artillery. The attack had been planned for months.

One group of "frogmen" would blow up a hindrance net suspended from a bridge to all the MTLs access to the harbour. The MTL pilots would race down the harbour and aim their exploding boats at ships before diving over their sterns. The plan almost worked, except that one of the Italians, Major Tesei, blew up the bridge and himself, blocking access to the MTLs, which found themselves helpless under the guns and floodlit by harbour searchlights.

This attack will be followed tomorrow night by Italian E-boats, who make an attempt to penetrate Grand Harbour and Marsamxett and destroy ships in harbour and the submarine base at Manoel Island. What the Italians do not realise is that the harbour is covered by radar, and the boats are engaged by guns from St Elmo and Ricasoli. The force is wiped out, with eighteen Italians being taken prisoner.

The US War and Naval Departments send a message to the Pacific commanders advising them that the President was going to close the Panama Canal to Japanese shipping and would freeze all Japanese assets in the US, and those of banks situated in Japanese occupied China. The commanders were advised to "guard against possible eventualities".

The British cruiser HMS Newcastle intercepts the German ship 'Erlangen' in the South Atlantic, which leads to the ship scuttling herself.

26th July

President Roosevelt incorporates the armed forces of the Philippines into the US Army and sends General MacArthur to take up the command of US forces in the Far East. MacArthur says that he is confident that the Philippines can be defended if war should spread to the Far East. The Army of the Commonwealth of the Philippines is called into Federal service.

MacArthur will continue as military advisor to the Philippine President. Upon learning of the mobilization of the Philippine National Army, he requests payment of the stipend of $50 per soldier serving in the Philippine National Army. This was provided for in his contract with the Commonwealth Government and had been approved by both Secretary of War Dern and the President in 1936. A number of other US Army officers had similar arrangements with the Commonwealth but one of them, Dwight Eisenhower, declined to accept his payment.

Soviet forces in and around Smolensk are cut off by the German pincer movement.

HMS Hood arrives in the US for a full refit. While the damage she suffered in the Bismark action has been fixed, the damage to her machinery and her general state means she is badly in need of a full refit, and dockyard space is not available in the

UK. She will receive a general update and new machinery. It is hoped she will be ready in a year.

28th July

The crisis in the Far East worsened today when 30,000 Japanese troops entered French Indochina. The build-up includes elements of the Japanese navy, which have sailed into Camranh Bay and aircraft which are flying into Saigon. Japanese troops have also begun disembarking in Cambodia where 8,000 men will be within striking range of Siam.

Malaya is now seriously threatened from Indo-china, which is providing the Japanese with a naval base within 750-miles of Singapore and airfields within 300 miles of northern Malaya. The Japanese move has isolated the Philippines and menaces the oil-rich Dutch East Indies.

The Vichy regime has given the Japanese a free hand in Indochina on the pretext that it was threatened by British and Gaullist plots. The fact that the Vichy regime no longer exists as a functioning government in France seems to have passed them by.

The USN forms its first experimental A/S group to be formed around a carrier. This will be escorting ships in the US section of the Atlantic, and is centred around the USS Ranger. The USA is building a number of escort carriers and merchant conversions for the UK, and has started to build additional ships for its own use. In addition to the escort duties the RN is using them for, the USN is interested in using an escort carrier for the transportation of planes. This would free up its fleet carriers for offensive uses, although they want the ships to ideally be faster and with a longer range for use in the Pacific. In the mean time, the Ranger will allow them to practice their own version of the RN escort tactics, which have been proving increasingly successful at keeping the U-boat packs away and shooting down long range reconnaissance planes.

30th July

Russia and the Polish government in exile signed a treaty of friendship in London today. The first result of the treaty will be the formation of a Polish army from prisoners of war held in Russia. Roosevelt's advisor Harry Hopkins arrives in Moscow to discuss ways to help the Soviet war effort.

Rolls-Royce has converted a Spitfire to use the new supercharged Merlin 60 engine. This has dramatically improved the high altitude performance. With the Gloster Sea Eagle due to come into service soon, the RAF has been putting pressure on the aircraft companies to improve Spitfire performance. It is hoped to have the new Mk8 with the new engine in production by the end of the year. A version of the Spitfire with the Griffon engine is expected to fly at the beginning of September, although the change to the much bigger engine means a longer development time is to be expected; it is intended that this aircraft will be the successor to the Mk8

2nd Aug

German forces attack Staraya Russa, south of Lake Ilmen, in their drive toward Leningrad.

US Lend-Lease aid begins for the Soviet Union, while the first Packard built Rolls Royce Merlin V-1650 aircraft engine is completed

The Royal Navy completes its assessment of shipping losses in July, and is quietly optimistic. Losses during the first six months of the year were running at over 400,000 tons of shipping in some months, but the losses have been steadily decreasing as the new escort carriers become available and more escorts allow proper escort groups to be formed. Escort groups are now formed on a long-term basis and practice as a group, and the combination is making losses drop steadily, although they are still concerned at what they see as the low level of U-boat sinkings. The biggest improvement has come from the decryption of the U-boat codes and the increasing use of HF/DF to locate U-boat packs, allowing evasive routing to slip through the searching submarines. This has been aided by using the carrier planes to keep U-boats closer to the evasive route down and allow the convoy to get through the gaps. The losses in July were around 90,000 tons. Losses need to be kept to under 200,000 tons a month to keep under the amount of new merchant ship construction in the Empire.

Centimetric radar is increasingly in use on the escorts, and its being fitted as fast as possible. It is also being fitted on the aircraft; the biggest limitation at the moment is the supply of radars. The new Leigh Light is just starting in operation, and the use of these even with the older metric radar on the Stirlings has sunk a number of U-boats. With the promise of the new Mediterranean route being open soon, the outlook for shipping resources is looking more promising. The new route will allow the ships supplying war equipment to return with full cargoes, and reducing the use of the Cape route will allow a good million tons of shipping to be reallocated. The southern route will also result in less shipping damage during the winter months. The one drawback is that the heavier use of this route will mean more air protection will be needed against Luftwaffe attacks from France, and it is seen as a necessity for these convoys to be covered by a carrier at least until range of Gibraltar.

A squadron of B-17's is delivered to the French in Algeria. This shipment has been redesignated as lend-lease as the USAAF want to see how the aircraft performs in actual combat. In addition to the planes there are a number of servicemen who speak French with a rather pronounced American accent.

New commands are put in place for Burma and Malaya, although the timing and composition of the additional forces are still secret.

British Far Eastern Fleet - Admiral Somerville
CinC India/Far East - General Auchinleck
CinC Burma General Cunningham
I Burma Corps
        1 Burma Inf. Division (in place)
        17 Indian Inf. Division (in place)
        7th Armoured Brigade (in place)
II Burma Corps
        12 African Division (arrives Nov 41)
        4 Indian Division (arrives Nov 41)
CinC Malaya General Alexander,   CoS Gen. Percival
I Australian Corps - General Blamey
        7th Australian Div (arrives Sep 41)
        9th Australian Div (arrives Oct 41)
        1 Armoured Division (arrives Sep-Oct 41)
III Indian Corps - General Heath
        9th Indian Div (in place)
        11th Indian Div. (in place)
        18th British Division (arrives Dec 1941)

RAF Burma - tbd, until then RAF Burma will come under RAF Malaya command.
RAF Malaya - AirMarshal Park
After considering his report, General Slim is promoted so he can take over one of the Indian divisions in Burma. It is emphasized to both the existing commanders and the new ones that training is seen as most important, this being one of the greatest deficiencies listed in the report. While the addition of some experienced and well-trained formations will help, the units already in place need to be brought up to standard.

5th Aug

The Germans have wiped out the "Smolensk Pocket", destroying the Russian Sixteenth and Twentieth Armies and capturing 300,000 Russian soldiers, 3,200 tanks and 3,100 guns. It is a shattering defeat for the Red Army. Smolensk itself, the "gateway to Moscow", fell on 16 July and the Russian forces east of the city were surrounded.

HMS Implacable leaves New York (after a goodwill visit) to return home after having her bomb damage repaired in the USA. She will receive an updated radar fit and then sail with a new airgroup for Trincomalee in Ceylon. She will be accompanied by HMS Prince of Wales and a number of destroyers.

The first successful sortie of a Mosquito reconnaissance plane flies a mission over French coastal ports. Intercepted by three Me109 fighters, it easily outpaced them. The Mosquito is being developed primarily as a bomber, but it is also to be used in small numbers as a long-ranged reconnaissance plane to supplement the Whirlwind, which is now being trialled for use as a long-range fighter.

9th August

The first British landings in the Dodecanese islands start. The men used are the Commandoes of Leyforce, covered by aircraft using the rebuilt Cretan airfields, although a carrier is stationed south of Crete in case additional support is needed.

The first islands chosen as targets are Kasos and Karpathos, as these are close to Crete and air cover. Both only have small Italian garrisons, and they are seen as a trial before the larger and better-fortified islands of Kos and Rhodes are assaulted. The force for Kasos is Leyforce, around 1,500 commandos, supplemented by 10 tanks. At the same time 1,200 men of the 4th Indian division, again supported by a small number of tanks, assaulted the small island of Karpathos. These forces were the maximum that could be used with the available shipping capability.

Both attacks went satisfactorily, although there were a number of problems caused by the troops lack of experience at assault landings. There was also a considerable amount of air support given to the defenders by the Italian air force operating from Rhodes. Indeed, without the RAF bases on Crete it was not certain if the landings could have been sustained, as even with fighter cover a number of landing craft and two coasters were sunk. However resistance on the islands themselves was light, and although some of the Italian troops fought well they were outnumbered and outmatched by the invaders.

As a result of these landings, further assaults were planned for September, once the lessons learn from the first two had been incorporated.

The battleship HMS Prince of Wales, with Prime Minister Churchill aboard, arrives at Placentia Bay with a destroyer escort. Churchill is here to meet with the U.S. President who arrived in the heavy cruiser USS Augusta two days ago. Churchill calls on Roosevelt on board USS Augusta and the two confer over lunch and dinner. This conference will result in the Atlantic Charter; a statement of principles governing the policies of Britain and America. The conference will last for four days.

The Australian Prime Minister, Menzies, is back in Australia. The Australian government and people are increasingly anxious about the Japanese, especially with the bulk of their men in the Middle East. Menzies has been criticised in particular by the Labor party (who have refused to join a wartime coalition, preferring to play party politics instead). Menzies has a good hand to play, however. With agreement from Britain, he announces that I Australian Corps, under the command of General Blamey, and including a British Armoured Division, will be sailing for Malaya later this month. Additional British and Empire forces will follow. He also announces that the battleships Warspite and Queen Elizabeth will soon be based in Ceylon, and they will be joined by additional ships, as well as Australia's cruisers which have been aiding the Royal Navy. This announcement - of considerably greater force than anyone had expected - is used by Menzies to justify his time spent in the UK, and shows that the Empire is indeed prepared to help Australia now that she also is threatened. He asks that Australia prepares additional forces herself to back up the Imperial forces. The whole presentation has rather derailed the Labor party and Menzies political opponents. By previous agreement, he does not mention the submarine force that is planned for deployment.

Britain and the USSR promise to go to the assistance of Turkey in the event of an attack by any European power. In identical statements presented to the Turkish foreign office by their ambassadors, the two Allies have also pledged themselves to "observe the territorial integrity of the Turkish republic."

The statements are seen as counters to German propaganda that Russia would take advantage of Turkey and invade should the latter enter the war.

A raid by 24 Wellington bombers on Monchen-Gladbach is the first to use the new experimental Gee system for radiolocation. The results are said to be 'encouraging'. Further tests will follow and it is hoped to have the system in production for the much larger bombing raids planned early next year when the new Lancaster bomber will be added to the increasing Halifax force.

12th Aug

The Free French offer the fast battleship Richelieu as part of the naval deployment to the Far East. They wish to show they are part of it, especially as they consider French Indo-China to be occupied territory no matter what the French government claim. The offer is accepted by the RN; she will act with the fast battleship squadron planned for the area.

In a supplement to his war directive no. 34, Hitler orders increased efforts by Army Group North to capture Leningrad and a new offensive by Army Group South to take Kharkov, the Donets Industrial Basin and the Crimea, suspending military activity by Army Group Centre in the central front around Moscow. Instead it is to aid the other Army Groups in achieving their objectives.

Production of the Canadian Grizzly tank starts. This will mount the British 6-pdr as standard, as O'Connor has stated that a reasonable HE shell capability is a specific requirement of any new tank. The tank is almost as heavily armoured as a Matilda, with superior speed and reliability, and with the 6pdr gun much superior firepower. Tests against German tanks in the desert have indicated it should be better than the current German tanks. The design has already started in production in the USA for the Free French, although the first batch will use the 2-pdr gun. Negotiations are taking place to produce the British 6-pdr under license for the French if the British production is insufficient.

A new version of the Valentine is put into production, which will incorporate the turret from the Grizzly. This is seen as an intermediate design until the new Churchill tank is ready. As there are, for the moment, sufficient tanks in North Africa for the perceived threat, the time is being used to work on the defects of the tank. This tank will also mount the Grizzly turret and 6-pdr, but will not be available until the defects are fixed. The current Valentine, with the 2-pdr, is still being manufactured for use in the Far East and to supply to Russia. Given the light armour of the Japanese tanks, the 2-pdr is seen as adequate.

A new cruiser tank has been in development for some time. This was specified with 75mm of armour and a large turret ring to take a bigger gun. The Cromwell tank will be available soon, but the biggest problem is lack of a suitable engine. It has been decided that the Mk1 will use the American engine as used in the Grizzly, with a turret mounting a 6-pdr. O'Connor would prefer heavier armour, and a new version is under development which will use a de-rated version of the Rolls-Royce Merlin engine, the Meteor. The extra power will allow thicker armour, and a new turret based on, but larger that, that used on the Grizzly will allow a gun of up to 75mm to be mounted. While the 6-pdr is currently adequate, now it is in production its successor needs to be considered, and a prototype 17-pdr gun is under development.

14th Aug

Evacuation of the Russian Black Sea naval base at Nikolayev begins. During the next three nights thirteen ships under construction will be towed away. Eleven remaining ships, including a battleship, will be blown up along with other supplies

Britain and the USSR protest to Iran about the large number of German "tourists" in Iran.

15th Aug

HMS Warspite and her escorting destroyers set sail for Ceylon. The ship will refuel there, and will then make a visit to Sydney and some other Australian cities before returning to Ceylon for exercises.

The first production Gloster Sea Eagle naval fighter is delivered. This plane, built around the Centaurus engine, is much more powerful and faster than the Goshawk. It is also capable of carrying some 2,000lb of bombs, thus able to act almost as a bomber in many circumstances. The first carrier to be equipped will be HMS Bulwark, due to commission in September. The other new naval plane, the Fairy Spearfish TBR, is expected next month. It also employs the Centaurus engine.

19th Aug

A joint Anglo-Canadian-Norwegian expedition lands on Spitzbergen to sabotage the coal mines and bring the miners back to Britain.

The Wake Detachment, 1st Marine defence Battalion, arrives in the cargo ship USS Regulus to begin work on defensive positions.

The first convoy leaves Iceland for the USSR. It includes the carrier HMS Colossus who is ferrying Hurricanes to Russia.

Hitler rejects proposals from General Franz Halder, the chief of staff, and Field Marshal Walter von Brauchitsch, the army C-in-C, for an attack on Moscow. Hitler also authorizes the development of the V-2 rocket

21st August

Hitler orders the investment, not capture, of Leningrad, and the transfer of several divisions from the North and Centre to capture the Crimea and the Donets Basin, an industrial region vital to the Soviet war effort. Hitler has been unimpressed by the arguments of General Guderian that Moscow should be the priority target.

In a ceremony at Rosyth HMS Theseus is formally renamed HMAS Brisbane. She will transfer to the Australian navy, heading out to the Far East once her new crew have worked up. HMS Eagle will return to Britain for a much-needed refit before being redeployed with the Atlantic convoys.

6th Sep

In Washington, the Japanese Ambassador Nomura hands Secretary of State Cordell Hull a draft proposal outlining what the U.S. and Japan will do to establish peace in the Pacific. Two of the items that the Japanese purpose to undertake are that Japan will not make any military advancement from French Indo-China against any of its adjoining areas, and likewise will not, without any justifiable reason, resort to military action against any regions lying south of Japan. Japan will endeavour to bring about the rehabilitation of general and normal relationship between Japan and China, upon the realization of which Japan is ready to withdraw its armed forces from China as soon as possible in accordance with the agreements between Japan and China.

Cadre from I Aus Corps and its divisional commands arrive in Singapore to prepare for the troop deployment. The first large troop convoy is expected in a few weeks, carrying the 7th Australian Division. Blamey and his senior officers and NCO's are not at all impressed by what they see of the troops already in place, and discussions are started immediately with General Alexander as to ways of bringing them up to what the experienced Australians think is a suitable standard.

8th Sep

HMS Warspite arrives in Trincomalee. She will be joined shortly by the cruisers HMAS Australia and HMAS Sydney, and then sail for Australia.

11th Sep

In a broadcast to the nation, President Roosevelt issues a "Shoot on Sight" order to naval forces in the Atlantic in regard to German U-Boats. This action is partly in response to the USS Greer incident of September 4th. In fact, it is more or less what is going on at the present. He describes the attack last week on the Greer as "piracy, legally and morally." He said that the outposts the USA has established in Iceland, Greenland, Labrador and Newfoundland would protect Atlantic shipping of all nations. He stressed that the US Navy only provides "invincible protection" if Britain's Royal Navy survived.

The president emphasized the difficulty of defending ships from torpedoes fired from submarines; "When you see a rattlesnake poised to strike, you do wait until he has struck before you crush him, these Nazi submarines and raiders are the rattlesnakes of the Atlantic - they are a menace to the free pathways of the high seas."

Admiral Stark advises Admiral Hart that Washington had declined to endorse Allied mobilization plans proposed by the British for joint operations in the event of war. Hart is ordered to defer plans to move the Asiatic Fleet to Dutch or British ports when hostilities began. Hart was ordered to ensure his fleet operations were "co-ordinated" with British and Dutch operations, although it is not made clear how this is to be done.

In Britain, the prototype Airspeed Horsa troop-carrying glider is flown. It has a crew of two pilots and can carry 20-25 troops. The failure of Operation Mercury has made the British more dubious about the viability of large-scale airborne attacks, but they see small-scale assaults on specific targets as being useful.

12th Sep

The 2nd and 3rd Panzer Armies join up near Rovno, completing the encirclement of Kiev and a pocket of 600,000 Soviet soldiers to the east of the city. However as they do the first snows of winter fall - General Winter has arrived early to help Russia.

The Free French air force try out their new B-17's for the first time, in a raid from bases in North Africa on Italy's royal arsenal at Turin. At the same time, the RAF strikes Messina and Palermo in Sicily, hitting merchant ships, oil tanks and a power station.

While it is not expected to match some of the other routes, supplies are starting to be shipped from Alexandria to Russia via the Black sea, using Russian coastal shipping. Turkey, keen to be seen to be neutral to both sides (both of whom are heavily armed and worryingly close to her) has allowed use of the Bosphorus for unarmed merchant ships. The small ships hug the coast as much as possible, hoping to evade the attention of the Germans, whose air force is at the moment rather busy supporting the army operations.

Two squadrons of Beaufighters (one RAF, one RAAF) arrive in Malaya from the Middle East. It is hoped that it will be possible to send more in a few months, but in the meantime they are waiting on the convoy carrying their support and equipment. The planes have flown in via India, where a new base is being fitted out in East India to handle and maintain aircraft in transit.

HMS Implacable, HMS Prince of Wales and four escort destroyers sail for Trincomalee via the Cape. Implacable carries the new Sea Eagle, but is still equipped with SeaLance TBR - her squadron of Spearfish will set out in a couple of weeks to meet her there, and the SeaLance will then go on to Malaya as a land-based anti-shipping force. The carrier also carries an additional 18 Cormorant divebombers which will be flown off to Gibraltar to make their own way to Malaya.

16th Sep

The last of the 'Formidable' class carriers, HMS Bulwark, enters commission. She will be the first RN carrier to carry both the Sea Eagle and the Spearfish planes, and her squadrons will embark with these next month once she is ready to deploy. It is intended for her and HMS Implacable to then join up in Ceylon where they will work up with the new aircraft. It is also hoped to send the squadron on a visit to Australia for propaganda purposes.

24th Sep

The first German U-Boat passes Gibraltar into the Mediterranean. Over the next two weeks six more U-Boats will pass into the Mediterranean. The German Submarine Force will later have about 50% of its active submarine force engaged in the Mediterranean, which is viewed by U-boat command as a major strategic error in taking the pressure off the vital Atlantic convoys to Britain.

The first 'Liberty Ship' is launched in the USA at Baltimore. The British government is becoming a little more hopeful about the Battle of the Atlantic. Sinkings in the first 6 months of the year averaged some 300,000tons a month. Since July, it has been under 100,000. The shipbuilding capacity of the Empire is somewhat more than 2,000,000 tons, so if the sinkings can be kept at the current level, and ships start to arrive in numbers from the USA, there is cause for some careful optimism. The new frigates will start to come into service in the New Year, and new weapons and asdic will soon be available for them.

Soviet forces in the Crimea have now been isolated by the German Army. Hitler orders all direct attacks on Leningrad to be stopped - the city will be besieged and starved out.

General Marshall requests Admiral Stark delay converting three freighters into escort carriers in order to increase the shipping lift for the reinforcements being sent to the Philippines.

29th Sep

Convoy PQ-1 leaves Iceland bound for Archangel with ten merchant ships, escorted only by one cruiser and two destroyers. There are no German attacks on the convoy, which reaches Archangel on October 11th. At the same time Convoy QP-1 leaves Archangel headed for Scapa Flow.

Hitler orders that Leningrad be wiped off the face of the earth and its population exterminated.

The troop convoy carrying 7th Australian division arrives at Singapore. The division is hoped to be operational soon, as the threat is increasing and the division has to work out how to fight effectively in terrain far different than the desert.

The first production Lancaster bomber makes its first flight. New tactics are being developed to attack German targets using the large bomb bay of the plane for heavier bombs to supplement those carried by the Halifax.

HMS Warspite, HMAS Australia and HMAS Sydney arrive in Sydney for a propaganda visit. They will remain in Australia for two weeks, visiting a number of ports filled with enthusiastic crowds before heading to Singapore. The first squadron of Cormorant divebombers arrives in Malaya, flown by RAF pilots.

2nd Oct

An Anglo-American mission led by Lord Beaverbrook has agreed to boost military aid to Russia next year. The USA will allocate 1,200 tanks a month to Britain and the USSR between July 1942 and January 1943, and a further 2,000 tanks a month for the following six months. This will mean initial US consignments of 400 tanks a month for the Soviets from 1 July. In addition the USA will send 3,600 aircraft to Russia between 1 July 1942 and 1 July 1943, over and above the planes already being sent by Britain. The Soviets in return will supply Britain and the USA with urgently needed raw materials.

The German attack on Moscow, Operation Typhoon, begins. 3rd and 4th Panzer Groups and the 4th, 2nd and 9th Armies join Guderian's forces which started their attack two days ago. This is the "last, great decisive battle of the war", according to a communiqué by Hitler to his troops, and today's attack makes rapid progress.

A national coalition government is finally formed in Australia. The leader of the Labor party, John Curtin, will become deputy Prime Minister. There has been considerable controversy over the last months, with the Labor party in particular wanting a greater emphasis on the threat from Japan. Menzies has used his speech to emphasize the substantial forces Britain is sending to the Far East to help protect Australia (and the arrival of 7th Australian at Singapore only days ago has not hurt his cause), and this has swayed a number of MP's who had been critical of what they had seen as a lack of support from Britain. As a result, although it will be far more fractious than its British equivalent, just enough support has been found to form a national government, although observers are worried that a war with Japan will strain it if defeats or setbacks occur.

5th Oct

Brereton is briefed by Marshall, Gerow, Arnold, and Spaatz about the situation in the Philippines. Brereton stated "in the event of war it was almost certain to incur destruction of a bomber force put in the Philippine Islands without providing adequate antiaircraft defence"; Marshall responded that he and Arnold were taking a "calculated risk". Brereton is worried that the lessons learned in Europe were being completely ignored in placing heavy bombers in the islands without adequate protection.

HMS Implacable and HMS Prince of Wales arrive at Trincomalee, where the carrier will conduct extensive working up of her airgroup and their new fighters. Eighteen of the carriers SeaLance will go on to Singapore, the carrier will retain twelve for

A/S and reconnaissance duties; eighteen of the new Spearfish will arrive next week having flown from Britain. Two squadrons of Goshawk fighters arrive in Malaya. They will be based at Singapore for defence of the naval base and as replacements for the carriers if needed.

12th Oct

Kaluga falls to the German forces advancing on Moscow. The worsening weather has caused problems with the advance, but has not been able to stop it. Today civilians start to be evacuated from Moscow.

14th Oct

British and French forces land on the island of Rhodes. Unlike their earlier attacks on smaller islands in the Dodecanese, Rhodes is both fortified and has a garrison of nearly 8,000 men. Every available landing craft is used in the operation, the initial attack being made by a brigade of the 6th Australian Division and a brigade of the French Foreign Legion, led by the commandoes of Leyforce. The initial landings are backed up by a British brigade and the 1st Polish brigade, and includes some 40 tanks.

The landings go as well as expected - although there were a number of problems, the experienced troops managed to overcome these, and the defenders were slowly pushed back in a series of actions. Air cover from the RAF on Crete stopped any serious interference from the Italian air force, although a number of RAF fighters were lost; for the first time the Italians were using the MC.202 fighter in numbers. This fighter was much superior in performance to earlier Italian designs, but still suffered from a light armament. The landing forces were also supported by two RN cruisers and the battleship Valiant, whose 15" shells cause a number of Italian positions to surrender.

The subdual of the islands defences takes some three days. The Italian navy does try to intervene - on the night of the second day a force of one light cruiser and two destroyers attempt to intercept the ships containing the second wave of troops in a night action. This proves unsuccessful as they run into the radar-equipped HMS Valiant and her escorting ships. The Italian cruiser was sunk, despite a desperate but unsuccessful torpedo attack by two of the destroyers, one of which was sunk in the action.

This was by far the biggest amphibious assault tried by the British, and like the earlier, smaller ones showed a number of new problems and shortcomings that needed to be addressed. Rhodes would be garrisoned by a reinforced brigade and the Italian airfields used to allow the RAF to dominate the skies over the Dodecanese.

Chapter 18 - The Road to Pearl Harbor

16th Oct

In Washington the Chief of Naval Operations sends the following message to the fleet commanders: "The resignation of the Japanese Cabinet has created a grave situation X If a new Cabinet is formed it will probably be strongly nationalistic and anti American X If the Konoye Cabinet remains the effect will be that it will operate under a new mandate which will not include rapprochement with the US X In either case hostilities between Japan and Russia are a strong possibility X Since the US and Britain are held responsible by Japan for her present desperate situation there is also a possibility that Japan may attack these two powers X In view of these possibilities you will take due precautions including such preparatory deployments as will not disclose strategic intention nor constitute provocative actions against Japan X Second and third addressees (in the Pacific) inform appropriate Army and Naval district authorities X Acknowledge XX"

18th Oct

Richard Sorge, one of the most successful spies in the history of espionage is arrested in Tokyo. The son of a German engineer and a Russian mother, he was brought up in Germany, joined the Communist Party, and became a Soviet agent in 1928, serving in America, China and Japan under journalistic cover. He then got permission to go back to Germany and become a member of the Nazi Party. He returned to Tokyo as correspondent for a Frankfurt newspaper. His greatest service to the Soviet cause was also his last. Just three days ago he was able to tell Moscow that the Japanese have no intention of attacking Russia. This means that Russia will be able to transfer divisions from Siberia to defend Moscow.

Japan's deadlocked political crisis has ended with the appointment of the army strongman General Hideki Tojo, aged 57, as the new prime minister in the wake of the Konoye cabinet's resignation. General Tojo retains his portfolio as war minister. It is the first time that Japan has had a serving general as prime minister. One of his first actions has been to extend the deadline for diplomacy to prevent war with the United States until 25 November. This overturns the decision of the last imperial conference, calling for a decision on war or peace with the US no later than 15 October, which divided the Konoye cabinet and precipitated its resignation. General Tojo insisted on being given a "clean slate" on this issue before accepting his appointment from the Emperor.

HMAS Brisbane arrives at Brisbane to a tumultuous civic reception. She will remain for a week, then she will join her sister carrier Melbourne at Singapore.

The French battleship Richeleau accompanied by two cruisers sail from Oran, headed for Gibraltar. There they will join HMS Bulwark and HMS Anson and go on to Ceylon, where she will join in exercises with the forming British Far Eastern Fleet before heading to Singapore.

The first two full RAAF Sparrowhawk squadrons arrive in Malaya. While flights of the aircraft have been based here for exercises and to test how the aircraft performs in the tropical environment, these are the first active squadrons to be based there

20th Oct

"Regarding the Japanese Air Force, which many people, he said, were inclined to discount as a second-rate body equipped with obsolete aircraft and lacking skilful and daring pilots, Air Vice-Marshal Pulford said that he certainly does not underrate its capacity. When it was suggested to him that it might be compared with the Italian Air Force, he pointed out how completely the RAF gained the mastery of the skies of the Middle East even when the Italians possessed great numerical superiority. He thinks that what the RAF has done in the Middle East it could certainly do in the Far East against the Japanese. One of the best Japanese fighters is the 'O' naval fighter, but the Sparrowhawks at present with the RAF in Malaya and Burma would have no difficulty in dealing with them.

The Japanese, he said, have two bombers of the Mitsubishi type, one of which is used by the Navy and one by the Army -they are about equal in performance to the Whitley bomber in the R.A.F. He believes that Messerschmitt 109s are being produced in limited numbers in Japanese factories."

-- "The Times", Oct 20, 1941

While reports as to the performance of the latest Japanese fighters is minimal, the RAF currently consider them to be similar to that of Italian designs, that is small, agile and lightly armed, but with longer range. Given that the RAF was able to dominate the Italian Air force, they see no reason why they cannot do the same to the Japanese.

General Alexander is very concerned at the lack of help his preparations are getting from the civil authorities in Malaya. After a number of increasingly vitriolic telegrams between him and the War Cabinet, he has a meeting which is later described as 'turbulent'. As a result, far more civilian labour is released, and local industry is forbidden to poach them. The most urgent need is to complete the protected shelters for the planes, first at Singapore then further north if time permits. Alexander has also discussed the possibilities for construction at least one defence line north of the city with his engineer and General Percival. The conclusion is that it would cause more panic than it was worth to start construction now, but that the defences would be planned and ready to be implemented the moment Japan attacks. Few people in the military think that an attack is more than a short time away, and pressured by Alexander preparations are going ahead as fast as possible.

HMS Bulwark and HMS Anson sail from Britain. The carrier will fly off a squadron of Cormorant divebombers to Gibraltar en route. They are expected to arrive at Trincomalee on the 10th November, where they will spend a month working up. Bulwark is the first carrier to sail with a full complement of the new Sea Eagle and Spearfish; as these are larger than the older aircraft they replace she has to carry eight planes on deck, but as this is now usual practice except in exceptionally bad weather it is not seen as a problem. They will be joined at Gibraltar by the French battleship Richelieu and her escorts.

21st October

The Foreign Office in Tokyo sends the following message to the Japanese Embassy in Washington: "The new cabinet differs in no way from the former one in its sincere desire to adjust Japanese-United States relations on a fair basis. Our country has said practically all she can say in the way of expressing of opinions and setting forth our stand. We feel that we have now reached a point where no further positive action can be taken by us except to urge the United States to reconsider her views. We urge, therefore, that, choosing an opportune moment, either you or Wakasugi let it be known to the United States by indirection that our country is not in a position to spend much more time discussing this matter. Please continue the talks, emphasizing our desire for a formal United States counter-proposal to our proposal of 25 September."

A squadron of Hudson bombers arrives to be used by Coastal command in Singapore. These planes have been very effective in use in Europe, and they will be used mainly for reconnaissance and anti-submarine patrols. A section of Whirlwind reconnaissance planes also arrives - the ten aircraft are expected to give the command better intelligence, especially as they do not think the Japanese have any planes capable of catching them.

The first part of 1st Armoured Division arrives in Singapore; the most urgent job they will have on arrival is to show the Malay and Indian divisions how to work with tanks - the Australians already know, but these divisions have never worked with tanks. It is not expected there will be time to make them expert, but at least a basic familiarity will be useful. To save time, the tanks are not tropicalised; this will be done once more of the division has arrived.

23rd October

The first four U-class submarines arrive at Trincomalee. It is intended to deploy them from Singapore shortly once work on the base has been completed to accommodate them. Further U and T class submarines will arrive over the next two weeks, as will a depot ship.

27th Oct

The sailing of two battalions of troops from Canada to Hong Kong has had to be postponed due to engine problems with the liner Awtea. This is not bad news for the Canadians, who consider the troops not yet sufficiently trained and ready for deployment. As no other liner is available, the troops will carry on with their original training program until new transport can be arranged.

HMS Warspite, HMAS Australia and HMAS Sydney arrive at Singapore to join Force Z. Talks have been going on for some time with the Dutch and (unofficially) with Admiral Hart for the Americans. Given the naval force the RN is assembling, the Dutch have agreed that their naval forces will be under RN command (subject of course to their need to defend the DEI), and work is proceeding at making it easier for the two navies to operate together. While Admiral Hart is unable to agree to anything similar, USN officers are included in the plans for joint operations, 'just in case'.

1st Nov

Japanese Combined Fleet Operational Order Number 1 - the plan for the attack on Pearl Harbor, Malaya and the Dutch East Indies is issued.

Joseph C Grew, the US ambassador to Japan, sends a second telegram to President Roosevelt warning that the Japanese may be planning an attack on an American target. The report is filed.

The first four long-range T-class submarines arrive in Ceylon for deployment, as does the depot ship and supplies for the two submarines squadrons.

The convoy taking 9th Australian Division arrives at Singapore. Due to the rising tension the division will deploy by the 16th; a number of the 7th Australian Division will be tasked with helping to get them ready for operations as soon as possible. They are accompanied by the second part of the 1st Armoured Brigade with 60 tanks. Only two of the division's brigades are on this convoy; the third and final one will not arrive until the 22nd November due to a shortage of suitable shipping.

3rd Nov

General Marshall states at a Joint Board meeting that there would only be sufficient B-17's in the Philippines to "have a deterrent effect on Japanese operations." The Joint Board concurred in opposing the State Department's hard line towards Japan and advocated the USA making minor concessions to buy time. Major General Brereton arrives on Pan American Clipper to take up his appointment as Commander, FEAF. He brings with him a draft of a revised Rainbow-5 plan for the defence of the Philippines.

5th Nov

General Marshall and Admiral Stark send a six-point memorandum to the President outlining the position taken by the Joint Board on November 3. He is specifically informed that there would be insufficient B-17's in the Philippines to serve as a "positive threat" to the Japanese until mid-December and that it would be February or March before air power in the Commonwealth was sufficient to be a "deciding factor in deterring Japan". This memorandum further sets out that a Japanese attack on British or Dutch possessions or a threatening Japanese assault on Siam would lead to an American declaration of war.

The RAF is having growing problems with the new Fw190 fighter in Europe. It has a better performance than the current SpitfireV or the GoshawkIII. A new two-stage supercharged Merlin 61 engine has been tried in one of the pre-production Spitfire VIII, and the increase in performance is said to be huge over the current SpitfireV. This engine is specified for the production run of the Mk8, and it is hoped to have these operational in March 1942. There has been pressure from the RAF to try the new Gloster Sea Eagle in operation, but the Navy is strongly resisting this as they claim it is not yet operational - the first carriers to carry the plane are still working up their air groups, and they are only just coming into full production. They also point out that it will not necessarily solve the problem; the Spitfire is more manoeuvrable, although the Sea Eagle has far more power, and the Sea Eagle has been optimized for performance under 20,000feet. The SpitfireVIII with the new engine is expected to have better performance above this height. In any case, numbers of the Fw190 are at the moment small, and with a steadily increasing prospect of war in the Far East, they would prefer to keep the performance of the Sea Eagle a secret.

Another four U-class boats arrive in Ceylon. The first half of the squadron arrives at Singapore yesterday, their arrival and deployment kept as secret as possible.

The 12th African Division arrives in Burma via India. This division has been freed up from East Africa by the finishing of the Ethiopean campaign; it is hoped its experienced troops, already used to hot conditions, will be able to be operational soon. The same convoy brings 40 additional tanks for the armored brigade in Burma, although these will need some weeks of tropicalisation before they can be put to use.

9th Nov

General MacArthur meets with Admiral Hart and advises him to "get a real Fleet". Hart bitterly resents this comment.

The first squadron of the new Mosquito light bomber becomes operational. The initial squadrons have been allocated to the bombing pathfinder squadrons; it is considered an ideal plane for them, and they do not need a heavy bomb load to carry their marking indicators. The pathfinder concept has slowly been improving the accuracy of the RAF bombers; a report by Justice Butt some weeks ago pointed out that while the accuracy was still poor, it was a great improvement on a year ago. As the marking planes skill increased, and new aids such as Gee were employed, it was felt the delayed heavy bombing campaign could go ahead in the spring as scheduled.

11th Nov

Battleship Mushashi, the largest warship in the world, is launched in Japan.

General Brereton, Air Force USAFFE Commander, is dispatched by General MacArthur on a three-week, 11,500-mile trip to Rabaul, Port Moresby, Townsville, and Melbourne, to comply with Marshall's directive of 30 September regarding the use of airfields in British Empire areas by the USA.

Although the largest island in the Dodecanese group, Rhodes, is now occupied and fortified by the British, low level air and sea activity continues across the islands. Italian and RAF and French planes stage raids and patrol the area, and the Italians have staged two raids by light craft against the small coastal ships supplying the British, in one case sinking or damaging a number of ships.

13th Nov

The Germans today resume their attack on Moscow now that frost has hardened the ground enough for operations. They have launched one of their customary pincer movements in a final attempt to capture the city before the winter

The plan is for the 2nd Panzer Group to take Tula, to the south of the Russian capital, and then sweep up behind Moscow to Kolemna. 3rd Panzer Group is to form the northern arm of the pincer with the task of driving eastwards to the Volga Canal and then wheeling towards Moscow while 4th Panzer Group attacks in the centre. The initial reports of the fighting show that it is going to be much harder for them to take Moscow than seemed possible last month when panic gripped the city.

The House of Representatives voted by 212 votes to 194 to revise the Neutrality Act of 1939 to allow US merchant ships to unload munitions in British ports..

15th Nov

The final four T-class boats arrive at Ceylon. This completes the two submarine squadrons deployed in the Far East. The rest of the U-class boats arrive at Singapore to take up their patrol stations. The T-class boats are headed further north, closer to the Philippines; they will refuel at Singapore at night then head out under cover of darkness.

The first of the latest version of the Valentine tank, mounting a 6pdr gun in a turret designed for the Canadian Grizzly tank arrive in North Africa. The first of the new Grizzly are expected to arrive in Britain shortly, and a small number will be shipped on to Alexandria for examination in the field by the British and French armoured divisions. Planning has been going ahead steadily for an invasion of Sicily in the spring and a more powerful tank has been eagerly awaited. General Montgomery has already pointed out that as amphibious forces are limited by sealift, especially until a port can be captured, having the best equipment in the initial landings is of especial benefit.

General Alexander approves plans for food rationing in Singapore. The engineers have been working on possible solutions for water; if the island is invested the water supply is so far north as to be very vulnerable to enemy attack. Singapore receives regular rain which can be collected; additional storage is being looked at. The administration is also drawing up plans for evacuation of civilians if Malaya is attacked; these will leave on small coastal shipping and on returning supply convoys for Ceylon and Australia.

18th Nov

General Brooke replaces General Dill as Chief of the Imperial General Staff. General Dill is assigned to Washington, DC. General Paget becomes C. in C. British Home Forces. These appointments will become effective in December.

General Brooke has a passion for innovation in military mobility, mechanization and gunnery, and this is expected only to increase the current progress for better mechanised forces in the Imperial Armies.

The Japanese Imperial Diet secretly approves a "resolution of hostility" against the United States. Admiral Yamamoto informs his staff to plan for an attack on the Royal Navy at Singapore once the strike at Pearl Harbor has been completed. This will have to be finalised later, as it will depend on how costly (and successful) the attack on the Pacific fleet is, and what force the Royal Navy have in Malaya at the time, but in principle and assuming the Pacific fleet is hit as heavily as he hopes, he wants to swing his forces around and cripple and drive back the Royal Navy Eastern Fleet as soon as possible.

Five mother submarines, each with a midget sub lashed to the deck, depart Kure Naval Base for Pearl Harbor. The submarines arrive off Oahu, Hawaiian Islands, on 6 December. Nine submarines from Kwajalein also sail for their stations.

A convoy containing supplies and a considerable amount of ammunition starts to unload in Singapore. In addition to army supplies, it carries additional shells for the ships which will be operating from the base, as well as torpedoes for the submarines and the new Torpex MkXV aerial torpedo. A similar convoy docked two days ago at Trincomalee.

The Dutch army in the Dutch East Indies receive their first shipments of the US 'Stuart' tank. These had originally been ordered by France, but after the actions in North Africa had shown they were really too light for use against German tanks, had been passed on to the Dutch - it was felt that it would be a very useful vehicle against the much lighter and poorly-protected Japanese tanks. The Dutch forces have been eagerly looking forward to their first modern tanks.

21st Nov

The Navy Department sends the following message to the Commanders of the Asiatic and Pacific Fleets. "Have been informed by Dutch Legation that they have received a dispatch as follows: "According to information received by the Governor General of The Netherlands East Indies a Japanese expeditionary force has arrived in the vicinity of Palau. Should this force, strong enough to form a threat for The Netherlands Indies or Portuguese Timor, move beyond a line between the following points Davao (Philippine Islands) Waigeo (Island, Netherlands East Indies) Equator the Governor General will regard this as an act of aggression and will under those circumstances consider the hostilities opened and act accordingly." Inform Army authorities of foregoing. Request any information you may have concerning development of this Japanese threat against the Dutch East Indies and your evaluation of foregoing information."

22nd Nov

The Japanese First Air Fleet arrives in Hitokappu Bay, Etorofu Island, Kurile Islands. This fleet consists of six aircraft carriers (HIJMS Akagi, Hiryu, Kaga, Shokaku, Soryu and Zuikaku), two battleships (HIJMS Hiei and Kirishima), two heavy cruisers (HIJMS Chikuma and Tone), a light cruiser (HIJMS Abukuma) and ten destroyers.

The German assault on Moscow continues. After bitter fighting, the Germans are now some 35 miles from the city.

23rd Nov

Carrier Striking Task Force Operations Order No. 1 is issued stating:

"The Carrier Striking Task Force will proceed to the Hawaiian Area with utmost secrecy and, at the outbreak of the war, will launch a resolute surprise attack on and deal a fatal blow to the enemy fleet in the Hawaiian Area. The initial air attack is scheduled at 0330 hours, X Day. Upon completion of the air attacks, the Task Force will immediately withdraw and return to Japan and, after taking on new supplies, take its position for Second Period Operations. In the event that, during this operation, an enemy fleet attempts to intercept our force or a powerful enemy force is encountered and there is danger of attack, the Task Force will launch a counterattack.

The second unit, the Midway Bombardment Unit (the 7th Destroyer Division less the 2nd section), will depart from Tokyo Bay around X-6 Day and, after refuelling, secretly approach Midway. It will arrive on the night of X Day and shell the air base. The unit will then withdraw and, after refuelling, return to the western part of the Inland Sea. The oiler Shiriya will accompany the bombardment unit on this mission and will be responsible for the refuelling operation."

24th Nov

Admiral Stark, Chief of Naval Operations, sends the following message to Admiral Hart, Commander-in-Chief Asiatic Fleet in the Philippine Islands; Admiral Kimmel, Commander-in-Chief Pacific Fleet in the Territory of Hawaii; Admiral Blakely, commander of the Eleventh Naval District at San Diego, California; Admiral Greenslade, commander of the Twelfth Naval District at San Francisco, California; Admiral Freeman, commander of the Thirteenth Naval District at Seattle, Washington; and Admiral Sadler, commander of the Fifteenth Naval District in the Canal Zone: "Chances of favourable outcome of negotiations with Japan very doubtful. This situation coupled with statements of Japanese Government and movements their naval and military forces indicate in our opinion that a surprise aggressive movement in any direction including attack on Philippines or Guam is a possibility"

27th Nov

The last Italian forces in Ethiopia have surrendered in Gondar. After holding out for nine months, aided by the mountains and the rains, General Nasi's troops were overwhelmed today. The British have taken 11,500 Italian and 12,000 native troops prisoner.

The Japanese carrier forces and Combined Fleet sail for the Pearl Harbor operation.

At 2000 unidentified aircraft were spotted at high altitude over central Luzon by Iba radar. All FEAF units placed on alert. Admiral Hart authorizes reconnaissance flights over Japanese troop convoys.

28th Nov

General Brereton requests permission to conduct high-altitude photo reconnaissance of Takao in Southern Formosa. General MacArthur refuses, citing "the War Department instructions to avoid any overt act" and directed that all Army reconnaissance, including that conducted in co-operation with the Asiatic Fleet, be limited to two-thirds the distance from Luzon to Formosa. The USS Enterprise and her escort group sets sail from Pearl Harbor for Wake Island to ferry Marine Wildcats to the island.

There is a meeting with General Alexander, Air Marshal Park, Admiral Somerville and their aides in Singapore to discuss the readiness of the area against attack.

While the defensive situation is much improved from even three months ago, it is still not close to what is desired, and it is felt that it will take another 3-4 months to bring the defence up to the standard required. None of the three officers think that they will have this time.

The ground forces have been reinforced, and more importantly reinforced with experienced troops. Not only has this given Alexander more options, the new forces have allowed him to conduct extensive training of the units already in theatre, which has improved their performance. He is especially pleased to now have armoured units available - despite some pre-war opinions, these have worked perfectly well in the jungle, as have the troops, who have found the plantations in particular quite navigable. He is still short of equipment - in particular AA guns, and as a result of the exercises showing that a considerable quantity of the pre-war stocks had deteriorated (having to be replaced), the stocks are less than optimal, although the reduced numbers of guns balances this out. Even so, only some 35% of the planned number of guns is available.

The situation of the air force is a little better. Earlier in the year, there were few modern planes in theatre, and the pilots were woefully short of training - indeed, Park would not have accepted them as fit for service when he was running 11 Group in Britain. Improving their training has been a major part of his preparations, and staff has been borrowed from Operational Training Units in Europe to improve efficiency. The quality is still variable, and a considerable number of the pilots need more experience, the general competence has improved. The overall situation has been helped by the arrival of more experienced pilots with some of the new squadrons (often men with combat experience), and judicious use of some of these to stiffen the existing squadrons has helped.

The radar and control situation has also improved. A number of the Army's AMES stations are in operation, Singapore Island and a considerable distance north of it now being covered. Thought was given to location a set in the north, but Koto Bharu, the best location, was considered far too vulnerable to attack. The control of interception has been improved considerably due to constant practice, although Park is still unhappy about the quality. Progress has been made on the airfields; many of those that were just strips six months ago are now equipped with concrete runways, thanks to the additional manpower made available, which is a huge help in the Malayan climate. Park has also instituted defence and demolition schemes for the forward airfields based on his experience in SE England during the Battle of Britain. Again these are not complete, but the northern airfields felt most likely to be at risk have been covered.

The air force has been reinforced with more modern planes, which has allowed the coverage of more of the peninsular; in particular he now has a small number of reconnaissance planes with radar for use at sea, and a squadron of night fighters to defend Singapore. More of the older planes than he would like are still in front line service, but some have been kept back for training. Since he has little accurate information on the capabilities of Japanese planes and pilots, he intends to decide later whether these aircraft (mainly Buffaloes) are capable enough to be used in combat.

The naval force has been heavily reinforced. Somerville points out that a number of his ships are not yet up to his standards operationally, but those are being held at Ceylon while exercises continue. About 2/3 of his force is ready, although he has serious worries as to having too many ships at Singapore - he sees no reason why the IJN cannot do to him what the RN has done to Germany and Italy, although the static defences of Singapore are rather more prepared and alert than Wilhelmshaven and Taranto were. He intends to keep only a small force at Singapore until more is known about the location of the IJN carrier force, accepting that this means he is less capable of stopping an initial invasion force.

29th Nov

A liaison conference among the Service Chiefs and Cabinet of the Japanese Government decides that the final proposal from the US is unacceptable. Their alternative is war. Their decision is prepared for an Imperial Conference, with the Emperor, which is scheduled for December.

30th Nov

MacArthur orders Fort Mills on Corregidor put on full alert.

The continuing reports of Japanese activity, and the reports of what could be troop convoys heading south, are putting Admiral Somerville in a dilemma. He cannot initiate action against the Japanese, yet concentrating his forces at Singapore means leaving them open to the possibility of a carrier strike. The IJN have at least six fleet carriers available, and a strike by them could devastate his fleet. However leaving them out at sea has its own drawbacks, the IJN has a strong submarine force and if spotted they could again be vulnerable to air attack. Once the Japanese commit themselves his task will be simpler, but until then he decides to keep the bulk of his fleet south and west of Singapore.

He has ordered a patrol line of U-class submarines south of French Indo China and oriented North-South to catch any ships heading for the peninsular. He also orders four of the larger T-class to sail tomorrow for stations between the Philippines and the China coast.

His surface force at Singapore consists of the light carrier Melbourne, the fast battleship KGV and three cruisers plus their destroyer escorts. These are at sea to the north-east of Singapore. If his reconnaissance detects a strong enemy force, he will either reinforce them with more of his fleet, or if the enemy force seems too large withdraw them and concentrate west of Singapore ready for a carrier strike.

2nd Dec

The Premier, Hideki Tojo, publicly rejects US proposals for peace. The Japanese carrier force "Kido Butai" sailing for the Hawaiian Islands receives a special radio signal: "Climb Mount Niitaka 1208", from Japanese Combined Fleet Commander Admiral Yamamoto. This is the order to execute the attack on Pearl Harbor.

German troops reach the outskirts of Moscow, 20 miles away. The Kremlin is in sight.

5th Dec

Despite the nearness of his advance units to Moscow, Hitler agrees to a halt in the Moscow offensive due to the growing exhaustion of his troops and the freezing weather conditions.

Japan assures the USA that its build-up of troops in Indochina is "a purely defensive measure"

In Australia the government cancels all army leave as the prospect of war with Japan grows more likely. Japanese convoys are on the move in Asia, and the only question now seems to be where, not whether, they will strike. Allied forces have been brought to the first degree of readiness. Australian service chiefs have been summoned and the Australian war cabinet has issued orders for emergency measures in the Pacific. Australia has two divisions in place in Malaya, and a new division, the 8th, has finished training in Australia.

All RN and RAN ships in theatre have been ordered to finish any boiler cleanings, hull cleaning and minor refits as soon as possible and be ready at eight hours notice. General Alexander has ordered the engineers to be ready to proceed with the defensive works as soon as he gives the order.

6th Dec

The Russian army launches a major counteroffensive on the Moscow front. The Germans are being hampered by the freezing conditions, for which they are not prepared, and the attack is a notable success

The first two brigades of the 4th Indian Division arrive in Burma, although only half its heavy equipment has arrived in the first convoy. The rest of the division and its equipment will arrive in two weeks

President Roosevelt again appeals to the Japanese Emperor for peace and asks for troop withdrawal from French Indochina. There is no Japanese reply. Later the first 13 parts of a 14 part Japanese message are transmitted. Unknown to the Japanese, this message is intercepted and decoded by US Intelligence

An RAF reconnaissance plane discovers a Japanese convoy heading west, south of Cambodia point. Bad weather makes it difficult to keep the ships under observation, so the Whirlwind is relieved by a series of SeaLance planes flying out of Kota Bharu and using their ASV radar to keep track of the convoy, which is sailing steadily into the Gulf of Siam. There are four U-class submarines in a patrol line that intersects the convoy, and they are ordered to concentrate on it during the night of the 7th. One of the submarines is ordered to move south to Koto Bharu, as the forward airfield is an obvious target for attack. The submarine is not authorised to take action unless the Japanese are not only inside territorial waters but also launching a landing. Air Marshal Park only has a small number of the radar-equipped SeaLance, so to supplement them sends out six Hudson patrol planes. If the convoy sighted is an invasion fleet, then a supporting force cannot be too far away if it is to give them cover, and he hopes that one of the Hudsons will spot them

Admiral Somerville can only consider this to be an invasion convoy (or at least ships acting like one). His big question is where is the covering force, and how large is it. At the moment it is not possible to say if the convoy is heading for Siam, or Malaya, or both. While he keeps planes covering the convoy, urgent attempts are made to try and find where the warships covering it are hiding. The ships at Singapore are brought to two hours notice for sailing (his advance squadron has been in port so the carrier can have her bottom cleaned). A squadron of RAF Beaufighters are put on alert for a possible torpedo attack, and the Army units in the north are alerted that an invasion may commence within 48hours. The RAF radar units on and north of Singapore Island have been on alert for some days. The RAF and Army units in the north will have to manage for the time being with the Malaysian version of the Observer Corps, the radar systems not having yet covered the entire country, but at least Park has managed to get a basic command system working, thanks in part to the availability of RN personnel trained in the similar job at sea.

Parks is also worried about air raids on Singapore. While there have been a number of air raid drills, there has only been one a month for the civilian population due to the disruption they cause (although the military have been tested more frequently), and he is concerned that an early raid could cause severe casualties. No-one is sure about the range of Japanese bombers, but it is considered possible they could raid the island with at least a light bomb load. There have also been problems in digging slit trenches in the often-wet conditions, although steady progress has been made in more permanent facilities for the airfields and some of the more important military targets.

7th - 8th Dec

Six Japanese carriers launch an air strike at the USN naval base at Pearl Harbor, using 184 planes in the first wave and 176 planes in the second wave, a much heavier strike even than the one the RN made against Taranto. The attack was made before a declaration of war, and resulted in massive damage to the US fleet, which seemed to be caught by surprise and without defensive measure such as torpedo nets fully or properly deployed.

Only 29 Japanese planes failed to make it back, although others were too badly damaged to be used again. Comments made seem to indicate that a daylight raid was not expected after the earlier examples of night raids in the European war by the Royal Navy.

The attack was a devastating success. Four battleships were sunk, and four more damaged, effectively destroying the US fleet in the Pacific. Also lost or damaged were three cruisers, three destroyers, an AA training ship and a minelayer. In addition the USAAF airfields were badly damaged, the USAAF losing nearly 200 planes.

Although reconnaissance planes took off from Hawaii, the Japanese attack force was not found. Although the damage done was serious, no further strike was launched (unlike the RN at Taranto), and, possibly due to the need to use a considerable force to neutralise the airfields, the damage to the fleet could have been even worse. Fortunately the US carrier force was not in the harbour at the time of the attack, and so was preserved for future missions.

Wake Island has received a warning from Pearl Harbour at 0650. The islands defences and the airbase were not fully operational, but they had received the second half of their fighters only a few days before. There were now 24 F4F3 Wildcats to defend the island. Unfortunately the radar set due to be delivered was till at Pearl Harbor, and so it was decided to rotate eight fighters at a time on CAP, as warning was expected to be minimal without radar.

At noon the airfield was attacked by 36 G3M bombers. Visibility was poor, and the bombers were not spotted until they began their attack runs. Only some of the aircraft were protected by revetments (these had only been built for the earlier group of 12 planes), and as a result the bombers destroyed five Wildcats on the ground. The control of the planes was poor, and the CAP did not succeed in intercepting the bombers before they made their escape.

Appendix One

This describes some of the aircraft in use by the Royal Navy and other air forces during the period covered by this book (1932 - 1941). Only naval aircraft or aircraft encountered in actions in the book have been included.

Aircraft in use by the Royal Navy

Gloster Goshawk Mk III (fighter)

The Goshawk is a single-engine fighter powered by the improved version of the Bristol Hercules engine. Performance is similar to that of the historic Spitfire at low level, but inferior above 20,000 feet - as was the usual practice with carrier aircraft of the period, performance was optimised for under 20,000 feet (since bombing above this altitude was too inaccurate for success against ships). Armament had increased to 4x20mm cannon over earlier version of the fighter. As with most naval planes, the Goshawk had rather longer range than its land-based equivalents, at the cost of a heavier aircraft (compensated for by the more powerful Hercules engine)

Fairy Swordfish (TBR - Torpedo, Bomber, Reconnaissance)

Developed in the early 1930's as a private venture, the 'Stringbag' as it was known would be used throughout the war in many different roles. No longer the frontline torpedo/bomber (although it was still to be found used in this role in the more remote theatres), due to its versatility and its ability to operate off of very small carriers in all sorts of weather, it would carry on as the anti-submarine plane on escort carriers and conversions throughout the war.

Martin-Baker Cormorant Mk III(Divebomber)

Developed in the 1930's, the Hercules-powered Cormorant was the Royal Navies first dedicated dive bomber. Initial versions carried either a 500lb HE bomb (on longer missions) or a 1,000lb against larger targets. With a later-version Hercules (with more power), it could also carry the 1,600lb AP bomb designed for use against battleships and similarly armoured targets

Boulton-Paul SeaLance (TBR - Torpedo, Bomber, Reconnaissance)

The replacement for the Swordfish, the SeaLance was an interim deign using the Griffon engine. Faster than the Swordfish, it was much more survivable against defended targets. With its increased performance, the Royal Navy carried on development of its aerial torpedoes to allow them to be dropped at a higher speed and from a greater height, also giving the crews more chance of surviving the attack.

Fairy Spearfish (TBR - Torpedo, Bomber, Reconnaissance)

The replacement for the SeaLance (which had originally been seen as an interim design), this plane was operational in late 1941. Performance was much better, thanks to the powerful Centaurus engine, but the limited availability of the engine limited initial deployment. It was the first carrier-based plane to carry the new, heavy MkXV torpedo, and it could deliver this at over 250kt. It was the first strike aircraft deigned to have an ASV radar equipped as standard, but production issues meant that at first only some aircraft were so fitted.

Gloster Sea Eagle (fighter)

This fighter started to replace the Goshawk in the autumn of 1941. Powered by the Centaurus engine, it was then the fastest fighter in the world, carrying 4x20mm guns. It could also carry some 1,600lb of bombs, allowing it to act as a naval attack aircraft as well as a fighter. Production was initially limited by low production of the Centaurus, and the weight of the plane meant it only operated off the later or modernised fleet carriers.

Aircraft in use by the RAF

Lockheed Hudson (anti-submarine)

The Hudson was a twin-engine light bomber in use by RAF Coastal Command as a reconnaissance and anti-submarine plane. The aircraft was bought from the USA, where it had originally been designed as a civilian aircraft, modified by the RAF to carry bombs and armed with a quadruple 0.303 gun turret.

Hawker Hurricane (fighter)

The Hurricane was a single-engines fighter powered by the Rolls-Royce Merlin. The first modern monoplane fighter in service in the RAF, its performance was similar to the Goshawk. Initially armed with 8x0.303" guns, by 1940 production aircraft were being armed with 2x20mm cannon and 4x0.303" guns, giving them more destructive power against German bombers. The plane would be one of the two mainstays of fighter command in 1940, before being phased out. The design did not benefit from a more powerful engine, and it was replaced in 1941 by the de-navalised version of the Goshawk, the Sparrowhawk.

Supermarine Spitfire (fighter)

The Spitfire was one of the great fighter aircraft of WW2. Developed before the war, it only entered service shortly before the conflict started. By 1940, it was already equal in performance to the best German fighters, and by the Battle of Britain was steadily replacing the Hurricane as the RAF frontline fighter. The airframe was far more capable of increasing performance when fitted with more powerful engines, and its development would continue throughout the war. Like the Hurricane, it was initially armed with 8x0.303" guns, but it was also upgraded to cannon by the time the Battle of Britain started.

Short Sunderland (anti-submarine)

The Sunderland was a long range, heavily armed flying boat, used for anti-submarine patrols. The heavy defensive armament led to it being used in areas like the Bay of Biscay where enemy fighters were encountered, and it was also capable of rescue.

Bristol Beaufighter (fighter, bomber, torpedo, attack)

The Beaufighter was the first true 'multi-role' plane in service in Britain. A powerful and heavy plane powered by two Hercules engines, it was capable of defending itself against all but the latest enemy fighters. Heavily armed, it was also used as a naval strike plane against light targets, and when carrying a torpedo, against larger ships. Its long range meant it was also used as a reconnaissance aircraft.

Consolidated Catalina (maritime patrol)

An American designed and built flying boat, this was used as an additional maritime patrol aircraft in the Atlantic and pacific theatres to supplement the limited production of the Sunderland, its long range being very useful in these areas.

Short Stirling (bomber)

The first four engined bomber designed for the RAF, it suffered from a number of performance issues, in particular its low ceiling of some 16,000 feet made it more vulnerable in operations. As the more capable Halifax was in production, and a long range aircraft was badly needed for convoy protection, many of the Stirlings were re-assigned to this job, some being fitted with ASV radar for an additional reconnaissance role.

Aircraft in use by the Luftwaffe

Heinkel He115 (torpedo)

Developed shortly before the start of the war, the He115 was a fast, twin engine floatplane designed to carry torpedoes and mines. Intended to fly from coastal bases, it was fast for the time and had a long range. However it was never manufactured in large quantities and its weak defensive armament made it vulnerable to fighters

Messerschmitt Me109 (fighter)

This single-engine fighter was the Luftwaffe's frontline fighter during the first part of the war. Agile and fast, it was the equal of the Spitfire (and in some respects its superior) at this time. Its main disadvantage was its short range and the delicate landing gear - although a version was produced for use on the German carriers, development shows a disheartening number of landing accidents.

Junkers Ju87 (Stuka) (dive bomber)

This aircraft was the iconic dive bomber of the war. A simple aircraft, its ability to dive extremely steeply made it very accurate. The early versions were limited in bomb load, but later versions with a more powerful engine had both a longer range and the ability to deliver a 500kg bomb at effective ranges. Fortunately for the Royal Navy the Luftwaffe neglected the anti-shipping role before the war, and so early attacks by the Stuka were often ineffective.

Junkers Ju88 (bomber)

Probably the best light/medium bomber of the early part of the war, this twin engine plane was fast and could carry a useful bomb load. Its performance was affected by the requirement that it be able to dive-bomb, a task it was never suited for (the Stuka being far more effective).

Heinkel He111 (bomber)

The standard Luftwaffe medium bomber of the early War years, this twin-engined level bomber was ineffective against ships at sea.

Messerschmitt Me110 (escort fighter)

A heavy twin-engine fighter, in some respects it resembled the Beaufighter. However its role was quite different. Intended as a long-range fighter to protect bombers, it was found incapable f protecting itself against the modern RAF and FAA single-engine fighters. It was also employed as a light fast bomber carrying one or two 250kg bombs.

Focke-Wulf Fw 190 (fighter)

This plane was introduced in 1941 as a replacement for the aging Me109. In fact the Me109 stayed in production throughout the war. A radial engine fighter, its heavy armament and high performance made it a dangerous threat to allied aircraft, and its performance was superior to the current RAF Spitfire MkV when it came into service.

Aircraft in use by the Italian Air Force

Savoia-Marchetti SM.79 Sparviero (bomber)

This was a three-engined bomber designed in the 1930's. It had a good performance for the time, and was the main Italian bomber of the war. One feature found useful by the crews in its naval use was that the wooden framework allowed the aircraft to often remain afloat for some 30 minutes. By 1940 its limited defensive armament was ineffective against the modern FAA fighters, making it very vulnerable.

Macchi C.200 Saetta (Mc200) (fighter)

The front-line fighter for Italy at the start of the war, this plane had excellent manoeuvrability but was slower than the equivalent RAF and FAA fighters, and poorly armed - 2x0.5" guns were not adequate, especially against the robust naval fighters it was to encounter. It also suffered from the common land-based fighter problem of limited range.

Macchi C.202 Folgore (Mc202) fighter

Introduced in 1941 after it was clear that the current Italian fighters were inferior to allied designs, this was a light and agile fighter. While more heavily armed than earlier designs, (2x7.7mm, 2x12.7mm guns), its armament was still inferior to alied designs, and had difficulty causing enough damage to the heavy allied aircraft. Rather rushed into service, the design had numerous problems that delayed its effective use.

Aircraft in use by the Japanese Air Force

Mitsubishi A5M Type 96 fighter (Claude)

A very light and agile fighter used by the Japanese Navy. By the end of 1941 it was being replaced by the Zero. Its main problems were its slow maximum speed (slower than attack aircraft like the Beaufighter), and poor armament (2x7.7mm machine guns) which made it difficult to do sufficient damage to the more strongly built allied aircraft.

Mitsubishi A6M Zero-Sen Type Zero fighter (Zero)

Probably the best Japanese naval fighter of the war, the Zero had only been operation since July 1940. Again a light and very manoeuvrable design, it was much faster than the Claude, and with a considerably heavier armament (2x7.7mm and 2x20mm cannon), it was far more dangerous to allied fighters.

Nakajima Ki-43 Hayabusa Type 1 fighter (Oscar)

A fighter used by the Japanese army, the plane was very agile, but again had a poor maximum speed and armament (2x0.5" guns).

Aichi D3A Type 99 dive bomber (Val)

Introduced to service in 1940, this was the dive bomber in use by the Japanese Navy when war with Japan started. Roughly comparable in performance with the Cormorant or Ju87, its main limitation was that it was designed to carry a 250kg bomb, which was of limited effectiveness against battleships or the Royal Navy's heavily protected fleet carriers.

Nakajima B5N Type 97 TBR (Kate)

The standard torpedo bomber in use by the Japanese Navy at the start of the war, this plane was one of the best torpedo planes in service. Broadly comparable with the SeaLance.

All Japanese planes were lightly built by comparison with Western designs. The advantage of that was it allowed them a much longer range, a very important characteristic in the vast Pacific theatre. The drawback was that this made them relatively fragile, especially to the heavy armament some of the allied fighter carried by 1941.

Appendix Two

Aircraft Carriers in service

Royal Navy

HMS Eagle

26,000t displacement, speed 22.5 kt ; 5x4" guns, approx 10x20mm. Normal aircraft complement 21

HMS Hermes

13,000t displacement, 25kt ; 4x4" guns, approx 10x20mm. Normal aircraft complement 20

HMS Argus

14,500t displacement, 20kt ; 6x4" guns, approx 12 20mm. Normal aircraft complement 20

HMS Furious

23,000t displacement, 31kt ; 12x20mm. Normal aircraft complement 36

HMS Courageous (sunk Oct 1940), HMS Glorious

27,500t displacement, 30kt ; 8x40mm, approx 8x20mm. Normal aircraft complement 48

HMS Ark Royal, HMS Illustrious

24,000t displacement, speed 31.5kt ; 16x4.5" guns, 64x40mm, approx 20x20mm. Normal aircraft complement 65

HMS Formidable, HMS Victorious, HMS Indefatigable, HMS Implacable

24,500t displacement, speed 32kt ; 16x4.5" guns, 64x40mm, approx 20x20mm. Normal aircraft complement 68

HMS Colossus, HMS Mars, HMS Vengeance, HMS Venerable (sunk April 1940), HMS Glory, HMS Ocean, HMS Edgar, HMS Theseus (renamed HMAS Brisbane), HMAS Melbourne, HMS Unicorn (repair carrier)

13,000t displacement, speed 27kt ; 16x40mm guns, approx 16x20mm. Normal aircraft complement 24 (40 maximum with deck park)

United States Navy

USS Saratoga, USS Lexington

39,000t displacement, 34kt; 12x5" guns. Normal aircraft complement (pre-war) 90

USS Ranger

17,500t, speed 29kt ; 8x5" guns, 40x0.5" mg. Normal aircraft complement (pre-war) 75 planes

USS Yorktown, USS Enterprise USS Hornet, USS Ticonderoga

22,000t displacement, 32.5kt ; 8x5" guns, 16x1.1"mg, 24 0.5"mg. Normal aircraft complement (pre-war) 90

USS Wasp

16,000t displacement, 29kt ; 8x5" guns, 16 1.1"mg, 24x0.5"mg. Normal aircraft complement (pre-war) 80

German Kriegsmarine

Graf Zeppelin (sunk 25th April 1941)

28,000t displacement, 35kt ;8x5.9"guns, 16x4.1" guns, 22x37mm cannon, 28x20mm. Normal aircraft complement 40

Imperial Japanese Navy

HMIJS Akagi

41,300t displacement, 31kt ; 6x8" guns, 12x4.7" guns, 28x25mm. Normal aircraft complement 72

HMIJS Kaga

42,500t displacement, 28kt ; 10x8" guns, 10x5" guns, 22x25mm. Normal aircraft complement 81

HMIJS Soryu

19,800t displacement, 34kt ; 12x5" guns, 28x25mm. Normal aircraft complement 63

HMIJS Hiryu

21,900t displacement, 34kt ; 12x5" guns, 31x25mm. Normal aircraft complement 64

HMIJS Shokaku, HMIJS Zuikaku

32,000t displacement, 34kt ; 16x5" guns, 42x25mm. Normal aircraft complement 72

HMIJS Ryuju

10,150t displacement, 29kt ; 12x5" guns, 24mg. Normal aircraft complement 37

HMIJS Chitose, HMIJS Chiyoda

15,300t displacement, 29kt ; 8x5" guns, 30x25mm. Normal aircraft complement 30

HMIJS Zuiho, HMIJS Shoho

14,200t displacement, 28kt ; 8x5" guns, 8x25mm. Normal aircraft complement 30

Notes :

(1) The displacement is given as a 'normal' displacement. The displacement of a ship varies as it uses fuel and stores, and even the 'normal' displacement is somewhat variable, especially when reported to keep inside treaty limits

(2) The aircraft capacity of a carrier can be quite variable. In addition to the 'complete' aircraft carried, most fleet carriers would also carry a number of replacements, broken down into parts in the hangar which could be used to cover normal operational losses. The US carriers carried the most planes as they used a full deck park - aircraft were held on deck. The RN carriers and the Japanese carriers normally kept all their planes in the hangar, although they could increase the number available by using a deck park if they wished. However there were also practical limitations due to the need to carry the extra flight deck and maintenance crews for a larger aircraft complement.

Irrespective of the number of planes actually carried, carriers were also limited to how many planes they could launch in a single 'strike' due to deck space. During this period in time it was about 30-35 planes, after which planes would have to be brought on deck, armed, fuelled and placed ready for a second strike, a process which usually took around an hour or so (depending on the skill of the carrier crews).

(3) Armament, especially of the light 20mm cannon which tended to be fitted on wherever they could fit, also varied through the War. The numbers given are those deigned in; where major changes were made these are listed with date

(4) Speed. This assumes the ship is in good mechanical condition and with a clean bottom. During wartime service the actual speed was often lower due to the inability to refit the machinery and dock the ship for bottom-cleaning.

Appendix 3

Report of the Committee on the application of airpower to defeat Germany (also known as the Dowding Report).

This report was produced in the Winter of 1940, detailing the current state of British aircraft and projects (both for the RAF and the FAA), and the ongoing tactics and strategy.

* * *

The committee has looked at the current range of planes in service and in development, and at the issues involved in causing the maximum amount of damage to Germany. Since it is obvious that the resources available are not infinite, consideration has been given to causing the maximum damage and disruption to the German war effort for the minimum cost to us. In addition the committee appreciates that there are political considerations involved in showing the public that we are hurting Germany. We have also examined the possible options for forcing Germany to make the maximum response (i.e. commit the most resources) for the minimum effort on our part, with a view to causing them to waste effort and resources. Finally we have also looked at the need to keep our defence strong, and protect the most critical of our needs such as the convoy system.

First, we have evaluated the planes currently available or being developed. We have also eliminated some current aircraft as obsolete or not filling their requirement (although some of these may well be useful in a training role)

Supermarine Spitfire. This is seen as our prime fighter/interceptor for at least the next year, and possibly beyond (depending on how far the airframe can be developed). It has effectively replaced the Hurricane in fighter command. Its short range means it is unsuitable (even with drop tanks) for offensive operations except in Northern France, but it is the best and most cost-effective short range fighter we have. Production should continue at as high a rate as practical, and ongoing development should be maintained to increase its performance as undoubtedly the Luftwaffe will be developing their own aircraft further. Now that the issues of operation of the 20mm cannon in the cold have been solved, the fit of 4x20mm cannon should be made standard. Work also needs to continue on the engine, to achieve both more power and better high-altitude (over 20,000feet) performance. It is also suggested that the possibility of fitting the Griffon engine is investigated to improve the performance. The version expected in the new year (the MkV) will not reach the performance of the Sea Eagle fighter when it enters service late next year; it is recommended that once the Mk V is in use development continues immediately on an improved version.

Hawker Hurricane. This has now been replaced as our best fighter, but it still has acceptable performance against all but top-line enemy aircraft. It also has the useful ability to be shipped and then put together easily, which makes it a very useful plane for deployment abroad. It also has a possible role as a fighter-bomber, as it can carry a 500lb bomb and defend itself after bombing. It is recommended that the production continues, though at a lower level than before, and that the obvious theatre of operation is North Africa.

Gloster Goshawk. This fighter will continue to be our main naval fighter until the new generation of aircraft are available in late 1941/early 1942. While production has started on two new aircraft (now that the pause due to the invasion precautions of the summer have been removed), they will not be available until the autumn(of 1941). In addition, the new planes are too large to be used on the escort carriers (and in any case the performance of the Goshawk is adequate against the long-range planes found at sea). Continued development of the Hercules engine will give higher performance until the new planes are available in numbers.

Gloster Sparrowhawk. This is the de-navalised version of the Goshawk; production was delayed during the invasion, but was restarted in September and the first production planes are expected next year. It is expected that this plane will fill both the role of fighter and attack, although its origins mean it is not optimised for high altitude performance, and so should not be the sole fighter in use where first-class opposition is expected. As its origin as a carrier plane means it is very suitable for temporary and poor-quality airfields, it is expected that this will become our main fighter for use outside the UK and northern Europe, replacing the Hurricane as production permits. This plane is also being produced in Australia; for efficiency in production, it has been agree that Australia will only build this version, and that Goshawks will be supplied by us for their carrier needs. We will need additional supplies of the Hercules for this to take place; production is already established in Canada and Australia as well as in the UK, but consideration should be given to supplies from the USA (as we are already doing for the Merlin).

Hawker Tornado. The cancellation of the Vulture engine and the continuing problems with the Sabre have caused Hawker to modify a development plane to be powered by the Centaurus engine. This has proven successful. However the performance of the plane is roughly comparable to the projected Mk V Spitfire, only its maximum speed being somewhat higher. It is therefore recommended that this plane does not enter production, as developments of the Spitfire will have similar performance at lower investment cost. Hawker have requested funding for a research programme to continue development of a land-based fighter with a high-powered engine, and we consider this a sensible precaution in case of failure of other development projects.

Hawker Typhoon. This aircraft looks like being extremely rugged and fast at low level, once the problems with the Sabre engine are sorted out. It is not yet clear if it will be superior to the Martin-Baker design; as the engine is still not considered suitable for mass production it is recommended that development continue for at least the next 6 months.

Gloster Sea Eagle. This is the replacement for the Goshawk as the FAA main fighter. It can also carry a considerable bomb load, and may be used in this role instead of the Cormorant (although it does not have the specialist dive-bombing features of the Cormorant); experience so far has shown that the ability to bomb targets such as harbours and ships at anchor, then act as a top-level fighter, would be useful. The plane is soon to enter production, and the first production models are expected in the Autumn. trials so far have shown that it has superior low-level performance to the Spitfire (assuming the improvements already developed for the next version of the Spitfire are in use by the time it enters service), although the Spitfire still excels at higher altitudes (as a naval fighter, performance has been optimised for under 20,000feet)

Martin-Baker Manticore. This is the second naval fighter development. As the performance of the Sea Eagle is seen as most satisfactory, and the radial engine is preferred by the FAA, it has been suggested that as production has been set up, that this aircraft is produced to complement the Spitfire, as it has better low-altitude performance and a longer range. However we will need to increase the production of the Griffon before it can be produced in the quantities likely to be necessary if it is to be used in Europe. A decision should be deferred until the details and probably performance of a Griffon-engined Spitfire can be determined.

Fairy Spearfish. This is the new TBR plane for the FAA, powered by the Centaurus engine. It has better performance than the SeaLance, and in production form will be the first naval plane designed to be fitted with AS radar (although due to shortages it is expected this will initially only be fitted to a limited number of aircraft). It has also been designed to carry the new (and heavier) Mk XV aerial torpedo. This plane will soon enter production, and the first of the production planes is expected in the late summer (of 1941). The Navy has informed us that if (as expected) the performance and handling show it to be better than the SeaLance for carrier use, they would like to standardise on it, making the SeaLance production available for land use. However as not all the fleet carriers have catapults capable of handling it at full load yet, it is expected to continue using the SeaLance at least until mid-1942, possibly later, as there is also a need to increase the production of the Centaurus engine.

Gloster Reaper night fighter. This has now started leaving the production line, and the first models are just entering squadron service. It is intended to replace the Beaufighter as the main AI-radar equipped night fighter, and when it does the

Beaufighter will return to its original role. Due to the need for night fighters, production will continue as planned, although it will require modification once the new centimetric AI radar is operational.

Bristol Beaufighter. Once the need for night fighters is met by the Reaper, production will resume of the fighter/attack version of this plane. It is intended to have three main roles; long range fighter (although it should be noted that it is inferior to the current best Luftwaffe fighters, it should be adequate in this role in all other areas, torpedo bomber, bomber (although it is not designed as a bomber its power allows it to carry a considerable load as a fighter/bomber - indeed, it carries considerably more load than the Beafort. It has also been suggested that a version with 4x20mm cannon and 4x0.5" guns would make a good attack plane for use against targets such as light shipping and craft, as well as other ground targets. This configuration would also serve for the fighter role, and if needed the machine guns could be removed for better performance, depending on the opposition. A suggestion has been made to test an aircraft with a heavier-calibre cannon such as the 40mm, or even larger. Once production allows we suggest a test aircraft is made available.

Bristol Beaufort. While the performance, even with the Hercules engines, is inferior to the Beafighter, the shortage of adequate Coastal Command patrol aircraft means we should keep it in production for at least the next year. It is superior to the Beaufighter as a patrol aircraft, as the extra crew are useful in the observer role, and its primary target, submarines, means the difference in performance is not relevant.

Bristol Blenhiem. This light bomber has been tried in a fighter role, but is inadequate at this except against 3rd-rate opposition. Its bomb load and durability are now inadequate for the bombing role, and we need to replace it as soon as possible. Due to a shortage of suitable UK-designed aircraft, this may have to be done by using a US import, but in any case the aircraft should be assigned to lower-threat theatres as soon as possible, not to waste pilots in an inadequate aircraft, and production phased out once a suitable replacement has been developed.

DeHaviland Mosquito. The initial flight reports of the prototype show an excellent performance. The testing program is expected to finish in a few months, but we suggest initial work be done of arranging manufacturing; due to the nature of this aircraft, it will need a differing arrangement than normal aircraft. While the bomber does not mount any defensive armament, it would seem ideal for the role of Pathfinder to the main bomber force. Once production allows it could also replace the Blenheim in the light bomber role. While its unusual construction minimises the use of many strategic materials, it also requires a specialised production line. We suggest a factory be set up in Canada to build the aircraft.

Westland Whirlwind. This is currently being produced as a long-range reconnaissance aircraft, but as these come into service in numbers some will be produced as a long range fighter . Before we commit to large numbers in this configuration, we should use a small number to evaluate their performance against the current Luftwaffe fighters.

Vickers Wellington. This is currently our best medium bomber. In addition to its use as a bomber, it is also in demand from Coastal Command for anti-submarine duties. We recommend that production of this plane continues at the maximum rate for at least the next year.

Avro Manchester bomber. The first of these are in use, but the performance is not as good as expected. There are continual and ongoing issues with the Vulture engine, and our recommendation is that it is cancelled - we have other engines in production in the power range if needed. A version using four Merlin engines (designated the Lancaster) has just flown before Xmas, and looks very promising, but the flight trials will not be finished for some time. Preliminary indications is that changing to four engines and a redesign may solve the problems, but this cannot be determined yet

Short Stirling bomber. This will be introduced into service in 1941. While superior to the older generation of bombers, there are issues which indicate it will be inferior to the Manchester and Halifax. These are its short range with a heavy bomb load, and its low ceiling which will make it very vulnerable to AA fire.

Shorts have offered two suggestions for versions. The first would be a high-altitude version with different engines and wings. The second using the Centaurus engine.

Since we have the superior Halifax in production, and a 4-engine version of the Manchester will be available soon, we recommend that we allocate the Stirling to Coastal command at present. This will fill their need for a long range patrol aircraft, the low ceiling not being a problem, and the load carried is adequate for the AS load carried. In addition, it can be produced in a second version without a number of the turrets, as many of the patrol areas envisaged will not encounter enemy fighters (in particular aircraft . Shorts should produce options on the re-engined low altitude bomber, and a high altitude version for evaluation and possible production alongside or instead of the Supermarine 318.

Handley Page Halifax bomber. This has now entered service in limited numbers, and is a considerable improvement on the existing bomber aircraft. It's one limitation is the size of the bomb bay which limits the size of bombs that can be carried; raids by the Luftwaffe have shown that heavy bombs have different effects to light bombs, and that the types of bombs need to be suited to the type of damage required by the raid. We recommend production to continue in order to build up a sizeable force of heavy bombers

Supemarine 318 (Coventry) bomber. This high-altitude bomber has undergone some trials, but a rework is necessary in order to achieve the high altitude envisioned in the original design. Data is now coming in from the high-altitude Wellington project, and this will be used to modify the aircraft. As Supermarine are heavily loaded with Spitfire work, the project has been passed over to Vickers, and development will continue under Mr Wallis. They expect to have a new prototype flying with all necessary modifications in the summer.

We currently see this aircraft as supplementing the lower altitude bombers. It will fly above the current German AA, and will be difficult for fighters to intercept, but is not ready yet and will be expensive. Until it is available in numbers, it will not be feasible to conduct raids using only this aircraft.

Use of our air assets.

(1) Air Defence of the United Kingdom.

While at the moment the threat of the day bomber seems to have been solved (or at least made it too expensive for the Luftwaffe), it is possible that at any time some new tactic or equipment may make this viable again. Given this, it is necessary to keep Fighter Command at its operational strength of around 1,000 planes. In addition the Navy needs some 2-4 squadrons to defend Scapa Flow and its convoy ports such as Loch Ewe in the extreme north of Scotland. These can either be flown by the RAF or Navy. The Spitfire is the best available fighter for daytime air defence, and we will shortly have the required strength available. There is also a need for a limited number of Spitfires specifically modified for high altitude to counter Luftwaffe high-level reconnaissance aircraft.

(2) Air Operations (North Africa and the Mediterranean)

In general, the nature of the airstrips and the size of the theatre makes it difficult to use the Spitfire (which find the general conditions too poor). We recommend a mix of Spitfires (for defence of higher value targets in the rear), and Sparrowhawks in their fighter role (these are much better suited for rough strips). The Hurricane is also more suitable for rough airstrips, and will be used until Sparrowhawk production builds up.

There are already Whirlwind and Wellingtons operating in theatre for reconnaissance and bombing, and these are proving suitable. We recommend that these retain the role for at least the next year, and that additional numbers are made available. Maritime strike by the RAF will either be by Beaufighter or Wellington (which can be modified to carry two torpedoes)

The role of army support will be by Sparrowhawk or Beaufighter in their fighter-bomber role. For heavier support, the Wellington is suitable, but we need a better light bomber than the Blenheim, although this is currently still usable in this theatre (unless Luftwaffe fighters are assigned there in numbers)

(3) Air Operations SE Asia

The air threat is much lower in this theatre, and we consider that any of the Sparrowhawk, Hurricane or Beaufighter will be suitable (depending on availability of the aircraft). Given the long ranges normal in this theatre, the Beaufighter and the Sparrowhawk are the better choice. Beaufighters would also be suitable for the maritime role in theatre, but until sufficient aircraft become available we can use older models as they are replaced in Europe. There also exists a need for limited numbers of long and very long range reconnaissance aircraft. The Navy has suggested that the SeaLance would cover the medium/long range need, and as it is currently only in use by the FAA it would be possible to provide the small numbers needed. For the very long range needs a number of Whirlwinds needs to be made available. Since this theatre is currently only at risk, we suggest a small number of squadrons of the different types needed will be useful to allow training and doctrine to be established in case there is need to counter Japan in this theatre. While this will complicate logistical support, we consider it a sensible precaution.

(4) Convoy defence

It was seen in the last war that the best defence of a convoy is a combination of air and light surface forces. Our analysis of the situation so far indicates this has not changed. The Navy is building light anti-submarine escorts as fast as possible, and we recommend no change to this priority. In order to maximise their effectiveness, we also need to provide air cover.

Air cover can be provided either from a carrier or by land based aircraft. Again, the escort carrier program currently ongoing is at about the maximum resources allow, but we recommend that it continues to be resourced at this level (there are indications that competing claims for shipbuilding may reduce the effort on the escort carriers). Ideally we need one per convoy, plus some additional ships, and the current building program will not provide these within 2-3 years. If possible, consideration should be given to building more ships in Canada, and if possible getting a number of the escort carriers built in the USA.

With respect to the land-based air support of Coastal Command, this currently is being given a very low priority by the RAF, with the suitable aircraft going to Bomber Command. We recommend that this policy is changed, and that Coastal Command is given a much higher priority for the aircraft it needs, especially over the next year which we see as the critical period in the North Atlantic. There is a specific need by Coastal Command for a long range four engine aircraft to supplement the Sunderland; production difficulties and costs mean the seaplane cannot be produced in the numbers needed. The US-produced Catalina flying boat is a useful supplement for the Sunderland, and it is recommended that purchases of it are increased.

(5) Operations over the North Sea and coastal regions.

The best planes available are the Hudson (US import) and the Beaufort. The Beaufighter will also be used once production permits. These are seen as adequate for the strike, reconnaissance and anti-submarine roles, the problem is that there are currently insufficient planes available and many of the existing planes are obsolete. We can see no quick solution except to increase production of the relevant planes. The Catalina is also suitable for the reconnaissance role.

Both the Beaufort and Wellington are suitable for minelaying, and in addition this low-risk mission can be supplemented by older, obsolescent models of bomber until the modern aircraft are available in sufficient numbers.

There are issues with providing protection to coastal convoys on the East Coast against aircraft. We do not have enough carriers to provide cover, and it has always been expected that the RAF would cover these convoys. The problem is (1) detecting enemy attack in time to allow interception, and (2) the range of the fighters. Detection is being addressed by fitting selected merchant ships with radar and communications to act as fighter control ships. This is currently slow due to availability of the needed equipment. The problem of the range of the fighters can be eased by using the Goshawk or the Reaper as the fighter, or a fighter version of the Whirlwind. It is recommended that the RAF and Navy undertake a specific analysis of this to work out an optimal solution.

(6) Operations in support of the Army

During the last year this has been the role of light bombers such as the Battle, which have proved unable to deliver the needed support. We have looked at the idea of providing a dive bomber (which has been used to great effect by Germany), either based on the Henly or the Cormorant, but are worried about the vulnerability of the dive bomber against fighters (we realise the Navy has specific requirements for which this limitation is accepted). We propose support be based on (1) a fighter-bomber which can defend itself after an attack - currently this is the Hurricane, but this will be superseded by the Sparrowhawk, and (2) a light bomber - again, we have no suitable British aircraft for this role. There is also the possibility of using the Beaufighter in this role, although it is only an adequate fighter, its range and load carrying capability makes it a good choice for overseas theatres.

(7) Attacks on Germany

After looking in detail at the possibilities open to us, bearing in mind the types and number of aircraft we have available, and the state of the German defences, we consider that the types of operation we can undertake fall into three broad categories

(a) Mine laying (also known as 'Gardening').

This is a low risk operation which nonetheless causes significant damage and disruption to German industry. Used coastally, it damages and sinks both naval vessels and coastal shipping, and requires a great deal of effort in sweeping the mines. In addition, as the Beaufighter becomes available it would be suitable for attacking or disrupting the minesweeping efforts, rendering the mine laying even more effective.

In addition, it is very feasible to mine the major German inland waterways, canals and rivers. these are used heavily for industrial transport (far more heavily that we use them in the UK)

Finally the lower level of risk involved means it can have the new, green crews assigned, allowing them to gain useful operational experience and perform a useful role while becoming seasoned crews.

We understand that there has been political opposition to this as it might cause Germany to respond in kind, but the Luftwaffe is in any case targeting our ports and coastal waters, and we make far les use of inland waterways than does Germany.

This operation can be conducted by the Wellington (indeed, by any heavy bomber) over the coast and estuaries; river attacks can also be a productive use of light and medium bombers since they do not need to drop the large sea mines needed to damage ocean-going ships.

(b) Pinpoint attacks on specific installations

The FAA have shown that precision attacks on targets, while often costly in planes, can drastically damage the target. While the losses are higher as a percentage than area raids, the damage done is such that there is no need to revisit the target, and so the actually losses (for a specific amount of damage) are actually lower. Since this type of attack can concentrate on small targets that cause severe damage to the German war economy, by attacking targets which cannot be easily replaced, the effects can be much larger than just the immediate damage indicates. We recommend that we build up a capability to do this type of attack on a regular basis.

The aircraft used by the FAA are not suitable except for some of the coastal/port targets. We need a fast, medium bomber capable of delivering some 1-2 tons of bombs precisely. In addition, the navigation of the crews needs to be improved significantly. Ideally, such raids should take place in daytime to make sure the maximum damage is done, but defences may make this impossible. If we decide on daylight raids, we will need a long range fighter capable of escorting the bombers. The only suitable long range fighter currently is the Whirlwind, and we need to use some of the current production to see if it capable of the task against the Luftwaffe's first-line fighters. Another possibility is the US-produced Mustang, currently undergoing testing with a Merlin engine. It would also be possible to use Spitfires or Goshawks (with overload tanks) for some closer targets.

A list of suitable targets by type should be drawn up, paying careful attention to the effects that destroying these targets would have on the German economy, assuming a bomber force of some 200 planes available carrying 200-400 tons of bombs. The Navy has asked specifically if some initial operations can target German naval facilities (particularly submarine construction and support), and we suggest this is not only a useful target, but will allow the force to build up experience on easier to locate coastal targets without having to also fight through Germany to get to their target.

(c) Area attacks on installations, transport & Communications, and the oil industry.

While we feel that the pinpoint raid is the most effective in terms of results for resources used, there are a considerable number of targets for which this type of raid is not suitable - they are either too large, too dispersed, or too heavily defended. For these the option of a large raid by heavy bombers is the most suitable choice. In order to be able to attack these successfully, we need to build up the requisite bomber force. We have had estimates from the Air Ministry of up to 4,000 bombers needed to achieve success with an area bombing campaign. We reject this scale of build-up for a number of reasons. First, the amount of fuel needed to prosecute such a campaign (and it would be a campaign, not limited to a few raids) exceeds our capability to import. Second, such an effort would virtually exclude the other services from investment in equipment. Third, the existing evidence suggests that the current accuracy of bomber command is so poor as to make this scale of attack extremely inefficient. We should also examine carefully the nature of the raids made on us by the Luftwaffe, to see why some raids have caused more damage than others, with a view to learning how to cause more damage to Germany.

Bearing in mind the need to do sufficient damage to neutralise (at least for a time) a large target, we consider that we should build up a heavy bomber force capable of operating 500 planes on a regular series of missions (plus allowance for maintenance and training). This will allow either a number of smaller raids or one large raid with the available force. This force will need support by Pathfinders to find and mark the targets, as we are seeing that the current training of ordinary crews does not allow them to find targets at night, especially in poor weather.

Studies are being prepared as to the best composition of this force. First indications are that a mix of high and medium altitude planes will be the best initial solution, using a mix of bombs to disrupt the ability of the target to protect itself, cause direct damage, and allow the use of a large quantity of incendiaries. Since we will not have the planes available in numbers for a year, these studies should be concluded in time to make sure we are building the correct mixture.

It is expected that initially the force will be comprised of the Halifax, supplemented by the four-engine Manchester once this passes evaluation trials.

(d) Raids or sweeps over Northern France and other areas covered by the range of our fighters

We view these and being an inefficient and costly way to use our fighters and light bombers. The number of targets in range is relatively small, and many of these have political issues (too close to the occupied countries civil population). We would meet a strong defence on any worthwhile target, and would suffer crew losses in the same way as the Luftwaffe did in its attacks on us - lost crew will not be recovered, while German crews will. It is an obvious aim to weaken the Luftwaffe fighter arm, but we consider a more efficient way will be to use our surplus of fighters against them in other theatres. It does not matter where we shoot them down, and playing them on their own ground puts us at an unnecessary disadvantage.

While the above covers the operational use of our bombers, it is realised that in addition we need to be seen to be hurting and damaging the enemy. Mine laying does not show this. Pinpoint raids may, as long as they are large and do a significant amount of damage (the FAA raid on Wilhelmshaven is an example of this), or hit a notable target, but otherwise they are not likely to be seen as causing major damage; the significance of their success will often not be obvious to the uninformed. The area attacks, although the last effective in terms or aircraft usage, do have the political advantage of being easy to use in propaganda terms. However we feel that effectiveness should be a higher priority than propaganda, as otherwise we risk diluting and damaging our bomber force for small results.

Summary of Recommendations for the next year.

The Spitfire and the associated Merlin engine should continue to be developed as our primary air defence fighter, especially for high altitude work.

The Sparrowhawk (initially the Hurricane) is seen as the best option for army support as well as air defence of the theatre, as it can deliver a useful bomb-load yet act as a first-rate fighter when unloaded. We have considered a dedicated dive bomber, but the vulnerability of these planes to AA fire and to fighter opposition leads us to think that the fighter-bomber is the more efficient option (we realise the Navy has specific and specialised roles for dive bombers, and note that this means suitable planes are available in small number if specialised raids are contemplated, although training will need to be given to RAF pilots in this case.)

The Beaufighter, while only a marginal first-rate fighter, is longer ranged and can also carry a significant bomb-load, or a torpedo for naval use. Production should be continued as planned, to replace part of the Beaufort force. We should also look into the suggestion of a very heavily gun-armed version (4x20mm cannon and 4x0.5" mg) for air support and interdiction of light shipping. The initial priority should be to coastal command, but a certain number should be retained to develop the concept of the heavy attack fighter properly.

Hurricane production should be reduced and replaced by Sparrowhawk as resources permit. The Hurricane will be supplied to overseas theatres where the fighter threat is less than over Germany.

Goshawk production will continue until the new fighters are available for the FAA. It will then either be discontinued or retained at a lowe level for second-line carrier operations.

Development of the Tornado should cease; development of the Typhoon should continue subject to ongoing monitoring of the situation of the Sabre engine.

The development of the new aircraft for the Navy is seen as acceptable by the Navy, now that the three new planes have entered production. Once these are available, the existing production will be reviewed to see if any of it should be made available for other usage. Although it is technically obsolete, the Navy has asked that production of the Fairy Swordfish be continued due to the characteristics that make it particularly suitable for the AS role on small carriers. This will be reviewed in one year when more experience with hew new escort carriers is available.

There is a problem with the performance and availability of the current light bomber force. The Blenheim is obsolescent, and not suitable for the fighter role against serious opposition. We recommend that production be reduced and phased out in favour of more useful aircraft. In the meantime it should be used in theatres such as North Africa where is performance is not such a drawback.

We have a lack of good new light bombers in development. Some of the roles currently tasked to them can and will be performed more usefully by the new fighter-bomber concept, but light bombers will still be needed. The Mosquito concept shows promise, but is untested, and until it has proven itself we cannot rely on it as the only plane to fill this role. In addition, while its construction has the useful benefit of not using many scarce resources, it also means that unlike a conventional aircraft there are limits on the number that can be produced. We therefore recommend we look for one or two aircraft from the USA to fill the light bomber requirement.

The medium bomber role is currently filled adequately by the Wellington. Production should be given priority, especially as it is also required by coastal command. The other planes being used in this role are seen as obsolescent.

The heavy bombers currently coming out of development and into service have a number of significant problems (please see detailed appendix on these). As a result, we cannot justify the huge investment in these demanded by Bomber Command, although development of the planes and techniques for using them should of course continue. We do not feel that any significant campaign against Germany using these planes is possible before 1942 at the earliest. In particular we are deficient in the means to find and mark the targets with suitable accuracy - until we do this, we are just wasting any heavy bomber force.

A marking or Pathfinder force should be established as soon as possible, and trained up to locate and mark targets of various kinds so that when the heavy bomber is mature we can use it effectively. This can be usefully tied in with the development of precision raids, as similar levels or marking/delivery accuracy is needed in both. The question of using a different aircraft for marking than bombing needs to be addressed.

Following successful tests of the prototype, a requirement has been put out for a twin engined jet-powered aircraft. Both Westland and deHaviland have presented suitable ideas, and prototypes from each company will be developed. While we see this advance as having great potential, after talks we have determined that the engines are currently the main limiting factor (they are currently unreliable with a short working life), and we recommend additional resources in this area to parallel to development of the planes.

Glossary

AA - Anti Aircraft (guns).

AI - Airborne Intercept (radar). A small light radar set capable of being carried on a plane to allow it to intercept another aircraft at night.

ASDIC - what later became known as SONAR, a high-frequency sound system designed to detect a submerged submarine. At this time, rarely usable above 1,500 - 2000 metres.

A/S - Antisubmarine

ASV - Air to Surface radar, a small airborne set designed to spot ships and, later, smaller objects such as submarines.

Avgas - Aviation Gasoline (fuel), very volatile and very dangerous.

CAP - Combat Air Patrol, the act of keeping a number of fighters in the air above the carrier or fleet ready to intercept enemy aircraft.

DB - Dive Bomber, an aircraft designed to deliver a single bomb in a very steep (normally over 70°) dive.

FAA - Fleet Air Arm, the aeroplanes flown and controlled by the Royal Navy

HA - also known as HA(AA), the guns capable of attacking a high-altitude enemy plane. Normally used against high altitude level bombing. While not terribly accurate at this time, the aim was to disrupt the formation of the attackers, making them miss, rather than to shoot them down. Level bombers depended on the 'shotgun' principle of bombing during this period.

Hammer-and-Anvil attack - a type of attack by torpedo planes. Two groups of planes will attack 90° apart, one the 'hammer', the other the 'anvil'. Dodging the torpedoes of one group will put the ship broadside on to the other group. The ideal torpedo attack against a moving ship.

HMS - His Majesties Ship (British); also HMAS - His Majesties Australian Ship, HMCS - His Majesties Canadian Ship, HMNZS - His Majesties New Zealand Ship.

HIMJS - His Imperial Japanese Majesties Ship (Japan)

Kriegsmarine - the German Navy

LA - Low angle guns, normally those unable to elevate above about 40 degrees, so unable to fire on a plane over the ship. In fact, these guns can be used as anti-aircraft guns, but only on aircraft some distance away (the angle of the aircraft increases as it closes the ship). Usually even less accurate than HA fire, as this type of gun was not usually matched with the control system designed to engage aircraft.

Luftwaffe - the German Air Force

MN - Marine Nationale, the French navy

Pom-pom - the name given in the RN to a fast-firing light AA weapon. Originally firing a 2-pdr shell, then the 40mm shell, given its name due to the sound the multi-barrel version made

RA - Regia Aeronautica, the Italian Air Force (Italy did not have a separate naval air force)

RAF - the British Air force

RDF - Radio Direction Finding, an early (British) name for Radar (so named to try and mislead what it actually did)

RN - Royal Navy, the British naval forces. Also the RAN (Australian), RCN (Canadian), and RNZN (New Zealand).

Round down - the aft part of a carrier's flight deck. This was 'rounded down' in a downward curve, which improved the airflow and made it easier for a plane to land. It also reduced the available deck parking area, and so was reduced on British carriers as larger strikes became more common.

SAP - Semi Armour Piercing

Shadow factory - A set of factories built in the mid-30's in Britain ready to be used as aircraft factories in war. In fact the need for aircraft due to the expansion of the Luftwaffe meant they were brought into use before the war, and more built. The term 'shadow program' came to be used for anything built in advance of wartime needs, such as the Japanese programme of 'Shadow Carriers', merchant ships built ready for easy conversion into light carriers.

TBR - Torpedo, Bomber, Reconnaissance. A class of plane used by most navies in these three roles. Bombing was normally level bombing with light bombs, although some aircraft like the Swordfish could dive bomb at shallow dive angles.

Twins - or the twins, the two German Battlecruisers Scharnhorst and Gneisenau.

USS - United States Ship (USA)

Information on the next book in this series may be found at

http://www.AstroDragon.co.uk/Books/TheWhaleHasWings.htm

Book 3, World War, is due for publication in the Autumn of 2013. This will cover the spreading of the war to the Pacific, and the actions of the allies against Imperial Japan, as well as continuing to show what is happening to the rest of the world.

6930982R00128

Printed in Great Britain
by Amazon.co.uk, Ltd.,
Marston Gate.